Praise for

The Oath, Book One of the Druid Chronicles

"Linden's well-researched tale eloquently brings to life a lesser-known period of transition in Britain. . . . The author has created a strong foundation for her series with well-developed characters whom readers can embrace. . . . [a] layered, gripping historical fiction . . ."

—*Kirkus Reviews*

"The story rolls along at a lively pace, rich with details of the times and a wide cast of characters. . . . [The] plotting, shifting points of view of the three engaging protagonists, and evocative writing style make *The Oath* a pleasure to read. Highly recommended!"

—*Historical Novels Review*

"Linden uses a fairy tale-like style almost as though this story has been passed down orally over the centuries."

—*Booklist*

"Thrilling historical fiction with heart and soul."

—Tim Pears, author of *In the Place of Fallen Leaves*

The
Valley

The Druid Chronicles
Book Two

The
Valley

A.M. LINDEN

swp

SHE WRITES PRESS

Published 2022
Printed in the United States of America
Print ISBN: 978-1-64742-409-1
E-ISBN: 978-1-64742-410-7
Library of Congress Control Number: 2021923482

For information, address:
She Writes Press
1569 Solano Ave #546
Berkeley, CA 94707

Interior design by Tabitha Lahr

She Writes Press is a division of SparkPoint Studio, LLC.

For Mark, renaissance man
and love of my life

Author's Note

The Druid Chronicles is a historical fiction series set in Anglo-Saxon Britain during a time known alternatively as the early medieval period or the Dark Ages. Books One, Three, Four, and Five are primarily concerned with events that take place in AD 788. Book Two begins a generation earlier and recounts the events that set the main story in motion. While considerable liberty has been taken in adapting the geopolitics of the period to the needs of the story, it is generally true that:

- At the time in question, the Germanic invaders (who in this narrative will be referred to as Saxons) had conquered the southeastern lowlands, while indigenous Celts retained control in the mountainous northwest.
- The majority of native Britons had converted to Christianity by the end of the fourth century. The Saxon conversion was essentially complete by the late 600s.
- Before the conversion to Christianity, both ethnic groups were polytheistic, and elements of those earlier beliefs and practices persisted after that transition was nominally complete.

Atheldom and Derthwald, the Saxon kingdoms in which most of the series' actions take place, are literary creations, as is Llwddawanden, a secluded valley in which it is imagined that a secretive Druid cult has continued its traditional practices despite the otherwise relentless spread of Christianity.

About Druids: Although much has been written about Druids, there is little verifiable information regarding what this apparently elite and possibly priestly class of Celts believed or what ritual practices they may have carried out. For the purpose of this series, it is conjectured that Druids were indeed priests and priestesses and that the Druids of Llwddawanden were matriarchal, subscribing to the belief that:

- There was a supreme mother goddess at the apex of an extensive pantheon of gods and goddesses.
- The spirit of this supreme deity inhabited the body of their cult's chief priestess.
- At the chief priestess's death, the goddess's spirit passed on to her daughter, if she had one, or else to a designated member of the priestesses' inner circle.

There is not, to the author's knowledge, any evidence that a community of practicing Druids persisted as late as the eighth century in the British Isles or elsewhere, and there is no reason to think that the views and practices ascribed to the Druids of Llwddawanden have any basis in reality.

Characters

FEYWN [FAY-un] . . . . Chief priestess

ARIANNA [ARI-anna] . . . . Feywn's daughter

ANNWR [ANN-ur] . . . . Priestess, Feywn's sister

CYRI [KER-ee] . . . . Annwr's daughter

GWENNEFOR [GWEN-eh-for] . . . . Priestess, Feywn's cousin

GWENYDD [GWEN-eth] . . . . Gwennefor's daughter

CALDORA [kal-DOR-a] . . . . Priestess, Feywn's cousin

CATA [KAY-tah] . . . . Caldora daughter

TARA [TAR-ah] . . . . Caldora daughter, Cata's twin sister

RHONNON [ROW-nun] . . . . Priestess, chief midwife

AOLFE [AHL-fee] . . . . Priestess, chief herbalist

LUNEDD [LOON-eth] . . . . Priestess, calendar keeper

BELODDEN [BEE-loth-en] . . . . . Priestess, guardian of the
women's quarters

HERRWN [HAIR-un] . . . . Chief priest, bard

LOTHWEN [LOTH-wen] . . . . Priestess, Herrwn's consort
(deceased)

LILLYWEN [LILY-wen] . . . . Herrwn and Lothwen's daughter
(deceased)

OSSIAM [oh-SEE-em] . . . . Priest, chief oracle

IDDWRAN [ITH-oo-ran] . . . . Ossiam's assistant

OGDWEN [OH'G-do-en] . . . . Ossiam's assistant

RHEDWYN [RED-win] . . . . Ossiam's disciple, Feywn's
first consort, Arianna's father

LABHRUINN [LAB-ruin] . . . . Rhedwyn's brother

MADHERAN [MAD-hair-an] . . . . Priest-in-training, later a member
of Rhedwyn's war band

OLYRRWD [OH-la-rood] . . . . Priest, chief physician

MOELWYN [MOIL-win] . . . . Priest-in-training, later Olyrrwd's
assistant

GOFANNON [GO-fan-on] . . . . Member of Rhedwyn's war band, later one of the shrine's guards

CAELENDRA [KAY-LEN-dra] . . . . . Chief priestess before Feywn (deceased)

ELDRENEDD [EL-dren-eth] . . . . Caelendra's son, later Feywn's second consort

CAELYM [KAY-lum] . . . . Caelendra's son, later Feywn's second consort

ARDDWN [AR-thun] . . . . Feywn and Caelym's first son

EALENDWR [EL-en-dur] . . . . Feywn and Caelym's daughter (deceased)

LLIEM [LEE-em] . . . . Feywn and Caelym's second son

BENYON [BEN-yun] . . . . Servant in the priests' quarters

NIMRRWN [NIM-run] . . . . Benyon's nephew

IDDWRNA [ITH-ur-na] . . . . Benyon's nephew

DARBIN [DAR-bin] . . . . Metalsmith

MAI [MY] . . . . Darbin's sister

AONGHUS [AHN-gus] . . . . Herder in charge of the shrine's sheep and goats

LLWDD [LOOTH] . . . . Villager, spokesman for the valley's farmers

NONNA [NO-na] . . . . Nursery servant

Place Names

LLWDDAWANDEN [LUTH-a-wand-un] . . . . . Site of the Druids' current shrine

CAENBWNSA [KANE-bun-sa] . . . . A village loyal to the Druids of Llwddawanden

CWMMARWN [KUM-ur-un] . . . . The cult's original shrine

CWDDWAELLWN [KUTH-way-lun] . . . . . . Site of the cult's original shrine

Author's Note: This list includes characters who died before the story opens or appear in later books. Names of minor characters who appear or are mentioned in a single context have been omitted.

Synopsis of The Oath

Book One of The Druid Chronicles

Book One (*The Oath*) opens with the arrival of Caelym, a young Druid priest, at the outer walls of the Abbey of Saint Edeth in search of Annwr, the sister of his cult's chief priestess, who was abducted by a Saxon war band fifteen years earlier and is rumored to be living in the convent.

Weary, wounded, and starving, Caelym is on the verge of collapse when he meets an elderly woman who takes him to her hut. In subsequent chapters it is disclosed that the woman is the Priestess Annwr, that she spent the first years of her enslavement as the nursemaid to Theobold and Alswanda's orphaned daughter, Aleswina, and that when Aleswina was consigned to the abbey, she brought Annwr with her and arranged for her to have lodging on the convent grounds.

Aleswina is well aware of Annwr's background and, acting out of devotion to her beloved servant, she hides Caelym in a secret chamber under a shrine in the convent's garden and nurses him back to health.

Just as Caelym and Annwr are about to leave together, Aleswina learns that her cousin, King Gilberth—a tyrant known for his cruelty and vicious temper, and for having had five wives die under mysterious circumstances—is going to take her from the convent to be his next bride. Terrified, she escapes with Annwr and Caelym. While Annwr, who's come to love Aleswina as a daughter, wants to keep her with them, Caelym is adamant that a Saxon Christian cannot be admitted into their cult and only agrees to deliver her to another convent.

Besides rescuing Annwr, Caelym also has to find his two sons, Arddwn and Lliem, who have not been heard from since they were sent out of the shrine to be fostered by Benyon, a servant believed to be faithful to Llwddawanden's priests and priestesses. But Benyon, it turns out, has converted to Christianity, assumed a new identity, and used the treasure trove he stole from the shrine to set himself up as a wealthy landowner ensconced in a heavily fortified manor.

On discovering that the man he entrusted his sons to has made them into slaves, Caelym is ready to break down the door of that manor with his bare hands, but Annwr and Aleswina hold him back. Instead, using subterfuge, Aleswina is able to get inside and trick Benyon into letting the boys go.

Despite Caelym's gratitude for Aleswina's rescuing his sons, he continues to refuse Annwr's demand that they take her back to Llwddawanden. The two continue to argue until, in an emotional confrontation, Caelym reveals that their cult's previously safe sanctuary has been betrayed, and that instead of returning there, they are embarking upon a perilous and possibly futile attempt to found a new shrine.

Wanting what is best for Aleswina, Annwr agrees to leave her at a remote lodge with an elderly servant who was the princess's first nursemaid and who promises to see that the princess reaches the safety of a convent beyond the border of Derthwald. In the book's closing pages, Aleswina is resigned to spending the rest of her life behind convent walls, and Annwr is ready, whatever dangers lie ahead, to rejoin her people.

Contents

PART I

Tales of the Hunt

"Until lions have their historians, tales of the hunt shall always glorify the hunter," is an African proverb quoted by the eminent Nigerian author and scholar Chinua Achebe, in an interview with *Paris Review* in 1994. Its applicability to the Druids of Northern Europe is manifest. Having left no written records, their early portrayals come from the accounts of foreign and often hostile commentators, while later depictions were the work of Christian authors intending to replace Druidic ideas with their own. It is not surprising, then, that by the eighth century, the priests and priestesses who had once been accorded a reverence bordering on worship were publicly reviled as sorcerers and witches.

That said, the superstitious dread of Druids that infected the Christians of that period was out of proportion with any apparent threat posed by a frail old man wrapped in a travel-stained cloak crouching on a rocky ledge overlooking the valley that encompassed what was then the Saxon kingdom of Derthwald.

In the wider scheme of things, Derthwald was a small kingdom, but to Herrwn, who'd rarely before been outside a valley barely four leagues long and only two across, the moonlit mix of woods and fields below him was a vast expanse almost dizzying in its immensity.

A sharp wind cut through his cloak and the robe beneath, both still damp from the downpour earlier that day, so the shiver that momentarily came over him was more likely from cold and hunger than a lack of personal fortitude. Still, physical hardship was a new experience for Herrwn. Until the unspeakable betrayal that laid open the entry of their previously secure sanctuary to their enemies, he'd led a privileged life—the life of a teacher and a poet within the shelter of a community that valued learning and poetry above gold. While this preferential treatment had not protected him from the aches of old age or the pain of outliving all his family and most of his friends, he had been spared much of the discomfort of living in a time that later generations would call the Dark Ages—although he would have been offended if he had heard the term and understood the implications that his time was a time of ignorance and depravity.

Having devoted his life to reciting the sagas that contained the ancient wisdom passed down to him from his father and his father's father going back to the night the first of those stories was told by the first storyteller, Herrwn would have expected more appreciation for his labors. Of course, the penchant of the young for giving themselves entirely too much credit was nothing new to a man who'd been a teacher for over forty years, and Herrwn would have considered anyone born in our time—twelve centuries after he was—to be very young indeed.

In the unlikely event that he had been able to do so, he would have been ready to answer the criticisms of those yet-to-be born scholars who had the conceit to pass such an ill-founded judgment on their elders. He would have straightened himself up to his full height, fixed the upstarts with the stern gaze that had subdued two generations of unruly disciples, and spoken with grave dignity as he challenged them to prove the boast that their age was better than earlier ones.

"So, I am to understand that in your time the wealthy gladly share their excess goods with the poor and the needy? And it must also be true that your rulers act only out of selfless consideration of what is best for those that they govern? And, certainly, in such advanced and civilized days, men do not resort to the crudeness of war to make their point but use reason and the thoughtful exchange of words instead!"

Here Herrwn would have paused to wait for the feeble rebuttal to sputter out before demanding to know whether all the wondrous advances of the future had served to make men and women more generous or more loving or more content—and exactly how they could be so certain that generosity or love or contentment had never been felt by those who lived in earlier times. Then he would have finished with a polite but pointed suggestion that "perhaps, instead of complaining about the flaws of other times, you should be putting your thoughts and actions into improving your own!"

Druids were like that—always ready to talk their opponents into submission on any topic whatsoever. And despite his shabby outward appearance, Herrwn was a Druid—and not just any Druid but a Druid born to the highest ranks of his elite order, descended from an unbroken line of Druids going back to the days when all of Britain worshipped the Great Mother Goddess and her ever-expanding family of divine offspring.

It was his ancestors who first chanted the sacred chants and danced the sacred dances celebrating the power of the Goddess, their bards who first recited the sagas recalling how the struggles between the Goddess's many children had shaped the world, their oracles who first foretold the future by augury and divination.

Even after other shrines sprang up in more accessible locations, theirs had held ascendency. The most important kings and queens did not marry without consulting with their high priestess, the greatest warriors did not go to war without the approval of their council, and the wisest farmers did not plant their crops before the day decreed by their calendar.

Secure in their primary position and elevated standing, they'd been tolerant when competing centers, out of either sincere misapprehension or unwitting envy, began to question their authority in determining the proper names, relative ranking, and exact powers of the vast and complex array of divine beings that had sprung from the Goddess's fertile loins.

The disputes, which at first had seemed no more serious than arguments over the merits of contestants in the footraces held at the summer solstice celebration, turned ominous when a rebellious faction of younger priests put forth the observation that men were bigger and stronger than women as evidence that gods must be more powerful and more important than goddesses.

This challenge to conventional wisdom was compounded by uncertainty about just how many gods and goddesses there actually were—a question that was only raised by common laborers complaining about the rising costs of placating the steadily increasing number of easily offended divinities before the invading Romans unleashed a whole new pantheon onto the lands they conquered. (The answer to this, of course, was, "So many that only someone with the highly trained memory of a Druid could keep track of them all.")

Herrwn's sect, the Shrine of the Great Mother Goddess, was, as its name implied, a conservative school of thought. Steadfast in upholding the preeminent role of the Mother Goddess both in the creation and the oversight of the world and unwilling to get caught up in what seemed to them to be juvenile squabbling, its chief priests restated the obvious—"All life begins with a mother"—and continued on with their own affairs.

Safely situated above the furthest reach of the Roman occupation, their shrine remained a prominent center of Druid belief and practice until a new and even more dangerous idea was put forth—first behind closed doors, then offhandedly at informal gatherings of priests-in-training, and finally out loud in open councils—and what began as a grassroots movement of the lower classes responding to the appeal of a simple idea of a single god, one who cared about the poor and maybe wouldn't expect so much tribute, took hold and spread like wildfire.

Well aware of the arguments for monotheism, the high priests of their cult had stood firm, saying, "You get what you pay for," and adding that what the converts to Christianity would get was one god who was every bit as demanding as a thousand had ever been but who wouldn't share with anyone else. It was Herrwn's great-grandfather's great-great-grandfather who'd answered the claim by proselytizing Christians that having one god was better than many, scoffing, "By that reasoning, having no gods or goddesses would be best of all." But neither humor nor reason prevailed, and almost overnight, the steady stream of tribute that had sustained their shrine for the past millennium dried up to a trickle.

As the tide of public opinion turned against them, they retreated from their original shrine to take refuge in an even more remote sanctuary that had previously been reserved for conducting their four highest seasonal rituals.

By the time the Romans were replaced by a second wave of foreign invaders, the schism between adherents of the old religion and the new one had grown so intense that there were some priests sitting on the shrine's highest council who considered the Saxons being polytheists to count in their favor. This guarded optimism faded, however, as it became apparent that the Saxons were undiscriminating in their warfare—killing fellow pagans as remorselessly as Christians.

With the eventual conversion of Saxons, the question of one god or many was largely resolved in favor of Jesus Christ, and while the widespread adoption of Christianity did not bring universal peace or justice, it did bring converted Saxons and Celts together to persecute nonbelievers of either race.

In spite of this growing hostility, the Druids of Llwddawanden had not yet been completely cut off from the outside world. They continued to meet with their relatives who'd become Christian for another two generations, although their family reunions had deteriorated into occasions for name-calling and acrimony by the time Herrwn was born. Then, the year that he turned eight, a delegation, led by his father and including his father's four brothers, went out for what was to be the last time. They left Llwddawanden expecting to be gone for at least ten days. They returned a week later with only half their number, and their kinship—which had remained intact in spite of all the arguments over the ranks and responsibilities of a thousand gods and goddesses—was permanently torn apart.

Of all Herrwn's childhood memories, the most vivid would always be the image of his calm, thoughtful father—a man known for his patience and open-mindedness, for his readiness to offer a sympathetic excuse for the bad behavior of others, and for his ability to smooth over rancorous disputes in the High Council—stamping in a circle around the sacred hearth, fuming and sputtering, repeating over and over how it was a travesty and an abomination that those who had once been their flesh and blood should spew the disgraceful, repellent falsehood that it was not the Great Mother Goddess who gave them life (as if you could look anywhere and find any creature that is born without a mother!) but instead chose to worship a despicable Christian god who claimed to have created the first man out of mud and the first woman out of the man's rib!

Huddled out of sight behind the back row of the benches in the great council chamber with his little brother and two of their cousins, Herrwn had stared in bewilderment at his father and uncles, the three highest priests on their highest council, almost incoherent with outrage, declaring that his two missing uncles were no longer kin and were never to be called by name again.

One of his uncles had a lively sense of humor and turned their outrage into laughter by pulling open his robe and counting his ribs and exclaiming in mock surprise that none were missing! The other two (usually dignified) men followed suit, each of them opening their robes and counting their ribs and trying to persuade Herrwn's mother and aunts to let their ribs be counted. Caught up in the game, Herrwn had pulled up his own shirt and counted his ribs, and then helped his brother to count his. The younger boy was ticklish and had fallen to the floor in uncontrollable peals of laughter and been left with a bad case of hiccups. Except for that, they all felt better, having proved that the number of ribs for men and for women was exactly the same and so settling, once and for all, that life was a gift from the Great Mother Goddess in whom they correctly believed!

With that, Herrwn's father and uncles agreed that while there was room in the world for a large and perhaps uncountable number of gods and goddesses, there was no place in their shrine for any god who claimed credit for the work of others.

Herrwn's mother and aunts did not need to be convinced. They had each given birth themselves and shared the view that men could never endure menstrual cramps, much less childbirth. It was Herrwn's mother who had the last word, startling them all by saying there might be some basis for Christian belief because (and she paused for effect), in the unlikely event that a male god were to give life, he would certainly do it in a way which did not require any real labor or discomfort for himself.

By then they all were in complete agreement not to demean themselves arguing over foolishness and decided that they would refuse to discuss the matter further and would wait for the absent uncles to return to their senses.

In the decades that passed since then, Herrwn and his cousins had risen to take their fathers' places as the shrine's chief bard, oracle, and physician, and, together with the shrine's highest priest-esses, they had continued to recite their ancient sagas, conduct their arcane rituals, and view themselves as the firstborn and favorite of the Goddess's mortal children.

The belief that the most important of all divine spirits had personally given birth to their ancestors, and that She continued to like them better than anyone else, was at best a tenuous conclusion in view of their reduced lot in life, but the Druids of Llwddawanden believed it. Dismissing the challenges of hostile armies and competing doctrines, they remained secure in their conviction that the living spirit of the Great Mother Goddess inhabited the body of their highest priestess— changing in form from tall to short, from svelte to voluptuous, from blond to dark as she passed from one generation to the next.

It had briefly seemed their faith might be rewarded when the ascendance of a mesmerizingly beautiful chief priestess brought the return of enthusiastic worshippers and their valley's population swelled—but that revival ended in catastrophe when her charismatic consort led his fanatically loyal but tragically ill-prepared band of would-be warriors in a doomed charge against a Saxon army.

In the fifteen years since that defeat, few children had been born, and the old had continued to die, so when their secret location was betrayed by one of their own, there were only a handful of them left to flee for other shelter. Still, the choice of staying faithful to the Goddess remained, and Herrwn had made it with his eyes open. It was a decision over which he had no regrets and one that gave him an inner strength beyond anything one would expect in a man of his age whose worldly possessions amounted to no more than what he could carry on his back.

Chapter 1:

The Manner of a Man's Death

Herrwn had left the relative warmth of the wayside shelter where Gwenydd and Darbin were bickering over which route to take in the morning—having nothing of any substance to add to the debate and knowing better than to take sides in a quarrel between a priestess and her consort. Instead of finding a spot out of the wind to practice his recitations, as he'd first intended, he'd been drawn by an irresistible urge to the brink of the cliff. There, after laying aside his staff and taking hold of a branch of a scrawny bush, he leaned out as far as he dared and stared down into the valley below, wishing that Olyrrwd was there to see it with him.

Thinking of Olyrrwd, Herrwn was reminded of a time they had discussed whether the manner of a person's death was a part of the pattern of the way that person had lived their life.

Olyrrwd had thought so, and, as their shrine's chief physician, he had watched a great many people die. And when Olyrrwd himself was dying, he had spent his final hours intent on seeing that his life's work would be carried on rather than wasting time in grief, anger, or regret. His had been a determined, purposeful death, just as he had been a determined, purposeful man.

The wind whipping across the valley cut through Herrwn's cloak and his robe underneath, reminding him of how chilled he'd felt—in spite of the fire blazing in their bedchamber's hearth—as Olyrrwd discussed the ebbing of his life with his young disciple as though it was only a matter of theoretical interest.

By then Herrwn had been an elder on the shrine's High Council for over two decades, but he only began to feel old when Caelym—himself suddenly aged beyond his nineteen years—with a now full-fledged physician's authority, firmly told him, "It's over," and "Olyrrwd is gone" (as if Herrwn were too dim to know death when he saw it). Sighing sadly, Caelym helped Herrwn to his feet, guided him to his bed (as if Herrwn would have become lost trying to find his way across the room), and sat next to him, patting his back (as if Herrwn were a colicky infant who needed to be burped instead of a wise and philosophical man weeping wise and philosophical tears).

Seven years later, Herrwn still felt the pain of Olyrrwd's absence every day, missing him as he would have missed a part of his own body. It was a familiar ache he welcomed, bringing with it memories so sharp and clear that it seemed he could reach out and touch them. What he regretted was his lack of grief for Ossiam, their fellow elder and the shrine's chief oracle and master of divination.

A theatrical and enigmatic man in life, Ossiam had departed in a dramatic display which, like his double-edged prophesies, had left behind more questions than answers—a fact that Olyrrwd would certainly claim as another proof of his assertion about the pattern of mortal existence.

Ossiam had only been gone for a matter of—here Herrwn needed to stop and glance up at the moon—five weeks, but already he seemed to have receded into the distant past, Herrwn's memory of him so shifting and elusive that he could not even recall his final words.

Of course, with everything that had happened since the dread night of the last winter solstice, one inexplicable catastrophe following on the heels of another, it might be expected that this final blow would overwhelm the senses of a man of Herrwn's advanced years—even one with the trained memory of a master bard. Feeling the loose gravel shift underneath him, he absentmindedly dug in his heels and pushed himself back a bit, still trying to bring those last days at Llwddawanden into focus.

Caelym had left on his mission to find the boys that Herrwn expected would be his last two disciples, assuming he managed to live long enough to pass his vast store of knowledge on to another generation of young Druids—as he very much hoped he would, having serious concerns about Caelym's ability to set his indulgence of his sons aside and maintain the firmness required of a teacher.

That was a tangential thought and Herrwn resolutely brought his mind back to task, recalling how, in the wake of the events now referred to obliquely as "The Betrayal," Ossiam had withdrawn to the oracle's tower, appearing only to share whatever omens he divined with their chief priestess in the privacy of her bedchamber.

There'd been no reason to think that the dark clouds gathering in the west presaged anything hopeful, and it had seemed almost inevitable that a massive storm would sweep in, toppling trees and whipping the lake into a froth of whitecaps.

While the rest of them huddled together in the shrine's main chamber or kept a tense watch for the impending enemy invasion, Ossiam had circled restlessly around the central hearth, muttering about evil signs and ominous portents. At a momentary lull in the sounds of the storm outside, he had abruptly stopped his pacing, raised his fists over his head, and cried out, "What is the meaning of this storm, and why does it come over us now?"

If Olyrrwd had still been there, no doubt he would have spoken up in the wry, sardonic voice he'd reserved for challenging whatever Ossiam said to point out that it was the season that storms happened, and that to be truly portentous, the clouds should be pouring toads or vipers down on them. As it was, Herrwn and the others had just shuddered as the oracle's next words—"The gods are angry and must be appeased! I hear their wrathful cries and will take them the tribute they demand"—echoed through the chamber.

Herrwn had tried to hold Ossiam back, protesting that it was too great a risk to take tribute out in the middle of the storm with the lake churning and heaving as if a vast swarm of sea monsters were at war with each other, but the oracle had repeated that the gods were angry and needed to be appeased and swept out of the room, taking with him a golden chalice that would have been a king's ransom in the days when they still had kings.

It was only now that Herrwn realized what had bothered him at the time—Ossiam had said the gods were angry. He had not mentioned the goddesses.

Still, the storm had subsided overnight and the lake was peaceful again in the morning, so when a boat had been found drifting upside down at the far end of the lake it was agreed that he'd been right and must be honored for the courage of his sacrifice. But for Herrwn, Ossiam's death had an empty and unfinished quality to it, leaving room for hope that he might return. His hope had lasted for most of the day, and he could not have said exactly when it turned into suspicion that Ossiam had taken the shrine's most cherished treasure and left to be a Christian.

With no way to know whether Ossiam was a hero or a traitor, Herrwn had not been able to settle on a single emotion, either grief or anger, about the oracle's disappearance. Now, without warning, the realization came over him that—in his heart of hearts—he wished that Olyrrwd was alive and hoped that Ossiam was dead.

The thought startled him, and it disturbed him deeply.

Chapter 2:

The Passage

Ossiam and Olyrrwd were Herrwn's cousins, sons of the two uncles who'd returned with his father following their last attempt to reconcile with the branch of their family that had left the shrine and converted to Christianity. Herrwn was the firstborn son of the shrine's chief priest and master bard. Ossiam, the son of their oracle, was born six months after Herrwn and six months before Olyrrwd, the son of their physician, and the three had spent their formative years studying, eating, and sleeping together in the quarters that included the classroom for priests-in-training and its adjacent dormitory.

A stranger looking at Herrwn and Ossiam would have taken them for brothers. Both were tall and slender with sharply defined features. Both had fine, straight hair that darkened from blond to brown as they got older and lightened to silver in their middle years. Both had gray eyes (although Ossiam's exact shade changed with the color of his robes and the light around him, while Herrwn's did not). Both of them had been handsome as young men and both remained imposing into old age, so it puzzled Herrwn that none of the shrine's priestesses had ever chosen Ossiam to be her consort.

Where Herrwn and Ossiam were tall and thin, Olyrrwd was short and stout. He had pale, protruding eyes, bristling, rust-colored hair, and a nose that was too small for the rest of his face. He looked, as Ossiam had sometimes remarked with an undertone that hovered on the edge of spite, "Like a changeling left in place of his mother's real child." Ossiam didn't actually say, "by trolls," but the implication was there.

It seemed to Herrwn that Ossiam and Olyrrwd had begun to quarrel as soon as they could talk. From as far back into their childhood as he could recall, the two were arguing about something—who could run faster, who could throw stones farther, who could recite the most words in a single breath. In contests where being bigger mattered, Ossiam had always won; in those that required aim and dexterity, Olyrrwd had—so the overall balance of victories and defeats stayed close. Now and again, however, one of them (usually Olyrrwd) would score a resounding triumph—like the time they'd been taking turns reciting sections of a particularly demanding epic that required the orator to switch back and forth in rapid succession between the voices of the Sea-Goddess, the mortal hero, and an entire family of ogres.

As Olyrrwd, whose voice had already completed its maturation into an unequivocal bass, was struggling with the lines of the goddess, Ossiam sneered, "You sound like a toad croaking in a bog."

At the time, Olyrrwd had just grinned and gone on, but he spent the following week training his cat to start wailing when he snapped his fingers. The week after that he hid the cat in a basket in the classroom's cupboard and snapped his fingers just as Ossiam opened his mouth to sing. The effect was an all-too-close approximation of Ossiam's erratic and unpredictable fluctuations between a boy's soprano and the high tenor where it would eventually settle. Instead of laughing, however, Olyrrwd had exclaimed, "Why, Ossie, that's the best you've ever done it!" in a tone of complete sincerity.

In spite of Ossiam and Olyrrwd's youthful disputes, the three cousins remained inseparable throughout their early years of study, sharing a chamber reserved for the most gifted and promising of the Druids-in-training even after they'd completed the second level of their instruction and been chosen as their fathers' disciples. At the time, in fact, Ossiam and Olyrrwd's squabbles provided a release from the strenuous demands of their studies.

◆◆◆

"Strenuous" was hardly sufficient to describe the studies required to become a priest in the shrine of the Great Mother Goddess, an indoctrination that began at the age of six and continued well into adulthood.

Starting with simple recitations, songs, and dances, the daily lessons quickly advanced to include oratory and the basics of ritual invocations. By the time boys destined for entry into the highest orders completed their second level of instruction, they were expected to answer any question put to them about any of the scores of interconnected sagas that comprised the nine major epics that lay at the heart of their cult's belief system and to have completely mastered the rites and rituals which, taken together, constituted the symbolic reenactment of the creation of the mortal world as well as providing an explanation for the seasons.

At some point between the ages of sixteen and nineteen, the best of the youthful initiates would be chosen for one of the three great fields of study and move on to the final stage of the indoctrination needed to become a bard, a healer, or an oracle.

For Herrwn, who earned his place as his father's understudy, this had meant not only learning to recite both the Eastern and Western versions of those epics from memory but also to draw on relevant tales in order to explain and defend their order's core convictions—that the Great Mother Goddess was the first and foremost of the world's vast array of gods and goddesses, that it was from Her that all life sprang, that they themselves were the descendants of the firstborn of Her mortal children, and that it was because of this—and because of their continued precision in conducting her rites and rituals—that She chose to remain among them, embodied within their highest priestess.

The belief that a supreme supernatural being of infinite power and importance would take the time and trouble to look after the welfare of a single cult, leaving the larger world to fend for itself, might seem foolish to outsiders, but Herrwn believed it. He had seen it happen.

•◆•

It was in early fall of the year that he was twelve. His father (whose name was also Herrwn, so that Herrwn was called Little Herrwn long after he achieved his adult height) had hinted that if he memorized the complete saga of the courtship of the Earth-Goddess by the Sun-God, he might be allowed to take part in "some very important rite."

The weather that day was sunny and clear, but there was a crispness in the air so that even with his eyes closed, concentrating on his delivery of the speech of the Earth-Goddess decrying her favorite consort's infidelity, Herrwn could tell that summer was ending and fall was setting in. Opening his eyes after what he was confident was a good, if not perfect, rendition, he had expected his father to say that he had done well and, at most, make a few corrections.

His father, however, remained silent, gazing out of the window with a preoccupied look on his face.

Herrwn was about to ask if he had made some grave error (he had just started using the word "grave," liking the profound and important way it sounded, and he also felt "error" was a more elevated word than "mistake"), but just as he was opening his mouth, a woman servant burst into the room.

That any woman should burst into the priest's classroom was startling. That it should be a servant was shocking. And then she spoke without waiting to be given permission!

"The Priestess . . . You must come now!"

While the title "priestess" could mean Herrwn's mother as well as his aunts and all of his grown-up female cousins, "The Priestess" was a term reserved for Eldrenedd, who had been chief priestess and the Goddess incarnate for all of Herrwn's life (and for twenty-eight years before he was born).

Instead of giving the servant a stern look or otherwise correcting her presumptuous behavior, Herrwn's father told her to take Herrwn, Ossiam, and Olyrrwd to the nursery and hurried out of the classroom.

There'd been nothing to do but follow the servant through the winding hallways that led out of the priests' quarters, circled around the central courtyard, and passed through the archway into the women's side of the shrine to the nursery, where Herrwn's little brother and the rest of the shrine's children were having breakfast.

Ignoring the three boys' questions, the chief nursery servant made them sit down at the table and set little cups of warm milk and little bowls of sweetened porridge in front of them.

"That's baby food!" Ossiam protested indignantly, at which Olyrrwd gleefully picked up his bowl and plopped the contents into Ossiam's, saying, "You'll need more because you're a big baby."

There was a moment of startled silence. Then the little boy sitting next to Ossiam picked up his bowl and dumped it into the bowl of the little girl sitting on the other side of him, saying, "Here, you're a baby!" starting a chain reaction of children turning their bowls upside down and shrieking, "You're a baby!" at each other.

Servants rushed around the tables, putting the bowls right side up and scraping up the splattered cereal, while the chief nurse scolded Ossiam and Olyrrwd, warning them to behave or she would go and tell their parents.

After a brief show of contrition, Olyrrwd and Ossiam left the table and began to fight over a toy that one or the other of them had left behind six years earlier until the nurse threw up her hands, left the room, and returned with Herrwn's father.

Although he hadn't been an active participant in his cousins' misconduct, Herrwn was hoping that once his father had given his usual calm admonishment to "take this chance to learn how to resolve your disputes with reason and compromise," he would explain what was going on. Instead, the elder Herrwn took Ossiam and Olyrrwd by the backs of their robes and handed them over to a man-servant with the stinging rebuke *"If you are going to bicker like servants' children, then you may go and stay with servants until you are ready to act like Druids"* and left.

Shaken by his father's uncharacteristic harshness, Herrwn spent the rest of the day doing whatever the chief nurse told him. He played games with his brother and the other children, and then, pretending to be a bard, he told them stories from his own lessons until the end of the afternoon when his father came back—dressed in his finest silk ceremonial robe and carrying a matching robe for Herrwn.

By then, Herrwn had guessed that the mysterious rite his father had been hinting at was about to happen, so he was on his very best behavior as the two of them went together to the shrine's main meeting hall, where all the shrine's priests were forming a line behind the chief oracle.

"Where are the priestesses?" What Herrwn really meant was *Where is my mother?* but he didn't want his father to know how nervous he felt.

"They're waiting for us."

Herrwn could see from his father's set expression that this was no time for questions. Pressing his lips together and bowing his head, he reminded himself that he was a pupil of the shrine's chief priest on the verge of taking part in his first great rite, and it was incumbent ("incumbent" being another word he'd taken to using recently) upon him to act accordingly.

Following close behind his father, he joined the line of priests. As they passed in single file out of the hall, their chief oracle handed each of them a lighted candle without speaking—something that was quite out of the ordinary for Ossiam's father, who always had something portentous to say on every occasion.

The rays of the late-afternoon sun filtered through the branches overhead, making a lacework of shadows on the ground as the procession wound its way deep into the forest. Leaving the paths that Herrwn was familiar with, they climbed upwards until they came to a massive granite outcrop that was split down the middle, as if it had been hewn open by a giant's axe. The priests, who had been murmuring a soft chant praising the Goddess and all of Her works, fell silent—except for the oracle who raised his voice in a long (and, to Herrwn, incomprehensible) incantation before he led the way into the dark crevice.

Herrwn edged along after his father, sliding one hand along the side of the rock wall and holding his candle out to see where he was putting his feet. The air in the narrow passageway was oddly warm and had a faint odor that reminded him of one of their physician's pungent healing potions.

The smell grew stronger as he stepped out of the rift to find himself in a small valley, a place the likes of which he had never seen or imagined.

Chapter 3:

The Sacred Pools

They were standing on the edge of a steaming pool dotted with smooth, flat boulders, the smoothest and flattest of which lay in an almost straight line across to a wide ledge. That ledge was the lowest and widest of a series of shelves that rose, step-wise, into a white cloud that glowed mysteriously with seven pinpoints of light hovering in a line just above where Herrwn imagined the top of the highest ledge must be.

More pools filled the depressions and irregularities in the rocky shelves, connected by ribbons of water that spilled over from one ledge to the next. The banks on either side of the valley floor were covered with a profusion of plants. Some were familiar—ferns and reeds and horsetails—but others were strange, creeping vines that coiled around the trunks of trees and almost covered a long, low wooden hut set back from the edge of the main pool.

Herrwn's father, who had not said anything to him or even looked back to check on him since they'd left the shrine's main hall, turned around and straightened Herrwn's robes, whispering, "We are at the Sacred Pools."

The Sacred Pools!

It was all Herrwn could do to keep his expression somber and earnest as he pictured himself telling Olyrrwd and Ossiam that he'd been to the Sacred Pools.

Ordinarily not even the highest priests were permitted to go to the Sacred Pools—only priestesses and their women servants.

Every month, Herrwn's mother would pack five days of clean clothes, kiss him, his brother, and his father goodbye, and leave with some of the other priestesses because, she said, "I need to rest and regain my strength." Once, when Herrwn had seen her gathering her things together, he'd run up and down the shrine's stairways until he was out of breath and then gone gasping to her, saying that he needed to rest and regain his strength too, but all he'd received for his efforts was to be sent to bed early.

When one of Herrwn's girl cousins, who was only a few months older than he was, smugly packed her clothes and left with the grown-up priestesses, he'd protested to his father that it wasn't fair that girls got to go to the Sacred Pools and boys didn't. His father had been sitting in a corner of the shrine's inner courtyard, talking with another priest who'd broken out in gales of laughter and fallen backward off his stool. Oddogwn picked himself up, brushed off his robes, and said, between wheezing gasps, "Oh, Little Herrwn, believe me when I tell you that you do not ever want to be there when women are resting and regaining their strength."

Herrwn's father, who had answered every question that Herrwn had ever asked him before, only said, "One day when you are grown and are some woman's consort, you will understand."

If he'd dared to move without permission—which he didn't—Herrwn would have loved to test the water in the pool with his toe to see how hot it was. Instead, standing still at his father's side, he waited until, finally, the oracle finished reciting another obscure chant and led the way across the pool, stepping from one dry stone to the next, his robes swishing around his feet, so it looked as if he were walking on the surface of the steaming water.

Keeping in an evenly spaced line and chanting a song usually sung at the winter solstice, the men wove back and forth from one ledge to the next.

As they reached the uppermost ledge, Herrwn saw the mist was rising from the base of a waterfall that plunged in a narrow stream from the cliff above and realized that what he had thought were lights floating in midair were the flames of candles held up by priestesses standing in a row, their gauzy white robes blending in with the mist around them. Their chief priestess, Eldrenedd, stood at the center, with Herrwn's mother on her left side, Caelendra, his mother's first cousin, on her right, and two lesser but still important priestesses on either side of them.

Following the oracle, the priests formed a semicircle facing the priestesses. The last rays of the setting sun turned the sky bright red. The water running around their feet and over the ledge behind them reflected the color overhead, making it seem as if they were surrounded by streams of blood. Suddenly, Herrwn didn't want to be there anymore. He pulled on his father's robe, trying to get his attention and his permission to go back to the nursery.

At that moment, the ancient chief priestess, who'd been glancing around the circle to make sure that everyone was in place, looked directly into Herrwn's face and winked at him, as though to reassure him that everything would be all right.

Then she began to sing.

Herrwn had been learning songs and chants since he was six years old and he thought he knew them all, the ones sung on the shortest day of winter and the longest day of summer, on the night of the full moon and the night there was no moon, after the birth of the first lamb in the spring and before the cutting of the first sheaf of wheat in the fall, but he'd never heard this one before—or any song so filled with passion for the colors and textures and sounds of the living world. The words and the music made him want to climb trees and dance in meadows and run splashing through the Sacred Pools all at once.

As the song went on, a nearly full moon rose above the eastern ridge while the sun was setting in the west, and the reds and pinks around them faded into dark green and darker grays. The light of the moon reflected on the mist so that the air sparkled as if each drop of moisture were an infinitesimally small star, while the real stars came out to fill the sky overhead.

Then the song stopped.

Speaking in a voice that was suddenly old and weary, Eldrenedd sighed. "But now I must leave all this behind and bid you farewell."

"No, please, don't go!" a deep and resonant man's voice rose up. It was Herrwn's father, and as he sang out all the other priests joined him, pleading for her to stay.

The flood of joy that had welled up inside Herrwn vanished, leaving a vast, empty ache behind. It was a feeling he'd only had once before—the one and only time that he'd ever heard his mother and father arguing. He and his brother had listened from outside the doorway to their parents' bedchamber, trembling, as his mother said that she was going to go back to live with her sisters (since Herrwn's mother didn't have any sisters, Herrwn had guessed she meant the quarters for the high priestesses without consorts). His father had pleaded with her not to leave him, promising that he would not fail her again. Herrwn had not heard the beginning of the dispute—and never did learn what it was about—but could feel the desperation in his father's voice as he said, "I will do whatever you ask, if only you will stay!"

"We will do whatever you ask, if only you will stay!" was just what his father sang at that moment, and the chorus echoed his words in an overlapping chant that bounced off the cliff walls.

Those seemed to be the words that Eldrenedd was waiting for, because, in an altered tone, she sang, "Will you honor me, and will you be forever grateful to me for giving you life?"

"We will honor you, and we will be forever grateful to you for giving us life."

"Will you keep a count of my days, and will you pay the tribute you owe to me and to my consorts and to all my divine children?"

"We will keep a count of your days, and we will pay the tribute we owe to you and to your consorts and to all of your divine children."

The chant went back and forth as Eldrenedd extracted their pledge to carry on their traditions in the face of any adversity. Herrwn sang along with the rest, one part of his mind filling with hope and determination, the other part doubting, wondering how the old priestess who seemed barely strong enough to walk could keep her promise not to die.

Eldrenedd put out her hand.

The chanting stopped.

The priestesses who'd been spread out on either side of her came together into a circle. Eldrenedd looked to her left—at Herrwn's mother—but her gaze moved on, looking into the face of each of the six priestesses in turn, until she got to Caelendra.

For a long moment, no one breathed. Then Eldrenedd closed her eyes. The candle that she was holding went out, and the candle that Caelendra was holding flared up brighter, and Caelendra, who was unusually tall for a woman, seemed to grow even taller before Herrwn's eyes.

Herrwn's father went down to his knees, and Herrwn, along with the rest of the priests, did too.

Lifting her candle high over her head with her left hand, Caelendra beckoned for them to rise with her right.

"You, Herrwn," she said, looking at Herrwn's father and speaking in a voice as soft and gentle as a mother comforting a frightened child. "Will you be my chief priest and master bard—giving me your wise counsel and telling the great legends of our past?"

"I will." Herrwn's father spoke in an equally soft voice that was somehow still strong and resolute.

"And you, Olyrrond . . ."

Caelendra went on to ask for and receive promises from each of the other priests. Then, she lowered her candle, spread her arms in a gesture that seemed to embrace them all, and said with surprising simplicity, "Thank you."

With that, Herrwn's father began the chant Herrwn knew from the daily sunrise ritual, and one after another of the priests and priestesses joined in. After the last note died away, Caelendra led them back down the way they came—all of them walking in a steady line, except for the old priestess, who was barely breathing and had to be carried by one of the younger priests.

Chapter 4:

Cididden

T he next morning, while his parents were busy with the preparations for Eldrenedd's funeral, Herrwn rushed to find Olyrrwd and Ossiam. He met them hurrying down the hallways toward him—Olyrrwd out in front for a change, carrying something wrapped up in a small woolen bundle.

Before Herrwn could tell them what had happened at the Sacred Pools, Olyrrwd launched into an enthusiastic account of his day in the shrine's kitchen—interrupted now and again by Ossiam, who seemed determined to continue some earlier quarrel.

Olyrrwd was more than ready to oblige, declaring, "Ossie was a big baby! He was rude to the cook, and she made him sit in the corner."

"She didn't make me do anything! I wanted to sit there! I was having a vision!"

"Were not!"

"Was too!"

"Were not!"

As Olyrrwd and Ossiam shouted at each other, the bundle Olyrrwd was holding against his chest began to move and give off faint mewing sounds. Olyrrwd dropped his voice to a whisper and, ignoring Ossiam's final "was too," abruptly changed the subject to say that he had watched the cook's cat have kittens.

"Seven of them! All black kittens, with no white on them anywhere!"

Too caught up in his story to keep up his quarrel with Ossiam, Olyrrwd retold every detail of the birth that he could remember.

"The mother cat yowled and heaved and looked like she was pooping, but instead of poop, kittens came out! They were all wet and gooey and covered with something like snot, only stickier! And the mother cat licked the sticky stuff off of the kittens, and the kittens crawled all by themselves to start nursing, even though they were just born!" Pausing to take a gulping breath, he went on, "But when the last and littlest kitten was born, her mother pushed her away and wouldn't let her have anything to eat, and the cook said that she was too weak to live, and that she was going to drown her!"

Here Ossiam broke in, paying Olyrrwd back for his earlier insult. "Oly cried like a little baby, and the cook gave him the stupid kitten to make him shut up! And it's just going to die anyway!"

"She will not!" Olyrrwd hugged the bundle closer and glared at Ossiam. "I'm going to heal her! I'll feed her sheep's milk and keep her warm so she will live!"

◆◆◆

Olyrrwd named the kitten "Cididden." For the next three days and nights, he cradled her in his arms, not willing to put her down for fear that she'd die if he wasn't holding her. He dripped milk into her mouth from a doll's spoon and stroked her tiny, frail body, all the time making soft purring noises in imitation of a mother cat.

Defying Ossiam's spiteful prediction, the kitten grew stronger until she could suck the milk off a rag wick and then lap it out of a bowl. The first of the many sickly or injured animals that Olyrrwd nursed back to health, she remained his boon companion for twenty-four years, the exact length of Caelendra's time as their chief priestess.

Once, somewhere in the middle of those years, when Herrwn, Ossiam, and Olyrrwd were resting in their chambers after their midday meal and Cididden was stretched out, sleek and content, on a sunny window ledge, Olyrrwd smugly reminded Ossiam of his "first prophecy," to which Ossiam retorted, "I said she was going to die, I didn't say when!"

But Ossiam was never able to pronounce his prediction fulfilled because, in the turmoil that followed Caelendra's death,

Cididden disappeared. No trace of her was ever found, and all Olyrrwd would say was, "She must have gone to be Caelendra's guide into the next world."

While there was no question that Olyrrwd mourned the loss of his beloved pet almost as much as he mourned for Caelendra herself, Herrwn always harbored a suspicion that his cousin had eased Cididden's exit from this world with a dose of poppy juice in her milk and then hidden her body among the grave goods surrounding the remains of their dead priestess. With Olyrrwd, anything was possible when it came to chafing Ossiam.

Chapter 5:

Rhedwyn

As they advanced through their training, all three cousins had excelled in their chosen field of study—Herrwn in recitation, Ossiam in prophesy, and Olyrrwd in healing—so it surprised no one when each was picked to be his own father's disciple.

Referred to collectively as the "Three Elders," the shrine's bard, oracle, and physician were the highest ranked of the priests, presiding over the High Council and acting as intimate advisors to the chief priestess. As the term implied, the Elders usually lived into venerable old age, and as young men, their understudies knew they could expect to have the benefit of at least twenty more years to fully master the intricacies of their roles before they needed to assume their full responsibilities.

This last stage of indoctrination, however, was cut short for Herrwn, Ossiam, and Olyrrwd by a wave of illness that swept through the shrine the winter after they completed their formal training, taking away almost the whole of the generation above them and leaving them "Elders" before their time.

For weeks afterwards, Ossiam was too busy making sacrifices to appease the malevolent spirits, and Olyrrwd was too busy tending the recovering survivors for them to argue about anything. But eventually, things returned to normal.

As they settled into their seats at the head of the High Council, Ossiam and Olyrrwd's bickering evolved into divisive debates over any question brought before them. While to Herrwn most of his cousins' disputes seemed petty and unnecessary, rising more out of habit than from real disagreement, one proved to be pivotal and to have lasting consequences for the shrine.

•◆•

The plague that left Herrwn, Ossiam, and Olyrrwd pronounced Elders while they were still in their mid-twenties carried a compelling message—so, as soon as they were able, they returned to the shrine's classroom to take up the task of training their own successors.

Before the epidemic struck, there had been a dozen boys of sufficiently high birth to become priests. Now there were only five. The oldest of them, Herrwn's brother, was the sole survivor of seven who'd reached the upper level of their studies. Three of the other four were still in their rudimentary lessons, and the youngest was only a toddler who would still be in the nursery if the women responsible for him hadn't been needed to care for the sick and dying.

Still, five was, as Olyrrwd, who was more accustomed to dealing with illness and death than Herrwn or Ossiam, put it, "better than none, giving us one apiece with two extras, just in case."

But it was not as simple as that.

Herrwn's brother, who'd always been a deeply sensitive boy, too kindhearted to kill a fly and liable to cry for hours over the body of a dead sparrow, withdrew from his training to wander in the high meadows and forests above the shrine, playing his harp and singing songs of unrelenting sadness.

That left the four younger boys—Rhedwyn, Madheran, Moelwyn, and Labhruinn—and it was clear that the handsomest of those four, Rhedwyn, outshone the others. Gifted with a quick mind, an astounding memory, and a flawless voice, he was taking part in all but the highest rituals—chanting the sacred invocations and dancing the sacred dances as if he'd learned them from the firstborn of the Goddess's immortal offspring—by the age of fourteen, and by sixteen he could recite the longest and most complicated of their sagas without so much as a misplaced pause while accompanying himself on a harp with unerring precision.

None of the other boys, with the possible exception of Labhruinn, were incompetent or stupid. Moelwyn actually had quite a good memory and was a quick learner, especially when it came to brewing potions, and—apart from a tic of blinking his right eye— had no major failings. Madheran had a strong, resounding voice and an impressive ability to recite and act out epic battle scenes, although his memory for the other portions of the sagas or for medicinal and oracular incantations left something to be desired.

Unfortunately, the best that could be said of Labhruinn was that he tried hard. At first, his struggles with the most basic of his recitations was put down to his beginning his training at three instead of the usual age of six. As time went on, however, the boy's failure to recite the simplest ode without stammering or to dance more than three steps without tripping over his own feet was an ever-increasing disappointment—especially since he was Rhedwyn's brother by his father as well as his mother.

In all, it was no surprise that the competition over Rhedwyn became a source of renewed contention between Ossiam and Olyrrwd. And being honest with himself, as he invariably was, Herrwn had to admit that he had been as determined as either of the others to claim Rhedwyn for his own calling.

To the best of Herrwn's knowledge, the only song Olyrrwd ever composed was a ditty about the boys that gave vent to his sardonic sense of humor. Almost four decades later, he could hear his cousin's gravelly voice warbling its facetious lines.

Madheran shouting, "I'm so brave!"
Boldly climbs a tree.
Moelwyn, paying him no mind,
Stirs two pots or three.
Labhruinn, rushing to catch up,
Stops to wipe his nose.
Rhedwyn, loveliest of all,
Brings we three to blows.

The first time he sang it, the three of them had been up late talking about their pupils' progress. Ossiam, who'd just finished a far longer and more erudite assessment, left the room in a huff. This was a mistake because it led Olyrrwd to repeat the lyrics so often that after a while he needed only hum the tune to make Ossiam grimace.

Herrwn reproached Olyrrwd about this, not just because he was being childish but because the choice of a disciple was entirely about the skills required to meet the demands of the highest levels of training and was not at all about physical appearance. It was Rhedwyn's abilities that mattered, not—and Herrwn had made this point repeatedly—that the boy was almost too good-looking to be mortal.

Perhaps it was mere chance—though Herrwn thought not— that at the moment he was picturing Rhedwyn in his mind, the night sky over the valley of Derthwald was lit almost as bright as day by a shower of meteors. Led by a fiery ball that dwarfed the others trailing in its wake, they made a blazing arc across the horizon before that brightest one flared in a final, blinding flash of light and the others flickered out one by one, leaving the heavens darker than before.

Given Rhedwyn's rapid progress through the most challenging of his lessons, it was no surprise that he passed all the final tests, including a uniquely spectacular dream quest, and was deemed ready to begin his formal discipleship as a bard, oracle, or healer a full year earlier than most.

So on the day of his sixteenth birthday, Rhedwyn, wearing the plain gray gown of an ordinary apprentice, sat waiting on a stone bench near the entryway to the stairs that led up to the priests' highest tower, while in the chamber at the top of that tower, Herrwn, Ossiam, and Olyrrwd met to determine the best course of his future (or, as Olyrrwd crudely put it—to squabble over who was going to get the pick of the litter).

Herrwn had carefully prepared his words well in advance, and after the obligatory round of ritual incantations, he asserted his right as the head of the High Council to speak first.

"You have heard Rhedwyn's voice, and you must know that he was born to sing the songs of our past. With practice and discipline, he will master the greatest of our tales—bringing alive the words of bards long dead."

It was not usual for Olyrrwd to disagree openly with Herrwn, but here he did, saying, "Those bards are, as you say, long dead, and they will stay that way, whoever sings their songs now." Then, unfairly, he sighed, put his hand to his chest, and said mournfully, "I will not live forever, and you will someday need a physician to take my place—maybe sooner rather than later."

Olyrrwd's words caused a spasm in Herrwn's own chest, and he hastily laid aside his own claim.

Then Ossiam spoke.

Ever since succeeding his father as chief oracle and master of divination, Ossiam had developed the annoying habit of responding to reasoned debate with prophecies of doom when he didn't get his way. Now he evoked the clustering of crows in the tallest oak in the Sacred Grove, the twisting of the entrails pulled out of a sacrificial hare, and the pattern of the clouds in the west that they could all see through the window of the chamber where they were standing as evidence that the Goddess Herself was commanding that Rhedwyn be given into training as an oracle.

Neither Herrwn nor Olyrrwd could muster an argument to counter this flood of omens, so Ossiam got Rhedwyn, although Olyrrwd got the last word, muttering a saying he'd picked up from the servants: "Beware of getting what you wish for."

Deaf to Olyrrwd's disgruntled gibe, Ossiam swept out of the room and down the tower's curving stairway.

Herrwn and Olyrrwd sighed in unison and stood side by side, staring into the smoldering embers of the chamber's hearth, until Olyrrwd sighed again and said, "Well, that leaves three—one for each of us and one left over just in case."

While disappointed, Herrwn was also oddly relieved that Rhedwyn was no longer a source of contention between the two of them. "You'll want Moelwyn, then?" he asked.

"He doesn't mind foul smells and likes stirring pots. I suppose I could do worse. And you'll be content with Madheran?"

"I can't complain about his voice; it's quite resounding and works well for opening odes and speeches of the conquering heroes. And after this . . ."

Herrwn stopped before saying what they were both thinking—that both the younger boys might look better with Rhedwyn gone.

Olyrrwd nodded his understanding and jumped ahead to say what was on the tip of Herrwn's tongue.

"And Labhruinn—"

"can wait." Herrwn picked up Olyrrwd's thought. "He may still—"

"show some promise at something, maybe—"

"as his brother's assistant. Or maybe—"

Going on in this comfortable exchange of half-sentences, they made their way down the stairs together. At the bottom, they parted ways, Olyrrwd taking the left turn toward the shrine's herb garden and Herrwn turning right, back to the classroom.

Chapter 6:

Lillywen

erched precariously on the edge of a cliff, overlooking an
alien landscape and thinking back forty years, Herrwn
regretted not trying harder to make peace between his
cousins. But at the time when he might have done something
to intervene, he had been preoccupied with his own affairs and
had not noticed how wide the rift between Ossiam and Olyrrwd
was growing.

Being literal minded, Olyrrwd would no doubt have pointed
out that the actual parting of their ways had begun when Ossiam
left their shared bedchamber to spend his nights as well as his
days in the Oracle's tower, descending only for the midday and
evening meals and then saying nothing of what he was learning
except that it was secret knowledge and that "his master" had forbidden speaking of it to the uninitiated—following the prescribed
practice of using honorific titles rather than any designations as
informal as "my father."

Meanwhile, Herrwn and Olyrrwd were each kept busy with
their own advanced studies, and while they still shared their
sleeping chamber and continued to spend time together when
their work allowed, they, like Ossiam, had time-consuming studies—and stern taskmasters.

Of their three teachers, Herrwn's father was, in Herrwn's
mind, the most—he was about to use the word "lenient" but
instead chose "wise." The elder Herrwn had not just allowed him
to take a break between his afternoon practice and his evening

recitations but had actually insisted he do so, saying, "Go and experience your own life so that you may more convincingly give voice to the lives of others!"

At first, this had felt more daunting than even reciting the most complex of poems, but his father had remained adamant (in later years, Herrwn had come to wonder whether this was at his mother's insistence). In any case, he soon came to look forward to those free hours. At first, he went with Olyrrwd on his rounds to tend ill and injured villagers—an experience that gave depth to his understanding of the minor characters in his sagas. Then he sought out his younger brother's company, developing a deeper friendship with him than they'd had when all of his time was spent with Ossiam and Olyrrwd. But gradually and increasingly, he was drawn to the shrine's central courtyard and herb gardens, the one location where priests and priestesses who weren't consorts or immediate family might mingle on an informal basis.

His excuse at the time was that this was an ideal location to practice his recitations, but the truth was that he liked being in the garden with priestesses-in-training who were his own age, especially Lothwen, who was his second cousin on his father's side.

As the understudy to the shrine's chief midwife, Lothwen was not free to choose a consort until she completed her apprenticeship any more than Herrwn was free to accept such an offer before completing his, but as they spent those months talking together, she became more and more open about who she would like to name and he became more and more open about his readiness to say yes. An array of their kin—parents, aunts, uncles, and older cousins—looked on from the sidelines with understanding smiles, and as the time approached when they would be free to make this choice, they were given tacit approval to start moving their things into a room of their own in the hall of the shrine reserved for priestesses with consorts and children.

It was considered a mark of a mature Druid to be able to maintain a calm demeanor in the face of the best as well as the worst of events—and Herrwn had managed, barely, to contain the pride and joy he felt the day he was named both a full-fledged bard and Lothwen's consort. The all-consuming bliss of the first months he and Lothwen shared was cut short by the plague but was subsequently replaced by something deeper and stronger as they held each other up and gave each other the strength to accept the loss of their parents and so many others.

•◆•

Herrwn had slipped out of the lean-to shelter where he and his companions had taken refuge for the night intending to make use of the time that Gwenydd and Darbin were arguing to catch up on a much-needed rehearsal of the fifth and final saga of the epic struggle between the Goddess and the giants of the northern mountains.

When the insistent hooting of an owl in a nearby tree brought him back to task, he was startled to realize that the moon was halfway up its eastern arc and he'd not yet completed so much as the hero's opening ode. Such lack of discipline was not acceptable for a bard of his rank. Straightening his posture, he started over, beginning with the names, lineage, and chief attributes of divine and semi-divine figures with major parts to be declaimed. Instead of focusing his mind, however, the familiar litany ran on of its own accord while his thoughts returned first to his beloved Lothwen, who had died giving birth to their only child, and then to his daughter, Lillywen—taken from him six years later by a childhood fever.

•◆•

The midwives who fought the long, losing battle for Lothwen's life had been too busy to notice that Herrwn had slipped into the birthing chamber. He'd stood in the shadows, drawing shallow, irregular gasps along with Lothwen until her breathing stopped and his kept going.

Rhonnon, the shrine's chief midwife, looked perplexed for a moment. When she turned around and saw him, her expression changed to vexation—leaving no doubt that she felt he'd done enough damage already. He flinched, expecting her to curse him as he was cursing himself, but instead she sighed and handed him his infant daughter, swaddled in woolen wraps that were damp with birth waters and Lothwen's blood.

It was well-known that Rhonnon did not hold men in much regard, so Herrwn was not surprised that she stayed close by, her hands stretched out to catch the baby in case he let her slip, but despite her misgivings, Herrwn did not drop his newborn daughter—he held her pressed against his heart until he was forced to surrender her to her nurse.

The next day, he used his authority as the shrine's chief priest to get past the guardian of the entrance to the inner sanctum of the women's quarters and found his way to the nursery. Brushing aside the nurse's objections, he sat on the only adult-size chair, placed Lillywen on his lap, and recited the silly rhymes he remembered from his own days in the nursery as she gazed up at him with her mother's eyes.

After that, he went to see Lillywen every day, getting up before dawn to cradle her in his arms before reluctantly relinquishing her to her nurse and leaving to attend to his own work, then returning as soon as possible—anxious to hold her again.

When she was weaned, he flouted tradition—and further displeased her nurse—by having his breakfast in the nursery sitting on a little chair at Lillywen's little table, his long legs drawn up so he looked like an oversized grasshopper perched on too small a leaf. His answer to Ossiam's querulous objections that he was spending more time in the nursery than in the priests' quarters was, "If you need me, you know where to find me." That was true—any time he wasn't presiding in the council chambers, reciting epics in the shrine's main hall, teaching in the classroom, or conducting sacred rites, he could be found playing dolls with Lillywen on the nursery floor.

As Lillywen grew older, Herrwn began to make up stories about a little girl and her foolish, stubborn father having humorous misadventures together and somehow coming through them without any harm to anything except that father's dignity. The stories became a saga about the fictional father and daughter's travels on a long journey to a distant and only vaguely explained destination. At the beginning of each story, the father would take the wrong path and get lost, and the daughter, who was brave and resourceful as well as beautiful, had to rescue him from one predicament after another with the help of the forest animals who, in spite of their fur or feathers, spoke fluent Celt and had complicated family relationships that crossed the boundaries between species with bunny children running to their uncle badger for advice or quarreling fearlessly, if illogically, with their cousin fox cubs.

Now, sitting at the edge of the cliff and gazing up across the valley as the moon moved through a swath of clouds, Herrwn could almost feel his small daughter's warm, sweet-smelling body snuggled against his chest and could almost hear her sleepy voice insisting that she was not tired and asking for just one more story.

After Lillywen died, Herrwn retreated back to his studies and to teaching other men's children. He took refuge in his work and was not willing to leave it even when his brother—his eyes once again bright with enthusiasm after seven years of pining—urged Herrwn to join him on a quest into the outside world to seek out those who still worshipped the Goddess and give them the comfort and strength of knowing that they were not alone. At the time, Herrwn did not think that he could offer anything to help the loneliness of others, and so his brother set off without him.

Of all the choices that he had made in his life, that was the one Herrwn regretted the most. He had, of course, no thought that his going along would have saved his brother from being captured by their Christian enemies—only that they would have been together and his brother would not have suffered and died alone. In the years that had passed since then, he had not ever forgiven either himself or the supposedly faithful servants who had promised to guide and protect his brother and had instead betrayed him to be tortured and burned at the stake.

Herrwn's daughter and brother died within a month of each other, giving rise to a communal sense of foreboding that settled over the shrine like a fog.

No one said what they were thinking out loud, but—

Ossiam stopped telling anyone what he saw when he looked into the entrails of sacrificial goats or watched the dark swarms of crows that flew over the shrine's highest tower.

Olyrrwd found reasons to remark, at least three times each day, that belief that bad things come in threes was a foolish superstition.

And as Herrwn passed people in the hallways, they would abruptly break off their conversations to smile unnaturally bright smiles at him.

While his friends and relations were treating him with the cloying kindness reserved for those who are fatally ill, Herrwn moved through his days with a feeling of profound clarity, relishing each act and each sensation, conscious that this might be the last time he laced his sandals, or bit into warm bread, or felt the sun on his face. His craving to savor each moment was mixed with his impatience to be reunited with those he loved the most, and he lived the next three months with an intensity of awareness that he'd never felt before or since.

As days and then weeks passed, however, Herrwn remained in glowing health—and one morning, he put on his sandals without paying attention to what he was doing. That same day, at breakfast, he had to ask twice for the salt, only to have a nearby servant fetch it for him instead of all his table companions reaching for it at once. As he left the table and went back to his classroom, Herrwn realized that all he felt was sad, and he resigned himself to remaining in the mortal world for the time being.

While Herrwn was disappointed, the rest of the shrine was relieved. Except for Lillywen, they'd all survived the illnesses of winter, and the pessimism and doubts that took hold in the dark of the year released their grip, giving way to the burgeoning hopes of spring—a spring in which Caelendra, their chief priestess, was going to give birth to the child everyone expected would be a girl and their next Goddess incarnate.

PART II

The Summer Solstice Ceremony

Caelendra's succession to the position of chief priestess had been unusual in that she was only distantly related to her predecessor. While in principle the spirit of the Mother Goddess taking leave of an elderly or gravely ill chief priestess might enter any ranking member of the inner circle of the elite women's council, the "Transition," as it was called, always seemed the most assured when the chief priestess had a daughter standing "at Her right side" (a phrase that described both the established order of ascent and the arrangement of the women's line in formal events). If she didn't have a daughter, a younger sister was thought the next best, and if—as was the case with the extraordinarily long-lived Eldrenedd—the chief priestess had no close female relatives left, the choice of her successor was usually made clear well before the final ceremony took place.

While Eldrenedd had been greatly loved and revered throughout the nearly five decades of her reign, she'd been known for putting off weighty decisions to the last possible moment—which accounted for the high level of tension surrounding Caelendra's ascension. As wondrously ethereal as that moment had been, it was generally hoped that the next Transition would not be as fraught with uncertainty—and that if Caelendra chose not to take a consort, she would make use of the Sacred Summer Solstice ritual to ensure that she would have at least one daughter when the time came.

Having decided to deny themselves the enjoyment of sex, the Christian priests of Herrwn's day bitterly reviled anyone they suspected might be having more fun than they did. That, at least, was what Herrwn's father had once told him.

"When I had the unfortunate occasion to see and hear their orations for myself," he went on to say (by which Herrwn understood him to mean the last time he'd left Llwddawanden to try to reconcile with their converted kinsmen), "I could not help but notice that those thundering the most loudly about the evils of physical pleasure were men so lacking in personal attractiveness that Christian priestesses choose each other's company over theirs." Here the elder Herrwn had allowed himself the sardonic speculation, "So perhaps they must make a virtue out of their failure to earn a woman's affections," before going on to describe in bitter detail how his two erstwhile brothers—who should have known better—had joined their benighted cousins in echoing the infamous accusation that the most ancient and hallowed rite of the Goddess, the Sacred Summer Solstice Ceremony, was no more than a lewd and licentious orgy.

Nothing could have been farther from the truth—and especially not in their shrine! While the priests and priestesses could not be held responsible for what overstimulated laborers and servants might be doing in the bushes, the Sacred Summer Solstice ritual was an act of devout homage.

Like all the shrine's highest rituals, the Sacred Summer Solstice Ceremony was the symbolic reenactment of critical events in the creation of the mortal world. Understanding it required an understanding of a complex series of sagas that began with the taming of fire (and of the Sun-God as well) and went on to an explanation for the seasons and of the special relationship between the first Druids and the Goddess.

The several variations on this legend fell into two basic versions, known among the shrine's scholars as the Eastern and Western Fire Tales. While there was disagreement between the two accounts over a number of significant details, both were in agreement that in the beginning, fire had belonged exclusively to the Sun-God and he carried it in a satchel slung over his shoulder from which he drew out a handful of flames to cast down to the earth whenever it amused him to watch the futile, panic-stricken scrambling of men and animals trapped in the wildfire's path, until the Earth-Goddess—who'd given birth to the human tribes and was fond of animals as well—caught him at it.

Perhaps the most disputed point between the two traditions was that in the Eastern version, the Goddess disguised Herself as an irresistibly beautiful mortal woman, while in the Western one, she transformed Herself into a white mare so dazzling that the Sun-God turned himself into a golden stallion to chase her down. In any event, it was well established that the Sun-God agreed to stop his wanton cruelty in exchange for the opportunity to make love to Her ("in the heat of passion" was a stock phrase in most versions—and saying that smoothly without any hint of humor or acknowledgment of the pun was the mark of a master bard). After exacting the Sun-God's promise to be kind to mortals—both human and animal—in exchange for becoming her main consort, the Earth-Goddess took a handful of flames out of the Sun's satchel, placed them in a bronze bowl, and gave the bowl to the firstborn of her mortal children—who, as it turned out, were none other than the first in the line of Druids leading down to their own elite fellowship.

Both the Eastern and Western versions were in full agreement that the summer solstice marked the anniversary of the night that the Sun-God and the Earth-Goddess first made love together, in the process conceiving a son who spent a short but brilliant life in human form, during which he bestowed the gifts of song and dance and healing on his mortal brothers and sisters.

The reenactment of that first summer solstice began each year in the largest of the valley's Sacred Groves with children's games—of which the most popular was one in which the village boys and girls, along with their pet dogs and goats, ran with shrieks of laughter away from an apprentice priest wearing a costume festooned with goose feathers dyed yellow in imitation of the sun's flames. For the rest of the longest day of the year, the young men and women of Llwddawanden, priests and priestesses, servants and laborers, took part in a flurry of contests—running, swimming, tossing lances, and shooting bows—intermixed with communal dancing, singing, and feasting.

Then, at the moment that the sun slipped out of sight behind the west rim of the valley wall, silence fell over what until then had admittedly been a noisy, raucous festival. As darkness gathered around them, the now motionless revelers scanned the shadows of the grove for the first twinkle of a lighted torch.

"There, look there!" would come not as a shout but as a reverent whisper, and the crowd would split apart and draw back as the priest chosen to act as the Sun-God passed by them dressed in golden robes, wearing a crown of summer flowers, and holding a blazing bundle of rushes above his head. Walking at a measured pace, like the stately march of the sun moving across the sky, the god's surrogate approached the sacred altar stone at the front of a ring of upright stone slabs that, according to tradition, had been placed there as a peace offering to the Goddess by the giants before they retreated into the higher mountains to become stone themselves.

The sight of the designated priestess, swathed in green silk and adorned with glittering gems, stepping out of the gap between the standing stones as if she had just emerged from earth itself was always breathtaking, but never more so—at least in Herrwn's mind—than the year that it was not a proxy for the Goddess but Caelendra herself who appeared holding out the sacred bronze bowl to receive the flames from the Sun-God's torch.

Chapter 7:

The Third Death

aelendra was a tall woman with erect posture but an otherwise undistinguished appearance. Unless required to don ceremonial vestments for rituals, she wore plain, unadorned robes and kept her hair, which had turned from drab brown to gray soon after her ascent to power, in a single long braid. Her eyes, certainly her best feature, were dark, serious, and thoughtful—two deep pools of care and wisdom set in a face so aged by the burdens of her office that even her most devoted admirers, and Herrwn was one of those, spoke of her inner beauty rather than her outward appearance. But that night, as she stepped through the space between the two frontmost of the tall standing stones, her face and form lit only by the flames of the single torch held up by the golden priest, Caelendra was resplendent.

Herrwn was standing close at hand, waiting for his part in the ceremony, so he could see for himself that she'd not resorted to any artifice—but with her hair released from its tight braid and flowing down in a shimmering silver cascade about her shoulders, it was as if, for once, her inner beauty shone through, and they were seeing for the first time the Goddess within her.

She stood there, radiant, her eyes for once not serious and thoughtful but bright with anticipation, her ordinarily sallow skin blushed a rosy pink, as her consort for the night—moving with the power and grace of a god—stepped up and reached out his torch to set the oil in her bowl on fire. She held the vessel cupped in both hands, her face aglow in its flames for a long moment before she gave it to Herrwn and stepped down from the altar.

As Caelendra's feet touched the ground, the shrine's musicians struck the opening chords of the song reserved for the sacrosanct dance of the Sun-God and the Earth-Goddess. The priest acting as the Sun-God handed off his torch to Ossiam and put his hands on Caelendra's waist. She put her hands on his shoulders, and, turning rhythmically in swaying circles, they danced their way down the path between the line of worshipful onlookers and off into the darkness, leaving the other priests and priestesses to pass out toy flutes and harps and drums to the drowsy children.

In the eulogy he gave for Caelendra nine months later, Herrwn spoke from his heart when he said, "She governed well and wisely, weaving the wisdom of the past into the actions of the present and carefully weighing the demands of the present against the needs of the future, but above all, she found the time to listen to those who came to her with their troubles, whether they were the highest priest or the lowest servant and whether that matter was of monumental importance or no more than petty gossip. Putting aside all else, she would take the worries and woes they brought to her up in her hands, as though they were a precious harvest of golden wheat, and then she would blow softly and gently on them with her warm, sweet breath, sending off the chaff of confusion and selfishness and keeping the best and the most worthy grains of truth to hand back, so the priest, priestess, laborer, or servant might know that within himself or herself was all the wisdom of the ancients, all the courage of any warrior, and all the glory of a god or a goddess."

Caelendra had, in truth, been a singularly skilled and judicious leader whose keen political acumen was balanced by her compassion and an innate sense of fairness. As their chief priestess and the living embodiment of the Great Mother Goddess, she could have named the virile young priest with whom she'd danced so perfectly on the night of the summer solstice to be her consort, but she'd never again favored him with more than an occasional pensive look.

Perhaps that was because overseeing the complex sequence of rituals that cycled through both the lunar and solar years, managing their shrinking treasury, and settling disputes took all of Caelendra's time and energy, or perhaps it was because her fair-mindedness kept her from favoring one of her subjects over the rest, or perhaps it was because she had enough problems without having a consort to cope with. Whatever the reason, however many others carried their desires and their cares to Caelendra, she did not speak of her own feelings—not even to Rhonnon, who was both her closest cousin and chief advisor—so no one ever knew whether the choice she made at the end of her childbearing years was an act of courage or loneliness.

There was, however, never any doubt in Herrwn's mind that Caelendra's decision to enact the first mating between the Earth-Goddess and the Sun-God was a selfless one, intended to be the start of a new generation, the conception of an infant desperately needed for its own sake and also the setting of an example to the childless priestesses still young enough to follow suit, whether they chose to take consorts or not. That was what he believed, and that was what he said whenever Olyrrwd muttered about the coincidence that, of all the available priests, she chose Rhedwyn.

Looking back, the risks of pregnancy so late in life should have been obvious. Caelendra, however, was a strong and resolute woman. Through the worst of her active labor, she did not curse, cry out, or groan but simply pressed her lips together and closed her eyes, as if the pain were only a problem brought to her for consideration at a meeting of the High Council—so even the most experienced of the midwives hovering around her did not expect the tragedy when it happened.

The birth was over. As chief priest, Herrwn had been admitted to the chamber to convey his blessing and had entered it to see Caelendra looking exhausted but otherwise well. Rhonnon, the chief midwife, had acknowledged his presence with a nod as she finished cleaning the fussing baby and placed it into Caelendra's arms. But instead of quieting with the chance to latch on to its mother's breast, the infant wailed louder—and instead of responding to its cries, Caelendra slumped back against the pillows, not just dead tired but actually dead.

The transition from life to death is always momentous, but for Caelendra to exit so abruptly, with no parting message about who was to be the next chief priestess, took them all by surprise, and for a time there was no sound in the room except for the plaintive wails of the dark-haired infant.

"She expected a girl and was going to name her Caelymna," Rhonnon said in a dull voice. Picking up the squalling baby, she sighed. "It's a boy and, I suppose, must be called Caelym." As she handed him to the wet nurse who'd been rushed into the room, she looked back at Herrwn, sighed again, and said, "You will tell the council."

"Of course." Too numb to say anything else, he turned away, leaving Rhonnon and her assistants to begin their final care of the woman who had shown so much foresight in every other way and yet never anticipated dying.

◆

It was the third death that they had all been dreading, and it left them stunned. Caelendra's decision to risk childbirth so late in life was the first injudicious decision that she had ever made. Dying so suddenly, without warning or preparation, was the second.

With no sign from Caelendra about who was to take her place, the shrine's leaders turned to their oracle.

Chapter 8:

Ossiam's Finest Hour

As Caelendra had died on the eve of the spring equinox, her funeral rites were carried out the next morning in place of the day's usual festivities. After the last of the odes and elegies were spoken, her body—wrapped in silk, blanketed with the first flowers of the year, and resting on a gilded litter—was lifted up by four of the younger priests. Followed by a procession of sobbing mourners, they carried her up the path that clung to the side of the western cliffs and then down again into the depths of the sacred catacombs, where she joined the remains of the other women who, like her, had been vessels for the Goddess.

Had her successor been named, the new chief priestess and Goddess incarnate would have led the way out of labyrinth and back into the daylight.

Instead, their oracle did.

It was Ossiam's finest hour.

Under Caelendra's cautious, circumspect leadership, the oracle's role had been entirely ceremonial. While she had consulted Ossiam on every expected occasion, nodding solemnly as he spoke and praising the skill of his prophesying, when it came to action she'd done whatever she thought best—never failing to give him full credit for his guidance even when her decision was the exact opposite of what he had actually said, as it often was.

Now he held the shrine's future in his hands.

The whole of the valley's population was gathered and waiting in the same grove where they'd celebrated the summer solstice nine months earlier when the procession returned from the catacombs. Now, as before, the crowd split apart and drew back, opening a corridor, this time to let Ossiam, leading the line of droning priests and priestesses, pass through.

Leaving the others behind him at the foot of the great altar stone, Ossiam swept up the steps to stand above them all.

The sun was directly overhead. The sky was a vast empty sea of blue—without a wisp of a cloud or a single bird in flight to offer any hint of what was to come.

"Bring me the sacrifice!" Ossiam's cry rang out in the stillness like the sound of ice splitting in a frozen lake.

Clearly, the goat—which had to be dragged, bleating and kicking, up the altar steps—foresaw nothing good in its own future. It took three strong men, pitting all their strength against its panicked struggles, to wrestle it into submission and lift it into place. As two of them gripped its flailing legs and one forced its head back to expose its throat, it gave a shrill cry that sounded almost human.

Ossiam stepped forward, raised the sacred dagger high over his head with both hands, and then brought it down.

The silence was so sudden and so complete that it seemed for a moment the audience had stopped breathing when the goat did. It was so quiet that those standing closest to the altar could hear the sound of the oracle's ceremonial blade slicing open the goat's belly. Barehanded, Ossiam scooped up its still-pulsing bowels and held them above his head as the assistant priests pulled its flaccid corpse out of the way.

Instead of the usual incantation, he simply cried out, "Tell us your will!" as he sent the entrails spilling across the stone slab. Then he stood staring into the quivering coils until it seemed that not even the pillars around them could bear the suspense any longer.

"Feywn!"

Looking up, Ossiam stretched out his right hand, still dripping with the goat's blood, to point at a golden-haired girl standing among the half dozen priestesses-in-training.

"It is she and none other whom the spirit of the Goddess

chooses! It is she and none other who is now our chief priestess and the vessel in whom the Goddess dwells!"

His pronouncement was met with a palpable shift in the crowd's silence, from awed to bewildered.

Herrwn, like all the rest, looked from Ossiam to Feywn to Rhonnon and back to Ossiam, in what an outside onlooker might have thought was an amusing imitation of a herd of deer turning their heads in unison toward an unexpected sound in the under-brush and then to their lead stag to see which way he would dart.

Most of the priests and priestesses were expecting to hear Rhonnon's name pronounced. After all, why would the Goddess pass over her closest kinswoman to pick a girl just sixteen years old and still in training? Though no one spoke it out loud, a question hovered in the air: *What if Ossiam mistook the message in the entrails—his vision affected by Feywn's youthful beauty or by Rhonnon's well-known aversion to taking advice from men?*

Perhaps Ossiam was aware that he'd lost his audience and perhaps he wasn't, but suddenly he staggered backward, as if struck by a spear in his chest. Drawing in a rattling gasp of air, he lurched forward again. Then his body went rigid. His back arched. His eyes rolled upward, leaving only their whites exposed. When he spoke again, his voice was high-pitched and shrill and seemed to come from a long way off as it howled, "Feywn! Feywn! It is Feywn whom the Goddess chooses!"

Then, just as abruptly, his stance relaxed, his eyes rolled back down, and his voice returned to normal—or, at least, to the normal of an oracle in the midst of his declarations—as he added, "And now she will come forth, and she will choose a consort, and he will reign at her side in a union that will change our destiny so that the power, the glory, and the riches of the past may once again be ours."

While Ossiam may have been right about the spirit of the Goddess entering Feywn (and after two long reigns spent within priestesses known for their reliability and diligence rather than their sexual allure, it did seem at least possible that She might choose Feywn over Rhonnon), Herrwn was absolutely certain the oracle had misread the identity of the consort that Feywn would choose to "reign at her side." He'd been watching his cousin closely and knew him well enough to read his expression even from a distance—and he saw the eagerness glow in his face as Feywn walked toward him—and saw it fade when she passed by him to place her hand on the arm of his disciple, Rhedwyn.

It seemed to Herrwn a youthful blunder, an affront to all the older and higher-ranking priests and especially to Ossiam, to whom she owed her amazing elevation in rank and authority, but whether Feywn's choice was inspired by girlish desire or by divine wisdom, it was an act that resonated.

Beginning as a whisper somewhere in the back of the crowd, the notion that the spirit of the Goddess had leapt from Caelendra's dying body into Feywn out of a deathless passion for the priest She'd chosen to take the part of the Sun-God nine months earlier gathered strength and spread through the gathered throng with the force of a powerful wind sweeping away their doubts and misgivings. As if on cue, Rhedwyn took the silk shawl embroidered with the symbols of the Goddess out of the hands of the priestess who'd been standing next to Rhonnon and draped it around Feywn's shoulders. In that moment, without any outward change beyond an almost imperceptible stiffening of her posture, Feywn assumed the mantle of absolute authority as their chief priestess and the living embodiment of the Great Mother Goddess.

"And you cannot argue that Ossiam was entirely wrong for, beyond any question, Feywn's union with Rhedwyn did change our destiny."

Startled to realize that he'd spoken out loud, Herrwn shifted his position on the edge of the cliff to relieve the numbness in his right leg and finished his thought silently—that while Feywn's union with Rhedwyn might now be seen to have brought tragedy instead of triumph, surely Ossiam would be able to explain the discrepancy if he were still with them.

Ossiam himself never admitted to either disappointment or resentment over Feywn's choosing his apprentice over himself. In fact, when Olyrrwd gibed him about it later, Ossiam affected studied indifference as he replied, "Who did you think I meant?"

Chapter 9:

Rhedwyn's Idyll

The spring equinox that opened with Caelendra's funeral rites and closed with the celebrations for Feywn's ascension and her nearly simultaneous union with Rhedwyn would long be remembered as a day set apart, a day when all the usual rules were suspended and the usual events were replaced by extraordinary happenings.

That night, it seemed like the wine was flowing from some bottomless vat, the plates were never empty, and the music and dancing would go on forever. It was long past midnight when Feywn and Rhedwyn left the great hall, late morning before Feywn called for breakfast to be brought to her bedchambers, and well past noon before Rhedwyn emerged and strolled back to the priests' quarters.

Normally, Herrwn would have had his pupils and classroom to himself at that hour, Olyrrwd would have been tending to the sick in the healing chamber, and Ossiam would have been ensconced in the oracle's tower, sorting out the patterns of the clouds and the flights of ravens. Instead, Olyrrwd was sitting at the classroom's only table, ostensibly sharpening and polishing his surgical knives, and Ossiam was rearranging the row of ritual chalices and talismans on their shelf by the classroom window.

Herrwn was in the middle of repeating the crucial opening stanzas of the tragic saga of King Derfwyn's Final Folly to his fidgety pupils when the door swung open and Rhedwyn walked in, his step as light and springing as if he were still dancing with Feywn.

"How kind of you to grace us with your presence," Ossiam said. "I trust your night away was a pleasant one."

Amazingly, Rhedwyn missed the derision in Ossiam's greeting and he puffed himself up—as Olyrrwd would say later—like a cock about to crow.

"It was"—here he paused to wink at Madheran and Labhruinn, who were staring at him in wide-eyed admiration—"very pleasant indeed!"

Speaking in a voice all the more ominous for its dripping syrupy sweetness, Ossiam looked at the amulet—a ram's head modeled in baked clay—that he was holding and not at Rhedwyn as he purred, "Far be it from me to keep you from your more pressing affairs. Do take the rest of the day off to continue the enjoyment of your union with our lovely chief priestess."

"Really? The whole day?" For an otherwise brilliant scholar, Rhedwyn's failure to grasp Ossiam's sarcasm was astounding.

Herrwn looked over at Olyrrwd and could see that he, too, was braced for the scathing rebuke to come—and that he was as startled as Herrwn himself when Ossiam, still looking at the talisman he was rubbing between his fingers, smiled a stiff smile and said, "Oh, as much time as you wish!" They were both left speechless when Rhedwyn took this as if Ossiam actually meant it, and cheerfully even cheekily called out, "Thank you," as he picked up a harp and left.

No one said anything until the sounds of his brisk and bouncy steps faded down the hall. Then it was Olyrrwd who broke the silence.

"Nice that oracles can take a day off now and again—wish it were so for healers." Gathering up his knives, he added, "But I've got a boil to lance and a diligent, hardworking apprentice waiting for me to show him how to do it."

While Olyrrwd hadn't complained openly about Moelwyn's performance since he'd officially taken him as his disciple, he hadn't said anything in his particular praise either, so Herrwn guessed this remark was meant to chaff Ossiam. It unquestionably had that effect. After Olyrrwd ambled out the door and down the hall, Ossiam dropped the figurine he'd been fingering and stepped on it, crushing it to red powder, before stalking off to his tower.

◆◆◆

Rhedwyn spent the rest of the day in an idyll with Feywn. The two rode off together into the hills. When they returned late that afternoon, both were wearing crowns of meadow flowers, and from the glow on their faces it was certain they had been doing more than gathering flowers.

There was feasting and celebration again the next day—and the next, and the one after that—and each night Rhedwyn and Feywn danced until nearly dawn before disappearing into her chambers, and each day they emerged at midday and spent the afternoon frolicking in the valley's upper meadows.

A week passed—seven days that had been notable for Ossiam's increasingly chilly silence. On the morning of the eighth day, just as Herrwn was about to start his lessons and Olyrrwd and Ossiam were on the verge of leaving to take up their own responsibilities, Rhedwyn reappeared, the stem of a wilted daisy tucked behind his ear.

"Welcome back," Ossiam said. "If it is not interfering with your other activities, perhaps you will join me in the oracle's tower so that we may discuss your studies."

It was equally remarkable that Ossiam's greeting to his truant disciple might only have been a casual comment on the weather and that Rhedwyn followed Ossiam out of the room without the slightest sign of contrition or concern.

Herrwn and Olyrrwd exchanged a cautious glance, sharing the same thought—that Ossiam, always proud and rarely forgiving, would dismiss Rhedwyn from his apprenticeship and then one of them could claim him.

Leaving Moelwyn, Madheran, and Labhruinn with hasty instructions to "recite the next twelve passages of the discourse between King Derfwyn and his wise men—paying particular attention to the reasons his counselors gave in attempting to dissuade him from his attempt to deceive the Sea-Goddess— while I attend to other duties," Herrwn hurried to catch up with Olyrrwd, who was already halfway down the hall.

Just as they reached the entrance to the stairway that led up to the oracle's tower, they heard footsteps coming down.

Acting as one, they stepped out of sight behind a pillar as Rhedwyn emerged and rushed past them off through the hall that led away from the priests' chambers. The moment he was out of sight, Olyrrwd charged up the stairs. Determined to be there to reassert his own case, Herrwn hurried after Olyrrwd and was only a step behind when he thrust open the door and rushed into the chamber.

"Well?" Olyrrwd demanded while Herrwn was still catching his breath and trying to think of some delicate way to open the enquiry.

"Well, what?" Ossiam was looking out the tower's window and didn't turn to face them.

"Have you dismissed him?"

"Why would I do that? Unlike healers, oracles can take a day off now and again."

Keeping his back to them, Ossiam continued to stare out the window, affecting a show of intense concentration on the shifting shape of a distant, wispy cloud that was floating just above the eastern ridge top on the far side of the valley.

For a moment, Olyrrwd stood with his teeth gritted and his fists clenched, just like when they were boys and Ossiam taunted him about being short and homely.

Ossiam continued to gaze at the cloud as though he were alone in the room.

After a long, tense moment, Olyrrwd uncurled his fingers and unclenched his teeth and turned to stalk down the stairs.

The owl whose earlier hooting had brought Herrwn back to the present called again, this time sounding so close that Herrwn startled and looked around just in time to see its black shadow leave a low-growing pine and swoop past him before disappearing down into the darkness of the valley below.

He should, of course, have resumed reciting the names of the divinities and mortals with key parts to play in the final battle between the ocean goddess and the giants of the northern mountains then, but he didn't. Instead, returning to his recollections, he tried once again to make sense of Ossiam's inexplicable change of attitude over his disciple's training.

•◆•

Had Herrwn been in Ossiam's position, he would have willingly given dispensation for Rhedwyn to sit next to the chief priestess at community meals and to have private time allotted to their relationship (though certainly not all night, as discipleship included the disciple's sleeping on a cot by his teacher's bed at night in case the elder priest should wake with a wise thought to pass on or a dream for them to decipher together). Yet Ossiam, who'd shown no inclination toward leniency in the past, never brought his disciple to task.

While Herrwn did not claim a personal expertise in divination, he knew that no skill worth having was gained without time and effort, but when he said as much to Ossiam, urging him to take his disciple in hand, Ossiam's answer was to make vague excuses that Rhedwyn was still young and not yet ready for serious study.

Afterwards, still troubled, Herrwn sought out Olyrrwd in the healing chamber. After making sure there was no one close enough to hear them, he repeated his complaint, adding, "I do not understand why Ossiam allows it! Instead of divining portends for himself, Rhedwyn looks to Ossiam and reads his lips—repeating his words as if they were his own."

Olyrrwd's response, "Maybe that's why," troubled Herrwn even more.

Chapter 10:

Declamation

"*Rise now all you who have sworn your lives to the Great Goddess who gave birth to us all! Take up your shining swords and gleaming lances, mount your rearing steeds, and follow me!*"

Herrwn nodded his approval as Madheran struck a noble pose, raising his empty hand above his head with his fingers so convincingly curled around the handle of his imaginary sword that Herrwn could almost see the flash of sunlight reflecting off its blade.

"*I will lead you to victory or to a death so valiant that no one will say of Pwendorwn, King of Llanamaeddwndod, that he or his warriors flinched from the threats of giants and ogres—*"

"King of?" Herrwn wouldn't have interrupted the flow of an oration so well delivered except this was the third time that Madheran had misnamed Pwendorwn's kingdom—and the last time, Ossiam had overheard and hissed "Llanamaeddwndod?" in derision. Caught up in his passionate declamation, Madheran had not noticed, but Herrwn had, and he'd felt his cousin's mockery deeply—both for himself and for his disciple.

"King of . . ." Madheran furrowed his brow—either trying to remember the correct kingdom or to keep from asking again why it mattered when all the names of the seven kingdoms in that particular saga sounded alike.

Stifling his own frustration that only the day before he had explained at length how each of those seven kingdoms represented an achievement of humankind and its name contained a clue to which of those endowments was threatened by the onslaught of the army of the ogres led by a terrible triad of one-eyed giants, Herrwn turned to Labhruinn. "Come to Madheran's aid and name the kingdom that the hero, Pwendorwn, is calling on his warriors to defend."

"It . . . it is, er, um, the name of the kingdom that Pwendordden—I mean, Pwendorwn—"

Startled out of whatever daydream had been preoccupying him, Labhruinn looked down at his nervously clenched fists and with a dint of effort out of proportion with the simple task he'd been given, uncurled his fingers, one after another, and counted off the seven kingdoms in the order that he'd memorized them, "Llanamaeddwndod, Llancerddysul, Llanddissigllen, Llandefodaerddin, Llangwehudd"—and instead of stopping here, as he should have, he plowed on—"Llanlendrwdd, Llanmeddelyderth."

Silently, Herrwn asked himself why he allowed as incompetent a pupil as Labhruinn to remain in his classroom, and equally silently he answered the question—besides the fact that Labhruinn was Rhedwyn's younger brother and so, by extension, was kin to the shrine's chief priestess, he simply didn't have the heart to dismiss a student who was so sweet-natured and sincere.

Suppressing a sigh, he turned back to Madheran. "Now, then, you may resume the recitation, beginning with, 'I will lead you to victory'—this time correctly naming the kingdom of Llangwehudd."

"I will lead you to victory or to a death . . ." Madheran had just resumed his heroic pose when a distant hunting horn sounded, signaling Rhedwyn's return from the hills. Keeping his arm raised with his fingers clutching at the empty air, he sped on, "so valiant that no one will say of Pwendorwn, King of Llangwehudd, that he or his warriors flinched from the threats of giants and ogres!" without pausing for breath, much less emphasis, in his eagerness to be done with the lesson and released to join the throng of priests, priestesses, servants, and laborers who were rushing from their chores to be in attendance when Feywn welcomed Rhedwyn back from his latest adventure.

It may have been that the intoxicating scent of the sun-warmed earth with her burgeoning new growth wafting in through the classroom's open window was affecting Herrwn as much as his pupils, because he was unable to summon the strength of will to hold his pupils captive when their minds had so clearly departed. He dismissed them both, calling, "I will expect you to return tomorrow able to state why it is the attack on Llangwehudd that finally brings together the greatest warriors of all the human tribes to rally under a single leader, rising up in defiance and charging into what seems certain death against the battlements of those apparently invincible giants," after them as they dashed for the door.

Madheran seemed not to hear, but Labhruinn skidded to a halt and turned back long enough to bow and gasp, "I thank you, Master, for the wisdom you have imparted," before racing off.

Left to wonder just what, if any, wisdom he had imparted that day, Herrwn walked over to the window, leaned out, and stared over the shrine's outer wall at the distant band of riders sweeping down the hillside toward the shrine, their pennants fluttering above them like a flock of gold-and-crimson birds.

Springtime was always the most difficult season for keeping his pupils' minds focused on their recitations, and having Rhedwyn galloping around and blowing his hunting horn was of no help whatsoever.

In the five years since Feywn had taken Caelendra's place as chief priestess, word of Ossiam's prophesy had spread, and, for the first time in Herrwn's memory, the valley's population had begun to grow as converted Britons were drawn back by the oracle's promise of victory over their oppressors and the return of their former glory.

No one believed that promise more than Rhedwyn.

At first it had seemed if not desirable then at least understandable that he was spending more time at Feywn's side than Ossiam's—but as time went on, it became clear that even when he wasn't closeted in Feywn's private chambers or entertaining her publicly with his songs and harp, Rhedwyn was spending less and less of his time in the oracle's tower. Apparently thinking that being the consort to the chief priestess in Llwddawanden was equivalent to being a king in ancient days, he all but abandoned his lessons of augury and animal sacrifices to go riding and hunting in the woods above the shrine.

Then—and looking back, Herrwn could not say with any certainty exactly when this began—Rhedwyn started to make perilous forays outside the valley, returning from each escapade with new recruits, captured horses and cattle, and enthralling tales of his exploits.

By the day Herrwn stood at his classroom window watching Feywn's consort and his band of boisterous companions careening down the hillside, Rhedwyn had ceased making even a token show of interest in his studies. If they weren't off raiding or hunting wild boar, he and his newfound followers were whipping their horses in frenzied races that thundered from one end of the valley to the other or fighting each other in mock battles that grew more like the real thing from one day to the next.

While the older generation of priestesses tut-tutted and shook their heads in disapproval, the younger ones were impressed, even enamored, with Rhedwyn and his band, informally dubbed "Rhedwyn's Riders." As their fawning admiration fed his swelling conceit, he took to making grandiose speeches at dinner or in High Council meetings as though he had wisdom to pass on to his elders, "as if," Olyrrwd muttered on more than one occasion, "he was chosen by Feywn for his brains."

Whatever Rhedwyn may have believed himself, there was no question among the shrine's senior priests and priestesses why he had been chosen over older and wiser men. Their impatience to see some result of all the time Rhedwyn was spending in Feywn's bedchambers grew as Feywn's two cousins, Gwennefor and Caldora, took two of Rhedwyn's favored companions as their consorts and each in turn became pregnant—not in a matter of years but months!

Herrwn, whose duties included overseeing the shrine's formal gatherings, disapproved of how often the eyes of his fellow priests (and many of the elder priestesses, as well) slipped furtively from Feywn's belly to Rhedwyn's crotch and back again—but understood why those flickering glances were accompanied by stifled sighs.

Either unaware of, or unbothered by, his elders' mounting concerns, Rhedwyn kept up his raiding and his war games. Over time, the crowding and jostling for position began to take a toll. The distinction between jokes and insults among the contestants blurred as their mock battles caused real injuries and wreaked genuine havoc. Olyrrwd was kept busy patching cuts and setting bones for the young would-be heroes, who hurried from the healing chamber determined to settle the score, leaving Olyrrwd shaking his head in frustration and muttering, "Why bother me with your broken bones, if you only mean to go out and break them again?"

Just how much Rhedwyn's undisciplined behavior was infecting the youth both outside and inside the shrine only came home to Herrwn the day Madheran abruptly announced that he was leaving his studies "to take up arms with Rhedwyn."

When he'd recovered sufficiently from the shock that his own disciple would think of such a thing, much less say it, Herrwn urged Madheran to reconsider, reminding him that "long after the warrior's sword has rusted, the words of the bard will shine anew each time his stories are told again."

Madheran's answer—"I would rather have adventures than talk about them"—was cocky, verging on disrespectful.

His cheeks burning as if he'd been slapped in the face, Herrwn kept his voice even as he responded, "Well then, you are dismissed to do as you think best."

He was, of course, deeply offended, but as he watched Madheran leaving the classroom for the last time, he heard his father's voice gently whispering in his ear, reminding him, "There is some good to be found in the worst of circumstances, if only one has the wisdom and courage to seek it out."

Madheran's departure left Herrwn with no disciple, and it was only too obvious that, however kindhearted and well-meaning he was, Rhedwyn's bumbling younger brother was not going to advance beyond the lowest level of sub-priest. Since both Ossiam and Olyrrwd had had their pick of disciples, he had every right to claim the next boy to enter training—and that would be none other than Caelendra's son, now ensconced in the shrine's nursery but due to be brought from there to the classroom on his sixth birthday, which was less than a year away.

Without consciously deciding to, Herrwn turned, walked over to the open window, placed both hands on the sill, and drew in a deep and satisfying breath.

Chapter 11:

Expectations

errwn was still standing at the window when Madheran emerged from the shrine's lower gate almost directly below him.

Although reconciled to this unexpected turn of events, he was bemused to see his just-discharged pupil sprinting toward a gathered group of mounted horsemen, having already shed his gray disciple's robes in exchange for the brown leggings, black tunic, and forest-green riding cloak that Rhedwyn had adopted as emblematic of his troop.

Rhedwyn held the reins of an extra horse with a hunting bow and quiver tied to its saddle. As if sensing Herrwn's eyes on him, Rhedwyn looked up. When their gazes met, he shrugged and smiled the self-effacing smile that had always melted away any reproach, however well deserved. Then, while Madheran was taking the horse's reins and scrambling onto its back, Rhedwyn shifted his gaze to the shrine's upper walkway where Feywn and a coterie of the younger priestesses were standing and raised his bow in a sweeping salute before he turned his horse's head, kicked it into a gallop, and led his men, now including Madheran, off to their hunt.

Glancing over at the cluster of girls and women waving silk scarves in farewell, Herrwn's own gaze lingered, just for a moment, on Feywn's younger sister, Annwr, before he turned away, went to get his harp, and began his practice for the evening's recitation.

He'd skipped the opening ode, as it was straightforward and undeviating from the traditional formula, and was concentrating on the lines of secondary characters that he'd been expecting his erstwhile disciple to deliver when the doors to the classroom cracked open and a tall, gray-robed figure slipped through. For a moment, Herrwn thought Madheran had reconsidered and returned, but it was Labhruinn, back early from his lessons in the healing chamber.

•◆•

When he'd started his formal training at the age of three, Labhruinn had been the youngest pupil they'd ever had in basic studies. Now, at nineteen, he was the oldest. Despite those extra years of instruction, he showed nowhere near the skill of memorization required of a bard and had even less promise for discipleship as an oracle or a physician—angering Ossiam with his carelessness in letting the birds and snakes escape on the way to the sacrificial altar and annoying Olyrrwd by fainting during amputations.

As none of them were willing to say there was no hope for the brother of Feywn's consort, Labhruinn's lessons in healing, prophecy, and oratory dragged on—falling mostly on Herrwn, since whenever Olyrrwd or Ossiam got frustrated, they sent Labhruinn back to the classroom, claiming the excuse that some critically ill patient or some particularly arcane incantation required their full attention. Olyrrwd, in particular, was always grumbling that if he didn't personally watch every single root and tincture Labhruinn put into a potion no patient would leave the healing chamber alive, so Herrwn could easily have taken Labhruinn's abject posture and downcast gaze as evidence of some toxic error Olyrrwd hadn't caught in time. Instead, feeling the tingle of a teacher's instinct, he asked, "Did you know Madheran was making plans to leave his studies?"

"Did I . . . er, hmm . . . Did Madheran . . . er, I, I couldn't say . . . I mean, I, he . . ."

Either unwilling to tell a lie or unable to think of a convincing one, Labhruinn stumbled to a halt. He looked, just for a moment, directly into Herrwn's eyes, as if appealing for understanding, and shrugged—raising his right shoulder higher than his left, a mannerism that was, so far as Herrwn could tell, the only family trait he shared with Rhedwyn.

Seeing that gesture gave Herrwn the seed of an idea, one which sprouted and blossomed so quickly he could almost see

Labhruinn's gray robes changed into brown leggings, a black tunic, and a forest-green riding cloak, and he could already hear Olyrrwd congratulating him for coming up with a practical solution that provided a face-saving way out for everyone involved.

Thinking how to phrase the suggestion that Labhruinn join his brother's horsemen without being too blatant, Herrwn beckoned for Labhruinn to come with him to the window where the departing troop of riders could be seen galloping up the hillside toward the meadows and woods beyond. Assuming his most gentle and understanding tone of voice, he began what he hoped would be the conversation leading to Labhruinn's decision, more or less of his own free will, to leave the studies for which he was so clearly unfit.

"Do not be troubled. Madheran's choice to ride with Rhedwyn is a noble one in its own way, one of which no one should be ashamed. Now be assured that you, too, may speak to me of anything that is on your mind."

Labhruinn shifted awkwardly from one foot to the other and cleared his throat. "I . . ."

"Yes?"

"I think . . ."

Several moments went by, during which Herrwn began mentally composing his speech assuring Labhruinn that there was no disgrace in choosing to join his brother's followers. In a moment of inspiration, he decided that he would borrow and adapt the words of Madheran's declaration. He was preparing to say, "Of course, I understand how you would prefer to have adventures than talk about them," when Labhruinn finally managed to finish his sentence.

"I think it was music."

This was not the opening Herrwn was waiting for, and he could think of no response except, "What was music?"

"The kingdom . . . er, the achievement that Pwendordden, I mean Pwendorwn, called on his warriors to defend."

It had been two weeks since Herrwn had dismissed Labhruinn and Madheran from their deteriorating lesson, directing them to return prepared to tell him which great accomplishment of humankind was symbolized by the kingdom of Llancerddysul and why the greatest warriors of all the human tribes had rallied to defend that achievement. He had, however, given the order in an uncharacteristic fit of pique, and he hadn't questioned them about it further but had simply gone on to the next section of the saga—which, being an account of the battle itself, had held their attention better than most.

Equally surprised that Labhruinn had been pondering this for the past fortnight and that he'd answered correctly, Herrwn stammered, "Wh-why, yes, how did you guess?"

If he hadn't been caught off guard, Herrwn would have done a better job of keeping the astonishment out of his voice. As it was, he did his best to cover it up by clearing his throat, giving a few thoughtful hums, and saying with due seriousness, "That is, how did you come to that well-reasoned conclusion?"

His effort clearly failed, as Labhruinn looked crestfallen and mumbled something barely audible about comparing the sounds of the sacred names for the things that mortals had achieved— growing crops, working metal, weaving cloth, healing, keeping a calendar, conducting rites and rituals, and making music—and that of all those, only music could not be stopped by giants.

It was an answer as profound as any Herrwn had ever thought of himself, and—this time making sure his tone was approving instead of incredulous—he said so.

Labhruinn looked up, his expression quite as astonished as Herrwn's must have been.

Still hopeful of Labhruinn's choosing to leave of his own accord—and thinking this was a positive moment on which to move forward—Herrwn smiled encouragingly. "And is there anything else you would ask now?"

Having apparently exhausted his store of words and capacity for coherence, Labhruinn sighed and shook his head.

Answering Labhruinn's sigh with one of his own, Herrwn changed the subject. "Well, the recitation for today is . . ."

Although Labhruinn's oration was as garbled as ever, Herrwn felt that he must somehow make up for the slight he'd unintentionally committed. While he was not so remorseful that he was willing to give the boy actual lines to recite in public, he solemnly entrusted him with the shrine's second-best harp and spent the afternoon listening to him strum the two alternating chords to be played in accompaniment to the saga's opening oration.

It was hard to say which of them was more nervous as they made their way to the main hall that night—or which was more relieved when they found that Rhedwyn had returned already and the evening's story was to be postponed to the next day.

The celebration of Rhedwyn's return from one of his outings—whether a single day's hunt or a weeklong raid—with music and dancing had become a custom over the past several years. In place of the bardic oration, Rhedwyn and Feywn would lead the younger priests and priestesses in a revel that would go on until the pipers and drummers were too tired to play.

That night, Rhedwyn and Feywn rose as if to begin the dance but instead remained in place—Feywn looking as radiant as the day Ossiam named her the living goddess. She said nothing but put her hands on her belly, drawing everyone's eyes to the slight mound where it had always curved inward. Rhedwyn stood erect at her left side, his face glowing with pride and his chest thrust out.

"Looking as if he'd made a score of women pregnant." Olyrrwd whispered the gibe in a voice that only Herrwn and Ossiam could hear.

"And what makes you think he hasn't?" Ossiam muttered back, and, for a brief moment, the two shared a smirk.

Then Ossiam composed his face, stood up, and—spreading his two arms in a gesture which seemed to embrace the entire chamber—restated his earlier prophecy that Feywn would join together with Rhedwyn in a union that was to change their destiny, before going on to pronounce his certain vision that "the child that grows within our Goddess is marked for surpassing renown, a child destined to outshine the stars themselves!"

At the time, Herrwn thought there was an undertone of something that might almost be spite in a prophecy that foretold Feywn being eclipsed by her unborn child. It worried him to think Ossiam would abuse his position to such a petty purpose—and to see the shadow of disquiet that passed over Feywn's face as the rest of the room burst into cheers that seemed to shake the stone walls of their shrine to its very foundation.

◆◆◆

Six months later—four weeks before the winter solstice and three weeks earlier than expected—Feywn entered the birth chambers. The labor went swiftly—the first cramps started at midnight, and the infant was born, dried, and handed to her wet nurse before dawn.

In keeping with Ossiam's prediction, the baby girl, named Arianna for the heroine of the Forest Queen's Tale, was born beautiful—a perfectly formed infant with a full head of bright red curls and blue-gray eyes that would turn emerald green before her first birthday.

Standing before the gathered crowd, Ossiam declared, "This child will ever be beautiful, ever graceful, ever wondrous to behold," in his most portentous voice. The solemn silence that followed this pronouncement ended when the chief midwife, Rhonnon, who was not known for her sense of humor, quipped, "This child will ever be in a hurry."

Chapter 12:

Annwr's Wish

The winter that Feywn gave birth was mild and gave way early to a bountiful spring. The crops that year seemed to burst out of the ground, the sheep and goats gave birth to twins and triplets, and the ducks and geese hatched broods twice as large as normal—all as if the earth herself was rejoicing with renewed fertility.

Inside the shrine, the infant predestined to be their next Goddess incarnate was fawned over and doted on, along with her three girl cousins and Caelendra's now five-year-old son, and two more servants were added to the nursery to be sure none of the children suffered from lack of attention.

Being one of the nursemaids to these highest born of the valley's children was a position of honor and distinction among the shrine's servants, second only to being a handmaiden to the chief priestess. Any word of theirs was attended to with as much regard as a priest's pronouncement, so when one of them was overheard whispering to another about needing yet another crib come the next spring equinox—and both looked toward the shrine's garden, where Feywn's younger sister was gathering medicinal herbs—the rumor that Priestess-in-Training Annwr was going to play the part of the Earth-Goddess in the summer solstice rites spread through the servants' ranks, setting off a buzz of speculation about which of the priests she was going to choose to stand in for the Sun-God.

•◆•

That matters pertaining to the most sacred of their highest rites should be a source of coarse gossip among their servants never occurred to Herrwn until Olyrrwd drew him aside and told him what he'd heard while he'd been in the shrine's kitchen tending to the cook's gouty toe.

Dismissing his protestations that it was unworthy for men in their position to pay attention to idle talk, Olyrrwd pushed Herrwn down onto a bench, looked him straight in the eye, and spoke in the tone he usually reserved for telling a recalcitrant patient to swallow his potion or take the consequences.

"Well, you can be sure that Ossiam and every other eligible priest in the shrine is going to pay attention, and if you want to be in the running, you'd better pay attention too!"

With that, he released the grip he'd had on Herrwn's shoulders and went back to his work in the healing chamber, leaving Herrwn to wonder, not for the first time, how Olyrrwd was able to see the thoughts that others kept hidden even from themselves.

It had been thirteen years since Lothwen died. While the unbearable grief Herrwn had felt at first had gradually subsided to a dull ache, the recollection of how good it was to share a woman's bed at night remained remarkably clear. And now, stirred by the warm spring breezes sweeping through the valley, that memory was growing stronger with each new day—in particular, with each sunrise ritual, where Herrwn's place at the head of the priests' line meant that for much of that ceremony he stood in close proximity to Annwr. It was a position of honor and trust, and he never would have abused it by shifting even a finger's width closer to her or allowing the sleeve of his robe to brush against hers. Still, had anyone had asked him later how often she had taken a breath during the morning's incantations, he could have answered with complete accuracy.

How Olyrrwd had divined Herrwn's growing passion before he realized it himself was puzzling. Thinking about it later, however, Herrwn decided that Olyrrwd must have overheard him murmuring something in his sleep that gave away his dreams.

And Herrwn's dreams had changed. There was no question about that.

In the years since Lothwen's death, he'd often dreamed of her doing things she'd done in life—teasing him for being so serious, sitting on the edge of their bed and combing her soft, silky auburn hair, even using his sacred staff, the emblem of his high office, to chase a bat out of their chambers.

But one night not long before Olyrrwd cornered him in the shrine's courtyard and warned him about what the servants were saying, he dreamed that he and Lothwen were walking together through the shrine's herb garden, and he had a sense that she seemed different than he remembered her. He must have looked quizzical, because she laughed the way she always had when she changed her hairstyle and teased him for not noticing. That was when he realized what should have been obvious—that instead of being tall and voluptuous she was short and slender and had much lighter hair.

The full impact of this dream only became clear to him after he'd pondered Olyrrwd's advice.

Annwr was shorter and more slightly built than Lothwen had been but was, in her own way, just as beautiful. At twenty, she was almost the same age as Lothwen had been when she and Herrwn had come to love each other. Herrwn, of course, was now two decades older than he'd been then, but his father had been that much older than his mother, and there had never been a happier or more harmonious union than theirs.

Taking Olyrrwd's admonition to heart, Herrwn began to choose the more romantic of their sagas (particularly those with wise and learned heroes and young and beautiful heroines) for his nightly recitations and took to dismissing Labhruinn earlier and earlier in order to give himself more time to refine his delivery. And his efforts seemed to bear fruit, as one day he returned to his classroom after the noon meal to find Annwr there, seemingly preoccupied with a small ritual vessel engraved with dancing deer. She was wearing a silk gown that fell in such alluring folds that his heart leaped into an irregular gallop, and he had to pause for it to resume its regular pace before he could say anything at all.

Recovering himself, Herrwn assumed the dignity he considered appropriate for a priest of his standing to use when addressing the sister of their chief priestess as he welcomed her, asking if there was any way he could be of service to her. Realizing the double meaning of what he had just said, he hastily rephrased his inquiry to whether she had some question regarding philosophy, or perhaps some point of contention from the last council meeting that he might answer for her.

Annwr, too, appeared to lose her composure for a moment, but then, blushing and stammering, she asked if he would recite a story for her.

Striving—successfully, he thought—to keep his voice steady, he assured her he would be most willing to recite anything she wished.

His heart went fluttery again when she whispered, "The Story of the River-Goddess and the Fire-God."

The Story of the River-Goddess and the Fire-God was among the most passionate and explicit of their tales, and for a priestess to ask a priest for a private telling was one small step short of an invitation to her bed.

Keeping his voice calm and steady—even solemn—Herrwn agreed, offered her his hand, and led the way out into the courtyard, where the bench under the single oak tree was just wide enough for two to sit side by side without breaching decorum. Once settled there, he began the tale of legendary love with Annwr so close he was almost overwhelmed by the intoxicating smell of her hair and skin.

She returned the next day and the next day, and every day after that for the next two weeks.

Just as the saga was coming to its climax and conclusion, Herrwn gathered his resolve and asked—cautiously and, he hoped, without appearing too eager—what she most wanted and wished for.

Twenty years later, Herrwn could see Annwr in that moment as clearly as if she were still alive and sitting next to him now. Her face glowed as she clasped her hands together, pressed them over her heart, and exclaimed, "A baby!"

This revelation came in a sudden burst of youthful enthusiasm as she went on to describe how she'd obtained Rhonnon's consent to conceive in the summer solstice rites and could name . . .

Here she looked directly into his eyes before blushing and looking away.

Chapter 13:

In the Garden

"$\mathfrak{I}$t was odd, very odd," Herrwn murmured, looking up at the cloud-veiled moon as if it might explain the mystery to him, "that I of all people should have so completely forgotten that the purpose of the Sacred Summer Solstice Ceremony was not love but birth."

He actually had not hesitated very long, but as he wavered—seeing Lillywen's sunken eyes in the last hours of her life, hearing her pleading with him to make her feel better, and wondering if he could bear to love and risk losing another child—the glow faded from Annwr's face. She spoke before he did, saying in a small, brittle voice that she was sorry to have taken so much of his time and that she had to go back to work in the garden.

Days passed. As each afternoon approached, Herrwn felt his hopes rise, only to have them fall when Annwr did not appear at the classroom's doorway. At last, he could no longer avoid the truth—that he loved Annwr, loved her so much that he had to overcome his fears and to go to her to plead that she choose him now for the night of the summer solstice, and later, when she was finished her training, to be her consort forever after.

The next morning, with the summer solstice only a fortnight off, Herrwn made a vague excuse to end Labhruinn's lessons early and stepped back as the boy (and Herrwn still thought of Labhruinn as a boy, despite his having reached his adult height some years earlier) dashed for the door.

With Labhruinn out of the way, Olyrrwd in the healing chambers, and Ossiam in the upper tower, mulling over the meaning of the drifting clouds, there were no witnesses to see Herrwn retreat into the dressing chamber, where he tried on robe after robe, discarding one as too ornate and the next as too plain, before finally picking the one he'd worn on the day that Lothwen had named him to be her consort and had placed a bracelet made of twisted strands of gold in the shape of a miniature torc on his wrist as a token of their commitment.

He'd worn that bracelet ever since—his only adornment besides the necklace denoting his rank as the shrine's chief bard. Looking at it for a long moment (and mentally pleading with Lothwen for understanding), he took it off and put it on a shelf beside the cloth doll that had been Lillywen's favorite toy.

Then he put on his best sandals and looked in the polished brass mirror on the wall. He was not, he told himself, too old—he was a Druid master at the height of his powers. Drawing a breath, he said aloud, "Worthy to join my fate with yours, if that is your desire, as it is mine." With that, he straightened his shoulders and set out to say just those words to Annwr.

He stopped along the way at the storage room where the musical instruments were kept, meaning to take his best gold harp. Finding it missing from its place on the shelf (all these years later, he remembered thinking that Rhedwyn must have taken it, and that he'd meant to complain about it to Ossiam since this was not the first time and he'd already chastised Rhedwyn, to no avail), he took up the next best harp, checked its tuning, and went on his way.

It was a perfect morning. The sun shone overhead. Wisps of white clouds danced with each other across the sparkling blue sky. Blossoms of columbine beckoned and waved along the edge of the laurel hedge that lay between the shrine's main courtyard and the garden of medicinal herbs.

Walking with measured steps, as if he were already wearing the golden robes of the Sun-God, Herrwn rehearsed his plan. He would open the gate and enter the garden quietly, see her working among her plants with her back to him. He would speak her name. She would turn to him and he would kneel down, pluck gently on the harp strings, and recite his declaration of love, promising to do his part in giving her the child she craved.

A flood of sensations he hadn't felt since his days of courting Lothwen came back, magnifying every sound, even the slightest fluttering of a leaf, and that was why he heard the voice on the other side of the hedge and stopped in his tracks. It was a man's voice—not Ossiam's or anyone that he immediately recognized, although there was something familiar about it. Puzzled, he quietly, stealthily, spread apart the branches of the hedge and peeked through.

Olyrrwd had warned him that he wouldn't be the only man courting Annwr, but, even so, never, not in Herrwn's strangest dreams, would he ever have imagined that his rival would be Labhruinn.

Almost as incomprehensible was seeing the tense, tongue-tied boy reciting in a confident voice as he strummed on Herrwn's harp—without so much as a misplaced pause or a false chord—while Annwr looked up at him, holding a single summer lily in her hand.

Drawing back, Herrwn let the peephole he'd made in the hedge close and walked away, back to his classroom, where he put down the harp and changed into his ordinary robes. Taking the harp up again, he tried to concentrate on that night's oration—only the echoes of his best harp, played by Labhruinn, continued to ring in his ears, and the sight of Annwr looking up at Labhruinn swam before him whenever he closed his eyes.

Chapter 14:

The Highest Tower

Several days later, Herrwn was still trying to think of something—anything—other than the coming summer solstice, when Annwr would be lost to him forever. He was so caught up in his inner turmoil at breakfast that he twice admonished his cousins to keep peace with each other when they weren't arguing.

"—as I'm sure Herrwn agrees," Ossiam's strident voice broke through his distracted ruminations. "In any case, it's time we go!"

Brought back to the present, he could see that Olyrrwd's shoulders were bunched up—a sure sign he was thinking of some retort to something Ossiam had just said. Herrwn, however, had no idea what they'd been talking about.

Feeling like he was one of his own students who'd fallen asleep during a lesson and had to guess the answer without admitting that he hadn't heard the question, he repeated, "As you say, it's time to go," as he looked around for some clue to remind him what they were supposed to do that morning.

Both Ossiam and Olyrrwd were dressed in their regular robes, so it wasn't a meeting of the High Council—Olyrrwd's, however, was clean and without noticeable blood stains, suggesting it was an occasion of some importance. But not a major or even a minor rite. Herrwn was sure of that. It wasn't the full, half, quarter, or new moon. They'd honored the spirits of the east winds last week and those of the spring rains the week before, and the Sacred Summer Solstice Ceremony (as he was all too keenly aware) was still a week off.

It was not any of their regular duties then, but some other commitment that they had to fulfill together.

But what?

Herrwn remained seated, nodding at Ossiam, in hopes of spurring some additional and more edifying pronouncement. When Ossiam only stirred restively, he asked, "So what do you propose we do?"

"We will go through the motions." Ossiam gave Herrwn a meaningful look.

"Of course." Herrwn nodded with a sage expression he hoped would cover his confusion.

"There is no point in putting it off any longer." Ossiam made ready to rise from his chair.

"No point at all." Herrwn tucked his feet under him and placed his hands flat on the table, ready to rise as well.

"And no point in wasting further effort on a fool." Ossiam pushed his chair back and stood up.

Olyrrwd stood up too, knocking his chair over backward in the process. Jutting his chin out, he declared, "He's not a fool!" in a bellicose voice before adding in a lower tone, hardly more than a mumble, "He's just not a Druid."

Ossiam's retort came in the dismissive tone of voice he used whenever Olyrrwd contradicted him. "There are fools and there are Druids. You are one or the other!"

It was an argument that his cousins had carried on ever since the two had been sent to stay overnight in the servants' quarters as a rebuke for their constant bickering—a boyhood experience that had left Ossiam embittered while Olyrrwd had made friends with the servants' children and had gone back to play with them as often as he could sneak away.

It was also the answer to Herrwn's unspoken question.

Today was Labhruinn's twenty-first birthday—the day that Herrwn, Ossiam, and Olyrrwd would hold their final council to determine whether he would be admitted to the last stage of his training. Already granted two extra years in basic studies out of consideration for his elite birth and family connections, there could be no further allowances. He must either be chosen by one of them as a disciple or his hopes of entering the priesthood were finished.

How strange that this should have slipped Herrwn's mind, especially as he'd spent his waking hours for the past week consumed by the misery of losing Annwr to Labhruinn. If none of them accepted Labhruinn as a disciple, he could not be a priest even of the lowest order, much less the consort to the sister of their chief priestess and Goddess incarnate or the surrogate Sun-God in the Sacred Summer Solstice Ceremony.

Outwardly calm, Herrwn rose from the table and led the way to the shrine's highest tower, keeping his eyes straight ahead as they passed through the antechamber where Labhruinn sat on a stone bench, gripping its edge with both hands.

As he ascended the steep, curving stairs, Herrwn weighed the chances that either of the others would admit Labhruinn to their order.

Ossiam was no more likely to claim Labhruinn than to turn himself into a crow and eat carrion.

But Olyrrwd . . .

Despite his admission that Labhruinn wasn't a Druid, Olyrrwd might take him on—if only out of a perverse need to irritate Ossiam.

Still, Herrwn could hope.

◆

Ossiam spoke out almost before the three men sat down at the polished oak council table. Blending sarcasm with the irrefutable authority of a prophet, he declared it his highest duty to protect the shrine from the doom and devastation that would come of Labhruinn's inability to read the simplest omen in a rat's entrails.

Ossiam turned to Olyrrwd.

Herrwn held his breath.

Olyrrwd sighed. "He tries hard and he means well, but . . ." Sighing again, he gave an regrettably vivid description of the night Labhruinn inadvertently dosed a chamber full of patients with a cathartic rather than a sleeping potion. He shook his head and turned to Herrwn.

Herrwn hesitated, considering how to phrase his answer with the right balance of firmness and regret. While they waited for his answer, Olyrrwd and Ossiam went back to bickering. Despite his own unwillingness to take Labhruinn on, Olyrrwd argued that Herrwn should, muttering, "A misquoted line of poetry won't change the future, and forgetting a hero's name won't kill anyone."

Before Herrwn could speak up to defend his vocation, Ossiam snapped back, "A misquoted line will change that poem forever, and forgetting a hero's name brings a second death for that hero."

Affecting a grave but resolute expression, Herrwn nodded at Ossiam, who nodded back in smug accord.

Olyrrwd gave the resigned shrug he usually saved for occasions when he'd tried against all hope to revive the dead. Rising together, they left the room in the reverse order that they had entered it—Olyrrwd first, Ossiam next, and Herrwn last.

As he descended the dark stairway, Herrwn drew in a deep breath.

It was done, and done without his having to say anything at all.

No one—not even Labhruinn himself—could accuse Herrwn of wrongdoing.

For he had done no wrong.

Not really.

Labhruinn was not worthy to be a Druid priest any more than he was worthy to dance with Annwr at the Sacred Summer Solstice Ceremony.

It was only right that they refuse him admission to their ranks.

Even if his jealousy played a part in that decision, he was the shrine's chief priest and he had only himself to answer to.

They reached the bottom of the stairway. Ossiam and Olyrrwd stepped aside and let him pass since, as the chief priest, it was his duty to deliver their verdict.

Labhruinn looked up at him from the stone bench, eager and hopeful—like an unwanted puppy, pleading to be picked up.

Herrwn stiffened his back, gathered his resolve, and sadly but firmly put his hand out to touch Labhruinn on the forehead—the time-honored sign of a master Druid's acceptance of a new disciple—because, in the end, he had to answer to himself.

Beaming with joy, Labhruinn dropped to his knees, kissed the hem of Herrwn's robe, and stammered an incoherent mix of oaths and promises to prove himself.

Taking a tight grip on his staff, Herrwn sighed and began, "To be a bard requires more than mere memorization and recitation. It requires the understanding of moral choices, and that is a grave undertaking not to be entered into lightly."

Olyrrwd and Ossiam, who had heard this speech before, went off to their own responsibilities, one smiling and the other shaking his head, as Herrwn, feeling oddly as if he were talking to himself, led his new apprentice through the hallway and back to his classroom.

Two weeks later, Herrwn stood at the side of the altar in the Sacred Grove and watched Labhruinn, dressed in golden robes, come out of the woods to meet Annwr as she stepped out of the gap between the great stone pillars wearing the green silk gown of the Earth-Goddess.

No, he told himself, *not Labhruinn but only his outward shape, serving as a vessel for the spirit of the Sun-God!*

He strove to keep that thought firmly in mind throughout the ritual, paying as little attention as he could to the pain of seeing the two of them dance off into the darkness.

It was only as the months passed, with summer surrendering to fall and fall fading into winter, that he found real solace in seeing Annwr blissfully happy, cradling her growing belly as though she were already holding the baby she so passionately wanted. Her joy, along with the knowledge that he had done the morally right thing, was his consolation for his heartache—and for the realization that by taking on Labhruinn he had inadvertently given up his first claim to Caelendra's son.

PART III

Initiation

While not precisely ordained, it was traditional that on the morning of a Druid boy's sixth birthday, his mother—or a mother surrogate—would wake him up before dawn with a breakfast of hot milk and sweet cakes, after which she would give him a ceremonial bath, dress him in his new apprentice robes, and escort him to the priests' quarters in time to cross the threshold of the classroom at sunrise.

Usually, the older disciples would have been there to welcome the new initiate. Rhedwyn, however, had chosen this day to take off for another cattle raid, Moelwyn was in the healing chambers brewing a potion that needed to be started at sunrise, and Labhruinn had somehow received word that Annwr was in labor and begged to be released from his duties, a dispensation Herrwn had given only after reminding his frantic pupil that he'd left his mortal identity behind him when he acted the part of the Sun-God in the Sacred Summer Solstice Ceremony, and it was that divine spirit that had engendered the child to whom the Priestess Annwr was giving birth.

It was just the three cousins, then, sitting together in their classroom as Herrwn's thoughts drifted back to the morning of his own sixth birthday—the sound of his mother's soft voice calling his name, the sweet taste of the honeyed cakes, the scent of the perfumed bath waters, the excitement of putting on robes that swished and swirled like his father's, the warmth of his mother's hand as she led him through curving corridors and up the steep stone stairway to stand in front of the great arched entrance with its towering double doors. Suddenly uncertain, he'd clung to her, afraid to let go, until she whispered in his ear, "They're waiting for you," and he'd stepped through the open doors to see his father, his uncles, and his soon-to-be classmates all smiling at him and had felt his fears fall away and be replaced with eagerness for his first lesson.

Ossiam and Olyrrwd were no doubt caught up in memories of their own as the first streaks of light began to brighten the horizon outside the window.

Chapter 15:

Do Not Grieve

Sunrise came, but Caelym didn't.

As the sun continued its upward climb, the tension in the room rose along with it. Ossiam's resentment that Olyrrwd, as the shrine's chief healer, was the only one of them to have free access to the women's quarters slipped out when he broke the meditative silence with the grumble, "You're the physician—why don't you go and ask when we may expect him?"

While his tone was unnecessarily abrasive, Herrwn thought, in all fairness, that Ossiam had a point. In any case, it did nothing to improve the general mood when Olyrrwd snapped back, "You're the oracle—why don't you gut a toad and tell us how much longer we need to wait?"

Not wanting the arrival of Caelendra's son to be marred by petty squabbling, Herrwn was on the verge of admonishing both men when the sound of scuffing came from the hallway and a shrill child's voice screamed, "I don't want to be a Druid! Druids are stupid! I hate Druids!"

"Shhh!" a woman's voice responded. "You mustn't say that! They'll hear you."

Startled, Herrwn, with Olyrrwd and Ossiam at his heels, hurried to the doors and opened them to see a disheveled servant clutching a struggling boy, dressed only in his nightshirt, who was hitting her with two parts of a torn toy, sending bits of stuffing flying into the air.

Before Herrwn could think of something soothing to say to calm the distraught child and coax him into the room, Ossiam lunged forward, grabbed the back of the boy's collar, wrenched him away from his nurse, and lifted him up to dangle at arm's length.

"Silence!" he screamed at the servant, who'd fallen, groveling, to the floor, and begun pleading with him not to turn her or the poor child into anything awful.

"And you." He shook the twisting, flailing boy so that he began to swing back and forth. "How dare you behave like the spawn of a Saxon she-beast? You are a disgrace to the goddess who died to give you life! You are a disgrace to—"

Ossiam's tirade was cut short when a surprisingly well-aimed thrust of the boy's bare foot struck him squarely in the stomach. Doubling over, he lost his grip on the thrashing youngster, who, still kicking his feet after falling to the floor, propelled himself backward through the door and across the classroom floor to the far wall, all the while emitting shrieks that were, fortunately, no longer coherent, or else Ossiam would no doubt have been cursed throughout his life and forever after.

This was no way to start the formal education of Caelendra's only child—and, determined to restore order, Herrwn, too, raised his voice.

"Ossiam, that will do!"

Whether because he was submitting to Herrwn's authority or was too preoccupied with trying to catch his breath to move, Ossiam remained where he was as Herrwn and Olyrrwd hurried over to where Caelym had wedged himself behind a fallen chair and was glaring out from between its legs.

Although he had never been faced with anything like this before, Herrwn felt instinctively that any move on his part to pry Caelym out from behind his barricade would only make matters worse, so instead he began the welcoming speech he had planned, amending its opening lines to acknowledge the boy's obvious distress.

"Do not grieve for the life you leave behind, my child, but rejoice for the one which lies before you now that you have crossed the threshold into this hallowed place of learning, where, with diligence on your part and devotion on ours,

you will be endowed with all the wisdom that has been passed down to us from the ages so that someday, when you have learned all that we have to teach you, you will be ready to enter the highest ranks of our sacred order."

Instead of the hoped-for calming effect, Herrwn's greeting only served to drive Caelym farther back behind the upturned chair. Clutching the remnants of his toy to his heaving chest, he pressed back against the wall, his knees drawn up and his dark, defiant eyes glittering with unshed tears.

At a loss for what to do next, Herrwn was relieved to step aside when Olyrrwd elbowed past him, muttering, "My turn."

Olyrrwd squatted down in front of Caelym, just out of kicking range, so that the two were eye level with each other, and said, "Your horse is hurt. How did it happen?"

At those words, spoken in the calmly concerned voice that Olyrrwd used in his healing chambers, Caelym's defiance dissolved into a flood of recriminations.

Herrwn presumed the servant, who was still groveling and whimpering in the doorway, had a real name, but it was usual for the children's nurses to be called "Nonna," and that was the name Caelym used as he pushed the chair aside and blurted out, "Nonna said that I had to go and learn to be a Druid and I couldn't ever come back! But Whinnie didn't want to go! He was hiding under the bed, and I was getting him!"

Stopping to draw in a long, shuddering breath, Caelym turned a baleful glare toward the door, where his nurse was now sitting up and wiping her eyes.

Olyrrwd nodded thoughtfully. "And then?"

"And then Nonna said I had to stop playing and hurry! But I wasn't playing! Whinnie was stuck! And then Nonna said to come or I couldn't learn to be a Druid! But I told her I don't want to be a Druid! But she said I had to, so come now! And then she said I was too old to play with Whinnie, and I should leave him for the new baby! But Whinnie doesn't like babies! And I told him he had to come, and I pulled him and I pulled him and . . . and . . . he came apart!"

At this, Caelym's voice rose to a howl of rage and remorse that continued for so long Herrwn had to wonder whether the boy would ever take another breath. When he finally did, Olyrrwd took advantage of the moment to put out his hand with his palm up and said, "May I see?"

Caelym held the remains of his toy tighter.

Olyrrwd kept his hand out. "I am a healer and it is my job to tend to those who are ill or injured, but if I am to help, I must first look to see what is wrong."

Herrwn was no healer but even he could see "what was wrong" was that the toy was torn in two and had lost almost all of its stuffing. Olyrrwd, however, gave no sign that he was less serious about this than about any other injured patient.

Caelym took another long, shaky breath. "Promise you'll give him back!"

"I promise."

Drawing in his lower lip and clenching it between his teeth, Caelym held out the bigger piece of the toy that he had gripped in his right hand and then, slowly, one finger at a time, opened his left fist and held out the rest.

Olyrrwd nodded twice, first in acknowledgment of Caelym's concession and then to dismiss the nurse, who scrambled to her feet and ran off. He then took the two parts of the torn toy and put them together, first one way, then another, apparently weighing its chances for recovery.

Caelym watched, his lower lip quivering. "Can you . . . ?"

The question came out halfway between a question and a sob.

"I can heal him, but I will need you to be my assistant."

With that, Olyrrwd handed both pieces of the toy back to Caelym, picked up the overturned chair, and set it right side up at the table where he'd left his healer's satchel. Caelym followed after him, climbed onto the chair, and wiped his nose with the smaller piece of the rag toy as Olyrrwd took his own seat and began to pull the things he used for real wounds out of the bag.

He threaded a needle with what Herrwn knew to be his best gut suture and held it up, looking at Caelym.

"Will it hurt?" the boy whispered.

"Perhaps, just a little, so you must hold him very still and tell him to be brave."

Bracing his elbows on the table, Caelym held the horse's head in his hands and whispered in its remaining ear, "Be brave," and

"Don't cry," and "It will only hurt a little," while Olyrrwd stitched it together, restuffing it with the sheep's wool he kept for sopping up blood or purulence from draining sores as he went so it gradually took the shape of a sturdy little pony that looked remarkably perky given all it had been through.

After tying off the thread, Olyrrwd handed the little horse back to Caelym, who hugged it in a grasp that would have suffocated a real pet and looked at Olyrrwd with worshipful awe.

Feeling it incumbent upon himself to instill good manners in his new pupil, Herrwn cleared his throat and prompted, "Now, what do you say?"

"Thank you" was, of course, the response he was looking for, but Caelym drew his lip in and seemed to ponder deeply, looking first at Olyrrwd, then down at the toy horse, and then back at Olyrrwd, before answering, "You can play with him." He held the horse out as he added gravely, "But you have to give him back."

Olyrrwd somehow kept from smiling as he took the toy and answered just as gravely, "Thank you, I will." Then he did smile— in fact, beamed—and said, "My name is Olyrrwd. What's yours?"

Caelym beamed back and said, "Caelym"—and, in his next breath, pelleted Olyrrwd with a volley of questions:

"Do all real animals have blood?"

"Why do birds get to fly, and we don't?"

"Can people eat worms?"

"What is poo-poo made of?"

An offended "humph" was the first audible sound to come from Ossiam since he'd had the wind kicked out of him. Drawing himself up to his full height, he announced that he was going to his tower to propitiate the spirits and to divine how best to make amends for Caelym's transgressions. Without waiting for any response, he swept out of the room, his robes billowing behind him.

Olyrrwd, who didn't pay much attention to Ossiam's pronouncements anyway, began to answer each of Caelym's questions in turn. He had just reached the one about poo-poo when a servant rushed into the classroom gasping that there'd been an accident at the archery practice.

Pausing just long enough to set the toy horse down, pat its head, and tell it not to hide under any more beds, Olyrrwd took up his leather bag and rushed off, leaving Herrwn alone with Caelym.

Chapter 16:

A Very Good Question

espite a vast store of knowledge, most of it profound and much of it arcane, Herrwn had no idea what poo-poo was made of. It was not a question that had ever been addressed in the ancient sagas, and he'd never thought to ask Olyrrwd himself. Instead of making something up, he took the now drowsy little boy over to a chair by the hearth, lifted him up onto his lap, and began telling a story that had been his own favorite when he was six.

"Long ago, in the time before the feud began between men and animals and we could all still talk to each other . . ."

Exhausted from his tantrum, Caelym fell asleep while Herrwn was reciting, *"there was a herd of wonderful wild horses that lived in a lush green valley . . ."* and Herrwn left speaking to gaze down at the little Druid-to-be they'd been waiting for since the day of his birth.

Believing as he did in the dogma that children conceived at the Sacred Summer Solstice Ceremony had no mortal father, he'd expected that Caelym would be a boyish version of Caelendra. Instead, curled up in Herrwn's lap, his head resting on his toy horse and damp ringlets of raven-black hair framing his almost impossibly beautiful little face, he was simply Rhedwyn born over again.

It was as though their chief priestess had been no more than a vessel—bringing forth a boy child without imparting anything of herself into him.

As he thought about what they had lost with Caelym's birth, Herrwn felt a wave of grief as overwhelming as the moment he'd realized that Caelendra was dead. With his next breath, he felt a sense of resignation and, with the next, acceptance that Caelym was the parting gift that Caelendra had given her people and she must have known what she was doing.

◆●◆

When Olyrrwd returned to the classroom, his robes were splattered with blood and he was grumbling, "Young idiots! Shouldn't be trusted with toy swords, much less real arrows!"

His expression softened, turning almost motherly, at the sight of Caelym asleep on Herrwn's lap.

"We'll share him, shall we? You make him a bard and I'll make him a healer, and together we'll turn him into the envy of all the gods and goddesses that ever were or ever will be!"

Seeing Olyrrwd's sudden shift to a tranquil mood as an opportunity to smooth over the rift between his cousins, Herrwn started, "And Ossiam will—"

"And Ossiam will never lay a hand on that boy again, or I'll—"

Just what threat Olyrrwd was about to utter was cut off by a muted tap on the door.

It was Benyon, the chief servant for the priests' chambers, carrying an armload of Caelym's belongings from the nursery.

As Benyon bustled about in the side chamber that was the apprentices' sleeping quarters, Caelym started to stir.

Murmuring, "I'm hungry, Nonna," he rubbed his eyes and looked up at Herrwn. "You're not Nonna!" He sat up, took hold of a fold of Herrwn's robe, and looked around the room. "Where's Nonna?"

As Herrwn was about to repeat his welcome-to-your-new-life-of-learning speech, Olyrrwd answered, "Nonna's gone back to the nursery to take care of the little babies who aren't big enough to go to the lake and hunt for frogs."

"I'm six! I'm big enough!"

"Are you sure?"

"Yes! Let's go now!" Releasing his grip on Herrwn's robe, Caelym leaped down and reached for Olyrrwd's hand.

"First Benyon will get you something to eat, and then we'll go."

After a moment or two, during which Caelym seemed to be

weighing the possibilities of his new situation, he opened his eyes wide and said in the sincerest of all possible tones, "Nonna always gives me cakes for breakfast and dinner and supper and never makes me eat anything else."

"It's your birthday, so Benyon will bring you some cakes and some apples and some cheese so you can be strong and fast for catching frogs—won't you, Benyon?" Olyrrwd glanced over at the servant.

"Of course, Good Master!" Newly promoted and anxious to please, Benyon was already bowing and backing out of the door.

Caelym, who'd kept a grip on his toy horse when he scrambled off Herrwn's lap, tucked it under his arm and regarded Olyrrwd, still with a deliberative look on his face.

"You're Olyrrwd."

"I am."

"You heal things."

"I do."

Caelym pointed at Herrwn. "He's Herrwn."

"He is."

"He tells stories."

"He does."

"Who was the mean one?"

Before Herrwn could intervene to say that Ossiam had not intended to be harsh but that sometimes even grown-ups got upset and acted in ways they regret later, Olyrrwd answered, "Ossiam."

"What does he do?"

Speaking quickly, before Olyrrwd could say anything disparaging about a fellow elder, Herrwn answered, "He is an oracle. He sees the future."

"Did he know I was going to kick him?"

Here Olyrrwd was faster than Herrwn. "That is a very good question! Maybe we should ask him."

To Herrwn's relief, Benyon came through the door carrying a tray laden with cakes, apples, cheese, and a pitcher of steaming goat's milk, diverting Caelym's attention from Olyrrwd's highly improper suggestion—and after the little boy finished his snack, he was so eager to go to the lake it was all Olyrrwd could do to hold him back long enough to change out of his nightshirt and into his new robes.

Chapter 17:

The Spring Equinox

Caelym's dramatic entrance into the shrine's classroom took place on the day before the spring equinox. The next morning, when Herrwn was getting up to join the other priests and priestesses in the performance of the morning's ritual welcoming the rising sun Olyrrwd stayed in bed, saying, "One of us has to be here when the lad wakes up," instead of making his usual excuse that he'd been up half the night with patients who didn't have the courtesy to be sick at some reasonable time of day and that the sun was going to come up whether he sang to it or not.

"Benyon is quite capable of giving Caelym his breakfast," Herrwn said sternly, "and on the spring equinox it is imperative—"

"Imperative?" Olyrrwd opened one eye and looked skeptically at him.

"Well, perhaps not imperative but highly desirable that on the one day of the year when servants and villagers are in attendance that we, the three chief priests of the shrine, be seen together, demonstrating our unity and setting an example for them to follow!" As he tied on his sandals, Herrwn repeated the point he made to Olyrrwd every year only to have the same grumbly retort, "They don't listen to me when I tell them to stay in bed and give their broken bones time to heal; why would they take notice of whether I sing along with Ossiam or not?"

Once Olyrrwd dug in his heels, there was no moving him, so Herrwn pulled on his best robe and hurried to join the priests and priestesses getting ready to start up the steep stone stairs to the shrine's uppermost courtyard.

As his eyes adapted to the faint light from the stars and the slender crescent of a waning moon, Herrwn could see that all the priests were there except for Olyrrwd, Rhedwyn (most likely still out raiding), and Labhruinn (presumably hovering outside the birthing chamber). Feywn lifted her staff and started up the stairs. Once the last of the priestesses-in-training passed by and started up the stairs, Herrwn raised his own staff and led the priests in single file after them.

Reaching the upper courtyard, Feywn led the way to the very edge, where she stood facing east. The other priestesses moved into a semicircle behind her, their timing so precise that Herrwn had no need to take even a half step in place before he led the priests into their places. Behind him, Herrwn could feel the space filling with worshippers from the servants' quarters and the village.

The last shuffling stopped, and all was quiet as they waited for the first rays of the sun to lighten the horizon above the valley's far ridge.

That day, as every day since he'd first been permitted to join the ritual, it thrilled Herrwn to hear the crystal-clear voice of the chief priestess singing the opening line of the ancient chant—a circular repetition of the original words for welcome, joy, and gratitude—which grew more complex as one after another of the priestesses joined in. After the full round was sung by the last of the priestesses, Herrwn sang his first line, followed in turn by each of the other priests, and then, just as the horizon was fully brightened, the men and women behind them sang out in a resounding chorus.

The sunrise ritual, whether on the spring equinox or any other morning, ended in a reversal of how it began. The last voice to enter fell silent first, and the song faded one voice at a time until the chief priestess sang the haunting final line and there was again silence as they filed out of the courtyard and down the stairs.

The sunrise ritual on the spring equinox served as the opening for revelries that had begun as a celebration of the birth of the firstborn child of the Earth-Goddess and the Sun-God, as well as the twin births of Her first two mortal children, a boy and girl from whom they themselves were descended. Over time, the spring equinox celebration had taken on a broader connotation and now included festivities in honor of all children, both divine and human. Conducting the day's public activities was delegated to the younger priests and priestesses, so Herrwn made his way back to his quarters in pleasant anticipation of an uninterrupted first day of instruction of the boy he hoped would someday take his place as the shrine's chief bard.

Opening the classroom doors, he found that Olyrrwd and Caelym had just returned from another expedition to the lake. There were tadpoles swimming in a ceremonial bowl on the windowsill, a jumble of birds' nests, pine cones, and pebbles was strewn across the table, and the sounds of scratching and scraping were coming from a wooden crate that had previously held Herrwn's extra sandals.

Olyrrwd and Caelym were sitting close together. Their heads were bent over a mound of brownish matter that Caelym was poking with one of Olyrrwd's surgical blades. Looking up, he announced with no small show of pride, "I know what owls eat! Mice and snakes and even other birds! They gobble them all up with their bones and everything! See?" He pointed to separate rows of tiny skulls, bones, and claws next to a scattering of mouse tails and went on, "Then instead of pooping like we do, they make the extra stuff into balls in their stomachs, and they spit them out!"

Hoping to avoid learning any more about owls' private habits, Herrwn hastily asked, "And what else did you find on your adventure in the woods?"

"A robin's nest and a wren's nest and pine cones that I'm going to plant and grow into trees, and—" Caelym leaped off his chair, knelt down, and reached with both hands into the crate. "See what I caught? Olyrrwd says I can keep him if I take good care of him, and I'm going to give him goat's milk so he'll grow up big and strong like me!"

Recalling the variety of injured or orphaned creatures Olyrrwd had brought home from his boyhood explorations in the marsh along the lakeshore and the wilderness beyond the marsh, Herrwn braced himself. It could be anything, although at the mention of milk his hope for a toad or a snake or anything not needing to be fed at all hours of the night vanished.

Of the creatures that would need milk, all could be counted on to wreak havoc in his classroom. Some (weasels, foxes, and badgers) had been worse than others (and Herrwn had actually become fond of one of Olyrrwd's several hedgehogs), but all could be expected to climb out of their crates and soil the floor and bite the servants who had to pick them up and put them back.

When Caelym finally managed to get hold of his scurrying quarry, he lifted it up and snuggled it against his chest, announcing, "I'm going to name him Hwppiddan, Hwppiddan the Hare."

Herrwn let out a relieved breath. It was just a bunny—a cute, fluffy bunny with ridiculously long ears and a twitching little nose. After badgers and foxes and weasels, how much trouble could a little baby bunny be?

Watching Olyrrwd show Caelym how to feed the baby hare warmed sheep's milk, Herrwn was deeply moved—both by the memory of his cousin as a boy nursing his new little kitten back to life and by the awareness that on the spring equinox, there could be no more sacred observance than watching Caelendra's son cradling an infant bunny in his arms.

Labhruinn returned to the men's quarters the next morning, gasping out, "It's a girl . . . She's fine . . . They're both fine . . ."

Until that moment, Herrwn hadn't been aware he'd been apprehensive, but now a flood of relief washed over him and he answered, "I am glad; I am most glad!" with what he hoped was not unseemly warmth.

"That baby can't have Whinnie! Whinnie is going to stay here and learn to be a Druid horse!" Caelym looked up from the moss and twigs he was arranging for a nest in the crate that was to be Hwppiddan's home because, as Olyrrwd had just explained, if Caelym held him all the time, Hwppiddan would never learn to hop. He eyed Labhruinn with suspicion, clearly ready to leap to his feet and grab his toy off the shelf if need be.

Whether Caelym's implied challenge penetrated Labhruinn's fog of bliss and fatigue or not, it at least drew his attention.

"You must be Caelym. You look just like Rhe—"

Before the confused and rambling Labhruinn could inadvertently suggest an earthly relationship between Caelym and the man who'd served as a vessel for the Sun-God six years earlier, Herrwn intervened, "This is Caelym, son of Caelendra, who was, as you know, conceived at the Sacred Summer Solstice Ceremony, just as was this new infant girl that the Priestess Annwr has borne! And Caelym, this is Labhruinn, who, like you, is learning to be a Druid priest."

"Who's Rhe?" Caelym cocked his head to the side, looking at Labhruinn.

"Er . . ." Labhruinn stammered.

"Not 'who,' 'what.'" Olyrrwd nudged Labhruinn aside and reached out to take Caelym's hand. "He means, 'Are you ready to go for your first lesson in how to stir potions and help heal people?'"

Grateful for the timely diversion, Herrwn stepped aside to let Olyrrwd lead Caelym away, promising to faithfully give Hwppiddan his milk while they were gone.

Chapter 18:

A Misunderstanding

"*And so all of the giants saw the wrongs that they had done and they were ashamed, and to make amends to the Goddess, to whom they also owed their birth, they built this shrine in Her honor, carving its halls and passages and stairways out of the pinnacle of rock where they had first declared their defiance, cutting out the stone blocks to make its outer walls and its three high towers, and putting the seven great stones in a circle in the Sacred Grove before retreating into the higher mountains to become stone themselves.*"

Herrwn had closed the shutters to the classroom window against the pelting rain that day, and Caelym's dark eyes were wide and luminous in the light of the hearth flames as he clapped his hands, exclaiming, "And the Goddess gave it to us!"

Herrwn nodded. "That is so—and why did She give it to us, of all her mortal children?"

"Because we fought the giants and made them say they were sorry!"

Nodding again, Herrwn took his lesson another step forward. "And what was it that the giants did of which they were rightly ashamed?"

"They were greedy and selfish."

"And?"

"They didn't honor the Goddess."

"And did they show kindness and respect to those who did them service?"

"No! They ate them!"

"But we are not like those giants were. We are not greedy and selfish. We do honor the Goddess, and we are kind and respectful to those who serve us." It was not enough, in Herrwn's mind, to memorize and recite the great sagas. Even in his earliest lesson he made certain his pupils applied the wisdom contained in those tales to their daily lives. Locking eyes with Caelym, he waited for a count of three before continuing, "And that means that when we ask Benyon to do something for us, we will say . . . ?"

Looking contrite, Caelym lowered his eyes and poked a finger into a crack in the stone floor as he murmured, "'Please,' and 'Thank you,' and 'We won't eat you!'"

There was no question in Herrwn's mind that the newly appointed chief servant for the priests' chambers had his work cut out for him, and, at a minimum, he should be spoken to courteously—especially since the duties he'd inherited from his predecessor had expanded to include the care and feeding of the assorted wildlife Olyrrwd and Caelym brought home from their explorations of the valley's woods and marshes.

Twenty years later, Herrwn could still hear his cousin's gravelly voice insisting, "They are a part the lad's learning about life!"—by which he clearly meant literal life, in all of its varied wriggling, creeping, hopping, flapping, hissing, croaking, and squawking variations—leaving, as he always did, the figurative, metaphorical meanings of the word, as well as the contemplation of how one might live a good life, to Herrwn.

Looking back from a cold and lonely perch above an alien landscape, Herrwn pondered—not for the first time—how it was that Olyrrwd, who paid so little attention to great precepts of philosophical thinking, had still lived the best of lives—if the value of a life was to be judged by its contribution to the welfare of others.

That day, however, he'd been preoccupied with keeping some sort of peace and order in his classroom, and that was difficult enough without the blithe attitude of entitlement Caelym had somehow acquired in the shrine's nursery.

The little boy's bossiness was a problem, but a lesser one than the challenge of protecting their beleaguered servant from being caught in the crossfire between Ossiam and Olyrrwd. Indeed, at that moment he had only to look over Caelym's bowed head to see Benyon wringing his hands as he agonized over how to obey both Ossiam, who'd ordered him to clean the mess off the classroom table, and Olyrrwd, who'd warned him not, under any circumstances, to touch the collection of birds' nests that he and Caelym were studying.

Recalling his father's words that achieving peace required sacrifice, Herrwn got to his feet and counted the separate piles of mud and twigs. He emptied the same number of engraved boxes in which he kept his precious quills, ink, and parchments, and—in order to assure that Benyon could truthfully say to Olyrrwd that he had not touched the nests—he himself lifted each of the mucky heaps into a box before handing them to Caelym to lay out along the windowsill while the anxious servant set to work scrubbing the table.

Whether it was out of frustration with the clutter in the classroom or a need to devote himself to his oracular duties without the distraction of Olyrrwd's growing menagerie, Ossiam rarely entered the classroom and took no part in Caelym's lessons.

Herrwn himself would have preferred a quieter, tidier space to do his instruction, but he could see the joy Olyrrwd took in showing Caelym the secrets of the natural world and the excitement in Caelym's eyes at each new revelation—besides which he would not venture to tell Olyrrwd how to teach his field any more than he'd expect Olyrrwd to tell him how to train a pupil in reciting odes or tuning a harp.

And, as Herrwn had tried to reassure Ossiam on more than one occasion, there was less risk of stepping in anything unfortunate before they'd had a chance to put on their sandals in the morning or of being startled by a snake slithering across the breakfast table now than there had been when they were growing up, since most of the varied creatures Olyrrwd and Caelym brought back to study were confined to their crates, baskets, and bowls.

"Most?" had been Ossiam's chilly response.

"All but Caelym's hare, and it's really no bother." Herrwn had found himself defending the animal as if it were his own pet.

Ossiam had humphed dismissively—but it was true. It really wasn't any bother at all to have the hare hopping around the classroom.

The little hare had taken the place of Caelym's toy horse. He carried it with him everywhere until it was big enough to hop along after him, and by then it could leap in and out of its crate at will.

As it got older and Caelym got busier with other things, the hare had made itself at home in the priests' inner courtyard, though it still came in to sleep with him at night and to sit quietly next to him during his lessons in recitation—looking inquisitively back and forth between Herrwn and Caelym as though it was following what was being said. By the end of the summer, when Herrwn was pleading its case with Ossiam, Hwppiddan had grown to be a strikingly handsome creature with such fastidious habits that it never left so much as a single dropping when it came inside.

Herrwn told his cousin all this, and while Ossiam did not appear convinced at the time, Herrwn noticed when he passed through the classroom a few days later, he paused to look at the now sleek and elegant hare with what for him was an appreciative expression.

Hoping to reduce the hostilities between his cousins, Herrwn made a point of mentioning that to Olyrrwd, only to have him bristle and growl, "He'd better not even think—"

Just what it was Ossiam had better not think was lost in the thunder of Labhruinn and Caelym returning from the herb garden, where Labhruinn was supposedly helping Caelym learn the names of plants—something he volunteered to do at the times when it was most likely that Annwr would be there nursing her now five-month-old daughter.

Before Caelym's arrival, Herrwn had wondered whether Labhruinn would resent the boy who was so certain to outshine him. Instead, perhaps because he had no other outlet for his overflowing paternal instincts, he'd become something between a loving brother and a doting uncle to the younger boy—which was, of course, a good thing and to be commended, as Herrwn told himself repeatedly whenever the exuberance of their friendship threatened to knock over the classroom chairs.

◆◆◆

While disappointed by his failure to soften Olyrrwd's attitude toward Ossiam, Herrwn did not mean to give up trying—especially as the increasingly snippy exchanges between the two were adding unnecessary divisiveness to the most contentious issue currently before the shrine's High Council: the complaints by the farmers and herders that Rhedwyn's horse races and war games were ruining their fields and frightening their flocks.

Returning to the classroom following a particularly strife-ridden debate—notable for Rhedwyn declaring that they needed to have an army "to be prepared for war" and the head of the village contingent retorting caustically, "I see, so now we have an army, it seems that next we will need a war!"—Herrwn opened the classroom door to hear the usually soft-spoken Benyon crying out, "Stop—*ouch!* Young Master, you must—*ouch!*—put that down! I'm—*ouch!*—only doing my job and following Master Ossiam's order to bring him this—*ouch!*—hare for his important sacrifice!" followed by Caelym's pure if shrill soprano, "YOU put HIM down, or I'll tell Olyrrwd and he will make a potion that will turn YOU into a hare, and Ossiam will sacrifice YOU!"

The door to the courtyard was open. Standing with his back to the classroom, Caelym was barring the way, wielding Herrwn's ceremonial staff like a war club. Beyond him, Benyon was holding up one hand to fend off the blows and clutching the struggling hare by the scruff of its neck with the other.

For a moment, Herrwn stood in the entryway, equally shocked that any pupil of his would hit a servant—moreover, hit him with Herrwn's own staff, the emblem of his order—and that, if what Benyon said was true, Ossiam would claim the hare without first getting consent from Olyrrwd, who must rightfully be considered to have prior title to it.

It must have been a misunderstanding, and one to be corrected as soon as possible. But first, he had to retrieve his staff—so he caught it as Caelym drew it back to strike another blow, saying sternly as he did, "You will return my staff to me, and you will say to our loyal servant Benyon that you are sorry and that you will never ever again raise your hand against him!"

Ignoring Caelym's heated protests, Herrwn planted his

reclaimed staff on the ground with a resounding thump, blocking the doorway as effectively as the boy had.

"And you, Benyon, you will give young Master Caelym the hare that you hold in your hand, and you will go to the village and find a hare being raised there for food, and you will take that hare to Master Ossiam for his sacrifice!"

"But Master Ossiam said he wants this hare—"

"I am sure you have misunderstood, for Master Ossiam has said nothing to me or to Master Olyrrwd of this. I will go to him myself and will assure him that you meant no harm and have gone to do as I bid you and will bring the proper hare as quickly as you can!"

Unable to disobey Herrwn's direct command, Benyon handed Hwppiddan to Caelym, who hugged the hare to his chest and, ducking his head, darted out of the classroom before Herrwn could repeat his directive to apologize.

Benyon stood where he was, pointedly rubbing his bruised forearm.

Herrwn's experience in his all-too-short union with his beloved Lothwen had taught him many things, not the least important of which was that it never hurt to call a dispute a misunderstanding and to apologize, regardless of whether he actually believed himself to be in the wrong. Putting that wisdom into practice, he bowed and said, "It is I, the teacher, who must ask forgiveness for my ill-trained pupil, and for any part I may have had in this misunderstanding."

Having done what he could to soothe Benyon, Herrwn dismissed the aggrieved servant to find another hare and made his own way to the healing chamber—where, he assumed, Caelym would have gone to enlist Olyrrwd in Hwppiddan's defense.

Neither Olyrrwd nor Caelym was anywhere to be seen, but Moelwyn was there, crumbling something Herrwn hoped wasn't an owl pellet into a simmering vat.

"They've gone to the upper meadows to set the hare loose."

Moelwyn's answer came before Herrwn could ask where Olyrrwd and Caelym were—and gave no hint of what Moelwyn might think about whatever account Caelym had given.

"When they return, ask Caelym to come to speak with me and tell Master Olyrrwd that I'm sure this has been a misunderstanding! You will say that, please? That it was a misunderstanding?"

After receiving Moelwyn's assurances, Herrwn kept his promise to Benyon and went to find Ossiam, where he repeated his assertion that this was a misunderstanding.

He'd hoped Ossiam would agree and explain, but had to be satisfied with getting a single, sullen nod before Ossiam turned his back and began to mutter incantations in a voice that was more irritated than apologetic.

Chapter 19:

The Ode

"**I**'m sorry I hit you with Master Herrwn's staff, which is the symbol of wisdom and judgment and which is not ever to be used for hitting, and I will never do it again."

Herrwn's finely attuned ear for nuance caught an element of ambiguity in Caelym's apology to Benyon. In an older boy, he would have thought it intentional, but he told himself that so young a child could not have the subtlety of mind to apologize for using the staff as his weapon rather than for the violence he'd done with it.

In any case, the sight of Caelym sadly picking up Hwppiddan's empty food bowl and putting it on the shelf next to his toy horse was so pathetic that Herrwn didn't have the heart to remonstrate further. In fact, he grew increasingly worried when the little boy sat listless and downcast through his lessons, left his noontime meal untouched, and spent the rest of the day on the stone bench in the priests' courtyard, rocking back and forth and silently moving his lips as tears trickled down his cheeks.

"Your beloved hare is happy, I am sure, being back with its own kin, and it would want you to be happy as well."

Caelym only shook his head as he sat on the edge of his bed that night, his dark curls tangled and the ties of his nightshirt hanging undone.

Herrwn tried a different approach. "But of course you are sad and must now put your sadness into words."

For a long moment, Caelym remained still and silent. Then, suddenly, he jumped off the bed, mounted a small stool, drew in a long, wavering breath, and—his chin thrust forward, his arms at his sides, his hands clenched into fists—cried out, "An Ode to Hwppiddan!" and began what was to be his first original recitation in a voice that cracked with grief.

Hwppiddan, Hwppiddan, greatest of hares,
He could leap over mountains
And up and down stairs.
As brave as a bear and as quiet as a mouse,
He never ran from danger
Or pooed in the house.

Oh, Hwppiddan, Hwppiddan, my very best friend,
I wish you were here
With me once again.
If ever I see him, a shout I will give—
"I'll love you forever,
As long as I live!"

Ending with a shuddering sob, Caelym stepped down off the stool, climbed into bed, turned his face to the wall, and pulled his blanket over his head.

Although somewhat awkward in its meter and unsophisticated in its pattern of rhyme, the poem, with its juxtaposition of the hare's imaginary and real virtues along with the depth of feeling it conveyed and the passion with which it was delivered, was a remarkable feat for a boy not yet seven years old. After blowing out the candle in the niche above Caelym's bed, Herrwn sat in the dark, feeling the weight of his responsibility for nurturing and molding such an amazing gift.

◆◆◆

The next morning, Herrwn was relieved to see Caelym fully recovered. He only wished he could say the same for Olyrrwd, who remained adamant that Ossiam had acted out of malice.

As Ossiam could not be persuaded to admit to either responsibility or regret for the previous day's misunderstanding, or to apologize for the grief that had resulted from it, Herrwn knew before he started that his efforts to mollify Olyrrwd would be to no avail.

He tried anyway, pointing out that even though Ossiam had ordered Benyon to bring Hwppiddan to be sacrificed, he surely must have meant for Benyon to obtain the proper consents before taking the hare out of the classroom—and might not have understood that it was Caelym's pet.

Olyrrwd continued to glower as Herrwn concluded what he considered to be a well-reasoned explanation by pointing out that from Ossiam's point of view, being sacrificed in a sacred rite was an honor for the animal involved. Resorting to a well-meaning, if clumsy, attempt at humor, he added, "And you must admit, it is a higher end than simply being killed and cooked for a common meal."

"And were you planning to eat him?" Olyrrwd stomped out of the room before Herrwn could finish saying, "Of course not!"

Chapter 20:

Ossiam's Dream

For months after what Herrwn continued to call "the misunderstanding," Olyrrwd stayed away from any ceremony that Ossiam was to officiate unless his attendance was obligatory, and, instead of exchanging snide witticisms at the communal meals, each of the two cousins acted as though the other didn't exist—Ossiam announcing to no one in particular that he'd like to have the salt pot and Olyrrwd picking it up and passing it without so much as shifting his eyes in the direction it was going.

Sitting in between them, Herrwn found he preferred his cousins' bickering to their chilly standoff and was almost relieved when the open antagonism between the two flared up again at the midsummer meeting of the shrine's High Council.

Held four times a year, the High Council met in the highest room at the top of their highest tower and was restricted to the highest members of their order—the chief midwife, the chief herbalist, and the keeper of the sacred calendar on the women's side, and the chief bard, the chief physician, and the chief oracle on the men's. The highest priestess might or might not attend. Caelendra always had, while Feywn, whose leadership seemed almost entirely defined by its differences from Caelendra's, appeared only on occasions when she had some edict of her own to announce.

The other high priests and priestesses were all expected to attend, however, and so Olyrrwd was there—ostentatiously fortifying himself with drink from the council's chalice of communal wine—as Ossiam rose to give the opening incantation.

Rhonnon was seated across from Olyrrwd. Wearing an immaculate white robe, the chief midwife was, as always, a model of decorum. Her eyes were focused on Ossiam, her hands folded in her lap. The shrine's chief herbalist, Aolfe, sat next to Rhonnon. Either placid by nature or from a life spent among aromatic herbs, Aolfe coped with council meetings the way she did with any forced separation from her garden—by weaving pine needles and stalks of dry grass into intricate baskets as she smiled pleasantly, ready to nod at whatever was being said. On the far side of Aolfe, the keeper of the sacred calendar sat with her elbows braced on the table and her chin propped in her cupped hands. Barely awake after a night spent tracking the movement of the stars, Lunedd's eyelids drooped, flickered up, then drooped again.

As he had at every council meeting since Arianna's birth, Ossiam included a new portent of the infant's future greatness in his invocation along with the (by now expected) prediction that hers would be an unusual and exceptional childhood. Instead of ending there, however, he went on to describe a dream in which he had seen their shrine transformed into a colossal boat in the center of a vast lake.

"The boat had decks that rose seven layers high," he murmured, "and in the top of the highest deck with the sun behind her back so that its light radiated out around her was a woman with glowing red hair. She sang a strange song in words I could not understand while flocks of ravens and larks circled in the sky above her and schools of silver fish leaped out of the lake's sparkling waters, swimming along with six long boats, each one laden with gifts and tribute, that were rowing toward the Goddess's floating shrine."

As Ossiam was given to showy dreams and visions, none of this was so surprising. What caught them off guard was his concluding pronouncement that since most of the affairs of that outer world were now conducted in the language of the Saxons, this was a message that Arianna must be sent out of the valley to be fostered among English-speaking Celts so as to be ready to rule when the time came for their resurgence.

Olyrrwd, who'd just taken another swallow from the ceremonial chalice, snorted, sending a spray of sacred wine across the table that splattered purple droplets across the front of Rhonnon's white robes.

Herrwn was equally startled. As Ossiam sat down, he stood up. He did not often use the power of his position to assert his views, but in this case he did, speaking in his most authoritative voice and beginning his rebuttal with an admonition against settling too quickly on any one interpretation of a dream's meaning.

"Although this dream was dreamed by an oracle—and so might understandably be assumed to be a revelation of the future—it could equally well be a vision from the past, when the spirit of the Great Mother Goddess first came to reside within the body of our first chief priestess, and our earliest ancestors built Her first shrine on Cwddwaellwn, the largest of the seven sacred islands of the sacred lake of Cwddwaffwn within the sacred valley of Cwddwandwn."

From there he went on to bolster his argument by noting the striking similarities between the scene that Ossiam had seen in his vision and the ancient descriptions of the islands of Cwddwandwn.

"Of course," he concluded with a solemn nod in Ossiam's direction, "I do not suggest that we disregard our esteemed oracle's urging to instruct Arianna in the language which so many of our people now speak, but it is my counsel that we do this prudently, by finding a servant who is able to give this instruction within her nursery and under the watchful eye of our chief midwife, whose duties have always included the oversight of the training of priestesses-to-be."

His words were greeted with vocal approval and applause from everyone except Ossiam, who rose up and walked out of the chamber—leaving them shaking their heads and looking at each other in bewilderment.

There were still several items of importance to be considered that morning, but as soon as they adjourned, Herrwn went to Ossiam's tower to soothe his cousin's hurt feelings and coax him back to reason.

The chamber was empty.

A sudden sense of foreboding came over him. What if Ossiam had gone to Feywn and actually made his mad proposal to her?

Lifting the hem of his robes, he ran down the stairs and through the hallways toward the priestess's chambers, filled with dread that Feywn, in a fury at the suggestion that she send her infant away, might expel Ossiam from their order.

He arrived at the entrance to the women's quarters just as Ossiam was coming out, his hood up and his face hidden in its shadow.

"Should I speak with her as well?" Herrwn spoke from his heart, ready to face Feywn's anger himself to ensure that she understood Ossiam meant well and, however mistakenly, sincerely believed that what he'd suggested was in the best interest of their people.

"There is no need." Ossiam's voice was calm, even peaceful.

Relieved that Ossiam had accepted his defeat gracefully, Herrwn fell into step with his cousin, and they walked back to the priests' quarters together in what seemed to Herrwn at the time to be a companionable silence.

Chapter 21

River's Gift

Except for Olyrrwd muttering, "Ossiam's up to something," nothing more was said that day of the oracle's peculiar prophesy, and Herrwn assumed the notion of sending Feywn's daughter out of Llwddawanden had been safely laid to rest. It was certainly not on his mind when he was waiting to start his recitation of the conclusion of the final saga of The Goddess's Golden Ring a fortnight later.

Poised and ready to begin his oration, he glanced around the great hall.

The chair to Feywn's left was vacant, as Rhedwyn had ridden off on a raid that morning, but otherwise all the priests and priestesses were in their places. He looked to the chief priestess in expectation of her usual small nod signaling him to begin. Instead, Feywn rose and held out her hand toward him in a gesture that somehow combined supplication with benediction.

"Tonight, Herrwn, Master of Tales, I wish above all things to hear you tell the story of the River-Goddess and her daughter."

Having been the consort to—and shared close living quarters with—an exceptionally beautiful woman, Herrwn was more able than most to accept Feywn's physical appearance as simply a part of who she was. Even he, however, was awed by her voice, a voice which was everything Rhedwyn sang about it—soft yet commanding, and so imbued with sensuality that most men's knees went weak just hearing her call them by name. The effect on Herrwn that night was all the more compelling as she rarely spoke to him directly and seemed at best only to listen politely when he recited.

Determined not to appear flustered, he took a firm grip on his staff and asked, "From the beginning?"

"From the part about the basket."

Acceding to Feywn's unusual request, Herrwn began in the middle of the story after a brief summation of the events that led up to "the part about the basket"—recalling for his listeners how Rhiddengwyn, the River-Goddess, had fallen in love with the mortal hero, Seddwelyn, spurning the advances of the demon Maelgwin, and how Maelgwin had pursued them in a jealous rage, finally slaying Seddwelyn, whose valiant last stand had given Rhiddengwyn the chance to escape with the child of their union, a baby girl named Halfwen, because she was half mortal, and how Rhiddengwyn, clutching Halfwen to her breast, had raced for the river that would have carried them to safety, only to be trapped in a magic net that Maelgwin had set at the river's edge.

Her strength sapped by the enchanted coils of Maelgwin's net, Rhiddengwyn managed to reach through the mesh and pluck reeds and lilies that she wove into a basket large enough to hold her newborn infant, then thrust the basket through a gap in the net and into the river just as Maelgwin came out of the trees behind her, armed with her beloved Seddwelyn's sword and shield.

Protected by Rhiddengwyn's spells, the basket, with its precious cargo, floated gently down the stream until it came around a bend in the river where a sheepherder, fishing from the shore, cast his line, caught the edge of the basket with his hook, and pulled it up onto the bank.

The sheepherder had six sons but longed for a daughter, so he carried the sleeping infant home to his wife. Delighted with the beauty of the baby girl, they called her "River's Gift" and agreed to raise her as their own.

One day, the sheepherder's wife accidentally dropped a spinning spool into the baby's cradle, and when she leaned over to get it, she was amazed to see that River's Gift had picked it up in her tiny hands and was spinning a strand of thread that shone like silver. As time passed and River's Gift grew into a beautiful young girl, the strands of wool she spun transformed into threads that shimmered in all the colors in the rainbow, and she soon began to weave wonderful cloth in patterns that changed with the mood and thoughts of the wearer.

Rhiddengwyn, however, had used the last of her waning powers to save her daughter and was helpless to defend herself from Maelgwin, who took her by force and dragged her off to his mountain kingdom. Kept locked in a windowless tower, she remained a captive there until she convinced Maelgwin that she loved him and enticed him to take off his armor and lay down his weapons. Coaxing him close, whispering seductively in his ear, she caressed his cheek with one hand while with the other she grasped hold of Seddwelyn's sword and, in a stroke, avenged both her honor and her murdered lover.

Once free, Rhiddengwyn searched in vain for her daughter, calling her name over and over to no avail. Eventually, she despaired of ever seeing her beloved child again and retreated in sorrow to the top of the highest mountain in all the world, where she remained, weeping and sighing, unaware that Halfwen was growing up in a valley far below—believing herself to be the child of the sheepherder and his wife and answering to the name of River's Gift.

As she ripened into womanhood, River's Gift became ever more beautiful and the cloth she wove became ever more wondrous. The sheepherder's wife cut the cloth and made it into garments that were not only lovely to behold but had magical powers that brought good fortune to the wearer. When the sheepherder took the clothes to sell in the market, everyone crowded around him, anxious to buy them and giving him any price he asked.

Over time, River's Gift's fame spread throughout the land. She had many suitors, but she refused one after another, saying she would only marry the man who could wear a shirt she had woven and tell her truthfully that he loved her for herself alone—not for the riches that came from her weaving. Many men put on that enchanted shirt and swore their love for her, but no matter how sincere their words seemed, the shirt always gave their inner thoughts away, its luminous colors swirling into pictures of their hands grasping for the gold that her weaving would bring them.

Of all River's Gift's many suitors, only the son of the king, who was exceedingly wealthy himself, could say that he loved her without thought of her weaving. He, however, was betrayed by the shirt as well, for it showed that his true longing was for her beauty and not for her wit or her strength of character. Seeing that he was, in his own way, as shallow as her other suitors, River's Gift sent the king's son away as she had all those others, except that—moved by his tears and pleading—she let him keep the shirt that she had woven.

Heartbroken, the king's son went off wearing the shirt which now showed only the picture of River's Gift's face, for that was the king's son's only thought. Lost in his long- ing for River's Gift, he wandered without looking or caring where he was going and surely would have perished from hunger or drowned in the sea or been devoured by wild beasts, except that the shirt had magical powers that made its wearer invincible.

Always full without the need to eat, able to walk on water without sinking, and shielded against all attackers, the king's son wandered on—down into valleys, across rivers, and up into the mountains—never stopping and never tiring, because the shirt's magic powers gave him the strength to climb the highest mountain with no more effort than walking along a gentle path through a garden.

It was at the top of the highest mountain that the king's son met Rhiddengwyn, who had taken on the appearance of a shriveled old woman from her years of lamenting.

All the while that the king's son had been wandering through the wilderness, he had been thinking himself the saddest of all beings. He'd never imagined that anyone could suffer more than he did until he saw the grief of a mother mourning for her lost child. Then, for the first time, he felt sorry for someone else.

Since he could not marry the beautiful woman he loved, he made up his mind to reject both joy and beauty alto- gether and marry the weeping crone. That was what he said to Rhiddengwyn—thinking that marrying a king's son and having all the wealth in the kingdom would at least make the old woman stop crying.

The audacity of a mortal feeling sorry for her did make Rhiddengwyn stop crying and she looked up, outraged and intending to cast a spell to make the king's son throw himself off the side of the mountain.

But as she was about to begin her incantation, she saw the face on the front of the enchanted shirt and recognized her long-lost daughter. So, instead of commanding the king's son to jump off the cliff, she greeted him like a son and listened with tears of joy as he told her how he'd come to have the shirt, and together they went to the sheepherder's cottage and told River's Gift the truth of who her mother was and why she had such wondrous gifts.

And that was how the River-Goddess's daughter was reunited with her mother and how the king's son learned to see beneath surface appearances.

Given the choice of marrying the king's son, who now loved her for herself, or going to the other world to be with her mother, River's Gift chose to go with her mother. But before she left, she kissed the king's son on the lips, and in doing so bestowed upon him the skill of singing songs in a voice of unmatched beauty. And while River's Gift was never to be seen again by mortals, she proved the meaning of her name, for the tears Rhiddengwyn had shed in the years that she had been mourning for her lost child became the crystal waterfalls that fall down the sides of mountains, the sighs that she had sighed became the gentle breezes that rustle the uppermost leaves in the summer, and eventually, when the king's son grew old and died, he was reborn as a nightingale and still sings his songs of love for the River-Goddess's daughter each spring.

Herrwn retired to bed that night feeling pleased with his performance, especially since it had been given without the benefit of advance preparation.

Rising the next day, he noticed that his cousin's bed was empty but thought nothing of it since, as Olyrrwd always said, patients seemed to go out of their way to get sick just when their physician was trying to get some sleep.

His first inkling that anything was out of order was a vague, indefinable difference in the tone of the singing at the sunrise ritual.

It was a usual sunrise ritual, and the usual priests and priestesses were there. Feywn sang the opening line of the ancient chant. Her voice, always clear, sounded oddly brittle in the still, cold air, and the other priestesses joined in a fraction of a beat out of time. None of the other priests seemed to notice the faint dissonance, however, and so Herrwn told himself that he was being overly sensitive.

When he got back to the classroom, Herrwn saw Olyrrwd talking to Caelym. Knowing his cousin as well as he did, Herrwn saw the tense set to Olyrrwd's shoulders and realized something was seriously wrong even before he heard Olyrrwd telling Caelym to be patient and that they'd go out to look for a new snake later, "after I have a little talk with Herrwn."

Thinking that what Olyrrwd had to talk to him about was that the adder he and Caelym had been keeping in their collection of animals had escaped from its vessel, there was more than a little urgency in Herrwn's first question as they stepped out of the classroom and into the courtyard.

"Have you told the servants?"

"They told me."

"So they are searching for it, then?"

"Searching for what?"

"The poisonous snake!"

"Oh, him—he's in his tower, plotting his next move."

Looking anxiously around for any movement in the grass, it took Herrwn a moment to realize that he had no idea what he and Olyrrwd were talking about.

"I am sorry, but I don't understand. What did the servants say, exactly?"

Whether or not what Olyrrwd shared was the servants' exact words (and Herrwn very much doubted that servants would have used the language Olyrrwd did), what they told him was, in essence, that Feywn had done as Ossiam directed and sent her infant daughter to be fostered in a village outside the valley.

The odd disharmony of the women's chorus that morning came back to Herrwn's mind.

"Did Rhonnon agree?"

"Rhonnon knew nothing of it until after it was too late."

"But why . . ." Catching himself on the verge of asking a fellow priest to divine what went on in the mind of the priestess who was the embodiment of the Great Mother Goddess, Herrwn stopped, cleared his throat, and reframed his question. "Why do the servants think Feywn would do such a thing?"

"Half of them say that Ossiam lusts after our high priestess and has conjured a spell compelling her to cast away the infant sired by Rhedwyn—and that Rhedwyn himself will be next. The other half say that Feywn is using Ossiam's vision as an excuse to send the infant off out of jealousy that Rhedwyn dotes on Arianna more than on Herself. Take your pick!"

Neither of these explanations was even remotely acceptable to Herrwn, and he regretted asking. Furthermore, he had no intention of asking which account Olyrrwd favored, knowing full well that Olyrrwd was always ready to believe the worst of Ossiam. Instead, he shook his head and sighed. "I am sure that this must be a misunderstanding."

Then, partly to change the subject and partly because he thought he saw something slithering under the shrubs at the edge of the courtyard, he asked, "And the snake you were speaking of to Caelym—is it the adder that is missing?"

Chapter 22:

Casting Stones

Whatever explanation lay behind Feywn's momentous decision, it was at least a relief to know that the escaped serpent was just a harmless grass snake. Accepting Olyrrwd's assurance that the creature would find its way out of the shrine eventually and that, in the meanwhile, they would have less bother with mice and rats, Herrwn returned to the classroom, where Caelym was waiting impatiently for Olyrrwd to take him snake hunting and Labhruinn was tuning his harp in preparation for his day's oration.

A scattering of broken strings lay strewn on the floor under Labhruinn's stool, and another one snapped as Herrwn stepped across the threshold and into the classroom. Suppressing a sigh, he went to the cupboard to get the spare harp he kept tuned and ready, saying as he exchanged it for the sadly abused instrument that Labhruinn apologetically held out to him, "We will review the proper way to tune a harp later, but now I would like to hear you recite the saga of Penddrwn and Ethelwen, starting where we left off yesterday, just after Penddrwn has been cast down in a pit and left there to be devoured by the avaricious one-eyed giant that has been terrorizing King Derfwyn's domain."

As Labhruinn began, *"Oh woe! Oh woe!"* Herrwn winced, wishing himself in the pit with Penddrwn—who, for all his misfortunes, would have struck the correct opening chord for the right lament.

◆●◆

In the year and a half since he'd entered his formal apprenticeship, Labhruinn had, by dint of sweating concentration and laborious practice, managed to learn the last of the dances and chants required for entry into the lowest rank of the priesthood and had, in addition, demonstrated satisfactory competence in the least demanding of his training requisites, which was participation in the shrine's Low Council.

The Low Council was held in a hall on the lowest level of the shrine and was attended by whatever priests or priestesses were willing to sit through hours of listening to laborers laying out their complaints about each other. As the shrine's chief priest, Herrwn presided over the Low Council. As his disciple, Labhruinn was required to sit next to him in respectful silence, nodding in agreement with his pronouncements and making a reasonable show of appearing interested in the long and tedious deliberations.

That Labhruinn actually paid attention to what was being said was something that Herrwn discovered by chance. On a whim, he remained in his place after the council ended and called on Labhruinn to "render his judgment" over one of the more contentious of the disputes they had just heard, and—much to his surprise—he found himself nodding in genuine approval at the fair and judicious answer he received.

The main responsibility of an assistant bard, however, was to speak the lines of the minor characters and to pluck or strum his harp at times in the narrative where a particular unison with or dissonance from chords being played by the chief bard was needed. To do that, Labhruinn had to master all nine of the great sagas, along with their accompanying odes and songs.

The songs were not an insurmountable problem. Labhruinn could actually sing most of them quite well—especially those that required a strong baritone voice.

The spoken lines were his downfall.

Listening to Labhruinn stumble from one mangled verse to the next, Herrwn could not help but recall Rhedwyn's flawless delivery. And while Rhedwyn was no longer in the classroom, Caelym was.

Gifted with Rhedwyn's uncanny ability to recall and repeat the most convoluted stories on a single hearing, Caelym had quickly surpassed Labhruinn—yet, for better or for worse, the two had become fast friends and Caelym had taken it upon himself to fill in the gaps in Labhruinn's orations.

Recalling one particularly beleaguered day in the fall of the second year of Caelym's training, Herrwn seemed to hear Labhruinn's rumbling baritone alternating with Caelym's shrill soprano.

"And so the goddess, hmmm (Eiriawen!) Eiriawen reached out her snow-white hand to touch . . . ahh . . . (Araddwn's) Araddwn's cheek (brow) brow as he lay wounded (no, dying!) no, dying . . . er, I mean, dying at her feet . . ."

Herrwn had sternly reminded Caelym that he should be attending to his own lesson and told Labhruinn to start from the beginning, but as Labhruinn was opening his mouth to comply, Caelym jumped to his feet, crying out, "It's my turn!"

Waving his hazel study stick like a sword, he began, *"I, Aiddan, Son of Araddwn . . ."* going on to vow vengeance against Hergest, the giant king, in as menacing a voice as a seven-year-old with missing front teeth was capable.

Labhruinn laughed a deep, throaty laugh that turned into a growl as he rose to play the part of the giant, and before Herrwn could object, the battle broke out in full force. Stools were piled up into tottering mountain peaks, rugs became lakes roiling with water monsters, and tables were turned on their side to be fortress walls as the mock war raged—only ending when Labhruinn fell to his knees and died a wild and convulsing death to the sound of Caelym's piping cheers.

When he was finally able to make himself heard, Herrwn chided them both, saying, "I see you have finished learning what I have to teach you, so now you may go outside to play games with the sheepherders' children."

That was the same rebuke his father had once used when his own attention had wandered off from his lessons, and it had served its purpose of shaming him into redoubled diligence and dedication. Labhruinn and Caelym, however, took him at his word, and he had to step out of the way to avoid being knocked over as the two dashed out the door together.

It was only mid-afternoon, but Herrwn felt drained. He left the room's clutter for Benyon to put right and went to the healing chamber to find Olyrrwd, hoping he'd be willing to come on a restorative walk along the lakeshore.

Not only was Olyrrwd willing, he was even more in need of a break than Herrwn. And as it turned out, he was no happier with Moelwyn than Herrwn was with Labhruinn.

Being so much taller, Herrwn usually had to adjust his stride so he didn't outpace Olyrrwd, but that day he was hard-pressed to keep up—and was soon too out of breath to do more than puff in sympathetic gasps that Olyrrwd did not seem to notice as he fumed, "Seeing people vomit makes him feel ill himself! Fevers frighten him since they could be catching! Can I ask him to lance a simple boil? Not if there's going to be pus! He doesn't like pus! Take care of a cough? Not if there's phlegm! He doesn't like phlegm either—especially not green phlegm! Blood, if there's not too much of it and it doesn't get on his sleeves, is all right, but it upsets him to have people scream when he splints their broken bones—or to have them die after he's given them a perfectly brewed potion!"

They were halfway around the lake before Olyrrwd finally stopped ranting, either out of breath or too disgruntled to go on. He plopped down on the bank, picked up a round, flat stone, and sent it skipping across the surface of the lake.

The stone skimmed across the water, touching down and rising up again a dozen times before it came down for a last time and sank out of sight.

"Twelve!" Olyrrwd said in a voice that seemed to be coming from somewhere very far away. "I have twelve years left!"

Then, sounding resolved and more like himself, he said, "Caelym will need to be ready! In twelve years, he will be old enough."

Ignoring Herrwn's objection—"You are not an oracle, and skipping stones is not augury!"—Olyrrwd grumbled, "I'd better get back before some inconsiderate sick person comes to the healing chamber and starts spewing in front of Moelwyn." He pushed himself up and started toward the shrine, walking with a limp that Herrwn hadn't noticed before.

Chapter 23:

Caelym's Close Call

Olyrrwd never gave any sign that he was saddened or worried about the fate he'd foretold for himself, and, despite the frustrations that both he and Herrwn had with their disciples, life within their classroom settled into a predictable pattern.

Caelym's mornings belonged to Olyrrwd while Herrwn, fortified with a goblet of mulled elderberry wine, labored through Labhruinn's lessons until the midday meal, after which Herrwn gave Labhruinn the mutually face-saving admonition to continue his rehearsal in some location "in which you find inspiration," which they both understood was tacit consent for him to spend the rest of the day in the herb garden with Annwr and her baby.

Herrwn's mornings with Labhruinn were the test of his mettle as a teacher. His afternoons with Caelym were his reward. Gifted not merely with an astounding memory but with an inborn musical ability, the youngster learned to tune a harp in a single sitting and was playing melodies of his own invention by the end of the day. Dancing came as naturally to him as walking and singing as easily as breathing. But it was the infectious joy Caelym exuded at each new accomplishment that gave Herrwn his greatest sense of success, even as he found himself worn out by the end of the afternoon when Benyon brought Caelym's supper tray.

Unless there were demands that kept him in the healing chamber, Olyrrwd would come in while Caelym was eating and afterwards the three of them would sit by the hearth and Herrwn would tell a story before the two men tucked Caelym into bed and left for the adult evening in the shrine's great hall.

The first of those "before bed" stories were simple tales with comic heroes and cheerful endings, but as Caelym got older Herrwn moved on to the more complex legends of mortal heroes fighting battles to overcome apparently undefeatable enemies and win the love of some beautiful goddess only to be brought down by their pride or by the envy of others—then rallying again to achieve a final moral triumph before dying and departing for the spirit world.

One evening, not long after Caelym's ninth birthday, Herrwn was concluding the tale of the noble and courageous though ill-fated Eddedrwn, seventh of the Great Mother Goddess's mortal lovers. He'd just finished saying, *"And so She lifted his body up in Her arms and carried him into the sky in a golden chariot drawn by three silver-winged horses,"* when Caelym asked, "How did my father die?"

Caught off guard, Herrwn pursed his lips, thinking quickly.

Certainly Caelym would have been told from the first that he was the son of Caelendra, who had been the shrine's high priestess and the living embodiment of the Great Mother Goddess, along with some gentle explanation that when he was born his mother had to go back to the other world and that she had left Feywn to take her place. But had anyone, either one of the priestesses or his nursemaid, actually explained the Sacred Summer Solstice Ceremony to him?

Apparently not.

So now, after having heard so many tales of goddesses giving birth to half divine children fathered by heroes who were subsequently killed by demons or dragons or poisonous serpents, it was only natural for Caelym to conclude he'd had such a mortal father himself and to wonder what had become of him.

Drawing in a deep breath and speaking in the solemn tone he used in his most serious lessons, Herrwn began, "If you are old enough to ask that question, then you are old enough to have an answer."

Caelym looked up expectantly, his dark eyes wide and unblinking.

There was no turning back now. Herrwn drew another deep

breath and went on, "You know that you were born on the day before the spring equinox."

Caelym nodded.

"And you know that the spring equinox comes nine months after the night of the summer solstice."

Caelym nodded again.

If Olyrrwd had been there, Herrwn had no doubt that he would have insisted on providing a graphic description of the specifics involved in conception, but left to his own resources, Herrwn fell back on the explanation of the Sacred Summer Solstice rites that his father had given him thirty years earlier.

"There was once a time before there were men or women or boys or girls—and in that time the earth was very beautiful, just as it is now, but it was also very lonely, so, on the night of a long-ago summer solstice, the Earth-Goddess sang and danced with the Sun-God, and nine months later, on the day of the next spring equinox, she gave birth to the first of her mortal children, a boy and a girl who were our people's own ancestors."

Recalling how profoundly private Caelendra had been about personal matters, Herrwn faltered. Then, gathering his courage, he plunged ahead.

"And that is why, if it happens that a high priestess feels the urge—that is, if, in her infinite wisdom, she decides that there is a man who is worthy to start a child within her, then, according to our custom, she may celebrate the Sacred Summer Solstice ritual as the Great Mother Goddess once did all those many years ago."

After pausing momentarily to touch a hand cloth to his forehead, where he could feel drops of perspiration starting to form, he finished as quickly as he could.

"So I will tell you now that, on the night of one summer solstice, your mother did choose such a man who chanted the ancient chant, turning himself into a god for that one night, and together they sang the sacred songs and danced the sacred dance so that you could be born."

Caelym's gaze remained fixed on Herrwn's face. "What happened to him after that?"

"He returned to being what he was before—a mortal like the rest of us."

"Is he dead?"

"No, he lives and is both happy and proud to have been chosen to sing and dance with the Goddess, your mother."

"Then who—"

Herrwn stood up, saying firmly, "Who he is in this world does not matter, for he was not himself when he was singing and dancing with the goddess."

"Who is he now?"

"Now"—Herrwn took Caelym's hand and pulled him gently toward his bedchamber—"the time for stories is done and the time for sleep is come."

Caelym seemed quieter and more thoughtful than usual the next morning, but he perked up when Olyrrwd told him that they were going outside the shrine to take care of the sick people in the village that day.

Glad to see that Caelym wasn't brooding, Herrwn waved them off and braced himself for the start of a new saga with Labhru-inn—one that required accompaniment with a harp tuned to a dark and difficult mode.

Even for a capable learner, the sea voyage of the three sons of Llaed-drwn, King of Llanddissigllen, was a challenging saga, intertwining as it did the separate adventures of the three heroes, each of whom assumed multiple guises with distinct but similar-sounding names that had to be kept straight for the final resolution of the story to make sense. Simply getting Labhruinn through the opening ode without reducing him to tears of despair took all of Herrwn's concentration, and he was caught off guard when the classroom door slammed open and Olyrrwd stormed in, thumping his staff with one hand and clutching Caelym's wrist with the other.

"Labhruinn!" he barked. "Take Caelym to the kitchen and get him some hot milk and a bowl of soup!"

Ignoring Caelym's protest that he wasn't hungry, Olyrrwd glowered at Labhruinn so fiercely that if Herrwn hadn't had his disciple directly in front of him for the entire morning, he would have believed him to be the cause of Olyrrwd's wrath.

Rising up to do as he was told, Labhruinn acknowledged the boy's protest by shrugging—his right shoulder lifted slightly higher than his left—in an appeasing gesture as he started for the door.

"Now!"

For a small man, Olyrrwd could produce a very loud roar. In this case, it sent both Labhruinn and Caelym running out of the room and down the hall without stopping to shut the doors behind them.

After stalking over to slam them shut, Olyrrwd turned back, paced over to the window, then stomped back and around the hearth, circling the room like an enraged bear, muttering, "Conceited, arrogant idiot . . . a danger to himself and everyone around him . . . ought to have his head banged against the wall to knock some sense into it . . ."

Herrwn had never seen Olyrrwd so angry—not even in his most heated disputes with Ossiam. Stepping directly into his cousin's path, Herrwn put out his hands and gripped Olyrrwd's shoulders. "Olyrrwd, calm yourself and tell me what has happened! Has Caelym done something wrong?"

"Not Caelym, Rhedwyn!"

"What did he do?"

Thrusting out his hand with his thumb and forefinger a hair's breadth apart, Olyrrwd thundered, "Came that close to killing him! If I'd come out a moment later, he'd have been crushed to a bloody pulp! And Rhedwyn—Rhedwyn wouldn't have stopped if I hadn't called him! And even then he didn't come back to see if the boy was safe, didn't even care—"

"But I care, so sit down and tell me how this happened."

Dropping his fist, Olyrrwd let himself be propelled over to the table where Herrwn pressed him down into a chair, before going to the cupboard and pouring him a cup of wine. Then the story came out.

◆◆◆

Halfway through his rounds, Olyrrwd had gone into the smith's cottage, leaving Caelym outside because the child he was going to see had what might be a contagious fever. Thankfully, the smith's boy had been sitting up and looking well, so Olyrrwd left the potion Moelwyn had brewed, told them to add it to some chicken broth and keep the lad in bed another day, and went back out—only just in time to pull Caelym out of the road when Rhedwyn and "his band of idiots" came racing through the village, trampling over anything that got in their way.

"But you called to Rhedwyn and he stopped! Did he ask your forgiveness when he saw what he might have done?"

"Not him! The fat-headed fool just smiled that 'I'm so charming' smile of his and did that 'you can't be angry with me' shrug of his shoulders and rode off, not giving a rat's ass that he'd almost killed his own son!"

Had it been anyone but Olyrrwd, Herrwn would have made the customary correction, but knowing his cousin's views on reproduction to be unshakably physical he just asked, "Was Caelym injured at all?"

"Not a scratch, except for the bruise where I grabbed his arm."

"But, of course, it was frightening—"

"For me, yes! It took a year of my life I didn't have to spare! But Caelym—that boy wouldn't know fear if it stood up and stared him in the face. If I'd have let him, he would have jumped up on a horse and ridden off with Rhedwyn, as happy as a lark."

His anger drained, Olyrrwd's tone shifted to something between melancholy and bitterness as he added, "Or if Rhedwyn had asked him."

In the silence that followed, Herrwn felt his heart filling with affection and admiration for his cousin. Another man loving a child as much as Olyrrwd loved Caelym would have been jealous of anyone else's claim on the boy's affections, but Olyrrwd was only saddened and resentful on Caelym's behalf that Rhedwyn rarely, if ever, even glanced in the boy's direction.

Hoping to ease Olyrrwd's mind, Herrwn reminded him that this would not affect Caelym at all, as it was absolutely forbidden for anyone to name Rhedwyn as his father. Refusing to be placated, Olyrrwd snapped, "And do you think he'll never look in a mirror?"

Chapter 24:

Which of the Young Priestesses

lthough most likely just a coincidence, Caelym's near-fatal encounter with Rhedwyn's riders marked a change from the carefree exuberance of his middle boyhood into the self-conscious intensity of early youth. Tall for his age and advanced in his studies, it was easy to think of him as twelve when he was nine and thirteen when he was ten.

Those were years in Herrwn's own life he recalled as being fraught with turmoil, when all his thoughts were confused, all his movements were clumsy, and all his mistakes were calamitous—but also the time when Lothwen suddenly turned from a gawky, gangly, and somewhat irritating cousin into a being so beautiful, so marvelous, so absolutely enchanting that his voice squeaked if he tried to speak to her and he blushed bright red when she smiled in his direction.

"Which of the young priestesses-to-be will someday have that effect on Caelym?" was a question that rose up in Herrwn's mind one day as he was passing through the shrine's central courtyard on his way to the midday meal.

It was a bright day in early summer, and the nursery servant had brought the little girls in her charge out to play while she sat spinning on a nearby bench. Gwennefor's dark-haired daughter, Gwenydd, was dancing her dolls in a line and singing made-up chants in imitation of a sacred ritual. Caldera's twins, their chestnut-brown hair in long braids, were darting among the stone pillars in a giddy, giggling game of tag while Cyri, Annwr's winsome red-headed toddler, was standing barefoot in a puddle of mud, pouring water from a child-size pitcher over a flooded clump of toadflax.

As Herrwn paused for a moment to watch, warmed by the summer sun and charmed by their sweet, innocent games, he realized how quickly they—and Caelym—were growing up.

He'd not thought about it before this, but of course there were four lovely little girls destined to become high-ranked priestesses (five when you counted Feywn's daughter, about whom there'd been no word at all in the two years she'd been gone but who, if Ossiam's prophesy was to be believed, would be the most beautiful of all), and as of now there was only one boy in training to be a priest. When one of the girls took Caelym for her consort, what would the other four do?

They needed more children—at least some of them boys— and the sooner the better. Resolving to speak to Olyrrwd, who in turn could bring the matter to Rhonnon's attention, who as chief midwife would presumably take the issue to the priestesses who were young enough to have babies, Herrwn took a firm hold on his staff and started back on his way just as the horn sounded the call to the midday meal.

While breakfast in the shrine was usually a simple, informal meal carried by servants to the priests' and priestesses' private quarters, both the midday and the nighttime meals were ceremonial events held in the shrine's main hall.

Seating at the high table (which, in keeping with its name, was set on a platform a step above floor level) was strictly ordered by rank, with the chief priestess in the center, the priests to her left, and priestesses to her right.

Like the seating arrangements, the discourse at the communal meals was tightly regulated, although an outsider might have assumed their conversations were simply congenial pleasantries being freely exchanged as the chalice of wine, the soup bowls, and the platters of food were passed up and down the length of the table.

As chief priestess, Feywn would call on Ossiam to give the day's omen, after which each of the elders would speak in turn—either offering some insight related to what had just been said or, if they chose, introducing a new topic with the proviso that all contentious issues were to be left to the formal council debates.

While it was true that Olyrrwd and Ossiam were sometimes guilty of sneaking in subtle digs at each other, the talk at the midday meal was, for the most part, congenial and pleasant. What an outside observer would have thought about the exchange that took place the day that Herrwn stopped to watch the four little girls at play in the main courtyard was something Herrwn was just as happy not to know.

Chapter 25:

The Most Beautiful Jewel

"I had a dream last night."

Having received Feywn's nod to pronounce his portent, Ossiam slipped into a dreamy-sounding voice as he went on, "At first I seemed to be walking down a long, winding path on a high hillside. It was dark around me, but I could see our shrine in the distance, and then a shimmering light appeared, a light that shone so brightly I thought it was the sun rising above the horizon. But then, out of the center of the light, there came a rider on a dark steed, wearing shining armor and holding up a silver sword. The light around him was so dazzling that I could not make out his face, but, as he passed me by, I heard him say in the wondrous voice of a god, "I go to seek the most beautiful jewel."

Ossiam's eyes had a faraway look, as though he were seeing the vision before him. Then he blinked. Looking at no one in particular, he spoke in a hushed tone, seeming to carry on a conversation with himself, first asking, "What does this mean?" and then answering in a voice that faded into a sigh, "I do not know."

Perhaps Ossiam, being an oracle, might be forgiven for not immediately recognizing the meaning of a heroic figure riding off in search of "the most beautiful jewel," but Herrwn was a bard and knew there was no more dangerous image in all of their great legends.

•◆•

The first of innumerable quests for "the most beautiful jewel" began at the conclusion of the story of the Goddess's Stolen Treasure. A good part of the remainder of that saga was taken up with the long and difficult search to recover the trove of golden jewelry and precious gems that was stolen from the Goddess by the devious demon king, Drogmwrg—and especially the most beautiful jewel that was its centerpiece.

After first vying with each other to win the glory of recovering the lost treasure, the surviving heroes came together and fought their way into Drogmwrg's mountain lair, defeating the demon hordes and slaying the demon king—only to discover that the spell Drogmwrg used to carry the treasure out of the spirit realm had died with him, and even the greatest of their Druids could not solve the puzzle of how to take the now earthbound trove back across the divide between the mortal and the spirit worlds.

It was at the very end of the first of the great sagas that the half-divine hero, Haerddrwn, managed to achieve that seemingly impossible task through a complicated series of incantations and at the cost of leaving his mortal body behind. Then, at the moment of Haerddrwn's greatest triumph, as he spread the recovered treasure out at the feet of the Goddess, it was discovered that the most beautiful jewel was missing, and the tale ended with the lines, "Unable to return to the physical world to complete his quest, Haerddrwn withdrew into the most remote corner of the spirit realm, where he has sat and sulked ever since, his angry frustration growing until he can contain it no more and he shoots his flaming arrows through the curtain dividing the worlds to strike down to earth as lightning while his curses against his fate can be heard in the roar of thunder."

The quest to find the most beautiful jewel was taken up by Haerddrwn's son, Haerddrael, and was thought by many to be the root cause of the everlasting quarrel between men and animals.

Reasoning the jewel must be somewhere near the site where Drogmwrg had made his last stand, Haerddrael ordered his armies to mine the mountains there and would not call them off, even though the task proved futile and the waste flying from their picks and sledgehammers filled the valleys below, burying lush meadows and pristine lakes in rubble. Caught up in his lust for the jewel, he refused to speak to the delegations of animals that came to tell him to stop destroying their homes until they in turn refused to speak and all hope for reconciliation or understanding between humans and animals was lost.

While the Druids of the day counseled making peace, Haerddrael scoffed at both them and at the animals, saying the men had steel armor and iron weapons and so could hunt down any creature that opposed them. On hearing that, some of the animals chose to accept human rule. Most of the others fled into the wild, but the smallest of them—the tribes of crawling and buzzing insects— armed themselves with pincers and stingers, waging relentless war against humans ever since.

Haerddrael's search, which left so much grief and bitterness in its wake, was in vain. When the men in his armies finally saw the futility of what they were doing they abandoned their king and went home to their farms and their families, leaving Haerddrael to die a sad and lonely death. His son, Haerddendwn, took up his father's quest but fared no better, in part because all those who had actually seen "the most beautiful jewel" were now dead and neither Haerddendwn nor any who came after him knew exactly what it was they were looking for.

So Herrwn's heart sank as he realized that, however unintentional, Ossiam's poetic description of seeing a rider on a dark steed leaving the shrine "to seek the most beautiful jewel" was all but an open challenge to Rhedwyn to take up that always-futile quest.

As Ossiam sat down, Olyrrwd stood up and raised the chalice to claim his turn to speak. Remembering Olyrrwd's earlier innuendos, which had gone more than halfway toward accusing Ossiam of plotting against Rhedwyn, Herrwn was preparing to intervene to prevent another outbreak of open hostility between them— but as it turned out, there was no need. Olyrrwd set the chalice down and said, quite cheerfully, "I have good news regarding the Priestess Ollowen's bowels"—and then, with not so much as a passing reference to Ossiam's dream, he launched into a protracted description of Ollowen's distress from abdominal bloating and noxious anal emissions, followed by an even more detailed account of the priestess's successful purging.

Brought out of his mystic reverie, Ossiam snatched up the chalice and, keeping his voice sufficiently controlled to meet the expected standard of mealtime discourse, asked Olyrrwd why he felt this was something to be announced at the high table.

"Why, out of my care and concern for you, our greatest oracle and also my own dearly beloved cousin," Olyrrwd said in a voice that seemed utterly sincere, "for I find myself suddenly worried that you may have need of some similar curative potion as that which relieved Ollowen's recent distress."

As the puzzled looks of the other priests and priestesses changed to suppressed smirks, Herrwn could see he was not the only one to catch the coarse comparison Olyrrwd was suggesting. Fortunately, before Ossiam was able to think of an adequate retort, Rhonnon took the chalice from Ossiam's hand and raised it in a toast to Ollowen's recovered health, adding a brisk expression of gratitude to Olyrrwd from all who shared the priestess's sleeping quarters with her, and then gave the chalice to Aolfe, the shrine's chief herbalist, who could always be counted on to give a pleasant and soothing account of how well the herbs were thriving in the shrine's garden.

Although there was something a little distant in Rhedwyn's expression during the rest of the meal, when his turn came to speak, he used it to recite his most recent poem in praise of Feywn's matchless beauty instead of making any rash vows to set out on an impossible quest to find the fabled jewel.

Returning to his classroom that afternoon, Herrwn was surprised (and somewhat annoyed) to find Labhruinn following at his heels instead of making his usual exit to spend the afternoon in the herb garden with Annwr and Cyri. As they crossed the threshold, Caelym looked up, and his eyes brightened at the prospect of acting out another titanic battle with Labhruinn—exactly what Herrwn had been determined to avoid when he separated their lessons.

He wasn't about to have the two of them create another jumble of upended furniture, as it always put Benyon out of sorts, so he might have sounded more irritable than he intended when he turned to Labhruinn and inquired sharply, "Have you a question for me that will not wait until the morning?"

At this implied rebuke, he expected Labhruinn to apologize and leave, instead of nodding and stammering, "Th-the most beautiful jewel—if no-no one knows what it is, th-then how . . ."

Realizing that Labhruinn must understand the danger of his brother setting out on a doomed quest, Herrwn answered more kindly, "That is right! No one knows what it is, so there is no way to find it!"

"But"—Labhruinn persisted, seeming oddly unsatisfied with this clear answer—"if no one knows what it is, then how do we know that it isn't found?"

No one, to Herrwn's knowledge, had turned the question around in that way, and he had to stop and think before finally saying, "I suppose that should someone claim to have found it and all who saw it were to agree that it is the most beautiful jewel . . ."

Unable to rid his mind of the suspicions Olyrrwd had planted about Ossiam plotting against Rhedwyn, Herrwn felt compelled to add, "That must, of course, include all of the shrine's elders."

For a moment he and Labhruinn locked eyes and Herrwn felt certain they understood each other—but then Labhruinn returned to his insistent questioning, asking again, "It could be anything—a diamond or a crown or, or anything—so long as no one said it wasn't the most beautiful jewel?"

By this time Herrwn was feeling the beginning of a headache. To end this fruitless exchange and get back to his lesson with Caelym, he agreed that "yes, if something were found and the finder claimed it was the most beautiful jewel and no one disputed that claim, then of course that would settle the matter!"

While Herrwn had lost track of exactly what he meant, Labhruinn seemed satisfied—at least, he bowed and backed toward the door, tripping over his own feet in his hurry to be gone.

Still uneasy, Herrwn made it a point to recite the full account of the tragic epic that evening.

Rhedwyn was missing from the sunrise ritual the next morning, which ordinarily would not have worried Herrwn but now made him apprehensive. His vague sense of disquiet took a clear shape when, as they returned through the gate into the main courtyard, they found Rhedwyn striking a valiant pose with his men, all of them dressed for travel.

Rhedwyn remained standing erect, his dark green riding cloak flapping in the morning breeze, until all the priests and priestesses had filed into the courtyard. Then, in a swift, graceful move, he dropped into a deep bow at Feywn's feet. Grasping a fold of her gown in both his hands and looking up into her face, he spoke, echoing the words that had doomed so many heroes of the past.

"I go now to seek the most precious jewel. I swear my sacred oath that I will return, bringing back to you what has been missing for too long."

As if she had not heard the cautionary tale of past quests for the lost jewel that Herrwn had recited the night before, Feywn said nothing to dissuade Rhedwyn—instead, she lifted a golden pendant inscribed with the shrine's three most sacred symbols off her neck and placed it around Rhedwyn's in a gesture that conveyed her acceptance of his vow. Glowing with pride, Rhedwyn stood up, signaled his men to follow him, and went striding out of the gate and down to the field, where horses were saddled and waiting.

Chapter 26:

Rhedwyn Returns

"Herrwn! Oh, Herrwn! Wait!"

Herrwn had left the courtyard, distraught over the dangers of Rhedwyn's quest and by the realization that Olyrrwd's suspicions about Ossiam might be right, and was starting up the stairs to the priests' quarters when he heard running steps and turned to see Ossiam coming around a bend in the hallway, his hood thrown back and his hair in disarray.

"I must speak to you!" his cousin called out between gasps for air.

Glancing over his shoulder at the sound of someone else's footsteps—most likely Benyon coming to collect Caelym's tray—Ossiam lowered his voice and said, "In private!"

With that he took a viselike grip on Herrwn's elbow and pulled him down the side hall and into a small storage room. Once inside, he let go of Herrwn's arm and turned away to light a candle, setting it back into its niche before he closed the door.

"What . . ." Herrwn stopped himself. What was the point in asking? Ossiam would never explain the meaning of any of his portends, much less admit that his ill-dreamed vision was to blame for Rhedwyn's newest and most misguided adventure, so Herrwn just sighed. "What is it you wish to speak to me about?"

"My vision! I think it is to blame for Rhedwyn's newest and most misguided adventure!"

Ossiam spoke in a broken voice, wringing his hands and making no attempt to wipe away the tears that streamed down his cheeks. "That cursed vision . . . how I wish I had never dreamed it . . . and oh, how I rue that I did not cut out my tongue before I ever spoke of it . . ."

Ossiam broke down, sobbing tears of regret and remorse that washed away Herrwn's doubts and suspicions. He did his best to comfort his cousin, reminding him that Feywn had given Rhedwyn her own sacred pendant and they must hope that its protective powers would prevail.

"Yes, so we must hope." Ossiam spoke in a hollow voice. Without another word, he pulled up his hood and walked away, shaking his head.

Hurrying back to the classroom, Herrwn met Olyrrwd leaving with Caelym and Moelwyn.

"Olyrrwd, you heard—" he started.

"I told you!" glancing at Caelym and Moelwyn, Olyrrwd broke off and muttered, "We'll talk later."

That night, when they spoke in private, Olyrrwd refused to believe that Ossiam's lamentations were genuine—dismissing Herrwn's description of how their cousin had berated himself and how tears of grief and regret had flowed down his cheeks with a caustic rejoinder, "And did you smell the onion?"

"That is most unjust of you!" Herrwn responded vehemently to Olyrrwd's implied accusation that Ossiam had resorted to trickery to feign the anguish he'd displayed—certain the pungent scent he now recalled noticing in the confines of the small, cramped storage room had been nothing more than the usual odor of Ossiam's lamentably strong breath. "Had you been there, you would know that such heart-rending feelings could not be contrived."

"You watch," Olyrrwd retorted, "if Rhedwyn comes back with a star plucked out of the heavens in the palm of his hand, Ossiam will sigh and shed some more tears and send him off to get a brighter one!"

Since neither Olyrrwd nor Herrwn could sway the other to his way of thinking, they left off arguing and went back to their separate responsibilities.

In the week that followed, a sense of expectancy and suspense settled over the shrine. Even though there was no reason to think Rhedwyn and his men would be returning any time soon, Feywn ordered that a watch be kept for them at the outer gate. She spent the time not otherwise committed to conducting rituals standing on the shrine's upper walkway and looking at the valley's west rim, her golden hair hanging loose and blowing in the changeable summer breezes. Her main servant and at least one of the other high priestesses stood watch with her, but the rest carried on with their usual duties, resigned to what they all expected would be a long and possibly futile wait for Rhedwyn's return.

Already in a flighty and distractible stage of life, Caelym fell victim to the tension and restiveness around him, and it took Herrwn's sternest looks and strictest admonitions to keep him even somewhat on task. On the afternoon of the eighth day after Rhedwyn and his men had ridden off, Herrwn was standing over his fidgeting pupil and correcting the errors in a poorly memorized ode when a cry came in the classroom's open window.

"They're back!"

Caelym was at the window before Herrwn gave him permission to go—leaning precariously far out and pointing at the distant line of horses descending slowly along the track that ran in a winding course down the valley's western slope.

"Wait for me!"

But Caelym had dashed out the door and was gone. Following after him, Herrwn was about to cross the courtyard and ascend the stairs to the upper walkway when he met Olyrrwd, who called out, "Come on, I may need help!"

That Olyrrwd foresaw the need for help was not a good sign—especially if he was calling on Herrwn instead of Caelym, who'd been acting as a nearly full-fledged apprentice in the healing chambers for more than a year. Without asking any questions, Herrwn turned and hurried after Olyrrwd out the gate and into the field where the riders would dismount before entering the shrine.

Once there, he could see why Olyrrwd was worried. Instead of galloping full bore, their horns blaring and pennants flying, as they always did on their triumphant returns from hunting or raiding, the riders came down the hill at a painstakingly measured pace. By the time the horses plodded up the path into the clearing outside the shrine's main gate, the walkway overhead was filled with priests and priestesses. Feywn seemed not to breathe at all as she stood waiting, her eyes fixed on the leader.

From where he stood, Herrwn could see that Rhedwyn's cloak bulged over his right arm and shoulder as if it was covering a thickly padded injury.

That was clearly Olyrrwd's thought. He was standing at Herrwn's side, muttering under his breath, *"Color is good, so no great blood loss; no sign of fever, so nothing's festered, more likely a break or dislocation, though you'd expect . . ."*

Rhedwyn, meanwhile, nudged his horse into the center of the open space below the wall where Feywn was standing.

There was a moment that seemed to stretch out as the suspense built. Then Rhedwyn spoke in a soft, subdued voice, one very much at odds with the triumphant pronouncement he was making.

"I have returned bringing the most beautiful jewel back to you, as I swore I would."

As he spoke, Rhedwyn took hold of the edge of the cloak with his left hand and, in a sweeping gesture, flung it open to reveal a sleeping child—a little girl with red hair.

A strong and resounding voice rang out from the gathered crowd, crying, "It is Arianna, the daughter of the chief priestess Feywn! Who here does not recall the prophesy by the greatest of our oracles that she would outshine the stars themselves?" Stepping out of the throng, wearing a ceremonial robe and holding up his staff, Labhruinn cried out in a voice that might have been a master Druid's, "Does anyone deny, then, that she is our most beautiful jewel and is returned to her divine mother in fulfillment of my brother's oath?"

Ossiam, standing at Feywn's right side, seemed momentarily frozen, but then he raised his staff in a salute as the rumbling of "no's" spread through the throng.

Later, Herrwn and Olyrrwd would argue over whether Ossiam's gesture proved he was sincere or whether it was "just another ploy," but at the time there was a burst of cheers from the onlookers that woke Arianna, who blinked and looked around, her emerald-green eyes sparkling in the sunlight.

Chapter 27:

War Games

$\mathcal{L}$eaving Olyrrwd grumbling about how Ossiam always found a way to claim credit for whatever happened, Herrwn went to find Caelym and pull him back to their day's lesson.

Instead of being where Herrwn expected—in the middle of the throng gathered around Feywn, Rhedwyn, and Arianna—Caelym was standing off in the shadow of a nearby post, his shoulders bunched up, his arms crossed, and his eyes narrowed and fixed on the ground. While he obeyed Herrwn's call to come along back to the classroom, he scuffed his sandals along the way and once there would only mumble, "I don't know," or "I don't remember," to any question put to him until Herrwn finally asked, "What is it that troubles you so greatly?"

"She's not a jewel!" Caelym shouted. "She's just a stupid baby! Why does she get to ride on Rhedwyn's horse with him? It's not fair!" Leaping up, he ran through the curtains that separated the apprentices' sleeping chamber from the classroom, threw himself down on his bed, and buried his face in the covers.

While Herrwn had never been so melodramatic about it, he remembered having fits of pique at the same age. Standing outside the chamber's curtain, he was pondering how much of the complexity that lay behind the shrine's rejoicing at Arianna's return he should attempt to explain once Caelym emerged from his sulk when there was a knock—somehow as diffident and earnest as Benyon himself—and the priests' chief servant entered to announce that they were being summoned to the great hall for the celebration welcoming Arianna back to the shrine.

"I will be there as soon as I have changed into my good robes." Herrwn kept his voice down and paused to peep through the curtain. Seeing that Caelym had his pillow pulled over his head, he felt it safe to continue, "Young Master Caelym, however, is, regrettably, indisposed, and I think we will not disturb him."

"I shall run with all haste to fetch Master Olyrrwd from the healing chamber!" Looking close to panic, Benyon hesitated long enough to ask, "What shall I tell him ails young Master Caelym?"

"That will not be necessary. It is not a serious ailment, and I will speak to Master Olyrrwd myself, but perhaps you will be so kind as to go to get my harp for me."

While the last thing Herrwn wanted was to have Olyrrwd come dashing in, alarmed at Benyon's overwrought report of Caelym's "ailment," it occurred to him that having the always attentive and sympathetic physician doting on him might be just the antidote to Caelym's injured feelings. After donning his robes, he picked up his staff, took up the harp Benyon had rushed to fetch for him, and set off for the healing chamber himself, buoyed by the knowledge that giving Olyrrwd an excuse to avoid sitting through a prolonged ceremonial event in close proximity to Ossiam was an excellent thing for all concerned.

On his way to the healing chambers to find Olyrrwd, Herrwn remembered Labhruinn's tenacious inquiry about the legend of the most beautiful jewel and his astute turn of the age-old question from "How does someone find it?" to "How does anyone know that it isn't found?"

Despite Labhruinn's occasional flashes of insight, Herrwn had never before considered the possibility that his reluctantly acquired apprentice had any true gift of intelligence. Now, he surprised himself by thinking that if Labhruinn were ever to succeed in memorizing the seven great sagas, he might someday deserve a seat on the High Council.

After finding Olyrrwd and sending him to coddle Caelym back into his usual high spirits, Herrwn continued to mull over

Labhruinn's feat that morning—how he had phrased his declaration that Arianna was "the most beautiful jewel" in words so
close to Ossiam's early prophecy that no one, least of all the oracle
himself, could challenge his claim, and how, as he stepped out
from the throng of onlookers, holding up his staff, he had looked
so much like a full-fledged priest.

When had Labhruinn shed his childhood pudginess to
become so tall and brawny? When had the stumbling awkwardness of his youth turned into the self-assured movements of a
powerfully built man? And when—Herrwn realized with some
embarrassment that he should have at least noticed this before
now—had Labhruinn learned to manage his burgeoning strength
so that he could tune his own harp to the right tension without
snapping its strings?

Recalling that it had been weeks—no, months, in fact, many
months—since he'd had to replace Labhruinn's instrument with
the spare harp he kept in the classroom cupboard, Herrwn realized there had been another significant change to which he'd paid
little attention.

Over the last winter, as Olyrrwd's knees had grown more
swollen and painful, Labhruinn had begun taking over bringing Caelym on his excursions into the woods. And even before
that there had been a subtle shift in his relationship with the
younger boy, a transformation from being a boisterous confederate
to something else—something less like a friend and more like a
father. Herrwn searched for the right word or phrase, and finally
found a metaphor that captured his thoughts—that if a spell were
cast that turned the two of them into a boat, Caelym would be
the sails, catching the winds to go soaring and swirling across
the waves, and Labhruinn would be the ballast and the rudder,
keeping them upright and on a safe course.

It was a change that could not have come at a better time
for, just as Labhruinn was emerging from the challenging years
between childhood and maturity, Caelym was caught in the throes
of youthful upheaval—pouting and complaining that he had to
stay inside and recite all afternoon only to argue in the next breath
that he should be allowed to perform real rituals like everyone else.

Pleased with his newfound metaphor, Herrwn expanded it,
musing that with Labhruinn's help and Olyrrwd's always steady

hand, they would see Caelym safely through the heaves and down swells, whirlpools and rocky shoals of the next few years. Yes, he was sure of it, and sure that—once the exuberant celebration of Arianna's return was over—life would settle back to normal.

◆◆◆

For the next year, it did.

Rhedwyn's raids outside the valley continued, as did the races and the war games, which were accompanied, in turn, by complaints to the Low Council from village delegates that those games were wreaking havoc on their fields.

Each time these protests were lodged, Herrwn would say that their points were just and valid, and that he would take them to the High Council—which he did, meticulously repeating the accounting of newly planted crops trampled, terrorized ewes that miscarried, and fishing streams that were ruined when Rhedwyn's racing riders charged across vital spawning beds. The debate then followed its usual course. Even though the sympathies of the council as a whole leaned toward the villagers, Ossiam stood staunchly with Rhedwyn, and they all knew that Feywn would not accept any ruling that went against her consort. At the conclusion of each session, Olyrrwd would again caustically point out that it was the farmers and herders who fed them all, and until they could survive on Rhedwyn's battle booty, they might choose to leave some crops and herds and fishing streams intact.

At each subsequent Low Council, Herrwn would deliver his now-routine speech, beginning, "So we have viewed this matter from all sides, and as it remains paramount that our valley be defended against our Saxon enemies . . ."

He knew that as he delivered this unwelcome message Llwdd, head of the village delegation, would roll his eyes and look away. Still, he was surprised and concerned when, at the conclusion of an otherwise subdued meeting, a voice he didn't recognize muttered, "Be defended against who? I don't see any Saxons trampling our crops!" from the back of the hall.

This outburst troubled Herrwn. Had Caelendra been alive, he would have gone to her, knowing she would listen to him and take his counsel that the villagers' just complaints must have a just response. But Feywn was not Caelendra. From the day Ossiam had proclaimed her their chief priestess and Goddess incarnate, she had acted with absolute dominion, seeking counsel from no one other than her consort—and she'd never paid Herrwn any serious attention at all. While he'd long since come to terms with this, Herrwn still thought privately that Feywn would be well advised to consider age and wisdom over youth and good looks.

Reaching the classroom in a pensive state of mind, Herrwn saw Caelym standing at the window, holding the toy horse he hadn't played with for years in one hand and idly sliding it back and forth along the ledge as he watched Rhedwyn and his men getting their mounts ready for a new expedition.

Turning to look up at Herrwn, Caelym asked, "Can bards ride horses?"

Herrwn had already lost one disciple to the lure of Rhedwyn's cavalier adventures, and he was not about to lose another. He crossed the room and put a hand on Caelym's shoulder. "Of course! Anyone can ride a horse, as that requires no special skill—only that you sit on it, take up its reins, and make it go!"

Herrwn had not ever ridden a horse but had seen it done and assumed there was no more to it than that. In any case, the actual demands of horsemanship were not the issue, and he saw no reason to belabor them as he moved on to make his point, declaiming, "But a bard! A bard can do far more than that—especially if he is a truly great bard, as I believe you will be someday. He can take his listeners with him, riding on dragons in the sky or swimming with selkies in the sea, going on more adventures in a single tale than any warrior can hope to have in a lifetime."

Whether or not Caelym followed Herrwn's line of reasoning was hard to say, as he just dropped his eyes, sighed, and went to sit in his place by Herrwn's chair—still holding the toy horse in his right hand.

PART IV

Insurrection

While the inhabitants of Llwddawanden were preoccupied with the valley's internal affairs, unsettling events were underway in the not-so-distant kingdom of Derthwald. There, unbeknownst to anyone outside of a small group of conspirators, the first steps toward over-throwing Derthwald's rightful monarch were underway.

In an act that would ultimately link the fates of the Druid sanctuary and the Christian kingdom together, the king's scheming nephew had sent his own men, dressed as palace guards, to a village in the north of Derthwald's border with orders to foment enough conflict to incite a local rebellion, hoping that the news of the insurgency would draw his uncle out of his fortress stronghold—to be waylaid and assassinated on the way home.

Had Gilberth picked any other village, none of this would have had any impact on life in Llwddawanden, but the village of Caenbwnsa was one of the few outside of Llwddawanden where the inhabitants continued to worship the Goddess and to send the best tribute they could afford to Her one remaining shrine. So as Gilberth's thugs were swilling ale and taunting the terrified locals, a badly bruised village elder slipped away and went to report this unprovoked assault to the Goddess's earthly representatives.

Chapter 28:

The Emissary

ord of the Saxon attack on Caenbwnsa reached Llwd-dawanden on what started out as a quiet afternoon in the shrine's healing chamber. With his beds empty and his shelves stocked, Olyrrwd had persuaded Herrwn to release Caelym early and go for a walk along the lakeshore. They'd reached their usual sitting spot and were watching a pair of ducks dabbling among the reeds when an out-of-breath servant came running up, calling, "Master Olyrrwd, Master Rhedwyn says you're needed at once!"

Grumbling about how much time he spent patching up the damage Rhedwyn's young idiots did to each other in their mock battles, Olyrrwd heaved himself to his feet, shouldered his pack of instruments and medicinals, took up his staff, and trudged off.

On a whim, Herrwn decided to take the path through the woods instead of going back the way he came. Lost in his thoughts, he took a wrong turn and wandered farther into the forest than he'd intended. He was about to turn around when he heard a voice singing a song he remembered from his long-ago childhood in tones so lovely that it seemed to him a nightingale must have learned to sing with human words or, seeing as that was close to impossible, then perhaps it was an elfin maiden.

He stopped and turned his head to locate the direction of the sounds. Knowing the risk of disturbing elves in their revels, he went cautiously through a grove of aspen, drawn by the sweetness of the song and the gaiety of the laughter that accompanied it.

Coming to the edge of the trees but still hidden within their shadows, he saw the shrine's little priestesses-to-be skipping along with Annwr, who was singing as she led them dancing in a ring.

While Herrwn had heard Annwr sing before, it had always been in a chorus behind Feywn, whose vibrant, shimmering voice overpowered the rest. He was standing there, transfixed in the delight of what he was seeing and hearing, when, suddenly, Annwr's song stopped and the five little girls squealed, "Down!" and dropped to the ground. Then Annwr held out her arms to embrace them all, and the girls, laughing and giggling, scrambled into her lap.

It was a sight that brought back the memory of how Annwr had confided her longing to have as many children as she could hold in her arms, and Herrwn—in a moment of pure selflessness, rare even for him—could feel her joy as if it were his own. Not wanting his intrusion to disrupt their game, he stepped away, into the trees, and went along his way, finally free of regrets for what might have been.

Herrwn's mood of quiet contentment lasted only as long as it took him to walk the rest of the way down the hill. As he reached the main path, he saw Benyon running toward him, gasping, "Olyrrwd sent me to find you, Master—there is talk of war!"

War? Thinking that this must be an exaggeration of some hot-headed dispute between Rhedwyn's men, Herrwn began to remonstrate with Benyon over his choice of words, for Herrwn was, above all else, a teacher, and he held the proper choice of words to be important, whether they were spoken by a pupil, a fellow Druid, or a servant.

But instead of rephrasing his message by replacing the phrase "talk of war" with "a serious disagreement," as Herrwn suggested, Benyon repeated, "Olyrrwd sent me to find you!" in a shrill tone that bordered on insolence. With that—and with only the briefest of bows—he turned and rushed back down the path to the Sacred Grove, losing a sandal along the way.

◆◆◆

If one ritual site among the many within Llwddawanden could be said to be more awe-inspiring than the rest, that one was the

Sacred Grove—an outer circle of ancient oaks that enclosed the seven stone pillars believed to have been placed there as a peace offering by giants to the Goddess.

There were festivals, including the coming Summer Solstice Ceremony, during which the ordinary people of the valley were permitted to enter the Sacred Grove. This was not any such occasion, and yet, as he drew closer, it seemed to Herrwn that every man and woman in the valley—Druid, villager, or servant—was there, all of them talking at once. As chief priest, Herrwn should have been consulted before any such gathering took place, and he meant to demand an explanation as soon as he could get to the center of the crowd and make himself heard.

Benyon pushed ahead into the crowd and was lost, but then Labhruinn emerged, and after gesturing to Herrwn he turned back and called in a commanding voice, "Master Herrwn is here! Make way! Make way!" as he plowed a path through to the center of the throng.

On either side of them, Herrwn heard the words he'd never before heard except in the recitations of the great sagas—"Arise! Arise!" "Death to our enemies!" "Victory or death!"

Benyon had not misspoken! These were calls to battle.

Then, cutting through the general commotion, he heard Olyrrwd's gruff voice, saying, "Be quiet! Let the man finish!"

When they reached the center of both the grove and the crowd, Labhruinn stepped aside so Herrwn could see a bruised and battered figure wearing a blood-spattered cloak and keeping himself upright by leaning on a makeshift crutch.

The man was tottering and barely able to stand even with the aid of his stick, his garments were torn, his head was wrapped in blood-soaked rags, and his face was so battered and swollen that it was only on hearing his voice saying, "We were peacefully tilling our fields when a Saxon war band, led by the captain of their king's guard, attacked without warning," that Herrwn realized to his shock and dismay that it was Asof, an elder from the village of Caenbwnsa and a well-known visitor to the shrine.

While most Britons living outside Llwddawanden had long since converted to Christianity, there remained a scattering of steadfast believers who continued to worship the Goddess and pay Her the homage She was due—faithfully gathering together their offering each year and sending it by their most trusted emissary to be added to the tribute that the highest of the shrine's priests carried to Her on the night of the spring equinox. While not everyone in Caenbwnsa belonged to the Goddess's clandestine cult, many did, chief among them Asof, who had been their go-between with the shrine for as long as Herrwn could remember.

When Herrwn had last seen Asof, just six weeks earlier, he had looked hale and hearty for his advanced age and had been, as always, cheerful and gregarious. Who would so brutally mistreat such a good-hearted man?

The answer to his unspoken question came in outcries all around him—"It was Saxons!" "Foul, filthy beasts!" "Curse them and the horses they ride on!"

"Let him finish!"

Whether Olyrrwd wanted to hear what Asof had to say or just get it said so he could take him to the healing chamber, the physician wasn't a man to be trifled with when he was in a temper. The crowd went silent and Asof went on—his speech slurred by his broken teeth.

"They surrounded us, cutting off any escape, laughing and jeering as we begged for mercy."

The clamor rose up again—"Beasts!" "Savages!" "Worse than ogres!"—and above the din, Ossiam cried out, "Will no one who loves the Goddess go forth to answer this outrage?" looking at Rhedwyn as he spoke.

Rhedwyn drew his sword and would, no doubt, have called his men together, had not Labhruinn interrupted, "Wait! I have a question!"

Stepping closer to Asof and lowering his voice, he asked, "You say you were attacked by the king's soldiers—how many were there?"

Although clearly distraught as well as fatigued and in pain, Asof drew himself up as he answered, "I do not know the exact number, but there were many of them, a score at least, all coming at us with their clubs!"

"Clubs? Not swords?"

"Were not their clubs enough? We were working in our fields! We were not armed to defend ourselves! All of us were injured. Idwal had his arm broken, Alpwn was beaten senseless, Maelwr was kicked so his ribs were smashed!"

There was no need for Asof to mention his own injuries, which were only too apparent.

"All were hurt, but no one was killed?" While not exactly rude or disrespectful, Labhruinn's voice had taken on the dogged tone Herrwn recalled from his inquiry into "the most beautiful jewel."

"Some may die yet, if that matters!" Asof remained adamant even as he swayed from the effort this conversation was costing him.

"Why do you badger this poor man? Has he not suffered enough at the hands of our enemies?" Ossiam's outburst struck a chord with the muttering crowd, but Labhruinn answered it as though it were just another question put to him in the classroom.

"Because this may not have been an attack by our enemies at all! Why would a war party attack farmers tilling their fields? And why with clubs? If these villains were soldiers of the king, would they not come armed with spears and swords? This sounds more like the work of local ruffians to me!"

"It was not!" Asof drew strength from some last reserve to refute this implied downgrading of what he and his fellow villagers had suffered. "I know the local ruffians, and these were strangers! And they were dressed in the king's colors! They carried his banner! And their king knows we stood against them and were the last to surrender to him!"

"But that was twenty years ago! Why wait until now to punish you and then send his troop across the kingdom just to break a few heads? If it was revenge they wanted, why not burn the village to the ground?"

"I don't know what evil lies in the minds of Saxons or their kings, but I know that after they'd done their foul deed, they went to the tavern, swilling ale without paying for it and boasting that their king challenged anyone who dared to come to do battle against him!"

"But that, too, makes no sense! You have said you were easily beaten down; why bother with such a challenge when you were already defeated?"

"Why does it matter?" Rhedwyn demanded while Asof was gasping in indignation. "Our honor is at stake! We will answer his challenge!"

"Because if this was the work of ruffians, then what you must do is go there and teach Asof's folk to defend themselves, perhaps

leaving some of your men to stand with them! But if it is an army—
or the forward contingent of an army—they may have done this to
draw you out into an ambush! Do you want to lead your men into
a trap?" Labhruinn retorted, now with a sharp edge to his voice.

Herrwn had never thought the two brothers bore any
resemblance to each other, but now, their face set in matched
stubbornness, it was clear to see they had come from the same
parents after all.

While Rhedwyn was searching for some fitting retort, Ossiam
broke into the debate, his sarcasm dripping like water from an icicle.

"And what, in your great wisdom, would you have us do?"

Labhruinn seemed to think this was a genuine question.

"We should send spies to see what force, if any, is gathered
against us, so we may prepare our counterattack if we need one."

The debate might have gone on longer, but Asof teetered on his
crutch and what little color was left beneath the purple bruises
drained away.

"Enough!" Olyrrwd barked. "This man is my patient, and I
am taking him to the healing chamber! And you, Labhruinn,
you will ask no more questions of him until I tell you he is recovered enough to answer!" Then, turning on Rhedwyn, he said with
equal force, "And, you, Rhedwyn—who anointed you our king?
And when did you get the power to declare war without going to
the High Council?" Pointedly ignoring Ossiam, he turned to look
at Herrwn.

Herrwn understood. He raised his staff, declaring, "The news
that Asof has brought, at great peril to himself, is a matter of
much importance, and we will consider what we are to do at the
meeting of the High Council."

For a moment it seemed that Ossiam would object, but instead
he raised his own staff and proclaimed, "This is a matter for the
next council!" as if it were his own idea. He then declared, "I will
go to my tower to seek the messages from the powers around us!"
and left with a dramatic flourish of his staff.

Pausing only long enough to roll his eyes and shake his head,
Olyrrwd put a protective arm around Asof's waist and guided him
through the crowd toward the healing chamber.

Maybe sensing that his older brother wasn't in a mood to listen
to anything that he said, Labhruinn edged over to Herrwn and

murmured, "I wonder, Master, if it might be wise for Rhedwyn to send his men to guard the outer gates in case Asof was followed?"

Herrwn thought this was very wise, and he repeated the suggestion word for word, breathing a sigh of relief when Rhedwyn called for his men to follow him and rushed off.

Chapter 29:

A Missed Message

With barely enough time to change his robes and get to the great hall for his oration, Herrwn still had to placate Caelym, who'd recently begun to chafe at not being allowed to eat his meals at the high table. Having repeated, "On the day of your fifteenth birthday, you will be seated there, just as I and Olyrrwd and each of the rest of us were seated in our turn," in answer to each of the boy's admittedly clever and persuasive arguments, Herrwn took up his staff and started for the door just as Benyon rushed in with Caelym's tray and six different reasons for being late.

"Of course, I understand and can see the delay was not any fault of yours."

Herrwn hoped his mollifying words would end the flow of Benyon's excuses, but the servant went on, "then Master Labhruinn stopped me on my way and—"

Speaking with an abruptness he'd later regret, Herrwn interrupted. "I am due at the high table, and young Master Caelym is anxious for his supper."

"But Master Labhruinn told me to tell you—"

"I will see him at dinner and he may tell me himself!" The horn calling for dinner sounded, and Feywn had no tolerance for late arrivals. With a final, "Now I really must go!" Herrwn gestured for Benyon to let him pass and hurried out the door. When he reached the final corridor leading to the shrine's main hall, he saw that the heavy curtains which served as the chamber's doors were already closed. He slowed his pace—both to catch his breath and compose his apologies. A simple *"I most humbly plead that you will show your eternal beneficence by forgiving my deplorable lateness which I shall lament for all of my days"* was likely to be sufficient so long as Feywn was in a charitable mood. Drawing in a deep, calming breath, he started through the curtains only to stop, step back, and let them fall closed again as he blinked and shook his head.

The great hall, which should have been bathed with the light of the bright summer evening, was shuttered in. A host of shadowy figures were gathered around a godlike being dressed in resplendent robes and singing a song from the saga of the River-Goddess and the Fire-God so that for an eerie moment Herrwn thought he was actually seeing that tale come to life.

Once his initial surprise subsided, Herrwn realized the chamber, though unusually crowded, was otherwise unchanged and that the godlike being was Rhedwyn, showing off as usual.

Hoping no one had noticed his undoubtedly comical look of astonishment, Herrwn edged his way around the side of the chamber and slipped into his seat. He needn't have worried, as no one paid the slightest attention to his arrival—least of all Feywn, whose gaze was fixed on Rhedwyn with such naked passion that Herrwn looked away, glancing around the chamber to see who all these people were.

Except for Olyrrwd—who, Herrwn knew, was in the healing chamber with his two injured patients—the chief priests and priestesses were in their places around the high table. While some of the spectral figures around the edges of the hall were the servants carrying flasks and trays of food, most were young men that Herrwn recognized as the new recruits Rhedwyn had gathered on his forays into the outside world. There were young women in the crowd as well, either wives who'd followed the men who followed Rhedwyn back to Llwddawanden or else girls from the village.

As he waited for Rhedwyn to finish his song, Herrwn looked around for Labhruinn. Normally picking out his oversized apprentice in a crowd would not have been difficult, but with the chamber filled as it was and with the shifting light of the torches turning people into shadows and shadows into people, he couldn't make out whether Labhruinn was there or not.

". . . no foe, not even death itself, will ever keep us apart!"

As Rhedwyn strummed the closing cadence of his song, Herrwn looked toward Feywn, prepared to deliver his apology as well as his night's oration, but she did not so much as glance in his direction. Instead, she nodded for the hovering servants to begin carving the roast boar and turned to listen as first Rhedwyn and then one after another of his men rose to boast about repaying the Saxon's attack in kind as if the deed were already done.

Once it was clear he was not to be called on for an oration that night, Herrwn exchanged a few pleasantries with Ossiam before excusing himself on the pretext of being tired.

Chapter 30:

The Secret Mission

errwn returned from the sunrise ritual the next morning to find Caelym sitting on the side of his bed, kicking the wall and muttering that no one ever took him anywhere and that he was always left alone with nothing to do.

Resisting the temptation to point out this was the first morning in the six years since Caelym had entered his formal training that Olyrrwd or Labhruinn had not, weather permitting, taken him around the lake or into the woods, Herrwn observed that the capacity to exaggerate events and dramatize emotions was key to being a successful storyteller, and dryly commended Caelym on his ability to do both before turning to ask Benyon, "What was the message that Labhruinn gave you to give to me?"

Pausing in his task of clearing away Caelym's breakfast dishes, Benyon did not exactly sigh, but he did take the sort of slow, deep breath that Lothwen had sometimes taken when Herrwn asked her about something she had just explained a moment before.

"He said for me to tell you that he was leaving on a mission for Rhedwyn, and that he would return in time for the council."

"On a mission for Rhedwyn." The words echoed Madheran's declaration that he was leaving his discipleship with Herrwn to "take up arms with Rhedwyn."

◆◆◆

With Olyrrwd unable to leave his patients and Labhruinn off on his "mission for Rhedwyn," Herrwn spent the next two days battling with Caelym's irascible mood and petulant complaints.

If it wasn't one thing, it was another!

Stamping back from his lesson in the healing chamber the next day, Caelym burst into the classroom out of temper because Olyrrwd wouldn't let him try his new potion on Asof, even though he'd put all sorts of good things in it—and glowered when Herrwn suggested that Olyrrwd must know what was best in such serious cases.

Instead of settling down with his recitation lessons, Caelym resumed the argument he had been making since the day after his eleventh birthday—that he was almost twelve years old and was ready to learn real rituals, not just to keep practicing silly chants that any baby could say.

Calling on the self-discipline he'd acquired through years of intense training, Herrwn repeated his counterargument—that the chants and sagas Caelym was learning to recite were far in advance of anything babies could say, and that they were the foundation on which his advanced studies would be built.

"But I know them now!"

"Very well, then." Herrwn met Caelym's vehement outcry with a reasonably calm retort. "What were the names of the rival contenders to the throne of the kingdom of Gwyddion in the seventh tale of the third saga of the wars between the Sea-Goddess and giants from beyond the northern mountains?"

"Heddrwn and Healyn!"

"Who was the true heir?"

"Heddrwn!"

"Why do you say so?"

"Because he was the firstborn son of the firstborn son of the firstborn son of the first king, Haerviu, who was the firstborn son of the Sea-Goddess by her consort, Headdreth."

"And can you name each of those forebears in their proper order?"

"Heddrael, Hilferann, umm, Hyaddan?"

This last question had not been entirely fair, as the earliest progenitor of Gwyddion's dynasty had not been named in any of the sagas except as Haerviu's beloved son or Hilferann's esteemed father. If Caelym had answered, "I don't know," or even "I don't remember," instead of hazarding a guess, Herrwn would have taken it as close enough. As it was—and also because he was beginning to despair of finding a question to stump his sometimes annoyingly precocious pupil—he simply complimented Caelym on what he had learned so far and said they would repeat that particular tale to clarify his recollection.

Then, hoping to cheer the boy up, Herrwn reminded him it was almost the summer solstice, where he would once again get to play the part of the firstborn son of the Sun-God and the Earth-Goddess in the festivities for the children from the village.

That was a mistake Herrwn would not repeat.

If Caelym's complaints had been vehement before, they were positively scathing at this reminder that he was going to be required to do exactly the same thing that he'd enjoyed so much in years past.

Beginning with how it wasn't fair that he had to play "stupid games with ordinary children" when he had already had his initiation into the second level of recitations, he ran on, decrying how he was being forced, against his will, to ride in a "stupid toy chariot pulled by seven stupid little goats" and bemoaning his having to say "the same stupid poem" he had to say every year—"and, worse, to dance stupid dances that are just hopping and skipping and not real dances at all"—before finally ending with the shrill pronouncement that he was "too old to wear a stupid make-believe crown that's just a bunch of stupid pink flowers!"

"That will do!" Herrwn softened his reprimand by saying, "None of us is ever too old to honor the Goddess."

Going resolutely on, he reminded Caelym of what a privilege it was to be chosen to enact the part of the firstborn son of the Great Mother Goddess in celebration of the day he danced on the banks of the river with his three mortal brides, wearing the crown they'd woven for him out of flowers that had sprouted up wherever his feet touched the ground.

Herrwn had just finished explaining that this was why, every year on the morning of the summer solstice, the priestesses wove their favorite flowers into the festival crown with their own hands when Olyrrwd, looking tired and careworn, came into the room to find the last of his remaining healing amulets.

Managing the lighthearted quip that "not everyone was lucky enough to have priestesses picking flowers for them" in answer to Caelym's attempt to get his sympathy, the weary physician shook his head at Herrwn's inquiries about Asof's chances for recovery and limped out of the room.

•◆•

"So, then, as you have no need to rehearse the poems and songs you will be performing at the Sacred Summer Solstice Celebration, I will now listen while you recite the seventh tale of the third saga of the wars between the Sea-Goddess and giants from beyond the northern mountains, beginning with the ogre king's challenge to Heddrwn, whom, as you correctly stated, was the rightful heir to the kingdom of Gwyddion."

Herrwn's back was to the door as he stood, looking as stern as he was able at Caelym's unintentionally effective rendition of the churlish ogre's speech, when Caelym suddenly shifted from surly to valiant and struck a noble posture more in keeping with the story's hero than with its villain—breaking off mid-phrase to say, "Master, I believe we have a visitor."

The visitor was Rhedwyn.

Dressed in his riding clothes, Rhedwyn scanned the room, looking for something or someone, before delivering his own greeting.

"Good day, Master. I am looking for Labhruinn. Where may I find him?"

It was an odd question under the circumstances, and Herrwn came close to stammering as he answered, "He . . . I . . . That is . . ." Unwilling to admit that all he knew of his disciple's whereabouts was what he'd been told by a servant, he cleared his throat and—speaking with all the dignity he could muster—finished, "It is my understanding that he has gone on a mission for you."

"What mission? I sent him on no mission!"

Rhedwyn's surprise surprised Herrwn.

Before he could decide how to respond, Rhedwyn spoke again, this time with the persuasive charm that few but the most strong-minded could resist.

"When he does return, I ask you, Master, that you release him from your charge as the time approaches that I will need all of the strong and courageous men of Llwddawanden at my command."

Herrwn was at a loss to answer this. All he could think of to say was, "I hold no disciple against his will, so if you see him before I do—and I expect that you will—you may assure him that I will listen to whatever requests he may have to make in this regard."

"My eternal thanks, Master!" Clearly assuming no request of his would be denied, Rhedwyn turned on his heels and strode off—leaving Herrwn completely baffled over Labhruinn's disappearance and also deeply disturbed that Rhedwyn was so certain that the council would agree to his cry for war. With nothing to be done about either question, he returned his attention to Caelym's lesson.

"So start again, if you will, from the passage in which the king of the ogres ridicules Heddrael's offer of a peaceful settlement of their differences."

But instead of resuming where he had left off, Caelym dashed over to the window, picked up a rock from one of his carefully arranged collections, and threw it out, heedless of anyone who might be passing below.

"Caelym, that is dangerous! Why ever would you do such a thing?"

Caelym answered Herrwn's sharp question with one of his own. "Why does Labhruinn get to go on missions and I have to just stay here and play stupid games with stupid babies?" With that he reached for the shelf again, and for a moment Herrwn thought he meant to hurl another rock—but instead he snatched up his bedraggled toy horse and stamped into his bedchamber.

Chapter 31:

The War Council

"**Y**ou know that joining in the Sacred Sunrise Ritual is a rare privilege to be granted to one so young?"

"Yes, Master!"

"You will recite the chant exactly as ordained?"

"Yes, Master!"

"You will follow the prescribed ritual precisely as I have instructed?"

"Yes, Master!"

"You understand that even the slightest misstep will shame us both in the eyes of our chief priestess, who is the living embodiment of the Great Mother Goddess?"

"Yes, Master!"

"Very well, it is time we go."

•◆•

Ordinarily Herrwn would not have given in to a pupil's sulks. Following a prolonged period of silence, however, Caelym had emerged from his sleeping chamber looking unbearably contrite. In answer to the question, "Have you anything you wish to say to me?" he'd collapsed to his knees, sobbed out a plea for forgiveness, and sworn never to be so bad ever again.

"You were not bad, you were angry," Herrwn had responded, "but in that moment of anger you had a choice—to regain control of yourself or to throw a rock. Was the choice you made one that you are proud of?"

Caelym's choked "No, Master, I am ashamed" was muffled as he buried his face in the hem of Herrwn's robe.

"And when you feel that anger rising up to overtake you again, will you allow it to do so?"

"No, Master, I will not!"

"How will you conquer it?"

"I'll . . . I, I don't know!"

Herrwn waited for the new outbreak of despairing sobs to ebb away before kneeling down and patting the boy's quivering back.

"That, my most esteemed pupil, is the correct answer! All wisdom begins in understanding what it is that you do not know—so now I believe that you are ready to begin the next steps in the long and difficult quest to become a Druid."

Besides the philosophically astute reason Herrwn had given Caelym for allowing him to attend the day's sunrise ritual, there was the practical consideration that with Olyrrwd ensconced in the healing chamber and Labhruinn still missing, it was safer to take Caelym along than to leave him to his own devices.

Later, in spite of everything, Herrwn was glad he did. That morning's sunrise was among the most beautiful in his memory, and all the more poignant for what was to come.

After returning to the classroom and sharing a sustaining breakfast of boiled oats mixed with goat's milk and blood sausage, Herrwn sent Caelym off to the healing chamber, took a final, fortifying sip of hot mead, picked up his staff, and left for the day's meeting of the Low Council.

When he'd declared that the question of what to do about the Saxon's attack on Asof's village must be brought before the shrine's council, Herrwn had meant the High Council—both because it was the proper venue for so serious a matter and because it would not be held for another three weeks, by which time tempers would have cooled and Asof would be recovered enough to give a full account for them to consider before deciding on the best course of action.

Meanwhile, knowing that Rhedwyn had redoubled his "training exercises," there was no doubt in Herrwn's mind that the morning's Low Council would be entirely taken up with the village delegation's renewed complaints about the riders wreaking havoc in their fields.

Herrwn left for the council on time, expecting that, except for the village delegation, he would be the first to arrive. Prepared as always for the awkwardness of sitting with them in the near-empty hall and waiting for enough of the other priests and priestesses to straggle in that they could begin, he was surprised that instead of being among the first to enter the main hall, he was close to the last. Every bench, chair, and stool except his own was filled. Neither Olyrrwd nor Labhruinn was there but Ossiam and Rhedwyn were and—for the first time since her ascendance—Feywn was seated at the center of the high table, with Rhedwyn on her left and all the ranking priestesses to her right, while Llwdd and the rest of the village delegation were crowded off to the side of the room by Rhedwyn's followers.

A veteran of contentious disputes in both the High and Low Councils, Herrwn guessed that Rhedwyn must have taken his case directly to Feywn and she was there to make a pronouncement in his favor regarding his use of the fields. It wasn't fair, but at least once she did the matter would be settled, and they could move on to other issues.

It was with this thought in mind that Herrwn bowed to Feywn and welcomed her with the formal greeting she no doubt expected.

"Most revered Chief Priestess, You who are the living embodiment of the Great Mother Goddess Herself, we thank You for so graciously honoring us with your sacred presence and await your words with wonder and awe."

Taking his seat, he was not surprised to see her nod to Rhedwyn—and to see him step into the speaker's place between the hearth and the high table, where he stuck a pose worthy of Elderond, the first and favorite of the Great Mother Goddess's mortal lovers, at the moment that hero swore his oath to go forth and defeat the hordes of one-eyed giants who'd declared war on Her and all Her divine and human descendants.

Instead of making his case for practicing his war maneuvers without restrictions, however, Rhedwyn repeated the charge that the foul king of the despicable Saxons had, without provocation, sent his warriors to attack a village loyal to the Goddess, and ended his speech with the declaration, "Their king has sent a score of his lowly minions against us! Now I will take our army to answer that challenge, returning with their heads and leaving their bodies to feed the crows!" and turned his fierce gaze on Llwdd. "It is for this we have trained and armed ourselves! Are there any of you that will join us?"

Caught off guard, Llwdd was saved from answering—first by the sound of pounding footsteps and then by the rustling and bulging of the entry curtains as someone struggled to get through.

Finally finding the gap in the draperies, Labhruinn stumbled into the chamber. Disheveled and unwashed, twigs and briers tangled in his hair, mud caked on his boots, he staggered between the crowded benches and across the space left open for speakers to grip the rim of the high table with both hands.

"Rhedwyn," he gasped, "I found their camp last night!" Reaching over to the table for the closest flask of wine and gulping it down like water, he forged ahead. "It's no pack of thugs! It's an army with a leader who might be the king himself!"

"Might be? You did not venture close enough to say for sure?" The first words Ossiam interjected were bathed in contempt.

"If there are three of their troops to every one of ours," Labhruinn snapped, "it doesn't matter who leads them!"

"And how do you know how many of them there were if it was dark?" the oracle demanded.

"I counted their fires." Making no apology for his brusque tone of voice, Labhruinn turned to Rhedwyn. "It's a trap."

For a moment, Rhedwyn seemed unsure, then, appearing to remember that the eyes of the room were on him, he bristled, "So you counsel that we shrink from battle? Hide from our foes like cowering hares?"

"Hares have the sense not to go to war with wolves!" Labhruinn's retort was not particularly noble or valiant, but in spite of that several of the priestesses, along with most of the village contingent, were swayed. Llwdd, who'd come to the council prepared to oppose Rhedwyn on any topic, nodded in approval, as did Rhonnon. Then Ossiam, who'd risen to his feet, presumably with the intention of making a caustic rebuttal, lurched forward, staggered back, and lurched forward again. Gripping his staff, he struggled to stay upright. His mouth went slack and his eyes rolled upwards so only the white showed—indications that Sarahrana, his inner spirit from the other world, was about to speak.

"Craven Coward!" he (or more properly, "she") screeched. *"Cast him out before his perfidy infects others!"*

Even for an oracular spirit, that was going too far! While Labhruinn's pronouncement merited criticism for its awkward and poorly ordered presentation, he was entitled to speak and to be heard—and Herrwn would have stood up to say so, but Rhedwyn moved first, stepping between Labhruinn and the possessed oracle and declaring, "No one calls my brother a coward!"

Holding up his shield in his left hand, he reached out with his right, gripped Labhruinn's shoulder, and spoke as if the two of them were alone. "You have counted Saxons by stealth at night—now let us count them openly in the daylight. Ride with me, and together we will tally their heads on our pikes!"

Then his eyes swept the room, seeming to take the measure of every man in it, and he demanded, "Who will join us?"

"We will!" The village delegation rose up as one with Rhedwyn's men.

Herrwn would always wonder whether, if he'd acted at once—stood up to say that he had not dismissed the council and declared that no final judgment had been rendered, nor would it be that day, and decreed that the decision to go to war or not was a matter for the High Council to decide following thorough deliberation—it would have changed the course of their history.

Before speaking, however, he'd looked to Feywn, expecting her to forbid this rash and reckless adventure, only to see her gazing at Rhedwyn with the besotted look of an ordinary girl in the throes of her first love.

By the time he did stand up, it was too late. His voice was lost in the uproar—heard by no one except for Labhruinn, who cast a long, despairing look back at Herrwn before he was swept along with the crowd that surged out of the chamber after Rhedwyn.

Chapter 32:

Where's Caelym?

s the curtains closed behind the last of the men following after Rhedwyn, Feywn rose from her place. No longer looking ordinary but regal and commanding—a war-goddess stepped out of a hero's tale—she led the other priestesses off, leaving Herrwn alone with Ossiam, who'd dropped back into his chair and was slumped facedown on the table. It wasn't unusual for Ossiam to collapse in exhaustion after a possession, especially one as intense as the one just past, but he didn't respond when Herrwn called his name or when he said, "I'll have Olyrrwd bring you a potion, shall I?"

Normally the very mention of Olyrrwd's name—to say nothing of the possibility of needing his help—would have roused Ossiam from the deepest trance, but the oracle only gave a long, ragged sigh and murmured something that might have been "please" without opening his eyes.

Now seriously concerned, Herrwn made up his mind. Since there was nothing he could do to call off the coming battle, he must see to his cousin's welfare. Ossiam's assistants were hovering nearby, and with an urgent "Help him to his bed. I will fetch Master Olyrrwd," Herrwn rushed off.

◆●◆

The healing chamber was dimly lit and filled with sulfurous fumes. Peering through the murky darkness, Herrwn could see

Moelwyn hovering over a steaming cauldron and Olyrrwd changing the dressing on Asof's head.

"Olyrrwd, Ossiam is—" Herrwn started, before choking on the acrid vapors. As he cleared his throat, he glanced around to see what Caelym was up to. Not seeing any shape resembling the tall, slender apprentice, a tingling of uneasiness made him change to asking, "Where's Caelym?"

"Isn't he with you?" Obviously preoccupied, Olyrrwd didn't look up as he grumbled, "He said you said that he was to join you today—Hold still, Asof!—and so I sent him back to you—Can you feel this?"

At a sharp "ack!" from Asof, Olyrrwd grunted, "Good," and went on, "You might have talked to me about it first. I want him to see these bruises while they're still fresh, so please be so kind as to send him here this afternoon."

"But I only took him with me to the sunrise ritual. I sent him to you after breakfast! You don't think . . . you don't think . . ."

"I am always thinking—wish I could stop sometimes!"

Olyrrwd's gruff sense of humor was something that Herrwn usually found endearing, but not now, when loud alarm bells were sounding in his mind.

"Olyrrwd, listen! I was at the Low Council this morning! Do you think he might have followed me there?"

"If he did—and if it didn't send him straight to sleep—I expect he's snuck off on some jaunt in the woods." Indulgent as always where Caelym was concerned, Olyrrwd smiled and added, "The rascal! I'll have a word with him when he gets back."

"But if he was there . . ." Herrwn swallowed hard and told Olyrrwd what had happened at the council, ending, "What if he took off after Rhedwyn—"

"Finish this!" Olyrrwd barked at Moelwyn, tossing a wad of bandages to his startled assistant. Without another words, he grabbed his staff and started for the door.

Even though Olyrrwd's gait had become stiffer and more lopsided over the past winter, he outran Herrwn as the two of them rushed to the field where the troops were gathering.

They arrived just as Rhedwyn's men were sorting through their weapons and the smith was passing out pikes and war clubs to men from the village. There, in the thick of it, was Caelym, who'd somehow gotten hold of a horse and was trying to mount it without dropping the sword and shield he had gripped under his arm.

Olyrrwd elbowed his way through the crowd, grabbed Caelym by the back of his collar, and had him disarmed by the time Herrwn caught up.

In his own early years, it was Herrwn's father who had been the firm hand, delivering stern reproofs when they were needed, while his mother had been an abiding source of sympathy, understanding, and approval. Somehow the same pattern had taken shape in the responsibilities he and Olyrrwd shared for raising Caelym. True to form, Olyrrwd did no more than pat Caelym affectionately on the shoulder and say, "Back to the classroom now, Caelie, Herrwn has some things to say to you," before he walked off muttering about needing to get to the healing chamber to relieve Moelwyn from the stress of actually having to put on a bandage.

Calling after him that Ossiam needed a reviving potion, Herrwn was relieved to have Olyrrwd call back, "I've got just the thing for him!"

Chapter 33:

But Everyone Is Going

Herrwn did indeed have some things to say to Caelym, and he began saying them once they'd reached the classroom and he'd shut the door behind them.

"So in return for being granted the privilege of joining in the Sacred Sunrise Ritual, you have abused my trust by telling Olyrrwd a falsehood—"

"It wasn't a falsehood!" Caelym protested. "You said I could join you this morning!"

"I said you could join me for the sunrise ritual! You know well that you were then to go to your lessons with Olyrrwd! And you know equally well that you did not follow me openly to the Low Council but came secretly behind and out of my sight!"

"But Olyrrwd won't let me do anything except stir stupid pots, and everyone else gets to go to the council!"

"Even if that were true, which it is not, and even if you acted with my knowledge and approval, which you did not, then it would still be incumbent upon you to return to the classroom afterwards!"

"But Rhedwyn said he needs all of the strong and courageous men of Llwddawanden, and I'm strong and I'm brave and—"

"And you are eleven years old!"

"Almost twelve!"

"And if you were twenty, which you are not, you would still be my pupil, and I have not and will not give you leave to ride off to any battle!"

"But everyone else is going—"

"Even if that were true, and it is not, everyone else is not in training for the highest level of the priesthood as you are!"

"You said you would hold no disciple against his will!"

With that defiant declaration, Caelym made for the door, but Herrwn was quicker and held it shut as he declared with equal vehemence, "Nor *will* I! So when you are of age and have completed the necessary training to be accepted as my disciple, then you may come to me and decline that honor! Until then, you are my pupil and I am your teacher, and now you will apologize for your disrespectful words and behavior!"

For a long, tense moment, the two stared, unblinking, at each other. Then Caelym dropped his eyes and muttered, "I am sorry for my disrespectful words and behavior, Master."

"I am glad to hear it! And I now want your solemn promise—your word of honor—that you will not go out of this door without my permission!"

There was another long, tense moment before Caelym mumbled, almost inaudibly, "Yes, Master."

"Let me hear you say it!"

"I promise." Caelym drew in a long breath and let it out in an equally long sigh. "On my word of honor, I will not go out the door without your permission."

Even in his most rebellious moments, Caelym had never broken his given word, so Herrwn took his hand away from the door and said in a quieter tone of voice, "And will we have any further argument about this?"

Glancing up and then dropping his eyes again, Caelym answered, "No, Master, we will not."

"I am glad to hear that as well. So now it is time we return to our lesson. Perhaps you will remind me where we left the hero, Heddrwn, yesterday."

No longer defiant, Caelym answered, "The too-trusting rightful king of Gwyddion was tricked by his devious half brother, Healyn, and was trapped in a deep pit and left there to be devoured by Talweddion, the voracious one-eyed giant."

"Exactly right. So you may begin from where Heddrwn sings his lament at his brother's betrayal."

"Of course, Master. Shall I get my harp?"

Still on alert, Herrwn suspected a ploy. The closet where the harps and other musical instruments were stored was down the hall, and agreeing to Caelym's innocent-sounding request would mean releasing him from his just-spoken promise, so instead Herrwn answered, "I will get it for you." With the storage closet only a short way off, he was there and back in a matter of moments, expecting Caelym to be in his place.

He was not.

Looking around the empty classroom, Herrwn realized his mistake—insisting that Caelym promise not to go out the door but saying nothing about the window.

Reproaching himself far more harshly than he'd reprimanded Caelym, he turned on his heels and dashed back to the field.

Herrwn arrived just as Rhedwyn was calling his final farewell to Feywn and signaling his men to fall in line.

The track out of the field was just wide enough for horses to go single file, and men on foot to walk two abreast. Herrwn stationed himself at its starting point, where he could see everyone who passed.

Once the last of the marchers had gone by, he scanned the crowd as it thinned—the servants returning to their duties and old men, women, and children from the village wandering back to their homes.

Caelym was nowhere to be seen.

Herrwn's heart lightened as he guessed that his truant pupil must have gone to Olyrrwd to plead his case and inveigle the permission he had not gotten from Herrwn. Hoping that Caelym was safely confined in the healing chamber, learning all there was to know about fresh bruises, Herrwn made his way there—only to meet Olyrrwd in the middle of the herb garden.

"It's true, then? He got away?" Some servant, probably Benyon, must have taken word to Olyrrwd that Herrwn was searching for Caelym.

Seeking to reassure himself as well as Olyrrwd, Herrwn explained about watching as Rhedwyn left for the upper gate and being absolutely sure that Caelym couldn't have slipped by.

"Did you check the lower gate to the tunnel?"

"He doesn't know that way!"

"He knows. I showed him."

Olyrrwd had more than once joked that worrying about Caelym was aging him before his time. Now, as he gave a disjointed explanation of wanting to "show him where to find that wretched herb," his bright eyes dulled, his shoulders slumped, and his face, which had remained unwrinkled through all his years of caring for the ill and the dying, grew saggy and wizened.

"We must go there now and look for him." Herrwn spoke as much to bring Olyrrwd back to life as out of any hope of heading Caelym off after so much time had passed.

It was too late.

There were some boy-sized sandal tracks here and there along the way to the lower gate and more leading into the underground passage that served as their secret shortcut to the outside world. The brush-covered screen that served as their "back door" was slightly ajar, but there was no sign of Caelym and no answer to their frantic calls.

Herrwn had not set foot outside the valley since his spirit quest thirty years earlier, and then he had just climbed the closest of the peaks above the upper end of the valley, where he'd spent a cold and uncomfortable night listening to shuffling noises in the bushes before finally falling asleep and dreaming that he was surrounded by bears.

Not sure if nightmares counted as fulfillment of a dream quest, he'd related his dream to his father, who'd been so proud that Herrwn had decided that, as unlikely as it seemed, perhaps his animal spirit guide was a bear after all. In the years since then, he'd never felt any need to test that assumption, but did so now, closing his eyes, raising his staff, and invoking his spirit guide to lead him to Caelym.

"Any luck?" Olyrrwd's inquiry was glum and he just muttered, "Well, it was worth a try," when Herrwn sadly shook his head. For some moments they stood there, Herrwn as crippled by his hopelessly poor sense of direction as Olyrrwd was by his swollen, painful joints.

Neither of them had to say aloud that their venturing out to search for Caelym would be futile. Instead, Herrwn whispered, "Can he find his way to the path that Rhedwyn is taking?"

"I hope not. Maybe he'll just wander around a bit and come back with some face-saving excuse." Olyrrwd did not sound hopeful, but with nothing else to do, the two men went back through the tunnel, leaving its outer door cracked open.

◆◆◆

Back at the shrine, Feywn was leading the other priestesses in warlike chants that were unlike anything Herrwn had heard outside of the most primitive of the ancient sagas.

Ossiam was in the shrine's latrine, waiting for the side effects of Olyrrwd's restorative potion to pass.

Olyrrwd still had two patients to keep him occupied.

Herrwn was not so lucky. Try as he might to think of other things, he spent the rest of the day wandering in circles around the classroom or going over to the shelves, picking up artifacts from Caelym's childhood—his stuffed horse, the empty bowl from his beloved pet hare, rocks and eggshells from his woodland collections—and putting them down again, until it was time for his evening's oration.

After reciting the tale of Trystwn and the Golden Stallion, a story that was one of Caelym's favorites, to the handful of priests and priestesses who came to the high table that night, Herrwn returned to his quarters to find Benyon taking away Caelym's supper tray.

"Kindly leave it."

Herrwn sent the servant off, wrapped a blanket around his shoulders, and settled into his chair for the night—alert for the slightest sound that might be an eleven-year-old boy sneaking in, trying not to wake anyone up.

Despite being certain he wouldn't fall asleep, he did, drifting into a dream in which Caelym climbed in through the window, followed by a gigantic brown bear, and started pleading to keep it for a pet.

When his dream self said, "Certainly not! It is much too big and dangerous!" the bear began to growl and then spoke in a voice that was just like Olyrrwd's, telling him to wake up—that Caelym was back.

Chapter 34:

Tell Herrwn I'm Sorry

It was Olyrrwd, and he was holding Caelym by the hand.
Herrwn's cry of relief caught in his throat.

Caelym's clothes were in shreds. His hair was tangled with brambles. His hands, feet, and face were covered with scratches. His eyes, wide open and staring, seemed blind to what was around him. He was breathing in odd, gulping gasps and his free hand kept opening and closing, its fingers writhing so it seemed as though it were something separate from the rest of him.

Olyrrwd shook his head, cutting off Herrwn's questions as he said, "We're going to get into our nightshirt and have a drink and go to bed," in a voice that was equally firm and matter-of-fact.

"Of course, I'll . . ." Herrwn grappled with his blanket, trying to get free of it while Olyrrwd went on, "You're home now, Caelie, and Herrwn will help you get ready for bed while I fix you a drink to help you sleep."

Now on his feet, Herrwn took hold of Caelym's hand and pressed it between his own to stop its twisting before guiding the boy into his bedchamber, stripping off his torn robes, and slipping a nightshirt over his head.

"You just drink this up." Olyrrwd came in with a cup of something that smelled of chamomile and poppies, held it to Caelym's lips, and eased it in, one small swallow after another.

"That's a good lad. Now, just a little more and then you can lie down and rest while I talk to Herrwn for a bit."

Somehow unaware that Herrwn was right next to him, Caelym whispered, "You'll tell him I'm sorry I didn't say my lesson like I was supposed to?"

"I'll tell him."

"He's going to be angry with me, but I didn't open the door—I didn't! And he didn't say I couldn't go out the window."

"He's not angry with you. He's just glad you're back and you're safe, and that's all that matters!"

"But what about Rhedwyn? He's dead. We buried him. They're all dead, but we could only bury Rhedwyn." Caelym went on as if still giving excuses for his delinquency, "There were too many of them. We couldn't bury them all."

"Of course you couldn't, and Herrwn knows that and he's not angry. He's glad you are back. Now you just lie down and rest."

"But what about burying the rest of them?"

"We'll take care of that."

"And you'll tell Herrwn I'll say my lesson in the morning?"

"I'll tell him, but now you must lie down and rest."

With a final "And you'll tell him I didn't go out the door?" Caelym lay down, drew his knees up, and covered his face with his hands.

"I'll tell him." Olyrrwd tucked a blanket around the boy's quivering shoulders, got up, and gestured for Herrwn to follow him as he tiptoed out of the chamber, through the classroom, and into the hall.

As soon as they'd closed the door behind them, Herrwn gasped, "Rhedwyn is dead? All of his men are dead?"

"That's what Labhruinn says."

"But Labhruinn—"

"—is back. He brought Caelym with him."

"If Rhedwyn and the rest are dead, how can Labhruinn be alive?"

"I don't know. He's in the main hall. Go ask him."

Whatever his disciple's other failings, Herrwn would have staked his own life on Labhruinn's courage and loyalty. It was simply unbelievable that he would have abandoned his brother instead of fighting and dying at his side, unless—Herrwn grasped at the one redeeming possibility he could imagine—Rhedwyn had realized

Caelym was there and had ordered Labhruinn to save the boy he'd never been able to acknowledge openly as his son.

Herrwn took up his staff and set out to find Labhruinn and get some answers, including why he had not come directly to the priests' quarters upon his return, as he had not been dismissed from his discipleship and should by all rights have come to Herrwn before speaking to anyone else.

Resisting the impulse to rush, Herrwn consciously kept to a dignified walk, using the extra moments this gave him to quiet his mind, frame his questions for Labhruinn, and decide on the tone with which he would put them forward.

Later, he would ask Olyrrwd if his arriving at the courtyard sooner would have made a difference. When he did, Olyrrwd said, "No," reminding him that the events that had taken place there had started while he was still asleep in his chair. While this was not entirely comforting, it was almost certainly accurate.

Chapter 35:

Banished

The shrine's great chamber was packed. Priests and priestesses pressed together with servants, all muttering and murmuring until, just as Herrwn was struggling to get through, Ossiam's voice rose from somewhere in the middle of the crowd.

"Silence!"

The crowd fell quiet, and Ossiam's harangue went on.

"You! You craven coward! You dare ask for mercy! You who hid like some slinking vermin while he who was the bravest and most valiant of heroes fought for his life!"

Labhruinn must have said something in his own defense because Ossiam shrieked louder, "Silence, I say! Do not dare speak his name again! You are not worthy to call him your brother!"

Finally managing to get to the center of the throng, Herrwn found Labhruinn kneeling like a condemned man before Feywn, while Ossiam, just off to one side, pointed his finger, crying, "How often have we heard of lesser brothers ill-wishing greater ones? How much venom did he store inside him for the brother who was as far above him as the sun is above a slithering swamp creature? Were we not warned to cast him out when he called on our brave warriors to act like hares—speaking of their defeat—dooming them with his words!"

That was wrong! The words Labhruinn had spoken at the council had been a warning, not a curse! He had not spoken to call for their defeat but to prevent the battle.

It was Herrwn's duty to refute this false charge, and he only hesitated to think of a way to phrase his rebuttal without suggesting that Feywn should have listened to Labhruinn instead of Rhedwyn. That would require some delicacy, and even as skilled with words as Herrwn was, he found it hard to concentrate with Ossiam ranting on, "And then this craven coward you see before you pretends to follow the brother he claims to love into battle only to betray him, fleeing like the despicable cur he is, abandoning that most noble and godlike of men to fall under the swords of the Saxon butchers."

Then, just as Herrwn was about to insist that Labhruinn be given the chance to come before the High Council and to speak in his own defense, Ossiam turned to Feywn and hissed, "It is he who is to blame for Rhedwyn's death! Cast him out! Banish him!"

Herrwn was stunned.

Without hearing what justification Labhruinn had to give for not fighting and dying with his brother, Herrwn could not say whether it was sufficient. If it was not—and this was a matter for the High Council to decide—Herrwn would do his duty as the shrine's chief priest and pronounce the decree stripping his disciple of his rank and sending him into exile with only the clothes on his back. But to be cast out by the chief priestess who was the embodiment of the Goddess was to revoke Labhruinn's very existence. Surely, even as consumed with grief as Feywn must be, she would not condemn Rhedwyn's brother to wander forever nameless and formless, neither living nor dead, not a part of this world and never to cross into the next.

To Herrwn's dismay, Feywn drew a breath and began in a voice that was all the more chilling for its ethereal beauty, *"You who were once one of us are no more—"*

It was a dire and dreadful spell, and once begun there was no stopping it—even to try was to risk being cast out as well.

Herrwn was not afraid of dying, and had the consequence of speaking out been only death he would not have hesitated. But to be cast out—to lose the hope of ever being reunited with Lothwen, Lillywen, his parents, his brother . . .

His vision blurred as Feywn's evocation ran on, *"I who am mother to all never gave birth to you . . ."*

He gripped his staff, focusing on the engraving by his thumb, which, by chance, happened to be a rearing bear pierced with lances. It was Cydderewn, a semi-divine hero who'd been changed into a beast by a jealous rival and slaughtered by the companions he'd run to for help.

Herrwn's vision—and his mind—cleared. He drew in what he assumed would be his last breath, bid a mental farewell to everything and everyone he cared about, and looked up, ready to speak in Labhruinn's defense.

But Labhruinn was already gone.

The low murmuring around him seemed only to be of grief and shock at the news of Rhedwyn's death.

Still, Herrwn knew he had to speak out, and he would have—only he felt a trembling hand clutch his arm. It was Annwr. She was standing beside him, looking to him for guidance.

Looking down into her searching eyes, he realized that if he were to speak, she would too—that she, in fact, was already on the verge of throwing herself into oblivion after her lover.

It was a terrible choice. If he did not speak out, he would carry the burden of his silence forever, and yet if he did—and if Feywn, in her boundless pain and rage, were to turn on her own sister . . .

He could not let that happen. Closing his eyes and willing Annwr to keep silent along with him, Herrwn was startled when Feywn called his name in a voice that no one could doubt came from the Goddess Herself, saying, "You, my chief priest, take what servants you need. Bring Rhedwyn's body back to me. The boy will show you where to find him."

Her command issued, she walked out of the courtyard with graceful, swaying strides.

Chapter 36:

Bringing Rhedwyn Home

Instead of going to the sunrise ritual the next morning, Herrwn left the shrine in the predawn darkness along with Caelym, Olyrrwd, and three manservants, one of them carrying a shovel, blankets, and two long poles, the other two armed with kitchen knives.

He'd expected Olyrrwd to object and was relieved that—understanding a direct order from the chief priestess could not be disobeyed—his cousin had just muttered, "Let's get it over with." After Olyrrwd cajoled Caelym out from under the covers, he helped the dazed and nearly mute boy get dressed, gave him a cup of hot broth, and asked, "Which way did you come back, over the ridge or through the tunnel?"

"The tunnel," Caelym answered, staring blankly at the wall.

"Let's go then," Olyrrwd said in much the same tone of voice he used when he and Caelym were going for a jaunt to look for wild herbs. With that, he took the boy's hand, nodded to the waiting servants, and started off.

When they came to the far end of the underground passage and made their way around the edge of the pool just below it, Olyrrwd murmured, "Which way from here?"

Caelym pointed into the start of a narrow opening into the undergrowth of the forest that lay beyond the pool. Crossing the pool's outflow on wobbling flat stones, they followed after Caelym, who seemed to be sleepwalking a step ahead of Olyrrwd, now and again coming to a stop at what to Herrwn was an imperceptible turn in the nearly invisible trail. Each time he stopped, Olyrrwd would ask, "Which way from here?" and Caelym would point to the right or the left, taking them along a route that ran mostly southeast, crisscrossing back and forth across a wooded slope and then over another before finally climbing up and coming out onto a hilltop covered with dense clumps of brush and blackberry brambles.

Before them, a trampled track made by hooves and boots ran across the bluff and over the far side. Thick plumes of brown smoke rising up from the valley below carried the smell of burnt meat.

The servants drew back and were making ready to flee when Olyrrwd said, in a matter-of-fact voice, "So, Caelie, you say you buried Rhedwyn. Where was that?"

"There." Caelym pointed to an apparently impenetrable mass of blackberry vines.

"You lead the way."

For a moment, Caelym stayed where he was, shifting from one foot to the other. Then he crouched down on his hands and knees and crawled into a gap in the tangled brambles. Olyrrwd followed him, the servants followed Olyrrwd, and Herrwn followed the servants, coming out, scraped and scratched, into a tiny clearing with a long, narrow mound of rocks at its center.

"Keep him with you," Olyrrwd muttered. Then he turned and told the servants to "start digging," and Herrwn, not ordinarily a man to be physically demonstrative with his pupils, hugged Caelym against his chest.

◆◆◆

The grave was shallow, so digging it up didn't take long—in fact, they hardly had to do more than move aside the rocks and scrape away a smattering of dirt and wilted plants. With Olyrrwd giving directions, the servants eased Rhedwyn's body out of the ground, wrapped it in blankets, and tied it to their makeshift stretcher. Then, bent over and fighting off the thorny vines, they made their way back through the brambles.

Slowed by the servants struggling along with the heavy stretcher, it was late in the day before they crossed back over the creek and trudged through the tunnel and up the path through the shrine's lower gate, where they were met by Rhonnon and another set of servants who took Rhedwyn and carried him the rest of the way back to the shrine.

Leaving Rhedwyn's final care to the priestesses, Herrwn and Olyrrwd took Caelym back to their quarters, where Olyrrwd used some last reserve of energy to drag the boy's cot to their sleeping chamber and shove it into the space between their beds before giving him a hefty dose of poppy juice–laced potion "to ward off nightmares."

After they'd gotten Caelym tucked in and were certain that he was asleep, Olyrrwd told Herrwn that Rhedwyn was laid out on a bed of pine branches, wrapped in his cloak with a broadsword and a ceremonial blade laid crosswise on his chest, and covered with Labhruinn's cloak and a layer of flowers.

Mulling over this—along with the fact that Olyrrwd had referred to Labhruinn by his name and not by the accepted circumlocutions of the "Banished One" or the "One Who Never Was"—Herrwn finally said, "So he didn't just run away," to which Olyrrwd replied, "No, he didn't."

Chapter 37:

A Toast to the Dead

xhausted in body and spirit, Herrwn slept until late afternoon, missing the sunrise ritual for the second time in his adult life. Caelym was still asleep in the cot next to him. The curtain into the main room was open, and as he sat up Herrwn could see that Olyrrwd was sitting at the table—a wine jug at his elbow, one cup next to it and another in his hand. Pushing back his covers, he got up, walked barefoot across the cold stone floor, and took the chair Olyrrwd had pulled out for him. "Will the funeral be tomorrow?" he asked as he sat down.

Instead of answering, Olyrrwd gave him the cup from the table. It was full to nearly brimming with what smelled like the potion Olyrrwd had given Caelym "to ward off nightmares." As he held the cup in both hands, Herrwn noticed that its dark surface was trembling. Reluctantly, and only because he knew there was no choice, he asked, "What now?"

"The priestesses were preparing Rhedwyn for his burial, and three of them went to gather King's Heal—"

"But why?" Had he been Olyrrwd, Herrwn would almost certainly have made the caustic retort that even if Rhedwyn were a king, it was too late for any herbal remedy to help him now. Being himself, he just shook his head in bewilderment.

"Not why, where!"

"I don't understand."

"King's Heal!" Olyrrwd spoke the plant's name as if he were spitting out something bitter. "I told you! I took Caelym out to show him the only place that wretched herb grows!"

It wasn't the moment to point out that Olyrrwd had not named the herb or said where it grew, so Herrwn just murmured, "I still don't understand, where does it grow?"

"On the north bank of the River Nevwrn, just above the first of the seven cataracts."

As limited as his experience outside of Llwddawanden was, Herrwn knew that the Nevwrn ran through the valley below the ridge where Rhedwyn had been buried, the valley where smoke had still been rising from the Saxons' bonfires.

"Surely they didn't go there . . . They must have known how dangerous—"

"They didn't know or they were too dazed with grief to care. When they didn't return by midmorning, servants were sent out to search for them." Olyrrwd took a swallow from his cup. "They found the tracks where they'd been overtaken and tried to escape by jumping into the river . . ." He lifted the cup halfway to his lips and lowered it again. "They found their bodies below the rapids. They'll be buried with Rhedwyn tomorrow, but we are going to drink to each of the three of them now."

Feeling not so much sad as numb, Herrwn asked, "To whom are we drinking first?"

"To Gwennefor."

"To Gwennefor," Herrwn repeated, picturing the quiet, gentle girl, seeing her dark, doe-like eyes and shy, sweet smile before him as he drained his cup.

Holding it out and watching Olyrrwd refill it, he asked, "To whom are we drinking next?"

"To Caldora."

Caldora, spritely and quick, always a winner in the summer swimming races. If she could not survive the raging rapids, who could? As Herrwn drank the second full cup of Olyrrwd's potent brew, the classroom started to spin around him, and so it was only to be expected that his hand would shake when he held out the cup for a third time.

Waiting for Olyrrwd to finish filling it and hand it back, Herrwn thought the room had gone entirely dark—then realized that he had just closed his eyes. Forcing them to open and meeting Olyrrwd's gaze, he heard himself ask, "To whom are we drinking now?"

"Annwr."

After Herrwn finished drinking, Olyrrwd took the cup out of his hand and told him to go back to bed. As the effects of three cups of the poppy juice–laced brew took hold, he could hear someone crying. At the time, he thought it must be Olyrrwd, but he woke up the next day to find that his own pillow was wet.

In years to come, Herrwn would remember the first half of the daylong funeral rites as if he'd been viewing it from a distance. He saw himself getting out of bed and attending to his morning necessities before donning the ceremonial gown Benyon held out to him, then moving on to have breakfast with Olyrrwd and Caelym and, along with them, leaving the priests' quarters to join in the procession to the Sacred Grove, where he watched himself deliver a well-chosen elegy in an unwavering voice.

For the most part, it all remained quite clear in his memory—the other odes and elegies, the careening laments of the lower ranks of priestesses, the three gilded litters set on stands before the altar—Rhedwyn's centermost, with Gwennefor and Caldora's to either side, each of their bodies swathed in embroidered silk and blanketed with fragrant herbs and summer flowers.

What Herrwn couldn't remember was when he'd found out that Annwr's body wasn't there. It was, of course, Olyrrwd who told him, and he must have taken him aside so Caelym wouldn't hear. What he did recall was asking, "Why not?"

"They didn't find her."

"Then there is a chance that she—"

"There is no chance."

"But how can you be sure?"

"Because they found the tracks where all three were together at the river's edge, and they found her shawl caught on a snag just beyond where they found Gwennefor."

Olyrrwd had seemed to think Herrwn wanted to cling to the hope that Annwr was still alive, but that wasn't so. As terrible as it was to know that she was dead, it would have been worse to think she might be alive in the hands of Saxons.

When the last of the public rituals were done, Olyrrwd told Moelwyn to take Caelym to the healing chamber, give him his next dose of calming potion, and put him to bed, adding, "Keep him there and don't take your eyes off him!"

When his assistant mumbled something in reply, Olyrrwd snapped, "No! Not even when he's pissing in his chamber pot!" so loudly that several of the nearby priestesses turned to stare.

Turning a brilliant red from the base of his neck to the top of his prematurely balding scalp, Moelwyn took Caelym by the hand and led him off as the strongest of the shrine's servants moved into place to lift up the three litters and begin the trek up the steep cliffside path to the priestly burial chambers.

PART V

The Catacombs

The cliffs above Llwddawanden were honeycombed with caves, and, with the limited land available for crops and grazing, it made sense to use these catacombs for interments. The lower and more accessible crevices—some of them no more than knee-high and just deep enough to accommodate an average-size body—served as graves for the departed villagers, while the elite dead were entombed in the spacious priestly burial chambers lying at the far end of an extensive labyrinth of tunnels and caverns that began at a deceptively narrow opening halfway up the western ridge.

As Herrwn led the line of priests up the steep and winding path to the ledge that formed the front stoop to the cavern's entrance, his sense of detachment diminished, and it left him entirely as he ducked his head and stepped into the cool, enveloping darkness. Without thinking about it, he joined hands with Olyrrwd on one side of him and Ossiam on the other, as he would have if this were the annual fall equinox ritual and they were about to begin chanting and dancing their way through the labyrinth of tunnels that led to The Hall of Distant Voices, where that highest of autumn rituals was conducted.

The Hall, as it was called for short, was a vast, domed cavern where the rustle of drafts overhead and the murmuring of unseen streams joined in a whispered conversation carried on in the ancient language of the earth itself. It was located just before the tunnel leading to the burial chamber for the highest of their priests and priestesses. As with birth, attendance to final rites of death was held to be a matter reserved for women, and even the highest ranked of the priesthood were expected to wait in The Hall while those rituals, secret even from them, were carried out. Chafing at this exclusion was one of the few things that Olyrrwd and Ossiam had in common, but Herrwn had always been glad to leave the death rites to the priestesses and simply experience The Hall's vastness, listening to the sounds around him.

Chapter 38:

Bidding Farewell

Ever since he'd first been allowed to join the fall equinox ritual, Herrwn had strained to hear the actual words in The Hall's voices. That day, he was nearly certain that he could hear his mother calling his name, his father reciting the words of an ode he could almost make out, and the faint sound of his brother's singing. As he strained to hear—not just with his ears but with every fiber of his body—he felt a draft of warm air on his cheek where Lothwen had always stroked it in their most intimate moments and felt a tug on his robes as though Lillywen was there, wanting to be picked up.

All too soon there came a soft tread of feet and swishing of robes. As the priestesses came out of the burial chamber, there was a nervous sort of murmur between the exiting women, and, listening as intently as he was, Herrwn heard Aolfe ask Rhonnon, "Is Feywn coming out?"

Herrwn understood why she might not. He, too, would have remained where he was if Olyrrwd hadn't taken hold of his arm and whispered, "They'll still be here when your time comes."

Rhonnon, who'd turned and gone back into the grave chamber, may have said much the same thing to Feywn, because the two emerged from the tunnel together and Feywn took her place at the front of the line to lead the way back out.

Herrwn's sense of peace and acceptance—wrapped around his shoulders like a warm woolen cloak—stayed with him all the way up through the tunnel and back down the trail to the

Sacred Grove, where it was traditional to close the funeral rites for their highest members with a final proclamation from the chief priestess.

Herrwn knew what Caelendra would have said, and since the Goddess was the Goddess regardless of who She inhabited, he half-expected to hear Caelendra's older and wiser voice bidding a final farewell to the departing spirits and reminding the living that they must put their grief behind them and carry on. But when Feywn spoke, it wasn't in any voice Herrwn had ever heard before—not her own and not Caelendra's but an ageless, sexless voice you would hear if a stone statue were to speak.

"Those who were his death, beware! He will be avenged!"

There was a long moment of silence when it seemed that not even the leaves of the sacred oaks dared rustle.

Although her voice was human again when she went on to swear by Rhedwyn's death wounds that she would be faithful to him until the end of time itself, never loving or dancing with any other man, it was just as eerie to hear those words spoken in the sensuous tones Feywn had used when she named him to be her consort.

Herrwn and the other priests remained frozen in place as Feywn stepped down from the altar and walked away, the priestesses falling into line behind her.

Olyrrwd was the first to unfreeze. He nudged Herrwn and muttered, "Maybe you should say something about bidding farewell to the departing spirits, putting our grief behind us, and carrying on."

Chapter 39:

Carrying On

Putting their grief behind them and carrying on was easier said than done. No sooner had Herrwn delivered his homily and lowered his staff than he was surrounded by priests and sub-priests, all of them wanting to know what to do next. Most of the questions were concerned with when and how to resume their schedule of ritual observances—in particular, what was to be done about the Sacred Summer Solstice Ceremony, which was less than a week away—but the most immediate was whether they would be having their communal meal in the main hall that night.

After repeating, "I will ask Rhonnon and see that you are informed," to each in turn, Herrwn was able to make his way out of the grove.

◆◆◆

The actual authority for ordering their lives lay with the chief priestess, but only a fool would have ventured after Feywn to ask about that night's dinner plans, and Herrwn had not reached his position as the shrine's chief priest by being a fool. While he did not have a particularly close rapport with their chief midwife, Rhonnon was next in the hierarchy, and she seemed the safer choice.

When he arrived at the women's quarters, Belodden, the guardian of the entrance, just waved him by instead of subjecting him to her usual sharp questioning about who he was there to see and how long he expected his business to take, which was in itself a worrisome sign of their world's disarray.

Reaching the birthing chambers, he found the door ajar, and through the crack he could see Rhonnon standing at a narrow side table chopping a pile of dried herbs. She looked up at his knock, her eyes red-rimmed and her cheeks streaked with tears.

"Yes?" As Rhonnon was always terse, Herrwn took this as permission to enter and to speak.

"I've come to ask—"

"I know"—Rhonnon put out her hand, cutting him off—"but even if we were willing—and I, for one, am not—it's been a year or more since any of us older ones have needed to take our time at the Sacred Pools."

Having been a consort to a woman with whom he'd shared the most intimate of confidences, Herrwn understood what Rhonnon was saying, but he wasn't sure why she was disclosing this private aspect of her life to him—and was equally unsure what the proper response should be.

He began cautiously, "And so . . ."

"And so, now that Feywn has sworn off men, there'll be no more births in this chamber until the girls grow up."

Realizing the larger impact of their tragedy, Herrwn stammered, "H-how long . . . I mean . . . how old . . ."

"Gwenydd is eight, and so nine years at least for her, eleven for the twins, twelve for Arianna, and thirteen for Cyri . . ." Here Rhonnon paused and gave Herrwn a look much like he'd once seen on the face of the village's chief herder when he was deciding which of the male sheep would be kept over the winter for breeding purposes and which would be slaughtered for meat. Then she sighed. "And so, unless you, Olyrrwd, or Ossiam hold up better than I expect, young Caelym is going be very busy."

What was there to say to that? Nothing that Herrwn could think of. He was trying, instead, to think of a graceful way to change the subject, but before he came up with anything, Rhonnon grew impatient.

"Is there anything else?"

Herrwn knew how trivial his next question would seem, but he had given Elfordd his word that he would ask it and so he cleared his throat and apologetically began, "I . . . that is . . . some of the other priests are wondering whether we will be eating in the main hall tonight, and I thought you might know what I should tell them."

Rhonnon stared at him for an interminable moment before saying, "Why don't you ask the cook?"

Assuming she was serious, he started to apologize and say that he would do so, but before he could get the words out she cut him off, telling him to go back to the men's quarters and that she'd find out and send word.

◆●◆

Seeing Olyrrwd waiting for him outside the classroom door, Herrwn guessed that another difficult conversation lay ahead—and the physician's first words proved him right.

"He's asking about Labhruinn. I gave him another calming dose so you could tell him."

"Couldn't you—"

"I've got to get back to work. I'm sure you'll explain it better than I would."

And Herrwn had to agree, albeit reluctantly, since as skilled as Olyrrwd was in discussing ordinary matters of life and death, he was not the one to clarify ritual banishment.

Caelym was out in the courtyard, sitting on the stone bench, as still as if he were made out of stone himself. Herrwn walked over and sat down beside him.

"Caelym, Olyrrwd says you have a question for me."

Caelym turned his head and looked up. "Where's Labhruinn?"

"The one you called Labhruinn is no longer among us."

"Is he dead too?"

"Not exactly, but he is gone."

"Is he going to come back?"

"No. I think . . . I hope . . . he has gone to some different kind of life and will find happiness there."

As Caelym didn't ask any more questions, Herrwn decided to put off a fuller explanation and, instead, stood up. "Come now." He put out his hand and was relieved when Caelym took it and allowed himself to be led back into the classroom.

There was an empty cup on the table and a plate with crusts of buttered bread, so Benyon must have brought something for

Caelym's midday meal. Herrwn had not eaten anything since breakfast and supposed he ought to be feeling hungry, although the aching emptiness he felt was not something that could be filled with food. Caelym, however, was young and needed nourishment. "You wait here and I'll go and see if I can"— he started, but before he could finish, "get you something to eat," Caelym gripped his hand and looked so frightened that he said, "It's all right. We'll stay here together and wait for Benyon to bring your supper."

Herrwn lost track of how long they sat by the hearth—Caelym clutching his arms across his chest and rocking back and forth—but it was long past the usual time for the evening meal when Benyon knocked his diffident knock and elbowed his way into the room with a tray clearly loaded to feed three.

Begging Herrwn's pardon for being so late, reminding him it had never happened before and promising he would do all within his humble abilities to see it never happened again, Benyon went on to explain that he'd gone to the kitchen to get young Master Caelym's tray as he always did, only to be told by the cook that all the priests and priestesses would be dining in their quarters that night and he'd had to wait while she filled the trays for the women servants to carry to the chief priestess and the other high priestesses.

It was not fair to be so bothered by Benyon's no doubt sincere obsequiousness and Herrwn knew it. Still, their previous chief servant had been entirely respectful without groveling, while Benyon's whiny excuses rained down on Herrwn's raw nerves like pellets of salt on an open wound, and he was relieved when Olyrrwd arrived and Benyon bowed his way out of the room. Not usually one for idle conversation, Olyrrwd chatted through the meal, pausing now and again to ask, "Isn't that interesting, Caelie?" or to say, "Eat up, there's a good lad!" or "Have some more boiled eel; it's good for you," while Caelym moved his food around on his plate, saying, "Yes," "I will," and "Thank you."

Caelym's numbed reticence lasted halfway through the next morning; then, without warning, he jumped up and began wandering around the room reciting fragments of odes and sagas—laughing at nothing instead of crying, when he had all the good cause in the world to do so.

Refusing to give him any more calming potion because "he can't be on it the rest of his life," Olyrrwd suggested instead that Herrwn take Caelym to the shrine's nursery, "where they can watch over him until his frenzy passes."

Chapter 40:

Lost and Found

"I'm not going to the nursery! I'm not a baby!"

"Of course you are not—and it is because I know how grown up you are that I have decided you have earned the right to help take care of the little children."

With that ruse, Herrwn managed to coax Caelym, who was still jumping and skipping like a skittish colt, to come along with him to the nursery, only to find the room was dim, the hearth dead, and the little girls' nurse nowhere to be seen.

Gwenydd was lining up a family of dolls—each one dressed in layers of clothes as if it were the dead of winter. The twins sat on a small bench, holding hands and talking together in something that sounded like a foreign language. Arianna was looking out the window. Herrwn guessed Cyri would be in the nursery's garden but saw no sign of her when he went to the door.

None of the children seemed to notice Herrwn or Caelym until Herrwn asked, "Where is your nurse?"

At that, Arianna swirled around, her arms crossed and her chin stuck out, and, stamping her foot, she declared, "I told her to go away! She's stupid! She didn't bring our breakfast, and she wouldn't stop crying about Rhedwyn! And he's not her father, he's *my* father, and I told her so, and I told her to shut up, and I hate her, and I never want her to come back ever again!"

There was enough fierce determination and authority in Arianna's shrill voice that it was quite believable that the five-year-old could command their servant to be gone—in fact, it took Herrwn some willpower of his own to keep from backing up as he said, "I see. And where is Cyri?"

"I don't care! She's stupid too! I told her I wanted her to play with me, but she just wanted her stupid mother!"

With that, Arianna stamped again, swirled back around, folded her arms on the window ledge, put her head down, and began to cry.

Caelym looked from Arianna to Herrwn and back again. Then, in an unexpected yet deeply touching move, he went to the sobbing girl and stroked her hair, saying, "It's all right. I'll play with you."

Turning to the other children, Herrwn asked again, "Where is Cyri?"

The twins spoke up first, their identical voices blending in unison as they said, earnestly and unintelligibly, something that sounded to Herrwn like, "Ulgo, meger'n ergabel náerwa spreg togû!"

At that, Gwenydd looked up from her play and said in the patient, soothing tone she'd been using to talk to her dolls, "Cyri went to find her mother."

The twins both nodded vigorously and added, "Éy spreg togû, nego hwp!"

Betraying none of his inner dismay, Herrwn murmured, "Well then, Caelym, will you please stay here and play with Arianna while I find the nurse—"

The door behind him swung open.

"I told you to go away and never come back!" shrieked Arianna, now stamping both feet and hitting herself in the face with her fists.

The tearful nurse, encumbered with a loaded tray, stepped back and cowered behind Rhonnon, who surveyed the room before asking, "Where is Cyri?"

Pandemonium ensued. The twins jumped up from their bench, yelling, "Éy spreg togû, nego hwp-hwp! Éy spreg togû, nego hwp-hwp!" The nurse sobbed, "She was here when I left! They all were!" Arianna shifted from shrieking at the nurse to shouting at Caelym that he had to play with her, while Gwenydd put her finger to her lips and told her dolls to talk quietly.

As Herrwn was trying to make himself heard above the uproar to explain to Rhonnon what Gwenydd had said about Cyri going to find her mother, he felt Caelym tugging at his arm.

"I will attend to you in a moment, but first you must allow me to speak with Rho—"

Dropping Herrwn's sleeve, Caelym pointed in the direction of the hall, shouted, "Éy spreg togû, nego hwp!" and dashed out the door, nearly knocking Rhonnon off her feet.

"Caelym, stop!"

Herrwn managed a brief, apologetic bow to the nonplussed midwife before calling "Stop!" again and running after Caelym.

Caelym waved Belodden a cheerful salute, calling, "Éy spreg togû, nego hwp-hwp!" as he ran past her, and was halfway across the courtyard before Herrwn could shout for her to stop him. Sprinting past Belodden himself, he was just in time to see Caelym take the turn to the shrine's side gate.

"Stop! Where are you going?" he called, only to have Caelym look back and yell, "Éy spreg togû!" without slowing his pace.

Herrwn raced after him, through the gate and along the trail, until he reached the fork where it split in three directions, sending one branch off toward the lakeshore, one up the hillside into the high meadows, and one on to the gate at the crest of the north ridge.

The reasonable thing to do was to turn back and get help, but that would mean facing Olyrrwd and telling him Caelym was lost again. So Herrwn stood still, closed his eyes, and quieted his mind. If he were Caelym, which way would he go?

The answer to that came as a question—"Not where did he go, *why* did he go?"

To find Cyri!

Herrwn opened his eyes and chose the middle path that led to the meadow where he'd watched Annwr singing and dancing with Cyri and the other little girls, somehow certain that he'd find Caelym and Cyri there.

The meadow was empty.

"Caelym! Cyri!" He called their names as loudly as he could and listened for some reply.

At first, he could hear nothing but the wind in the trees overhead, the chattering birds, and the babble of water from some nearby stream. Then came a rustle in the bushes and a child's piping voice, asking, "Can I keep it?"

It was Cyri's voice, and Caelym's answered, "You have to take good care of it and give it sheep's milk to drink until it's old enough to eat grass."

The two children popped out of the brush behind Herrwn as if they just appeared out of a hole in the ground. Caelym, who had his arm around Cyri's shoulders, continued, "—you can call it Hwppiddan if it's a boy and Hwppiddena if it's a girl." Cyri, who was cradling a fuzzy ball of brown fur, lifted her face to ask, "How can I tell?"

As Caelym was giving a detailed anatomical explanation, Herrwn gave silent thanks to whatever spirits had seen to the children's safe return. Once the little creature was turned right side up again, he herded the two children back to the shrine, past the glowering Belodden and down the hall to the nursery where Rhonnon had restored order. The hearth was relit, the nurse was at her post, and the breakfast was set, including a place for Caelym. There was a minor skirmish between Arianna and Cyri over possession of the baby hare, but that was resolved when Caelym, showing diplomatic skills beyond anything Herrwn had seen in him before, promised first Arianna and then the rest of the girls that he'd get bunnies for them too.

Chapter 41:

Back from the Dead

"**S**o it's settled that he'll stay there until he's calmed down?" Relieved after hearing Herrwn's report, Olyrrwd even managed something close to a smile at the news that Rhonnon's fastidiously well-kept nursery would soon be jumping with a drove of hares.

"Yes, it is, though I had to promise Rhonnon—"

Herrwn was about to detail the conditions of his arrangement with the shrine's chief midwife when Egwn, one of the two servants who'd been assigned to guard the upper gate, came running in, crying, "Back from the dead! Back from the dead!"

By the time Olyrrwd managed to calm the rattled man enough to get anything more out of him, a half dozen gaunt men riding wasted, stumbling horses could be seen through the classroom window. From their ravaged appearance and the severed heads strung from their saddles, Herrwn was ready to take Egwn's assertion at face value. Olyrrwd, however, was a skilled physician who could tell live men from dead ones even from a distance. He ordered Egwn off to tell Moelwyn to prepare six beds and snapped, "I'll need help," at Herrwn as he grabbed his bag and dashed out the door.

Determined to be of any assistance he could, Herrwn followed on Olyrrwd's heels and was the one to catch Madheran as he slid off his horse, gasping, "Rhedwyn . . . tell Rhedwyn . . . we have brought our trophies to hang with his . . ." before his eyes closed and he became a dead weight in Herrwn's arms.

None of the other exhausted survivors were in any better shape than Madheran, and so it was the next day before any of them were recovered enough to tell their story.

•◆•

Following Rhedwyn's command, they'd split off from the main body of their force on what they'd understood to be a suicide mission—riding headlong into the Saxon's mounted frontline to open the way for the rest.

Madheran had led the charge, crying out, "For the Goddess! For Llwddawanden! For Rhedwyn!"

As they careened down the slope, the phalanx of advancing riders spun around and thundered away. Caught up in the mindless rage of battle, they raced after their fleeing foes, over the next ridge and into the valley beyond, where the Saxons turned their mounts around, drew their swords, and jeered. Outnumbered two to one, Madheran's men answered with catcalls of their own and plunged into battle.

Horses reared and men screamed in a confusion of thrusting spears and slashing swords. Then it was over.

As the dust cleared, they looked around at the fallen men and horses and realized that they'd won.

•◆•

They hadn't known it was a hollow victory—that the band of Saxons they routed was a decoy, a fraction of the actual forces that had been poised out of sight and closed in on Rhedwyn when he'd led his charge after Madheran's.

Dazed but triumphant, they bandaged each other's wounds, collected their trophies, remounted, and rode back, joking about how surprised the others would be to see them turn up alive.

When they reached the crest of the ridge and looked down at smoldering piles of burning bodies, they assumed they were seeing Saxon corpses and rode on disappointed that their comrades had left the battlefield without coming to look for them.

•◆•

Neither the men nor their horses had come through the battle unscathed. With blood loss, festering wounds, and hunger taking their toll, the trek back turned into an arduous three-day ordeal. Still, sustained by the water they drank from streams and the berries that the least damaged of them were able to find along the path, the six had made their way home unaware they were the sole survivors of what was otherwise a total massacre.

Worried that learning the truth would be more than Madheran and the others could endure in their weakened condition, Olyrrwd would allow no one into the healing chamber except Herrwn, Moelwyn, and servants sworn to silence, and he would not leave it himself. When Herrwn asked him what to do with the pile of severed heads the stable workers had left behind when they'd come to collect the horses, he gave the shrug he reserved for those beyond healing and grunted, "They were brought back for Rhedwyn; take them to him."

Chapter 42:

A Matter of Great Significance

Ossiam would later demand to know why Herrwn hadn't consulted him before having servants gather up the heads on a pallet and carry them up to be placed in niches by the entrance to the inner burial chamber, but at the time the oracle had closed himself in his tower and refused to answer Herrwn's knock, calling through the door that he could not be disturbed while he was exorcising the malevolent spirits that had gained ascendance through the evil wishes of "The One Who Never Was."

Besides that, Herrwn had other pressing problems, not the least of which was to find out what was to be done about the rapidly approaching Sacred Summer Solstice Ceremony. Feywn had decreed months earlier that Gwennefor was to take the part of the Earth-Goddess, and Gwennefor had naturally named her consort, Arrodden—not a priest but one of Rhedwyn's high-born recruits—to act as the Sun-God.

Both were now dead.

The responsibility for naming their replacements lay with Feywn, but aside from her appearances at the Sacred Sunrise Rituals, she remained in seclusion in her chambers, and Herrwn, though a brave man in his own way, did not even consider knocking on her bedroom door. Instead, he decided to go back to Rhonnon.

◆◆◆

"And your business with the High Priestess Rhonnon would be?"

Far from being offended at the chilly interrogation, Herrwn was relieved to have the guardian of the women's quarters again accosting would-be entrants with the severity of a judge on the High Council, and his answer to her challenge—"A matter of great significance"—though fully in keeping with his own dignity as the shrine's chief priest, was accompanied by a deep and respectful bow.

"You may enter." Belodden's formal reply was normally all he would have expected, so he was gratified, even flattered, that she unbent enough to add, "You'll find her in their private courtyard."

And he did find her there, pacing in a circle, muttering to herself with her hands clasped behind her back.

The door was open, so Herrwn cleared his throat and began, "If I'm not disturbing you . . ."

Despite its awkward moments, Herrwn felt that his last encounter with the shrine's chief midwife had ended well and thought that they had reached some closer rapport in light of their mutual concern for the children's welfare.

That idea vanished when she turned on him, her eyebrows lowered and her mouth fixed in an ominous scowl.

When she didn't say anything to explain her anger, Herrwn hazarded a guess. "Has Caelym been any trouble? If it's the hares—"

"It's you!"

"I?"

In point of fact, Herrwn led an exemplary life and he knew it, so he was incredulous at the accusation that he had done anything to earn the withering glare she was directing toward him.

"And me!" Still glowering, Rhonnon snapped, "She named us!"

"Who named us? For what?"

"Feywn! The Solstice Ceremony! I am to take the part of the Earth-Goddess and you—"

"I?"

"You!"

•◆•

There was, of course, no refusing a command of the chief priestess and embodiment of the Great Mother Goddess, so on the night of the summer solstice, Herrwn found himself wearing a crown of primrose, yarrow, and lilies and carrying a bundle of blazing rushes up to the altar in the center of the shrine's Sacred Grove to meet Rhonnon, who came out through the gap between the standing stones as stiffly as if she were stepping out of her grave.

Avoiding any eye contact, Herrwn dipped the tip of his torch into the bowl of oil that she thrust out in his direction and then hastily passed the flaring torch over to Ossiam. Equally quickly, Rhonnon handed the still-smoking bowl to her attendant. As the first chords to the Sacred Solstice Dance were struck, Herrwn hesitantly put his hands on her waist. She clenched her teeth and put her hands on his shoulders, and after one or two false starts, they managed to move more or less in time with the music, off and into the woods.

Once safely out of sight, they drew apart with a mutual sigh of relief and sat down at far ends of the ritual bier, making small talk about how things were going in the nursery, until enough time had passed to return to their separate bedchambers.

Chapter 43:

Children's Games

"Herrwn, Herrwn, Herrwn, I am sorely disappointed in you—given a once-in-a-lifetime opportunity to consort with a goddess without assuming any ongoing obligations, and you wasted it!"

Herrwn fended off Olyrrwd's good-natured ribbing about how he'd spent his solstice interlude with Rhonnon by saying he had found the evening quite rewarding in its own way.

And he had.

First of all, he now understood Rhonnon's stipulation that, in exchange for taking Caelym back into the nursery, he agree to assist the Priestess Lunedd in overseeing the children until arrangements could be made to replace the nursery servant to whom Arianna had taken such an intense dislike.

Surprised that a grieving child's temper tantrum would be taken so seriously, he'd ventured to say that, in his experience with childish outbursts, it was best to remain understanding but firm, at which Rhonnon had dryly commented that in most cases she would agree, but, as it happened, there was a reason for the young nurse's intense and personal distress at Rhedwyn's death, and that it was best for all concerned that she be sent to live with kinfolk outside Llwddawanden before that reason became apparent to Feywn.

Rhonnon crossed her arms and looked Herrwn in the eye.

Recalling his father's often-repeated advice that "if a priestess—your consort or any other—crosses her arms, looks you in the eye, and tells you to do something, just do it and don't argue," he'd nodded and asked only how long his assistance would be required.

Rhonnon had nodded back and gone on, saying rather briskly, "Having lost most of the village men between fifteen and fifty in Rhedwyn's final deb"—here she stopped abruptly, drew a breath, and then went on—"battle, I have sent all of the shrine's able-bodied servants, excepting those that are indispensable—Benyon and Iddwrna—to help with work that has to be done if we are to have supplies to get us through the winter. I will see that a new nurse is found and trained as soon as possible, but until then"—here, another deep breath—"it would be of great help if you would watch over the children in the morning so Lunedd, who, as you know, spends her nights tracking the movement of the stars, can get some sleep before taking over their care for the afternoon."

That was by far the longest statement their chief midwife had ever made to him outside of a formal council meeting, and it contained two revelations that seemed noteworthy to Herrwn—that of all the shrine's workers, only the priests' chamber servant and the cook were indispensable, in Rhonnon's view, and that of the possible words beginning with the sound "deb" that she'd started to say following the phrase "Rhedwyn's final," only "debacle" seemed the likely choice.

Needless to say, he kept those thoughts to himself and said, in his most reassuring tone, that he was not merely willing but deeply honored to do his part for so long as it was necessary.

As Rhonnon exhaled in what seemed to Herrwn to be a sigh of relief, her rigid posture relaxed and her voice softened.

"You'll want to know something about each of the girls and what they will require by way of supervision."

"Of course." Herrwn nodded gravely—giving, he was sure, no hint of his admittedly prideful assumption that having been in charge of a classroom of rambunctious boys, he was fully capable of taking those sweet little girls in hand. It was a supposition that seemed borne out as Rhonnon began with Gwennefor's daughter.

"Gwenydd is eight but acts older. She is doing well in all her lessons and is by nature kind, conscientious, and motherly. She will expect you to learn the names and personalities of each of her dolls." Here Rhonnon paused, appearing to do some mental calculation before going on, "There were eleven of them at last count. She is quite responsible and will give you no trouble—in fact, will be a great help in looking after the others."

"Learn the names of eleven dolls," Herrwn repeated solemnly. "I believe I can do that."

"And their personalities."

"I will do my best. And now about the twins?"

"The twins . . ." Rhonnon shook her head, giving Herrwn his first hint that not all his new charges would be as easily managed as Gwenydd.

"As you may recall, the twins were given the same name as they were so much alike at birth it was supposed that they must have begun their life in the womb as a single girl that was somehow split into two. When it is necessary, they are distinguished as Catara-the-First-Born and Catara-the-Second-Born. In the nursery, the elder is called Cata and the younger one Tara, although you will do best to call either or both of them Catara, as even . . ." There was a catch in Rhonnon's voice, but she cleared her throat and went on, "As even their mother could not tell them apart." She finished up with the admonition, "They like nothing so much as convincing you that each is the other, but since they are usually up to the same mischief, it hardly matters which one you reprimand."

"And what is the language they speak?"

"Oh, that! When they first began to talk, it was in words that they made up and taught to each other, and with the recent events they have fallen back to it. Although they learned real language late, they came to speak perfectly well and I assume they will again, unless they find that pretending they do not speak Celt serves as a joke—so do act as though you understand and do not give them a reason to keep it up!"

Rhonnon's tone had shifted from approving when she spoke of Gwenydd to amused exasperation when she described the twins. The exasperation remained, but the amusement was replaced with an undertone of uneasiness as she moved on to Arianna, "who, I don't need to tell you, is Feywn's daughter and will, in all likelihood, reign after her. It will be best that you strive to withstand both her charm and her temper, or you will find yourself and the nursery being ruled by a five-year-old."

"And Cyri?" While he meant to have no favorites among the

five girls, Herrwn was especially interested in what Rhonnon had to say about Annwr's daughter.

"And Cyri . . ." Rhonnon faltered before saying, somewhat out of context, "You need to know about her blanket."

"Her blanket?"

"It's just a scrap of cloth now, but it was the baby blanket that"—a shadow crossed Rhonnon's face—"her mother wove for her. She calls it "Lovie" and never goes anywhere without it." "Only her mother could get her to let go of it when it needed washing, and then she'd stand under the line where it was hung to dry, talking to it as if it were alive and suffering through some frightening ordeal. And if it ever got lost, she—Annwr, I mean—would drop everything to hunt for it. I don't know how many times I told her she was coddling the child—that she needed to leave her alone and let her grow up." Rhonnon stopped there and was silent for a long moment before adding, in so low a voice that Herrwn almost missed hearing her murmur, "I wish I had never said that."

Rhonnon had seemed to run out of words at that point, and for the next while they'd sat in silence at their opposite ends of the Sacred Summer Solstice bier. Eventually, Herrwn had said, "I'll make sure she has her blanket," and Rhonnon had said, "Thank you," and they'd both stood up and made their way along the dark, overgrown trail to the shrine's side entrance.

Feeling that Rhonnon's unintended revelation of her innermost grief was something that needed to be treated as a private confidence, Herrwn skipped over that part of their conversation and returned to Olyrrwd's earlier question about how Caelym was doing and whether he was ready to resume his regular studies.

"Caelym has thrown himself into caring for the little girls with all the enthusiasm of which he is capable, and that, as we both know, is considerable . . ."

Slipping into his narrator's voice, he went on, "As agreed, I go directly from breakfast to relieve the servant who sleeps in the nursery so she may go to her other assigned tasks. By then the children have finished their own meal and are packing little baskets with the things each considers indispensable—Gwenydd her family of dolls, the twins some balls and hoops, Arianna several changes of little dresses, and Cyri their five bunnies—while Caelym takes charge of seeing they are well supplied with cakes and sweetbreads for their mid-morning snack. After seeing to it that the last of the dolls and hares are securely stowed, he will announce, 'Follow me!' and lead the way, marching solemnly out to the herb garden—and the girls do, each taking her own basket, except for Arianna, who allows me the honor of carrying hers along with their basket of treats. Once there, Caelym will play whatever games the girls ask him to, shifting on demand from a father to Gwenydd's dolls to a goblin chasing after the twins to a king in Arianna's court, while I console whichever ones may be left out by telling them the stories my Lillywen loved so much."

Drawing a satisfied breath, Herrwn reverted to a conversational cadence, saying, "So I believe she"—and by this point both Olyrrwd and Herrwn understood that unless otherwise specified, "she" or "her" referred to Rhonnon—"is satisfied with my fulfillment of these duties, though she had some doubts about my ability to successfully discharge my responsibilities in spite of my having been a teacher to boys in training—"

"—for the highest ranks of our priesthood for over twenty years and having dealt quite successfully with the challenges which that entails," Olyrrwd finished for him. "I, for one, never doubted you for a moment—but what about Caelym? Has he gotten over his frenzy?"

"I believe so . . . or . . ." Herrwn weighed his next words thoughtfully. "Or has at least channeled it in a useful way."

"So once Rhonnon has found a new nursery servant, he will be ready to resume his own lessons?"

"Perhaps. But do you think it wise for him to go to the healing chamber so soon, and so newly recovered from his own shock, while it is still occupied by . . . what I mean is . . ."

"I know what you mean, but I haven't been entirely idle myself these past few weeks. Asof is fully recovered and gone back to his village, and Madheran and the rest—"

"—are recovered as well?" Herrwn had been afraid to ask about his former disciple, having had a dream in which Madheran, drenched in blood, came into the classroom and staggered toward him carrying a basket of severed heads and asking, "Where is Rhedwyn?"

"Are reasonably patched back together and I've discharged them as well, so the healing chamber is as free of unpleasant reminders of Rhedwyn's final debacle as any other place in the shrine. So, about Caelym's lessons . . ."

While Herrwn had some remaining apprehensions he could not explain either to Olyrrwd or himself, he agreed to bring Caelym back to the priests' quarters and resume his regular lessons.

Chapter 44:

The Autumm Equinox

"Well, what do you think now?" Olyrrwd stifled a yawn as he spoke and Herrwn shook his head—partly out of discouragement and partly to keep from yawning himself.

They had been up late into the night, talking about whether Caelym would be ready to take part in the Fall Equinox Celebration. The hearth was burned down to embers and Herrwn's bed called to him from the next room, but he remained where he was, reluctant to give the answer Olyrrwd was waiting for.

It had been two months since Caelym returned to the priests' quarters and resumed his studies. By Olyrrwd's account, he was doing "well enough" in the healing chamber, where his lessons consisted mainly of tending to the aches and pains of servants unaccustomed to the rigors of working in the fields. He was not doing at all well in the classroom, however—especially for a pupil who had moved through his basic studies with such ease, and by his last birthday had already been close to completing the memorization of the last of the major sagas, something that Herrwn himself had not achieved until he was almost sixteen.

"Before the battle" and "since the battle" were phrases that Herrwn found himself and others saying frequently, and he'd used both earlier that night, telling Olyrrwd that before the battle he'd had no doubts that Caelym would be ready to take part in the Fall Equinox Celebration, but since the battle . . .

While the rituals of the Fall Equinox Celebration had to be carried out with exacting precision, the actual words, steps, and harmonies were quite simple and Herrwn had not expected that Caelym would have any difficulty mastering them—in fact, had started his instruction earlier than he'd thought necessary only as a way of easing the still edgy and distractible boy back into his studies.

He began by reciting the first of the required chants and demonstrated the accompanying dance steps, and Caelym, as expected, had no difficulty following along. But when he stepped back, saying, "Now show me what you have just learned," Caelym started on a false note, took a few faltering steps, and then stopped, looking bewildered. Herrwn's going through his instruction a second and a third time only increased Caelym's frustration and his own dismay. It was no better the next day, or the next. And now, with the equinox just three weeks away, there was no longer any reason to hope for some miraculous improvement.

◆●◆

"Well, what *do* you think?"

When Olyrrwd repeated the question, Herrwn sighed. "It's like trying to carry water in a sieve. He'll never be ready in time!"

Knowing Olyrrwd's own reservations, Herrwn wasn't surprised to hear his cousin grunt, "Just as well. This is not the year for him to go dancing with the dead!"

Only Olyrrwd could so oversimplify the most complex and profound of all their high rituals. Conducted in the hallowed Hall of Distant Voices in the depths of the sacred catacombs on the night when the dwindling light of day and the expanding dark of night were equally balanced, the rites of the Fall Equinox Celebration opened a gap in the otherwise impermeable curtain that separated the ordinary from the ethereal, allowing the spirits from the next world to pass through and join the living in a mystical dance of universal oneness. Far from being grim or macabre, it was for Herrwn and for most others a source of solace and comfort.

◆●◆

Later, it occurred to Herrwn that Caelym must have overheard what he and Olyrrwd had said that night, because the next morning the youngster was up, still in his nightshirt, with his teeth clenched and his eyes squinting almost shut as he plodded dog-gedly through the steps for the first of the five autumn equinox ritual dances, and for the next three weeks he exhausted himself in an unrelenting effort to learn every word of the chants and every step of the dances.

So, despite Herrwn's doubts and Olyrrwd's reservations, Caelym was ready to join the line of priests and priestesses as they filed out of the shrine's great hall at twilight on the night of the autumn equinox.

Holding Caelym's hand, Herrwn could sense the same tingling of excitement he'd felt at the start of his own first journey into the labyrinth of tunnels that led deeper and deeper into a world without moon or stars, sun or seasons, where the only light came from their flickering torches and time went faster or slower in keeping with the rhythm of their chants.

As the men's line followed the priestesses' through the cavern's entrance, they linked arms and began the first slow dance that would carry them—three steps forward, one to the left, one back, three forward, one to the left, one back, three forward—down the long, descending tunnel, the tread of their feet echoing like the heartbeat of the earth itself.

As they came out into the great underground hall, the priest-esses' line moved to the left and the priests' line to the right, each singing and dancing their separate rites with the shadows cast by their torches dancing between them. Both the men's and women's parts of this chant were quick, even spritely, characterized by spar-kling gaiety and light, skipping steps. One of the critical points in the ceremony was when, at the same exact moment and on a single note, they shifted from the second chant's bright, open harmonies to the darker, tenser tones of the third. But it was between the third and the fourth chants that the most crucial of the ceremony's rites, the Oracle's Invocation, took place.

While the rest of the rituals were strictly prescribed and rigidly carried out, the Oracle's Invocation sprang from the inner depths of the oracle's being and was well known to be unpredictable—even to the oracle himself. In all the years that Herrwn had been taking part in the Fall Equinox Celebration, the Oracle's Invocation, enacted by Ossiam or his father before him, had never been the same, sometimes a brief, soft whisper and sometimes a resounding and prolonged oration, sometime delivered from a motionless stance and sometimes accompanied by sweeping gestures or spinning steps. Assuming that in keeping with the pall of their recent tragedies, this year's invocation would be more subdued than usual, Herrwn was startled when, without any preliminary ode or accompanying song, Ossiam broke out of the men's line and into the center of their circle in a wild and erratic dance and then, just as suddenly, gave a shrill, spine-chilling shriek and dropped, fainting, to the floor.

Alhwran and Oddogwn, the sub-priests whose duties included seeing that the oracle wasn't injured in the course of being possessed, sprang out of the men's line in time to break his fall and catch his torch and staff. After they lifted his head and gave him a reviving dose from a small silver flask, Ossiam let out a moan and rose, slowly and awkwardly, as if he were being lifted by some outside force. Once upright, he began to sway and swirl, pointing into the shadows, and then called out in a shrill and eerie voice, *"Look there! They have come! See how they move among you! See how they beckon! See how they reach out their hands to you!"*

Standing next to Herrwn, Olyrrwd muttered, "See how only he can see them," despite Herrwn's elbowing him to be quiet.

He needn't have bothered, as Olyrrwd's muffled jibe was lost in the murmurs of, *"There! No, there! No, over there!"* echoing through the line—murmurs that changed into a single gasp as Feywn stepped out of her place.

Moving so silently and gracefully she might have been floating, the chief priestess walked toward the entrance of the tunnel leading to the burial chamber. At first it seemed that she might be going into the tunnel, but she stopped before she reached it. Then, looking up and smiling as if there were someone in front of her, she raised her arms, embracing the empty air, and began to turn in a circle, dancing what they all recognized as the Sacred Summer Solstice dance.

As mesmerized as everyone around him, Herrwn watched her finish the dance's final steps, kiss the tips of her fingers, reach out to touch her invisible partner's lips, and nod at words no one else could hear before walking back to her place, where she retrieved the staff she'd left in Rhonnon's hand and lifted it to signal the start of the next chant.

Herrwn and Olyrrwd had agreed to keep Caelym between them, and it was a good thing they did as he stood dazed, staring at the entrance of the burial chamber, and would have missed the cue for starting the fourth dance if Olyrrwd hadn't taken hold of his arm and muttered the opening lines of its chant in his ear. Fortunately, its steps began slowly, so Caelym was able get his feet moving in unison with theirs before its tempo increased, going faster and faster, until their circle became an ecstatic cyclone of solid figures and shadows spinning and swirling together.

There was no clear demarcation between the fourth and fifth dances—the former simply slowed gradually until they were no longer flying and the wild, exuberant chorus that accompanied it quieted into the solemn chant bidding the spirits farewell and promising to return next year.

Counted separately, there were actually six dances, but the last was the same as the first—three steps forward, one to the left, one back, three forward, one to the left, one back, three forward—back up the passageway to emerge sometime past midnight and make their way down the narrow trail.

Even after they reached the shrine and the rest of the priests and priestesses went their separate ways, Olyrrwd would not let go of Caelym's hand. As he pulled him through the corridors to their sleeping quarters, Caelym kept asking, "Who did Ossiam see?" and Olyrrwd kept repeating, "Nothing! He saw nothing!"

It had been a long and exhausting night, and Herrwn had told Caelym he could sleep late the next morning. While he himself managed to get up for the Sacred Sunrise Ritual, he'd skipped breakfast and gone back to bed. It seemed he'd barely fallen asleep when he felt Olyrrwd shaking his shoulders and crying, "He's got him! What are we going to do?"

Herrwn had been in the throes of a bad dream—not one he was ever able to remember clearly afterwards, but Olyrrwd's anguished voice seemed at first to be a part of it, and in a last, strange, and very unnerving flash he saw a cadaverous Rhedwyn gripping Caelym's arm with a skeletal claw of a hand—dragging him along as he leaped into a mist-filled void.

It took several moments for his heart to slow and his head to clear, and by then Olyrrwd was halfway through a garbled account of Ossiam taking Caelym as his disciple that was so interspersed with curses as to be almost unintelligible.

Chapter 45:

Share and Share Alike

Olyrrwd's tirade broke off in a choking sob. He collapsed onto the chair next to his bed, buried his face in his hands, and rocked back and forth, moaning, "He's got him! What are we going to do?"

Herrwn had never seen his cousin like this. Throwing off his covers, he got up, hurried to the cupboard, poured a goblet of the potent ale Olyrrwd kept there, and brought it back.

"Drink this and calm yourself! You say Ossiam has taken Caelym as his disciple? Tell me what you mean, and then we will decide what is to be done."

Olyrrwd took the cup in both hands, drained it, and heaved it across the room. "I mean Ossiam has taken Caelym as his disciple—and I know what I'm going to do! I'm going to . . ."

What followed was an outpouring of the various ways Olyrrwd meant to murder Ossiam—all extremely violent and some quite implausible—that left Herrwn sputtering, "But . . . but . . . you are a healer!"

"And I'm going to heal our shrine by getting rid of that pestilent vermin."

"No, you are not! And we both know you are not!"

Realizing that by implication he had accepted Olyrrwd's derogatory description of their shrine's chief oracle, Herrwn drew a breath, cleared his throat, and spoke in the authoritative voice he usually reserved for making declarations at the High Council.

"And we also both know that Ossiam, whatever his flaws, is not a pestilent vermin but an honored priest in the highest ranks of our order—so, if you are finished venting your spleen, tell me what he has done to aggravate you this time."

Grumbling, "He is too a pestilent vermin," Olyrrwd walked over to retrieve his cup, refilled it, and carried it back into the bedchamber, where he set it on a side table within easy reach before sitting down and beginning, "I woke up needing to void and was coming out of the latrine when I saw them—"

"Them?"

"Caelym and Ossiam!"

"But Caelym should still be in bed."

"Should be but isn't! Now, are you going to hear me out or not?"

"Of course I am."

"Then please do! It was Caelym and Ossiam, and they were coming from the door to the back gate and heading toward the entrance to the oracle's tower."

"How was Caelym dressed?"

"What does it matter?"

"Well, if he was in his nightshirt, perhaps he was just visiting the latrine as well and only happened to meet Ossiam, and it may just have been a kindness that Ossiam was walking him back here."

"First, he was wearing the robe he wore last night. Second, I just told you they were going to Ossiam's tower. And third, you are supposed to be listening to me, not interrupting!"

"I'm sorry and I won't—"

"—say another word until I've finished. Good! Don't! So, seeing them and knowing that Ossiam was up to something—"

"You don't know that!"

"I do, so will you let me finish?"

"Of course I will!"

"So, knowing that Ossiam was up to something and that I had to get Caelie away from that conniving snake—"

"He's not a—"

"He is! And if you will stop interrupting, I'll prove it."

"I certainly don't mean to interrupt."

"Then may I go on?"

"Please do."

"So I went after them, calling for Caelie that it was time for his healing lessons."

"Which it is, so what . . . Ah, sorry . . . do continue!"

"So Caelie stopped and turned around, but Ossiam grabbed his arm and held him back, crowing, 'He doesn't want to be a healer; he wants to be an oracle!' and turned to Caelym, sneering, 'Isn't that right, boy?'"

"What did Caelym say?"

"Nothing at first . . . just looked embarrassed and gave his please-don't-be-mad-at-me shrug, but Ossiam shook his arm and shouted, 'Tell him!' I don't know what Ossiam did to cow the poor lad, but he mumbled, 'I want to be an oracle,' not looking me in the face, but that wasn't good enough for Ossiam, who shrieked at him, 'Look up and say it louder!' and he did, though he looked like he wanted to drop into a hole and hide. 'Tell him why!' Ossiam shrieked again, and Caelym—closing his eyes and speaking as if he were under a spell—recited the words that Ossiam had obviously put in his mouth, 'Because the study of divination is for those not afraid of seeking answers beyond the reach of ordinary minds.' Then Ossiam—that vile, venomous vermin, that slithering snake—smirked at me and jeered, 'So, if you will excuse us, my disciple and I need to begin his lessons,' and he dragged Caelym off to his tower."

After waiting a moment to be sure Olyrrwd had finished his diatribe, Herrwn shook his head, saying firmly, "It is a misunderstanding, I'm sure."

Herrwn was sure, and he would have explained why if Olyrrwd hadn't drowned out his next words in a flood of invectives so foul it made his earlier outburst seem restrained.

"Olyrrwd, you must stop this!"

"Me? What about Os—"

"You and Ossiam both! He taunts you and you badger him, and that is what this is about—not whether Caelym is to be a healer or an oracle! If there were three Caelyms and we could each have one, you two would find some new reason to torment each other!"

"But there's only one, and Ossiam has no right to him!"

"He has the same right as you or I to impart his wisdom to the one pupil we have left—the pupil that you yourself have said that we must share."

"He never showed any interest in the boy before."

"But before, he had a disciple—one who is now lost and for whom he must be feeling great grief and pain."

"Him? Feel pain or grief over Rhedwyn? He cares nothing for anyone except himself! He destroyed Rhedwyn and will do the same to Caelym!"

"Stop! I will not allow you to say that about our cousin and our shrine's chief oracle."

As Olyrrwd was drawing his breath to retort, Herrwn put up his hand.

"I insist that you look at this from Ossiam's point of view. Like us, he knows that he must have a disciple to replace him, and so you and I must share the one pupil we have with him."

Olyrrwd was not ready to be reasoned with or pacified. "But Ossiam doesn't share! He's claimed Caelym as his disciple! I told you what he made the boy say!"

"You told me what Caelym said to you, colored by your suspicions and your readiness to think the worst of Ossiam! What you heard is that Caelym wants to be an oracle, which is as honorable a goal as to be a physician or a bard!"

"But—"

"But, in any case, Caelym is only beginning the second level of his training, and it will be four years, at the earliest, before his discipleship, or discipleships, will be decided. Until then, he will remain under my supervision, and he will continue his studies in healing and recitations, along with the lessons in divination that Ossiam now offers to him."

"Offers? He's poisoned the boy's mind, I tell you, convincing him that being a healer or a bard is just for those of us too stupid to be oracles!"

"Even if that were true, which—"

"It is!"

"—which I am sure it is not, the choice of whose disciple he will be is not decided by the pupil but by his teachers! It is a decision that we three elders will make together when Caelym has completed his second-level training, and if none of us relinquishes our claim—and I do not foresee that any of us will—then he will be a disciple to all three."

"But if Ossiam keeps him until then, stuffing his head full of—"

"He will not 'keep him'!"

"But Ossiam said—"

"Ossiam is not the chief priest in this shrine. I am. And I have just said that Caelym will remain under my supervision and will continue his lessons with both of us!"

"But—"

"But his most important lessons will be seeing his three teachers treating each other with courteous respect and honoring the wisdom that each has to impart."

Olyrrwd snorted. "Maybe you should tell Ossiam that!"

Herrwn sighed. "I will, but now I am telling you."

Herrwn did speak with Ossiam and was relieved at the oracle's ready acquiescence, as well as his assurance that he had simply been elated by Caelym's unexpected interest in the wonders of divination and had never imagined Olyrrwd would take his light-hearted jesting so seriously. He had no objection at all to Herrwn's stipulation that Caelym's time be divided evenly between the three of them, asking only that occasional allowance be made when intensive preparations were required for critical incantations.

That, Herrwn had to agree, was entirely reasonable, and he said as much when he repeated his exchange with Ossiam to Olyrrwd. He was disappointed, but not surprised, that Olyrrwd's only response was, "Harrumph!"

Chapter 46:

Truce

While Olyrrwd made no further threats against Ossiam's life, the truce between the physician and the oracle remained tenuous. Still, in spite of periodic flare-ups, it endured over the next four years, lasting almost to the end of Caelym's second-level training.

The second stage of priestly studies was demanding for pupils and teachers alike. It was during those years that the initiate advanced from the basics of ordinary invocations and minor rites to mastering the chants, songs, and dances required for participation in the shrine's high rituals, moved from mere memorization of the common versions of the great sagas to acquiring a working knowledge of the important alternate accounts, and was introduced to the intricacies of reasoned debate.

Just finding time to fit in all of the intense and time-consuming instruction when a usual day's schedule now included the rites dictated by the seasonal and lunar calendars, along with attendance at the Sacred Sunrise Ritual, communal meals, and following orations would have been a challenge even if the chief oracle and chief physician had been on excellent terms and were able to amicably work out the conflicts that invariably arose when a rash of accidents required both tending to the victims and placating the spirits. As the current holders of those high offices could not speak to each other directly without their exchange degenerating into a volley of recriminations, it fell to Benyon to carry their missives back and forth.

Benyon, however, could not presume to alter any word of those messages on his own initiative, so Herrwn could expect to have the beleaguered servant come rushing to wherever he was, gasping out, "I have been ordered by Master Ossiam to say to Master Olyrrwd that Master Caelym is to come to the oracle's tower at once, as there is a portentous cluster of ravens circling overhead."

Knowing any peremptory demand from Ossiam would evoke an equally adamant refusal from Olyrrwd, Herrwn would sigh and say, "I believe what Master Ossiam meant to say was, 'There is the fortuitous opportunity for a crucial lesson in the interpretation of the flights of sacred birds, and it would be of great benefit to young Master Caelym if he might be excused briefly from your always invaluable lessons in the honored arts of healing. To grant this dispensation would be a kindness on your part for which I would be eternally grateful'—and I think it would be a good thing for you to phrase it in that way when you speak to Master Olyrrwd."

At that, Benyon would bow and back away, only to return shortly afterwards to say, "Master Olyrrwd told me to tell Master Ossiam that young Master Caelym is busy saving the life of a patient just now, and, as he has said before, a physician-in-training can't abandon his duties every time a flock of birds flutters by, so Master Ossiam should find himself a toad to sacrifice while he's waiting."

"I believe you may omit the last part of this message, as Master Olyrrwd has made mention of it before," Herrwn would say, stifling another sigh before going on, "and I think you would do well to rephrase the first part to something more like, 'Master Olyrrwd sends his deepest regrets to Master Ossiam that Master Caelym must remain a little while longer to complete his care of a patient who is in the throes of the acute phase of his illness, but assures Master Ossiam that he will send young Master Caelym to his vital oracular studies at the earliest possible moment, lest this invaluable lesson in the high art of divination be lost to him,'" at which Benyon would go off muttering, *"vital oracular studies"* and *"invaluable lesson in the high art of divination"* under his breath.

Interceding in these exchanges became a ritual of its own, and Herrwn soon lost track of the actual disputes he had to mediate. It was, in his view, pointless to waste time bickering over whose lessons were more important but, he had concluded, likewise futile to try to convince his cousins that their time would be better spent working together to give the only pupil they had the preparation he would need for his final induction into their three callings and to be ready to assume the immense responsibilities that awaited him.

The belief that any boy, however promising, could succeed in achieving all that was required of him to enter into a triple discipleship encompassing all three of the priesthood's highest callings was a leap of faith. Even Rhedwyn, whose passage through his first and second levels of training had been so stellar, had only been expected to become fully proficient in one field of wisdom. And despite his almost daily resolutions not to, it was impossible for Herrwn not to compare Caelym with the man who'd taken the part of the Sun-God on the night of his conception.

Like Rhedwyn, Caelym had been an exceptionally beautiful little boy and was to become an exceptionally handsome man. His transition from one to the other, however, was not as smooth and straightforward as Rhedwyn's had been.

Destined to be as tall for a man as his mother had been for a woman, Caelym seemed to grow overnight, getting up in the morning looking as though a pair of giants had caught him by his arms and legs and used him for a game of tug-of-war—stretching him out into an ever longer, ever leaner version of himself. Meanwhile, his nose and ears appeared to be in competition to see which could most quickly outgrow the rest of his head, which by then had given up on any sense of proportion in its race to keep up and simply got longer, reminding Herrwn of the legendary sprite Bervin as he was being changed into a horse.

Lost along with his childhood's physical perfection was the pure boy's soprano that had made Caelym's most childish whines almost unbearably sweet-sounding. Now his voice cracked and broke during his recitations, turning heroic passages into parodies. This, of course, could be attributed to the growing process, although Herrwn couldn't help but notice it had gotten worse since Gwenydd, the oldest and most advanced of the young priestesses-in-training, had begun to attend the evening orations.

Recalling his own youth, Herrwn made allowances when Caelym slipped away from his lessons at times when the girls were most likely to be in the central courtyard or its nearby gardens, and it was on one of those occasions that Herrwn realized that Caelym's disparate surges of growth were finally coalescing into a coherent whole.

It was an unusual day in that there were no monthly or seasonal rituals to be conducted, no one ill or injured in the healing chamber, and no augury happening in the oracle's tower. Taking advantage of the momentary calm, Herrwn had not only told his hardworking pupil to take the afternoon off but had done so himself and was standing at the edge of the garden watching Caelym, now fifteen, playing a raucous game of tag with the younger girls while Gwenydd, now a self-consciously grown-up twelve-year-old, sat demurely on a bench, sorting herbs.

Arianna had just announced that they were going to play "The Hero and the Goddess Fight the Ogres," and that she would be the Goddess and Caelym would be the hero and the others would be the ogres.

"We don't want to be ogres! We want to be dragons!" As Rhonnon had predicted, the twins had quickly resumed speaking perfectly good Celt, although they retained the unusual habit of saying exactly the same thing at exactly the same time.

"No, I want you to be ogres!" Arianna turned to Cyri, obviously expecting her younger cousin to give in.

Cyri, however, seemed to weigh the matter seriously before saying, "You can be the Goddess. Cata and Tara can be the dragons, I will be the hero, and Caelym will be a horrible one-eyed ogre!"

At this, Caelym obligingly closed his right eye and gave a resounding roar, turning the play into a melee of exuberant mayhem that ended with all four girls jumping on Caelym and burying him in a shrieking, giggling pile. From under the heap a muffled but mature tenor voice called out, "That's enough, I'm dead!" and as the girls, still laughing, rolled aside, it seemed to Herrwn for a single, very unsettling moment that he was seeing Rhedwyn get up and dust off his robes.

PART VI

The Bottomless Falls

Of the numerous natural features within Llwddawanden that were held sacred, four were especially revered—the Sacred Grove, a circle of ancient oaks that enclosed the seven stone pillars believed to have been placed there by giants; the Sacred Pools, where the shrine's priestesses retreated to celebrate their monthly menstrual flow; the Hall of Distant Voices, the cavern within which the autumn equinox rituals were conducted; and the Bottomless Falls, a thundering torrent that poured out of a fissure in the valley's northernmost rim.

Located in the farthest recess of a sheer-sided ravine, these falls could only be viewed by taking an arduous trail up to a ledge across from which the flume plunged down the side of the cliff. Needless to say, the "Bottomless Falls" were not actually bottomless, although they appeared to be from that ledge since the torrent of water disappeared into a thick, swirling mist that covered the basin below.

Mixed with the roar of the falls was a whistling of winds that rushed along with the falling water and the shrieks of hawks that swooped in and out of the canyon, sounds that by some fluke of acoustics blended together into semi-human cries. It was because of this seemingly uncanny clamor that the falls were considered the particular province of the shrine's oracle, whose job it was to interpret communications from the spirit world.

Just how generations of oracles had been able to derive meaning from the noise of a powerful but otherwise ordinary waterfall was a secret known only amongst themselves and those disciples able to grasp the unspoken fundamental of divination—that the point was not to be truthful but to be convincing. Without this crucial underpinning to aid in resisting the pull of the rushing water and the mesmerizing din, an apprentice sent to the falls "to listen to its wails until their meaning becomes clear" was at risk of joining others who had not returned from the same rite of passage.

As his cult's chief priest, Herrwn was fully aware of the risks that the falls posed to the unwary, but he reassured himself that Caelym, with his essentially divine parentage and his brilliance at any task he took on, would master whatever Ossiam demanded of him.

Chapter 47:

The Lull before the Storm

"It was in the lull before the storm that Llaedderan, the youngest son of Llaeddrwn, King of Llanddissigllen, bade farewell to his beloved Eleri, the beautiful forest nymph who had taken him as her consort, and—despite her warnings—prepared to set sail into the deceptively calm sea, unaware of the dark clouds that were gathering beyond the horizon."

Herrwn was reciting the opening lines to the third saga in the epic adventures of the three princes of Llanddissigllen on a crisp fall afternoon.

Standing at the point of a rocky outcrop that jutted into the lake like the prow of a ship, and imagining himself as the tale's young hero, he turned back to face the forest as he prepared to deliver Llaedderan's farewell speech to the heartsick sprite whose gift of foresight gave her both the premonition of the perils awaiting her mortal lover and the knowledge that he would refuse her pleas to remain with her in the safety of her glade.

With the shimmering beams of the late-afternoon sun filtering through the trees, it was not difficult to picture a slender, silver-haired nymph holding her arms out "with the grief of a thousand previous abandonments in her deep green eyes." What *was* hard was deciding exactly how to deliver the hero's speech, a declamation that served the primary purpose of setting the stage for Llaedderan's departure on the first stage of his journey and only secondarily addressed his grieving lover at all.

The usual choices were either to proclaim it with chest-beating bravado or with quivering, tearful regret, but Herrwn had never been satisfied with either, feeling that the first portrayed Llaedderan as a self-absorbed braggart and the second made him out to be a peevish whiner—neither one suggesting a figure capable of inspiring Eleri's love.

It was in this opening moment that the tone of the entire tale was set—so, with only a few hours before the evening's performance, Herrwn had come to this secluded spot at the upper end of the lake to resolve the question of how to reconcile the demands of the speech's practical function with his own sense of Llaedderan as a more complex hero than either of the traditional narrations conveyed without being interrupted by Benyon asking how to tell Olyrrwd that Ossiam was going to keep Caelym overnight in preparation for some vaguely described rite he was to perform in the morning.

Shutting his cousins' incessant squabbling out of his mind, Herrwn concentrated on how Llaedderan might feel as he stood "between the beckoning of the sea and the beseeching of his lover." He himself had once been young and in love. How would he have spoken those lines if he had been forced to choose between his duty and Lothwen? Somehow, he could not picture it.

But why not?

There were two answers to the question he asked himself—first, that his love for Lothwen, though deep and passionate, had been entirely suitable to their caste and circumstances, far different from the inherently tragic love between a moral hero and an immortal sprite, and second, that even if there had been some barrier of race or rank between them he would not have given up without going to his father to ask what to do. Then his father, always kind and understanding, would have helped him come to the best decision for all concerned.

That was it! Llaedderan wasn't the son of a wise and gentle Druid priest but of a harsh and unbending warrior-king, and so he would have been compelled to deliver his lines as his father expected—sounding strong and resolute but with poignant pauses when he would look at his beloved, silently pleading with her to understand what he could not say, before uttering his final words, *"I go boldly now to my destiny!"* in a falling, dying voice as Eleri turned her back and walked away from him, vanishing into the forest.

Pleased with this new interpretation, Herrwn spoke the passage to the space between two beech trees where he mentally placed Eleri, letting the silence that followed speak the grief the words could not.

He had just turned to directly face where his audience would be and resumed his narrator's stance, and was about to go on, *"Calling on his twelve loyal followers to cast off the lines and raise the sails, Llaedderan left his love and the shore behind . . ."* when he saw Olyrrwd stamping up the path from the shrine.

Determined to finish his preparation for the evening's performance, Herrwn put out his hand. "If it's about Caelym's lessons with Ossiam, I have told you before and I will not tell you again—"

"Good! Don't tell me again!"

Herrwn's authority as the shrine's chief priest carried no weight with his cousin, who tramped out onto the spit where Herrwn was standing and slammed the points of his two walking sticks down to either side of him so that Herrwn was effectively trapped.

Sounding more forceful than most men gasping for breath could, Olyrrwd snapped, "Now I'm telling you . . . Ossiam is going to kill the boy . . . making him brew vats of vile concoctions emitting who-knows-what noxious fumes . . . ordering him to fast for days on end . . . keeping him up all night chanting gibberish until he doesn't know who he is . . . all for some 'special ritual' so secret Caelie can't tell me what it is . . . and don't you sigh and say . . .'It's a misunderstanding and one that . . . could be resolved easily if only . . . you and Ossiam could speak to each other with courteous respect . . . honoring the wisdom that each has to impart.'"

As it happened, Herrwn was about to sigh and say exactly that. Overcoming the temptation to point out that whatever concoctions Caelym might be brewing in the oracle's tower, the fumes could hardly be more noxious than those in the healing chamber, he sighed and said, "Of course Caelym can't tell you what it is—oracular lessons are always secret. When Ossiam was in his training, he would never tell us what he'd learned that day."

"That was because he knew it was all fakery . . . and anyway, it just made him think he was important . . . knowing something we didn't!"

"I don't think he thought that," Herrwn managed to break in as Olyrrwd took a particularly long gasp for breath.

"Well I do! But it doesn't matter, because Caelie isn't keeping secrets from me because he wants to . . . either he doesn't know himself what this 'special rite' is about . . . or he's afraid to say!"

"Why should he be afraid? He knows we all cherish him and want only to endow him with the wisdom that has been passed down to us from our fathers, preparing him to enter the highest ranks of our sacred order—"

"That's what . . . you want and . . . that's what I want . . . but what does Ossiam want?"

"The same thing, surely! What else would he want?"

"I don't know . . . but Ossiam has been hounding the boy ever since—"

This time, when Olyrrwd stopped, it seemed he couldn't draw his breath at all.

"Ever since?" Worried, Herrwn urged Olyrrwd on in hopes that his need to speak would force him to breathe.

"Ever since Caelym turned into the image of his father!" Olyrrwd's eyes widened, and he went rigid.

In some long-ago exchange, excited as he always was about his most recent experience in the healing chamber, Olyrrwd had told Herrwn about treating a villager who was having fits—first going rigid, then falling over and jerking—and how he'd had to put a stick between the man's teeth so he didn't swallow his tongue. The thought of Olyrrwd swallowing his tongue was dreadful, and in his haste to find a stick that would serve to prevent it, Herrwn forgot to correct his cousin's use of the word "father." Not sure what size stick to pick up, he was relieved that Olyrrwd remained on his feet and did not start to jerk but instead drew a breath and spoke with a calm but authoritative voice, quite different from the emotionally intense pitch of moments before.

"You may be the chief priest in this shrine, but I am the chief physician, and I am going to get Caelie and he will be confined to the healing chamber under my supervision until he isn't starved and has had enough sleep to think straight!"

While Herrwn could see there was no way he would be able to entirely dismiss Olyrrwd's worries, he had no intention of letting the physician, whose own health suddenly seemed fragile, go running back to the shrine, climb the steep stairs to the oracle's tower, and engage in an angry confrontation with Ossiam. Still hoping for a little more time to prepare his recitation, he reached out and put a restraining hand on Olyrrwd's shoulder.

"Wait! I agree that Caelym's well-being is of paramount importance. I will speak to Ossiam at supper and will insist that he send Caelym to you tonight or tomorrow at the latest."

"See that you do!" Olyrrwd snapped, and with that curt rejoinder, he turned and limped back down the path toward the shrine.

Neither Ossiam nor Caelym appeared in the main hall that night.

As he finished his oration, Herrwn saw Olyrrwd looking pointedly at him.

Keeping the promise he'd made, he went to the oracle's tower instead of returning to his quarters after leaving the main hall.

Reaching the top of the staircase, he could hear Caelym's voice coming through the closed door, chanting in a peculiar drone that was quite unlike his usual flowing tones.

When there was no answer to his knock, Herrwn tried the door and found it barred. He knocked again, this time announcing his wish to be admitted.

Caelym's dull chanting droned on.

Herrwn raised his staff, meaning to make his next knock one that couldn't be dismissed, but the door cracked open and Ossiam poked his head out, streams of acrid vapors flowing past him. Appearing somewhat edgy (which might have had to do with seeing Herrwn's staff swinging above his head), he hissed, "What is it?"

Herrwn lowered his staff. "I have come to find out why Caelym hasn't been to his meals for the past two days." The words he'd meant to speak firmly and with authority came out as a croak as he choked on the acrid fumes, but he managed to clear his throat and finish, "And to tell you that it is time for him to resume his studies in healing and oration."

Ossiam's expression shifted from perplexity to irritation. "I told you that intensive preparations were required for the crucial rite he is to perform before dawn. Nothing must disturb the incantations he is in the midst of now."

"Until tomorrow, then." Herrwn sighed. "But you must promise me that you will release him to resume his other studies as soon as that rite is concluded."

"You have my word that I will release him as soon as he is finished with this one last rite!"

With that, Ossiam drew his head back in and pulled the door shut. Herrwn heard the iron latch sliding back into place. He sighed again and went down the stairs to reassure Olyrrwd that he'd spoken with Ossiam and had his promise that Caelym would be finished in the morning.

Chapter 48:

Absolutely Unthinkable

The next morning, Olyrrwd got up at the same time Herrwn did, put on one of his least stained robes, picked up his walking sticks, and announced that he was inspired to attend the Sacred Sunrise Ritual. It was Herrwn's guess that what inspired his cousin to attend the ceremony he hadn't been inspired to attend for the past six months was his impatience to reclaim Caelym and override any plan Herrwn had of getting him back to the classroom before he was ensconced in the healing chamber.

Not willing to forgo his own sorely overdue instruction, Herrwn responded with studied mildness that he, too, was looking forward to seeing Caelym again and also to discussing at breakfast how best to divide his day between his always valuable studies in healing and the equally necessary, and perhaps more pressing, need for him to be prepared to take his part in that evening's recitations.

"Just so long as we see him!" There was a startlingly grim— almost threatening—note to Olyrrwd's retort, and he started for the door as Herrwn was still in the middle of saying that when Ossiam had promised Caelym would be finished in the morning, he'd naturally assumed it meant he would be at the sunrise ritual, but Ossiam had not actually said so.

◆◆◆

Joining the other priests and priestesses in a predawn gloom that was darker than usual because of a dense layer of low-lying clouds, they wouldn't have seen Caelym even if he was there and standing close enough to trip over. Herrwn's trained hearing, however, was even sharper without his eyesight to interfere. He could easily name those around him by the tread of their sandals and knew with certainty that neither Ossiam nor Caelym was among them.

Whether Olyrrwd could tell or not didn't matter at that point since, even as cavalier as he was about the norms of their society, he would not walk out of a sacred ritual once it had begun. Knowing that (and hoping this irregular and mysterious rite of Ossiam's would be over by breakfast), Herrwn raised his staff and followed the sound of the women's footsteps as they started up the steep stone stairway to the uppermost of the shrine's courtyards.

As they were ascending, the clouds were dropping down to lie in wait for them when they reached the top.

Haze, especially during the transition from night to day, was usual at this time of year, but there was something eerie about the suffocating mist that engulfed them now, a mist so dense that it muffled their chants and reduced the rising sun to a faintly glowing red disk beyond an otherwise impenetrable wall of fog.

A bout of coughing illness the previous winter had left Olyrrwd with a faint but continuous wheeze, and it was by that—along with the tapping of his two walking staffs and the uneven sound of his limping gait—that Herrwn could tell his cousin was close on his heels as they made their way back into the shrine after the ritual was over.

In keeping with the custom that each one passing through the inner doorway would turn and greet the one behind, Herrwn started to say good morning to Olyrrwd but seeing his grim, accusatory glare, he instead found himself saying somewhat defensively, "I'm sure he'll be at breakfast."

"If he's not—"

"If he's not, it's because the rite he was conducting took longer than expected"—Herrwn hurried to finish before Olyrrwd got wound up again—"in which case I will go and make certain that Ossiam sends him to you the moment it is done."

◆◆◆

Before Rhedwyn's defeat, the upper ranks of the priests and priestesses had enjoyed the luxury of having their breakfast brought to them in their private quarters. Since then, except for Feywn, they all ate together in the main hall in order to ease the burden on the servants, whose duties continued to include helping the surviving villagers with their work in the fields. While breakfast was somewhat more informal than either the midday or the evening meals, they still took their usual seats, and Herrwn could see on his way in that both Ossiam and Caelym's chairs were empty.

Unwilling to display any concern of his own over their absent apprentice, Herrwn set about resolutely filling his bowl from the communal pot of porridge and carrying it to his place.

In fact, he had no concerns—or at least no concerns that Olyrrwd's suspicions about Ossiam hatching some nefarious plot against Caelym could be true. It was simply unthinkable that the shrine's chief oracle—or any high priest—would set out to intentionally harm an initiate in their order, and especially not Caelym, who was, after all, not just an exceptionally gifted priest-in-training but also the son of the Goddess incarnate.

Absolutely unthinkable! Herrwn told himself, resolutely dipping his spoon into his steaming bowl of oatmeal. *Unless.* While the faint tendrils of vapor rising from the porridge had little in common with the dense mist outside, seeing the wispy swirls somehow set off an alarming question in Herrwn's mind. *Could there be a connection between that really quite otherworldly fog and the streams of acrid vapors that escaped when Ossiam cracked open the door to the tower room last night?*

There had been something furtive about the oracle's manner, something evasive in his response. At the time, Herrwn had assumed it was no more than Ossiam's habitual secretiveness, but now he recalled how as a boy Ossiam had been fascinated by the forces of nature and how he'd boasted that one day he would not just predict the weather but actually command it. None of his youthful attempts had been successful, and he'd stopped trying (or at least stopped trying openly) after his own father had admonished him in front of Olyrrwd and Herrwn—leaning over him and shaking a finger in his face as he delivered the warning that "the forces of nature are the province of the Goddess and the highest of her divine consorts and are not to be trifled with."

But had Ossiam truly given up? Or was he still driven to achieve this perilous goal? Could it be that he'd decided to try again, this time through the intermediary of a pupil who was not only extraordinarily talented but was, at least symbolically, the son of the Earth-Goddess and the Sun-God? Might Ossiam's obsession, combined with Caelym's always intense fervor for whatever his current pursuit might be, have come together to call forth that morning's uncanny fog?

Suddenly aware his hand had stopped and his spoon was hovering halfway between the bowl and his mouth—and that Olyrrwd was staring at him—Herrwn made a show of blowing on his porridge to cool it and began to eat.

He could, of course, be needlessly concerned—making a causal connection based on the temporal association between otherwise unrelated events. But if he was right, then the worst possible thing would be for Olyrrwd to go charging into the Sacred Grove, breaking into the intricate oracular spells being woven there, and wreaking who knew what havoc.

Knowing the one way to divert Olyrrwd's uncomfortably keen attention was to ask him about some patient, Herrwn took a swallow of elderberry tea to wash down the glutinous mush and asked, "How is Iddwrna's toe?" The cook's gouty foot could be counted on to be a problem at almost any time, and he was relieved that Olyrrwd took the bait.

Only half-listening while the physician described the cook's current symptoms, along with the ingredients of his most recent medicinal unguent, Herrwn continued to wonder whether Caelym's exceptional parentage might have tempted Ossiam to delve into rites that were not just perilous but actually forbidden. There was a sinking feeling in the pit of his stomach. What if Ossiam had forgotten his father's warning, along with the moral of the saga Herrwn himself had recited not more than three months ago—its very name, "The Wizard's Ill-Fated Apprentice," a dire warning?

Chapter 49:

The Wizard's Ill-Fated Apprentice

"The Wizard's Ill-Fated Apprentice" was the opening story in the saga of the Great Flood, or as it was sometimes called, "The War between the Land and the Sea."

While the name of the title character was either lost or else had been intentionally expunged from the extant versions of the Great Flood, his description as the half-mortal son of a high though unnamed goddess and a golden-voiced minstrel seemed uncomfortably close to how an only partially informed narrator might describe Caelym in some distant time in the future.

Like Caelym, the wizard's ill-fated apprentice was an unusually capable and gifted student in the ancient day when the three high fields of wisdom were still combined into one and were imbued with magical skills long since lost. There were passages that depicted him as performing amazing feats at an early age and several lines saying he was predicted to be the greatest wizard of his time, even outshining the brilliance and renown of his own master, the great Alhwradd. Without intending to, Herrwn slipped into a silent recitation of the story's opening lines, and once he did, the rest of the ill-fated apprentice's tragic tale ran on despite his efforts to think of something else.

> . . . defying Alhwradd's warning not to venture into realms reserved to the highest divinities, the apprentice persisted in these dangerous incantations until he began to think he was so powerful he could command the sea. Early

one morning, while the elder wizard was still asleep, the ill-fated apprentice donned his master's robes, took his master's sacred implements, and went to a cliff overlooking the sea, where he began an invocation commanding the seas to rise and come to him. It was a dangerous thing to do, and it awakened a force best left undisturbed—the long-smoldering dispute between the Earth-Goddess and her eldest daughter, the Sea-Goddess. As the sea below the cliff began to heave and swell, the apprentice was pleased with his apparent triumph. His conceit turned to terror as the waters gathered into an immense wave that rose up high over his head and came crashing down, followed by others that swept over the land, drowning everything that lay in their path.

By the time Alhwradd awoke and realized what was happening, it was too late to do a counterspell. He was, however, able to give warning so that the king had time to gather his most valuable subjects and take refuge in the highest mountains in the world.

The remainder of the epic told how the survivors managed to overcome the effects of the spell gone wrong and were eventually able to return the sea to its proper shores. The apprentice himself was never mentioned again and was presumed to have been the first victim of his own folly.

In the time he'd been ruminating, Herrwn had finished his breakfast. Now, pushing his empty bowl aside, he wiped his mouth before addressing Olyrrwd with a careful balance between authority and conciliation.

"I am pleased to hear that things are going well for our most excellent cook's ailing toe and have no doubt its improvement is a tribute to your skilled craft. Knowing how vital it is that Caelym resume his instruction in that very artistry, I will go at once and see that he returns to do so as soon as possible."

Half-expecting Olyrrwd to demand to come along (or go instead), he was relieved when his cousin merely wiped his hands on his robe and said, "You do that. And tell Caelie I will be there just as soon as I've checked with our cook to see how her toe fares today."

It was like Olyrrwd that he always found time to minister to the needs of a servant's ailments in spite of his private grumbling that for all her complaining, Iddwrna's toe was not as swollen and painful as his own knees.

"Why do you go to treat her so often?" Herrwn asked, but again it was like his cousin to cover over his own tender compassion by grunting, "How else would I know what's really going on around here?"

Once Olyrrwd was safely out of sight, Herrwn made his way through the thick and choking fog to the Sacred Grove, only to find it empty except for the remains of a disemboweled baby goat. This was worrisome in itself, as it was incumbent on an apprentice to clean up after himself if there was no servant in attendance.

Now gravely concerned, Herrwn made his way back through the fog. As he was starting down the hall in the direction of the oracle's tower, he saw Ossiam striding briskly toward him.

"Ossiam, what's happened? Where's Caelym?"

Ossiam stopped midstride. Ignoring Herrwn's admittedly brusque questions, he raised his staff and called out, "Oh, Herrwn, I was just coming to find you."

"Caelym's rite is finished?"

"It is."

"And you have released him?"

"I have."

"And the fog is only a coincidence, and not . . ." Suddenly feeling quite foolish, Herrwn fumbled to close his sentence, not wanting to admit to what he now realized were groundless fears.

Still, he was relieved when Ossiam said, "The fog—as all forces of nature—is the province of the Goddess and the highest of her divine consorts!"

Readily agreeing, "Indeed, it is!" Herrwn reached forward to pat Ossiam on the arm. "Well then, I will go to the healing chamber to see that he and Olyrrwd know that I'll want him to come to the classroom to prepare for his part in tonight's recitation as soon as possible."

Herrwn was, in fact, quite determined to have Caelym back in the classroom in time to rehearse his role in that night's recitation and in particular wanted his backup in playing the dissonant chords depicting the raging storm that would first buffet and then swamp and sink the hero's ship.

He was turning to deliver exactly that message directly to Olyrrwd when Ossiam snapped, "Wait!"

The sharpness of Ossiam's tone seemed to startle the oracle as much as it did Herrwn, because he softened it immediately as he went on, "Wait, Herrwn, my dearest cousin, before you rush off. As I have the morning free, I was hoping you might want to go play a round of Stones."

Herrwn wavered. The part he had planned for Caelym in the night's recitation was not a speaking role but simply strumming rising and falling arpeggios in the background. And in view of how anxious Olyrrwd had been over Caelym's welfare, it would be a generous act to give the two of them some uninterrupted hours together, as well as a gracious one to accept Ossiam's conciliatory overture. Swayed by these considerations—and overtaken by a sudden yearning to take his beloved game board down from its place on the classroom shelf—Herrwn cleared his throat and said, "Well, if you are sure you are willing to risk being beaten, I suppose I could make time for one game."

Chapter 50:

Ghost Stones

tones" was short for "Ghost Stones," a complex game of strategy and calculated risk at which Herrwn, Ossiam, and Olyrrwd were acknowledged masters. It was played on a five-sided board with a pair of dice and thirty-three polished stones, of which fifteen were white, fifteen were black, and three were gray.

The object of the game was straightforward. Opposing players began with a set of the white or black stones, and the one who got the most of his stones all the way around the board won.

The remaining three playing pieces—the "Ghost Stones" that gave the game its name—were gray. Except for their color, the black and the white stones were indistinguishable, but each of the gray stones was engraved with one of the ancient symbols for fate, most commonly read as Chance, Fortune, and Destiny. One of the Ghost Stones moved after the players had each taken three turns at tossing the dice—Chance going forward three places, Fortune six, and Destiny nine—so, in addition to keeping track of their own pieces and those of their opponent, players had to take into account the movements of the Ghost Stones.

While game boards varied from simple planks to ornate heirlooms, they all shared the same basic features. There were eighteen numbered spaces zigzagged along each side and a space at each corner that was not numbered but was instead designated with a symbol depicting some feature of nature (usually an oak tree for the earth, horizontal arrows for wind, drops from a cloud for rain, undulating lines for the sea, and a fan-shaped cluster of spirals for fire). Taken together, the numbered and corner spaces were the game's "track" where the active play took place. In the center of the board was a shallow depression—called the "hole" by some players and the "hold" by others—where out-of-play "captive" stones were kept.

A game of great antiquity, each facet of Ghost Stones was governed by deeply entrenched traditions, beginning from the moment the board was set out and all the stones, black, white, and gray, were placed in a strictly prescribed pattern around the "earth" corner of the board. This done, the two opponents stood up and bowed to each other, then sat back down and each picked up one of the two dice. On a count of three, they tossed their die, and the one with the higher score subsequently tossed both dice to set the "luck" of the track—an even number coming up making the even-numbered spaces "lucky" and the odd-numbered spaces "unlucky" for that game. The other player then got to choose whether to take the black or white stones. (Most picked black, as that was generally felt to be the stronger color.) With the colors decided, they tossed a third time to see who went first, and the play began.

A stone being moved onto the board had to go the full number that was tossed. Once stones were on the track, the number thrown could be split between two pieces. A game stone was taken "captive" and put in the hole when the opposing player's stone landed on the same space. Having a gray stone land on a black or a white one was good for the player whose stone it was if the space was "lucky," because the game stone was then sent forward to the next corner space. It was bad if the space was "unlucky," because that meant the player's stone was "struck down," by which it was meant that the piece was permanently out of play (and it was for this reason that the gray stones were called the "Ghost Stones").

Key to the game's outcome was that a player who could get three of his pieces on a single corner (a placement that was called a "wall") could bar the passage of his opponent's stones, and that would begin the central intricacy of the game—the negotiation over how many turns would be skipped or how many captive stones in the hole would be released (or "ransomed") in exchange for the wall being "taken down" and its stones moved back into play.

The position of the playing pieces at any particular time was called the "lay" of the track. There were certain strategic positions that players aimed for, and opponents intent on their game could often be heard muttering to themselves about getting a good or a bad lay.

A "round" of Stones between two well-matched players might last for hours. Before the schism between Olyrrwd and Ossiam, the three cousins had often stayed up all night—two of them "at the board" while the third moved the Ghost Stones—and Herrwn continued to practice in private, playing against himself, in order to be ready when one or the other of his cousins wanted to "go a round" with him. Now, carefully nonchalant, Herrwn went to get his board and the embossed leather bag holding the stones and the dice while Ossiam moved Olyrrwd's healing paraphernalia off the table.

From the outset, it was clear that the game was going to be a close one. On the opening toss, Ossiam threw a 5 to Herrwn's 4, then cast a 2 to set the even numbers as lucky.

Herrwn chose the black stones.

On his first regular toss, Ossiam rolled a 9, while Herrwn's first throw was a 6—equally good if you accounted for its being on an even number rather than an odd one. From there play went on, growing in intensity as one of them jumped ahead only to be overtaken by the other's lucky throw.

They'd both made it past the first corner and both had succeeded in getting two stones in place on the second corner and were in competition over which of them would complete his wall at this critical juncture in the game. It was Herrwn's turn. Deep in thought over how best to use the 2 and the 5 he'd just thrown, he was leaning back, balancing his chair on two legs, when, without warning, the classroom's double doors slammed open and Olyrrwd stormed in, roaring, "Where is he?"

The next thing Herrwn knew, he was lying on the floor, his legs hooked over his toppled chair and pieces from the game scattered around him.

He must have been, at least momentarily, knocked senseless, as he had no memory of Ossiam standing up or of Olyrrwd crossing the room, and yet the next thing he saw was the two of them poised just beyond arm's length of each other, their mouths moving in some heated debate—although at first all Herrwn could hear was a loud buzzing, as if the room were filled with swarming bees.

Chapter 51:

The Witness

here was a dreamlike quality to the entire scene. The room was spinning, carrying his two cousins with it, and when Herrwn could finally hear what they were saying, their voices seemed to be echoing around him.

As he struggled to push himself up on his elbows and then to keep himself at least somewhat steady, the buzzing in his ears rose and fell, letting bits and pieces of his cousins' exchange break through. The first thing he heard clearly was Olyrrwd shouting, ". . . comes to any harm, I will bring you before the High Council. I will tell them that you hated the boy for what his father did—winning first Caelendra and then Feywn—and so you drove him to suicide! And they will curse you and cast . . ."

The buzzing rose again, so the next thing he could make out with any certainty was the end of Ossiam's rejoinder, ". . . has come to harm, it is by his own hand! Herrwn will be my witness! He will admit that he gave the command that I release the boy after his rite was completed!"

"But that was not what I meant!" Herrwn wasn't sure whether he actually spoke his objection aloud or only thought it, but in either case Ossiam continued without the slightest pause, "He will swear that I have been here all morning! And as to the rest, it will be only your word against mine, and no one will believe you over me!"

"OssiamOssiamOssiam," Olyrrwd spoke the oracle's name three times before going on in a voice that came out like the hiss of a venomous serpent, "you must hope that they believe me, for if they do not, I will curse you myself! And beware, Ossiam, for it is in my power to curse you so that your bowels twist into knots and your body swells and festers with sores and the stench of your rotting skin drives all others away from you! If I curse you, you will spend all the remainder of your days and nights in the healing chamber alone—except for me! But I will be there with you every moment to make sure that you do not die quickly—and it will do no good for you to call out to the Goddess for mercy, for the Mother-Goddess sees all things and knows all things, and She does not need me to tell Her what you have done. Where has he gone? Use your foresight and use it now, or never eat from a plate that I pass you without wondering what's in it!"

The two stared at each other without blinking as the room rotated another three turns. Then Ossiam's lips moved again, and Herrwn heard something that sounded like, "I told you, I don't know . . . but . . . but it's possible he might have gone to the overlook above the Bottomless Falls . . . but not because I told him to! I never once told him . . ."

Herrwn's vision, like his hearing, came and went. One moment he was watching Ossiam and Olyrrwd locked in verbal combat, the next he was seeing Olyrrwd grab Caelym's battered toy horse from the shelf, and the next both Olyrrwd and Ossiam were gone.

Exhausted from the effort of keeping his head and shoulders raised, he eased back down flat and closed his eyes. He couldn't tell how long he lay there on the cold stone floor, his head throbbing and his feet caught in the rungs of the overturned chair, but sometime, sooner or later, Benyon appeared—leaning over him and telling him not to move. Then he had a pillow under his head and a suffocating pile of blankets on top of him and could hear Benyon saying over and over again that Master Olyrrwd had said he must stay where he was, and not try to get up, and then he must have slipped off to sleep because suddenly he was sitting upright at a meeting of the High Council.

●◆●

While there had been a dreamlike quality to the scene between Ossiam and Olyrrwd, Herrwn's dream afterwards was starkly real.

He was in his place at the council table and knew by feel that he had a bandage wrapped around his head. That and other details of the council chamber and of the people in it were clear and precise, down to the smallest detail.

Feywn was in the chair next to him. On her right, where Rhonnon and Aolfe normally would have been, were her two predecessors, Caelendra and Eldrenedd. That should have been startling but seemed quite ordinary, as did the fact that his father, along with Olyrrwd's father, Olyrrond, and Ossiam's father, Ossaerwn, were seated to his left—all three of them dressed in the robes of judges at a solemn tribunal. In the center of the room, in place of the stone hearth, was a hole in the floor filled with fog—a hole that must have been deep, because Caelym was in it with only his head showing above the swirling mist.

Ossiam and Olyrrwd were standing on either side of the pit, Ossiam holding a handful of white stones and Olyrrwd holding a handful of black ones. Each made sweeping bows, first to Herrwn and then to one another.

Olyrrwd spoke first, saying gravely, "I must regretfully inform you that my dearest cousin, Ossiam, has vilely plotted against his own disciple out of jealousy and bile—driving him to suicidal despair and sending him to the edge of the cliff above the Bottomless Falls—so it was only right that he have his rank and his staff taken from him, and that he be sent to the kitchen to be the cook's servant, chopping wood for the fire and carrying slops to the pigs."

When he finished, he bowed again to Herrwn and the other priests and priestesses and then to Ossiam, who bowed back before speaking in his own defense.

"It grieves me deeply to say how wrong my beloved cousin Olyrrwd is—but no matter how much it may appear that I did those things of which I am wrongfully accused, I never did—or, if I did, it was only a jest to tease Olyrrwd, besides which it wouldn't really have been me who did it but Sarahrana, my female spirit guide, who regrettably may have spoken through me. And so I say that for making this false accusation, it is Olyrrwd who should have his rank and staff taken from him and be sent to the kitchen to be the cook's servant, while I should be forgiven and named to take the part of the Sun-God at the next Sacred Summer Solstice Ceremony."

It was clear from the murmuring between Feywn, Eldrenedd, and Caelendra that the priestesses were fully persuaded by the thrust of Olyrrwd's arguments.

On his left, the priests were divided—Olyrrwd's father naturally siding with his son as Ossiam's father sided with his, while Herrwn's own father sought to resolve their differences by saying that Ossiam's being so decisively defeated by Herrwn at Stones was surely punishment enough. This, however, led to a further argument between Herrwn's father and Ossiam's over whether Ossiam's throwing the stones and the board off the table constituted an admission of defeat. Their dispute was becoming heated when Olyrrwd's father intervened, saying that the question of who won the game depended on how many playing pieces or turns Herrwn was prepared to give in exchange for ransoming Caelym.

It was at that point that Caelym, who'd been entirely silent up until then, asked urgently, "How many, Master?"

Herrwn opened his eyes to scc a hand in front of his face—one that was badly in need of washing. He would have said so except that he saw Caelym's face behind the hand and knew there was no point in telling a figure in a dream to do anything.

Remembering the question his pupil had just asked him, Herrwn answered firmly, "As many as necessary! All of them!"

Without moving his hand, Caelym (and as the fuzziness in his head was replaced by a throbbing headache, Herrwn realized that he was awake and Caelym was actually there) turned to look at Olyrrwd, who was standing behind him.

"What do I say to that?"

"Ask again, making sure that he understands your question."

Nodding, Caelym turned back and asked, "How many fingers am I showing you, Master?"

"Four." At first, this seemed the obvious answer to an easy question, but while four was the correct count of the fingers Herrwn saw, he could also see that Caelym's hand was not wide open but half-fisted. Focusing very carefully, he realized he was seeing two forefingers and two middle fingers, so he amended, "Two, that is. Two of each."

He was not sure whether this was correct and apparently Caelym was not either, as he lowered his hand, looked at Olyrrwd, and asked, "Which means?"

Herrwn wondered about this as well.

"Seeing double means your patient is still in the early stage of his recovery, but his knowing he is seeing double is a good sign, considering the resounding thud I heard when his head hit the stone floor."

This was not entirely reassuring, although Olyrrwd going on to say, "When he sees just one of each finger that you hold up, he will be ready to take a quarter measure of chicken broth, along with a half measure of tea brewed from willow bark and chamomile," seemed hopeful—especially as Herrwn realized how parched his mouth was.

While Olyrrwd and Caelym were talking about broths and brews, Herrwn had time to take stock of his situation.

He was no longer lying on the floor in the classroom. He was on a bed in the healing chambers. Caelym was sitting on a stool by the edge of the bed, his face as dirty as his hand. Olyrrwd was at a nearby table, where he was wrapping something that looked like the liver of a sheep (and smelled exceedingly foul) in a linen sheath as he continued in a lecturing tone of voice, clearly meant for Caelym rather than for Herrwn, "And so, after applying the compress of goat's liver preserved in equal parts ale and urine—which serves what two purposes?"

"Cushioning the swollen lump and fending off the spirits of brain fever and bewilderment!"

"Excellent! When and how should it be changed?"

"Precisely at midnight, while reciting the chant to repel those spirits, taking care that the windows are open so that they leave the chamber and do not remain inside, waiting for another victim!"

"Correct again! And what are the rest of your directions for his care?"

"That he should remain lying in bed until morning, at which time he may sit up and, so long as he does not grow pale or queasy, take a half measure of willow bark and chamomile root brewed as tea, along with a light breakfast of wheat bread softened with sheep's milk, but nothing containing blood, fat, or inner organs for at least . . ."

Neither as confused nor as feeble as they apparently thought, and done listening to the two of them discuss his treatment as if his views on the matter had no bearing, Herrwn pushed himself up to sitting and announced that he had the second tale in the third saga of the Three Princes of Llanddissigllen to recite that night and needed to return to his quarters to change his robes.

"Oh please, Master, it is too soon for you to rise, and I must plead that you do not strain yourself." Caelym held out both hands, as if he expected Herrwn to topple off the bed.

Olyrrwd did not speak to Herrwn but to Caelym. "What you say is correct, only you must say it remembering that you are a physician! He is not your master now, he is your patient, and you do not plead with patients! You tell them what they must do, reminding them, if need be, that it is you—and not they—who know the secrets of healing! Watch me and I will show you!"

Standing at his full height, Olyrrwd was just barely eye level with Herrwn sitting up in bed, but crossing his arms and affecting an unyielding and immovable posture, he declared, "You have suffered a serious injury to your head due to striking it on the stone floor and are fortunate not to have cracked it wide open. It is the considered opinion of my skilled disciple that you will remain in bed until he determines you are fit to stand, and that would be tomorrow at the earliest!" with such a blast of authority that Herrwn would have lain back down even if he hadn't been so woozy that he had to.

Speaking up from his flattened position, he protested, "But my oration!"

"You have a disciple who will do the oration tonight in your stead!" Olyrrwd put a hand on Herrwn's chest, pinning him in place, as he turned back to Caelym and said, "And speaking of that, I expect that you will want to go change into bardic robes and get a harp—so, with your permission, I will take over the care of your patient, carrying out your directions precisely."

As Caelym swung around and started off, Herrwn could see he was wearing Olyrrwd's cloak—which, with the differences in their height, came only halfway down his thighs. Below that, his bare legs and feet were even dirtier than his face and hand. Seeing this, Herrwn, despite Olyrrwd's restraint, managed to half raise himself and call out, "Do not put on my robes without bathing first!"

The effort drained him so that, when Olyrrwd pressed him back down, he obeyed his cousin's order to "go to sleep!"

Chapter 52:

Dy Na Ma

Waking up later that evening, Herrwn correctly answered "three" to Olyrrwd's question of "How many fingers am I showing you?" and was given enough pillows that he could sit up and start sipping his allotted portions of broth and tea.

"Now, I insist that you give me a full account of what happened when you went to find Caclym." Pleased that his voice had come out sounding stern and resolute, he added, "And why—"

"Why I say that Ossiam was responsible for Caelym almost jumping off a cliff? I told you, he's . . ." Olyrrwd had poured himself a stronger brew than he'd allowed Herrwn, and here he paused to take a swallow, which gave Herrwn a chance to head off the impending tirade.

"No, not that! I know what you believe Ossiam guilty of. What I want to know is how you found out Caelym had gone off—and, while you are at it, you may also explain why you took his toy horse when you went to look for him."

Olyrrwd pursed his lips and stared down into his cup. "Why *did* I take the horse?" The stress he put on the word "did" made it clear that this was not a rhetorical question but one he was genuinely asking of himself. "I don't know. I just saw it on the shelf and somehow knew that I'd need it. As to how I knew Caelym had gone off, Nimrrwn told me."

"Nimrrwn? Benyon's nephew?"

In all truth, Herrwn would not have known the young serving boy's name except that in the shifting of roles and responsibilities that had taken place in the wake of Rhedwyn's defeat it had been necessary to start sending Benyon to trade for salt and spices at a village outside the valley, and Benyon had spent what had seemed to Herrwn to be an inordinately long time introducing the youngster who would be cleaning up their chambers in his absence, particularly in view of the fact that the trip to the market would require that Benyon be away from his regular duties for less than a day only once or twice a year.

As the physician to all of the valley's population, Olyrrwd knew the name of every servant in the shrine as well as every villager, along with their extended kin, and he answered with an emphasis that implied Herrwn should be equally well-informed, "Benyon's nephew on his mother's side and our cook's grandson on his father's!"

Olyrrwd went on to say that Benyon had turned some of his chores over to Nimrrwn, including the task of carrying food trays up the steep stairs of the oracle's tower "whenever Ossiam decides that he's too busy to come down and eat in the main hall with the rest of us."

After digressing to grumble that this was lucky, since the boy had a considerably keener wit than his uncle, Olyrrwd returned to the topic at hand. "Nimrrwn noticed that the plates and bowls he'd dished out for Caelym these past three days had been left untouched and told his grandmother, who guessed it was because he was fasting in preparation for some special rite and told him to keep paying attention since, as Benyon's sister's son, he will be the priests' chief servant himself someday."

The idea that servants had their own lines of succession was new to Herrwn and one he found extremely interesting, but he didn't interrupt the flow of his cousin's narrative to say so. Instead, he paid close attention as Olyrrwd continued. "Being a bright lad, he did. So last night, as he was going back to get the tray he'd taken up to the tower earlier in the evening, he saw Ossiam, dressed for a high rite, coming down the hall toward him, and he ducked out of sight.

Here Herrwn did break in. "Why?"

"Because he's afraid of Ossiam—all the servants are. Anyway, he was just about to go on when Caelym, dressed in plain white robes, came along, carrying a ceremonial knife and reciting, '*Dym naw ma llut hwnan, Dym naw ma llut twnan, Dym naw ma llut nwffan,'* under his breath."

Herrwn was sipping his chicken broth as Olyrrwd said this last part. Hearing it, he choked.

Usually spoken of by the initial sounds of its first three words, the Dy Na Ma was no intermediate chant but a powerful and dangerous invocation that began by reciting all seven sacred names of the Great Mother Goddess and went on to deliver a message to—and compel an answer from—the other side of the curtain that divided life from death. Those were not words that any fifteen-year-old novice should be reciting! Even Olyrrwd, though he was as high a priest as Ossiam, clearly had no grasp on the possible consequences of reciting it without proper preparations and precautions. And for a servant boy to have uttered the words . . .

"Stop," Herrwn commanded, "just tell me what happened next," and he listened as Olyrrwd explained that Nimrrwn had watched Caelym disappear down the passageway to the sheds where the sacrificial goats were kept, then had gone on to climb the stairs to the oracle's tower to get the tray. While he wasn't surprised to see Caelym's portion left over, he hadn't been sure what to do. He couldn't just leave the tray there, because then it might be thought he hadn't done his duties, but (Nimrrwn said) since Master Caelym had been fasting for three days, he'd want something to eat when he was finished with his rite, so he decided to wait downstairs in the antechamber and be ready to hand him his meal when he got back.

"That was thoughtful of him!" Herrwn was impressed and made a mental note to have Olyrrwd tell the cook to give his personal thanks to her grandson.

"He's a thoughtful lad—thoughtful enough to pick a dark corner and stay out of sight."

Olyrrwd drew a breath and took a drink from his cup before going on.

"That was why—when Ossiam returned alone—Nimrrwn saw Ossiam but Ossiam didn't see him. Expecting that Caelym would be along any moment, the boy settled back to wait and fell asleep, waking up at the sound of Caelym coming through the antechamber and going up the tower stairs 'all eager and excited.' It must have had taken Nimrrwn a few moments to get to his feet and gather up the tray. In any case, he said he was just starting up the tower stairs when he heard voices overhead. What he heard then, and what happened next, made him run to tell his grandmother—and, thank the Goddess, I was in the kitchen tending to Iddwrna's toe when the lad came in, calling to her and saying Master Ossiam had just said terrible things to Master Caelym. Well then, Iddwrna gave me a look, and I gave her a nod, and she spoke firmly to the lad, saying, 'You must tell Master Olyrrwd all about it!' And he did, speaking in an earnest, forthright manner, no more nervous than you'd expect of a half-grown boy talking to a gruff old man like me, up to the point where he'd heard Ossiam talking. Then he lowered his voice, so I had to lean forward to hear him repeat, 'He said terrible things.'

'Well,' I said, lowering my voice to match the boy's, 'Master Ossiam is always saying terrible things. What exactly did he say this time?'

The boy looked at his grandmother who gave him a nod, so he whispered, 'He called Master Caelym bad names and said that he'd failed and he wasn't ever going to be a Druid and sent him away.'

'I see,' I whispered back. 'What happened then?'

'Then,' he said, 'Master Caelym came down the stairs crying and talking about drinking poison and stabbing himself!'

'Hmmm,' I said, trying to be matter-of-fact so the boy didn't clam up on me, 'and did Master Caelym happen to say where he was going to do this?'

'No,' he said, 'he just went off, and I came to tell Grandmother.'

'Well,' I said, 'I'll just be off to the tower and will ask Master Ossiam if he knows, because we don't want young Master Caelym to hurt himself.'

At which the boy looked to die of fright and gasped out, pleading, 'You won't tell him that I told you—'

'I won't!' I said, not saying out loud that I'd be too busy wringing his neck to get the truth out of him!"

After taking another swallow of ale, Olyrrwd went on, "I would have wasted time running back to the tower, only Iddwrna—who knows more about what's going on in the shrine than the Goddess Herself—said, 'He's in the priests' chambers with Master Herrwn!' So off I dashed, and though you may not remember it, I slammed open the classroom doors and you fell over backward, knocking yourself out, but Ossiam just sat there as calm and smug as a cat who'd caught a bird and was wiping its feathers off its lips.

'Where is he?' I demanded, but he just smirked, said, 'Where is who?' and rolled the dice."

"But it wasn't his turn! I hadn't made my move!" In its own way, the thought of Ossiam failing to adhere to the game's strict rules was as shocking to Herrwn as hearing that the perilous lines of the Dy Na Ma had been recited by a servant.

Olyrrwd shrugged. "That, Herrwn, is the difference between you and Ossiam. You follow the rules whether they work in your favor or not. Rules only matter to Ossiam if they benefit him. Anyway, he tossed the dice, getting a five and a four, which you'd think would have been good enough for him—getting his next stone out of the starting corner and all the way to nine—but he acted as if he'd only just noticed you'd fallen over and pointed to you with his right hand, saying, 'Oh, look at Herrwn!' while with his left he turned the die from a four to a five, changing his score to ten, and then jumped his stone to the corner to finish his wall."

While cheating at Stones was not as serious a wrongdoing as driving a pupil in his care to the brink of suicide, Herrwn would never have imagined any member of their order capable of such a transgression. "What—what did you do?"

"I knocked the board off the table and threatened him with every dire thing I could think of until he told me that Caelym 'might have gone to the overlook above the Bottomless Falls.' That was what I'd come to find out, so, much as I regretted leaving you, I dashed off to try to get to Caelym before it was too late. I passed Benyon as I ran down the hall, and I called for him to go and cover you up and keep you from moving until I got back. Then I just ran on as fast as I could."

Olyrrwd drained the last of his drink, got stiffly out of his chair, and hobbled over to refill his cup. After limping back and sitting down, he raised his cup in an unexpectedly exultant gesture before taking his next swallow and said, "I wish you could have seen me tearing up the side of that mountain, jumping over logs and dodging around boulders—Caelie's toy tucked under my arm like it was the chalice in the summer solstice relay race and I was sixteen again!"

Chapter 53:

On the Brink

The triumphant tone in Olyrrwd's voice shifted abruptly to something much grimmer as he described how he'd scrambled up to the top of the last ridge to see Caelym at the brink of the cliff *"stripping off his clothes, casting them over the edge and getting ready to leap after them."*

Picturing his cousin there, exhausted and out of breath but still fiercely determined, Herrwn ventured, "So you rushed on to take hold of him and pull him back!"

"The Goddess knows I wanted to, but I didn't dare! Not when he was so close to the edge that any wrong move would have sent him over."

"Then what did you do?"

"I hid! Ducked behind a tree to catch my breath and try to think of anything I could say to call him back to me."

"And that was?"

"Nothing!"

"But—"

"There was nothing I could say, because I'm not Rhedwyn."

"You've given him more love and care than—"

"That didn't matter! What mattered was that he'd walk through fire to have Rhedwyn look in his direction, so I guessed he'd walk away from the edge of the cliff if I could make him believe I was Rhedwyn's ghost calling his name and offering to take him for a horseback ride!"

"But how—"

"How could I hope to look—or sound—like Rhedwyn?"

Herrwn hadn't meant his question to be quite so blatant, but Olyrrwd waved his apologies aside, going on, "Well, if he were still alive, there wouldn't be much chance of it, but I thought that—with the fog to help—I might look and sound as good as a man who'd been dead for going on five years. Anyway, thinking back to our beginning oratory lessons and how your father always said you needed to become the character for whom you speak, I imagined myself as a ghoul returned from the spirit world and called out, 'Caelym, oh, Caelym, I've come for you!'—throwing in, 'I have your horse!' for good measure."

"And he believed you—"

"He did at first—at least long enough to turn around and take a step away from the edge. He realized it was me before I could reach him, though, and I would have lost him then and there, but I held out the toy horse to show I wasn't lying to him and he snatched at it, shouting, 'That's mine! Give it to me'—no doubt meaning to take it with him when he jumped. Seeing my chance, I tempted him with it, waving it just out of his reach and keeping him arguing with me about it, until I'd backed far enough away from the edge that I dared grab hold of him. At first he tried to break free, but he was chilled to the bone and shaking like a leaf and I got my cloak wrapped around him and held him fast, and finally he gave up and just clung to me, sobbing like a baby, saying over and over how he had to be an oracle to see and hear Rhedwyn and now he'd failed his test and wouldn't ever get to see him or hear him!"

"What did you say?"

"Whatever I could think of. Most of it was just silly nonsense—something about if it was a ghost he wanted to talk to, he'd do better to come along back to the healing chamber, where there are ghosts aplenty and all of them ready to talk, especially when it comes to complaining about what I should or shouldn't have done—as if they know more about what killed them than I do."

"Did that help?"

"Not particularly—he just went on about how he'd done everything right when he sacrificed the little goat, but its entrails hadn't told him anything except that it wanted its mother, and then he'd found the baby owl that he'd had to sacrifice to tell the future, but all he'd seen was that if he did it would just be dead, so he hadn't, but that was wrong and he was a disgrace to his mother, and Ossiam had told him he couldn't be a disciple or learn answers beyond the reach of ordinary minds but hadn't told him whether he was supposed to drink the poison first and then stab himself and then jump off the cliff or stab himself first and then drink the poison and then jump off the cliff or jump off the cliff first and drink the poison and stab himself on the way down, until I'd had enough of it and I said, 'Ossiam has said you are not his disciple, and for once he's right—you are my disciple, and I am commanding you to come with me!' Then I took him by his hand, like I used to when he was little, and I led him back here and gave him some warm mush and put him down for a nap. Leaving Moelwyn to watch over him, I took a litter and got Benyon to help me move you here, tucked you in, and waited to see which of you would wake up first. Caelym did, so I put him to work being a healer, with you as his patient."

With that, Olyrrwd concluded his rendition and shifted quite anticlimactically into a discourse over what other cures might still be necessary if Herrwn did not lie back down and let the current one do its work.

Herrwn put out his hand—partly because he was certain that the fetid goat's liver bound to the back of his head was quite sufficient to fend off any malevolent spirits within smelling distance of it whether he was sitting up or lying down, but also because there was something in Olyrrwd's account that didn't add up.

While his recollections of the previous day were cloudy, when Herrwn tallied the time that Olyrrwd had spent questioning the cook's grandson, the time he spent confronting Ossiam, and the time it would have taken to climb up to the overlook above the Bottomless Falls—and while Olyrrwd was rightfully proud of his remarkable burst of speed, Caelym certainly would have been faster—it must have been approaching noon before Olyrrwd reached the top of the cliff, and by Nimrrwn's account, Caelym had left the shrine just after dawn.

Glad to have an excuse to change the subject, he interrupted Olyrrwd's enthusiastic description of having once cured a patient who'd suffered an injury somewhat similar to Herrwn's by drilling a hole in the top of his head to say, "The one thing that still puzzles me—mind you, I am grateful for whatever the reason might be, but—starting so long after him, how were you able to reach Caelym in time?"

"I wondered about that as well but didn't want to put the question to him in a way that suggested he should have gone quicker—and it turned out I didn't need to because, as he was crying about all his dismal failures, he moaned, 'What if Rhedwyn was there calling me, like Ossiam said, but got tired of waiting and left?' and then sniffled that he had come as fast as he could but he kept getting lost in the fog. That was it! Just the stupid, dumb luck that by the time I set out the fog was starting to lift, and it kept on rising up above my head all the while I was climbing up the trail—and don't think I am not grateful to be short, because I could see my way under it, and that was how I got there in time!"

It was then that all the pieces fell into place for Herrwn.

While Olyrrwd now insisted it was simply a matter of luck that the fog had come and gone when it did, had he not proclaimed to Ossiam that "the Mother-Goddess sees all things and knows all things"?

And had Ossiam himself not acknowledged that the forces of nature were "the divine power of the Goddess"?

So was it mere coincidence that the eerie mist had swirled into the valley so soon after Caelym sent his seemingly ill-advised invocation to the next world, or could it have been that Caelendra had heard her son's message, seen the danger he was in, and sent the fog—wrapping it around him like a mother's cloak and keeping him back from the edge of the cliff until Olyrrwd could get there?

That was what he thought happened and that was what he said to Olyrrwd, fully expecting his cousin, who had little faith in mystical explanations of events, to dismiss it out of hand.

Instead, Olyrrwd seemed to ponder this seriously and said, "Well, I suppose it could be." And then, with the first glimmer of puckish humor Herrwn had seen on his cousin's face since Ossiam had taken Caelym into oracular studies, he added, "And I think I will say exactly that to Ossie the next time I have a chance."

Chapter 54:

The First Oration

T here was something in Olyrrwd's tone that was reminis-
cent of a time when his clashes with Ossiam were more
than half in fun. The accusation that Ossiam had deliberately plotted against Caelym, however, was no boyish squabble.

"I suppose you will bring this to the High Council." Herrwn
spoke reluctantly, heartsick at the thought of presiding over that
council meeting.

"What good would that do?" Olyrrwd's tone changed from
lighthearted to bitter. "Do you think Feywn will take my word
over his?"

At first, Herrwn was taken aback that Olyrrwd would reduce
the substance of the High Council meetings to a mere stage for
their chief priestess's pronouncements. On reflection, however—
and recalling the preference Feywn had shown for Ossiam's
pronouncements over anything anyone else had to say ever since
Rhedwyn died—he was forced to concede Olyrrwd's point.

"So you will let the matter drop?"

"So I will come up with something else."

"But you wouldn't . . ." Herrwn hesitated, not sure how to
phrase his next question but, remembering Olyrrwd's previous
threats against Ossiam's life, more than a little concerned with
the way the physician was surveying the line of potentially lethal
potions he kept on the highest shelf on the far wall of the room.

Olyrrwd said nothing for a long moment. Then he sighed.
"You're right. I wouldn't."

Relieved, Herrwn lay back against his pillows and let his mind wander from picturing Caelym dressed in formal bardic robes and reciting his first independent oration to the night that he himself donned those same robes for the first time.

Herrwn had been rehearsing for months for what was to him a far more important rite of passage than the spirit quest he'd gone on before entering his formal discipleship the year before.

His fingers had shaken as he fastened the ties of his robe. Gripping his harp with sweaty hands, he'd walked what seemed to be leagues through the torch-lit hallways, his pulse pounding in his ears, his mouth and throat so dry he could barely swallow.

He reached the curtained entrance to the great hall and froze there, suddenly unable to recall a single word of the saga he was to recite. As he stood trembling, unable either to move forward or run away, his father stepped in front of him, laid a hand on his shoulder, and murmured, "All the sensations that you are feeling now are not just normal but necessary, for how else would you understand and convey the feelings of a hero setting out on a perilous quest?" Adding, "And I know that you, too, are a hero, and you will conquer your fears, and you will triumph!" he stepped aside, pulled the curtain open, and pointed through it. "Now go!"

Herrwn went.

Walking through the entrance to stand in the center of the floor—the chief priests and priestesses seated at the high table in front of him and the ordinary ones at their lower tables stretching around him on both sides—he understood truly for the first time how Pwendorwn must have felt facing the ranks of the giants and surrounded by an army of ogres.

Then, as his father had promised, his fear of forgetting his lines fell away and the power of the tale came over him. Instead of reciting from memory, he found himself describing what he was seeing before him—and sensed that his audience was not just listening to the story but was living it along with him.

When he'd finished, he heard the wave of applause and saw his uncles slapping his openly grinning father on the back, but what he remembered most clearly was his mother looking at him with love and pride and speaking loudly enough for her words to carry across the room, "That was wonderful!"

His mother's praise had capped off the intoxicating sense of fulfillment he'd felt at that moment—a sensation he felt again each time he completed a successful oration, which he'd done almost every night for the past forty-five years.

But instead of being there to bolster and encourage Caelym on the night he gave his first independent oration in the shrine's great chamber, Herrwn had sent his disciple—Caelendra's son—off with nothing more than a querulous admonition to wash himself before putting on his robes.

Herrwn shook his head at the memory, reviving the headache which had almost faded entirely and causing a dribble of slime to ooze out from his soggy headdress and down the back of his neck.

As if reading his thoughts, Olyrrwd said, "It may not be the best oration ever, but he's there to give it and not floating dead at the bottom of the Bottomless Falls."

There was no arguing with that. Herrwn rested against his pillows and began composing his list of reassurances to help revive Caelym's spirits when he got back, beginning with stories about great orators whose first performances had been dismal— condolences that, it later turned out, were unnecessary.

"She—she—praised me! She said I told the tale well! She looks forward to hearing me tell another!"

It was close to midnight when Caelym returned to the healing chamber. Barely able to contain himself, he danced around the room, repeating segments of his oration that had gained Feywn's particular nod of approval.

In view of his own failure to support his disciple's first independent oration, Herrwn was both touched and grateful that Feywn—who, in all honesty, had never seemed to view Herrwn's nightly performances as more than a ritual she was required to sit through—had been so kind and encouraging about an underprepared beginner's performance.

Olyrrwd, however, just grumbled, "I'm sure it was a top-notch tale and can see that you are terribly proud of yourself, but you do have other duties and—as you've seemed to have forgotten—it is almost midnight!"

The remark (and the gruff tone in which it was spoken) brought Caelym both literally and figuratively down to earth. He'd just capered along a bench and leaped into the air in a spinning pirouette. Landing on his toes, he dropped his heels down and brushed his hands off on his (actually Herrwn's) robe, his expression and tone of voice suddenly solemn. "Forgive my excessive and undignified display, Master. As you say, it is almost midnight and so time to open the windows through which the fleeing spirits of brain fever and bewilderment will rush out at the sound of the 'Be Gone' chant."

After hurrying to the window and then to the counter next to Herrwn's bed, Caelym fished another slimy goat's liver out of its crock, wrapped it in a linen band, and changed it for the older dressing around Herrwn's head, chanting, *"Be gone from this place of rest and healing! Be gone into the dark from whence you came! Be gone! Be gone! And trouble us no more!"* in a reasonably grave voice with only the faintest undertone of elation.

Whether it was the restorative effects of the goat liver compress, the protection of the "Be Gone" chant, or just getting a good night's sleep, Herrwn woke up the next morning feeling entirely fit and, after nodding obediently at the lengthy list of precautions Caelym recited to him, escaped from the healing chamber determined to re-establish himself as the master of his classroom—where Caelym was his disciple and not his physician.

While Caelym was practicing his part in that evening's saga, Herrwn had time to think about the previous day's events, and he came to the conclusion that even though Olyrrwd had decided against bringing his accusations before the High Council, it remained Herrwn's duty as the head of their order to confront Ossiam and hear what defense he might give.

Chapter 55:

Herrwn's Judgment

Following a subdued and awkward midday meal during which neither Olyrrwd nor Ossiam made eye contact with each other, Olyrrwd herded Caelym off to the healing chamber without any of the usual departing salutations.

Taking advantage of the scraping of chairs and murmuring of priests and priestesses leaving the table, Herrwn turned to Ossiam and said softly, "I must speak to you in private," at the precise moment Ossiam said the exact same words to him, adding, "Will you come to my chambers, or shall I come to the classroom?"

The conversation Herrwn anticipated was not one he wanted to have where anyone else could hear—so, realizing Benyon was likely to be in and out of the classroom, he answered, "Your chambers will do."

◆◆◆

Herrwn hadn't been inside the room at the top of the oracle's tower since his long-ago lessons in the basics of augury. Looking around through the haze of the steaming cauldron, it seemed to him that nothing had changed. Dismissing the feeling that his uncle, Ossaerwn, by whom he'd always been somewhat intimidated, was standing in the shadows, he cleared his throat and began, "You must explain what happened yesterday!"

"I? You might ask Olyrrwd!" Ossiam's opening words were irate and became more so as he went on, "Only I see you already have—and I can well guess what groundless accusations he has made in private to you that he does not dare make openly before the High Council!"

Unwilling to be put off, Herrwn crossed his arms and looked Ossiam straight in the eye. "I have spoken with Olyrrwd, and now I am speaking to you—and *I* will decide whether this is a matter for the High Council."

"And what is it that I must answer for?"

"That, whether intentionally or unintentionally, you put the apprentice entrusted to your care in mortal danger—and before you say anything more, I must tell you I know that to be true, and I know that if Olyrrwd had not rescued him, Caelym would have thrown himself over the edge of the cliff above the Bottomless Falls! And now I want to know why you have done this!"

"I—I never—"

There was something in how Ossiam clasped his hands to his chest in a gesture of offended innocence that was so much like the scene in Herrwn's recent dream that he half-expected to hear his cousin protest, "I never did—or, if I did, it was only a jest to tease Olyrrwd . . ."

But Ossiam only said, "I never imagined," as he staggered backward to collapse on a chair. He slumped forward and buried his face in his hands, and for several moments his shoulders shook and heaved before he looked up and repeated, "I never imagined . . . How could he have thought I meant . . ." He managed to steady his voice. "You must believe me—I never thought—"

Though touched by Ossiam's abject distress, Herrwn persisted.

"What did you think? That you could put the words of the Dy Na Ma into the mouth of a fifteen-year-old boy, whatever his parentage, and have its spell succeed? That the blame for its failure rested with your pupil and not with you? That telling that pupil to whom your word is law that he was unfit to join our order and sending him away with a vial of poison in one hand and a knife in the other would have no untoward result?"

"But that's not how it was!" Ossiam put his hands up and grabbed fistfuls of his hair as he shook his head. "True, I set the boy a test to see whether he had the gift to be an oracle, but I left the choice of the incantation to him, never imagining that he would use that one. I regret now that I spoke so harshly to him, but I did so out of my fear and dismay at the risk he took in using it. It was out of my last hope that I gave him a second chance with a simpler task, which he failed as well, leaving me no choice but to accept the truth—that even though he is the son of our forever mourned chief priestess, Caelendra, he has no aptitude as an oracle, and so I could do nothing else but dismiss him and could not—for his sake as well as our shrine's—give in to his pleading to continue in studies for which he was ill-suited. I assumed that he would recover from his disappointment in time and would keep up his lessons with you and Olyrrwd. Whatever Olyrrwd may have claimed, I swear to you on my sacred staff and necklace, I didn't put either the vial of sacred elixir or the ceremonial dagger in his hands; I but cast both down on the floor in my deep disappointment. How could I have imagined that when he picked them up, it was for such a purpose?"

Rallying enough to straighten his shoulders, Ossiam regained something of his earlier injured dignity as he added, "If I had any thought that a pupil in my care had left my chamber bent on self-destruction, do you think I would have calmly come to you and started a game of Stones?"

Herrwn hadn't planned to bring up the painful revelation of Ossiam cheating at Stones, but it slipped out. "I would not have believed that—but then I would not have believed that you, my cousin and our shrine's chief oracle, could have taken advantage of my indisposition to toss the dice out of turn and change their score to suit yourself!"

"Is that what Olyrrwd told you?"

"It is!"

"Well, I am telling you that he charged into the room shouting incoherent accusations—so crazed that he, our shrine's chief healer, never even looked to see how badly you were hurt when he knocked your chair over! I, of course, was more concerned with your welfare than any attack on myself and demanded he do his duty as a physician. If, in my shock at his behavior and out of my concern for you, I dropped the dice or accidentally shifted any of the stones, I cannot recall it now—nor does it matter, since he tossed the board off the table and continued to shriek until I finally came to realize that he was saying some servant claimed Caelym had left the shrine intent on self-destruction. It was not out of any thought that this was true but only to send Olyrrwd away so I could see to your needs that I said the one thing I could think of—that when Caelym first pleaded with me to become my disciple, we'd been standing together on the overlook above the Bottomless Falls, and since he'd just been dismissed from his studies, he might have returned there. But now . . . but now . . . if what you say is true . . ."

In his vigorous denials of intentional wrongdoing, Ossiam had risen from his chair, waving his arms and stamping his foot. With this last, faltering line, he sank down again, and again covered his face with his hands. "But if what you say is true . . . If Caelym took my dismissal so wrongly and might actually have . . ." Looking at Herrwn, his eyes brimming with tears, Ossiam said in a hollow voice, "And if you, the head of our order, truly believe that I did this out of malice, then you must take my staff and my necklace."

Herrwn looked back at Ossiam as he pondered what to say. Considered side by side, both of his cousins' accounts fit the facts before him. There was no question in his mind about Olyrrwd's version of the actual events, but knowing the readiness of both men to infer the worst motives in each other, it was not impossible that Ossiam was equally sincere. And to take the symbols of a high priest's office from him was an act as irrevocable as the chief priestess casting him out.

"I will not take your staff and necklace, for I do not believe that you did this intentionally. But hear me, my cousin, if I should ever find out that I am mistaken—dear as you are to me, I will take those things from you, and I will expel you from our order. Now, it is my greatest wish that we will never need to speak of this again."

Chapter 56:

The Fourth Corner

"And then I told him I would take his staff and his necklace if I ever found out he'd used the power of his position to do harm instead of good!"

Olyrrwd had rolled his eyes when Herrwn told him how shocked and distressed Ossiam had been to learn that Caelym had almost thrown himself over the edge of the cliff above the Bottomless Falls. He raised one eyebrow and lowered the other at hearing Ossiam's explanation that he'd dropped the dice accidentally and moved the playing stones without thinking about what he was doing. He muttered, "Like what?" at hearing Ossiam's account of giving Herrwn aid until Benyon arrived.

And now, as Herrwn repeated his own stern parting admonition, he scoffed, "Well, that must have made him shake in his sandals!"

In view of Olyrrwd's open skepticism of an innocent explanation for Ossiam's actions, Herrwn was braced for an escalation of the hostilities between his cousins. He was both surprised and relieved that, over the ensuing months, relations between the two took a turn for the better.

No longer deriding Ossiam's every pronouncement and prophesy, Olyrrwd reserved his challenges for matters of substance—and then began his refutation on some point of agreement (if only their shared devotion to the Goddess) and delivered his rebuttal calmly, respectfully, and without even a hint of sarcasm. Ossiam likewise adopted a more civil attitude so that their exchanges, both public and private, were conducted with courteous formality.

Herrwn had not been fully aware of how much the hostility between his cousins had weighed on him until it ended, and he said as much to Olyrrwd, who responded with touching sincerity, "I should have listened to you sooner, for you were right all along—I badgered him and he tormented me, and since I cannot make him a better person, I must be better myself."

They'd just returned to the classroom and were still talking over the unexpected and unorthodox outcome of what had started out as an impromptu and informal meeting with Ossiam, during which the oracle had eloquently waived any claim to Caelym and, going further, had given effusive blessing to both his entrance into the third level of study and to his double discipleship as both a bard and a healer.

It was precisely the sort of thing that in the past would have led to a prolonged and fruitless exchange between them over the oracle's motives, but while Olyrrwd had countered, "It's just his way of weaseling back into your good graces," when Herrwn asserted that this had been a peace offering, he said it without rancor and with an undertone of resigned forbearance. And when, still pondering the unexpected turn of events, Herrwn insisted, "In any case, he could not have meant for Caelym to think that this was to be the council determining his entrance to the priesthood, and he must have been just as surprised as we were," Olyrrwd merely said, "So it would seem."

As that was an ambiguous response, Herrwn felt it necessary to press the issue further, pointing out that Ossiam had not said what it was he wanted to speak about when he asked them to join him in the high tower that morning, that he had not given Caelym any more than a casual nod as he stood up from the breakfast table, and that he had looked genuinely astonished when the three of them came down from the tower stairwell to see Caelym sitting on the stone bench in the antechamber, dressed in pristine robes, his hands clasped together in the traditional pose of an initiate-in-waiting.

Whatever had given Caelym the notion they had gone to the tower to decide his future as a Druid priest, it was clear from how he'd looked at them—his dark eyes shining with expectation—that this was what he thought.

Herrwn had glanced at Olyrrwd, who shrugged and nodded. They both knew that Caelym was already doing lessons well in advance of the second level of studies. They'd long since agreed to share the final phase of his training. Now, with Ossiam's approval to proceed, there was no reason to wait another two years, so Herrwn had nodded back and they simultaneously put out their fingers to touch Caelym's forehead, acknowledging him as their disciple and welcoming him to the fellowship of priests of the shrine of the Great Mother Goddess.

Sliding off the bench and down onto his knees, Caelym had recited the traditional pledge of his eternal gratitude. Then, having run through a flowing litany of the high deities by whom he solemnly swore to prove himself worthy of the honor they bestowed on him, he asked in an anxious, boyish voice, "And will I be given a quest?"

"Of course you will be given a quest!" Ossiam spoke out before either Herrwn or Olyrrwd could respond.

Overjoyed, Caelym leaped up, announced he had to tell "the girls" he was a real priest now and was going on a spirit quest, and went off dancing and turning cartwheels before Herrwn could temporize that so long as he continued to attend diligently to his studies, he would, in all likelihood, prove himself ready to undertake his quest at the ordained age of eighteen.

As Caelym bounded off, Herrwn turned to remonstrate with Ossiam for speaking out of turn only to see the oracle's shadow flitting up the stairs to the tower.

"Well, that's that!" Olyrrwd said in a surprisingly restrained tone of voice.

He didn't say anything else until they'd walked back to the classroom and he'd gone to the cupboard where he kept his private store of medicinal brews, poured two cups of elderberry wine, handed one to Herrwn, and lifted his own, saying, "Here's to our new disciple!"

After sharing the toast, Herrwn had begun the conversation cautiously, opening it with praise for the exceptional civility of Olyrrwd's interactions with Ossiam. Now, encouraged by Olyrrwd's calm demeanor, he ventured to ask, "So what do you think of Caelym's going on his spirit quest when he will be but sixteen on his next birthday?"

They'd gravitated to the warmth of the hearth and were standing side by side, looking at the flames rather than at each other. Out of the corner of his eye, Herrwn could see that Olyrrwd, who tended to gulp down his wine when he was upset, was drinking it slowly and swirling it between sips.

"Sixteen is too young for some things"—Olyrrwd lowered his bushy eyebrows and gazed into the little whirlpool he'd created—"but may be just the right time for him to go hunting for his animal spirit."

"Do you really think so?" Herrwn was surprised and disconcerted that Olyrrwd did not see the risks of Caelym's undertaking his spirit quest two years earlier than normal.

Instead of clarifying why he thought Caelym, young and impulsive as he was, was ready to leave the safety of the valley for the dangers of his spirit quest, Olyrrwd shifted his gaze from Herrwn to the shelf where he kept his Ghost Stones board and back to Herrwn again before saying, "What I think is that we've rounded the fourth corner."

To someone unfamiliar with Ghost Stones, Olyrrwd's reply would have made no sense. Herrwn, however, knew both the game and his cousin so well that its meaning, though layered, was all too clear.

In the game of Stones, "rounding a corner" referred to a player moving the hindmost of his stones past a corner space and onto the next side of the game's track.

Rounding the board's fourth corner had a particular significance. With only this last section of the track left to play, all banter and bravado fell away and it was rare to hear more than the tumbling of the dice, the soft tap of the stones being moved, and, perhaps, the drumming of a player's fingers on the table.

So, in part, what Olyrrwd meant by saying they'd rounded the fourth corner was that Herrwn should not hold out hope for a genuine reconciliation between his cousins but rather accept that they were simply too caught up in their stratagems against each other to waste any effort in open hostilities.

There was more to it than that, however.

Because "rounding the fourth corner" meant playing out the game's final phase, it had become a euphemism for the coming end of a person's life.

This latter meaning reminded Herrwn of the afternoon seven years earlier when they'd stood together on the shore of the lake and Olyrrwd had skipped a stone across the water. He'd counted the number of times it bounced that day and announced, "Twelve! I have twelve years left."

Unable to envision his future without Olyrrwd in it, Herrwn repeated what he'd said then—"You are not an oracle, and skipping stones is not augury!"

Evading the thrust of Herrwn's assertion, Olyrrwd muttered, "You're right, I'm not an oracle—and I have real work to do if Caelie's going to be ready for his quest."

With that, he put down his cup, picked up his walking sticks, and lurched out of the classroom, leaving Herrwn feeling deeply disconcerted.

PART VII

Spirit Quest

Within the shrine of the Great Mother Goddess, it was felt to be in poor taste to imply that some Druids were better than others, so regardless of whether an initiate was expected to be an ordinary or an elite priest he was inducted with the same formulaic words of welcome. The unspoken distinction between those who were embarking on the nine years of intensive study required to become high priests and those who would complete the training required to carry out routine ritual functions within a matter of months was that the former were sent on a spirit quest and latter were not.

The quest might be as brief as overnight or last for weeks, but it always entailed accomplishing a task divined by the shrine's oracle in the expectation that through fulfilling that task the quester's spirit guide—most often an animal, bird, or fish for bards and healers, and a spirit from the other world for oracles—would reveal itself in a dream or a vision.

Not only was a disciple's spirit quest his initiation into the long and arduous path to joining the highest ranks of their order, for most it was the only time in their lives they ventured outside of the valley.

Chapter 57:

Provisions

"Caelym can take no more on his quest than he can carry in a pack." Herrwn held open the curtain to what Olyrrwd now referred to as his workroom, although Herrwn could see little space for anyone to work between the piles of provisions and paraphernalia that filled most of the chamber.

Huffing, "We'll pick the best of it and keep the rest for later," Olyrrwd dumped his armload of leather goods onto a bed already buried under a stack of tunics, capes, and cloaks.

By "later" Herrwn supposed Olyrrwd meant some future time when the entire population of the valley decided to go off on a quest, since all the other beds in the chamber that had once served as the sleeping quarters for a dozen Druids-in-training were as full as that one.

When Caelym moved his things out of the students' sleeping quarters and into the bedchamber with Herrwn and Olyrrwd, Herrwn had presumed the vacated room would be left in readiness for the next generation of pupils. Olyrrwd, however, quickly appropriated it to store his growing collection of "things Caelym might need on our . . . er . . . his quest."

Unlike Herrwn, who continued to have grave misgivings about Caelym's undertaking his spirit quest at so young an age, Olyrrwd threw himself into preparing for the event with a zeal that recalled the enthusiasm with which he'd planned for his own spirit quest forty-five years earlier. Sacrificing time that might otherwise have been devoted to lessons in the healing chamber, he sent Caelym off with the best of the village hunters and fishermen to "learn those arts from masters" and busied himself gathering supplies and implements for what he regularly slipped into calling "our quest."

Copper cups, bowls, and cooking pots and an assortment of waterskins were stacked on a bed just inside the doorway. Clothing—deerskin shirts and pants, fur-lined cloaks and hooded tunics—were separated into piles on two beds that had been turned sideways and pushed against the wall. A bed at the far end of the room was covered with layers of hides and furs that Olyrrwd had explained could serve as sleeping mats, blankets, or tents.

Caelym's former bed was spread with fishing spears of all shapes and sizes, along with hunting bows and matching quivers of arrows. The only clear space was on the table next to the bed, and half of that was taken up with surgical implements, pouches of powders and flasks of elixirs, along with a mix of oddments—extra arrowheads and spear points, coils of twine and rope, a tinderbox, and a rugged-looking knife presumably meant for cutting wood rather than lancing boils.

Sighing, Herrwn let the curtain drop.

The spirit quest was a sacred rite of passage—not, as Olyrrwd seemed to think, a chance for Caelym to spend the summer hunting and fishing. With this clearly in mind, Herrwn's own teaching sessions included careful rehearsal of the preparatory rites and rituals, and repeated admonitions that Caelym's time in the mountains be spent in intense introspection, delving deeply into his innermost uncertainties and yearnings.

It had been Herrwn's hope—and, frankly, his expectation— that once the short, dark days of the late fall and winter set in, he would be able to get his student's attention back to his own demanding field of study. Instead, Olyrrwd decided it was not enough for Caelym to know how to hunt and fish, he had to know how to make his own bows and arrows and fishing spears, so Herrwn found himself sharing his disciple with an odd assortment of village artisans Olyrrwd had enlisted to teach Caelym their crafts.

"Arrows get lost and spear shafts break, and knowing how to make his own is half the fu—" Olyrrwd paused and cleared his throat. "Umm . . . spiritual revelation."

With mountains of implements and supplies filling the side chamber, some of the excess had spilled out and was beginning to encroach on the classroom itself. Looking at a dozen pairs of boots lined up on the shelf under the wall, Olyrrwd muttered, "Two pairs should be enough. He can wear the high ones and carry the short ones. Which do you think he should take?"

"The ones that will keep his feet the driest!" It was the sound of rain drumming against the window shutters that put this answer into Herrwn's mind, and he was relieved to have Olyrrwd nod vigorously, saying, "The sealskin then! I thought so myself!"

The storm outside was the first of many to sweep through the valley in what was the most severe winter in Herrwn's memory.

By comparison, the atmosphere within the shrine was remarkably peaceful.

Ever since Olyrrwd's cautionary hint that the schism between himself and Ossiam was as deep as ever, Herrwn had been bracing himself for a resurgence of their hostilities, especially at the autumn equinox and then the winter solstice. Both rituals had, in the past, been occasions for particularly incendiary prophesies from Ossiam (or, more correctly, from his frenzied and unpredictable spirit guide), and he shuddered to think of Olyrrwd's response to any vision that foreshadowed doom in Caelym's coming quest.

As it turned out, he need not have worried. Both the equinox and the solstice came and went with only mild and generally reassuring portends delivered in Ossiam's own voice.

Meanwhile, Caelym managed to keep up with his recitations and his work in the healing chamber, along with the lessons in arrow-making and excursions to the upper reaches of the valley to practice making shelters out of evergreen branches, while still finding time to spend with the five young priestesses, the older three of whom were showing signs of ripening womanhood.

Chapter 58:

The Task

Late-season storms continued to batter the valley, adding to Herrwn's misgivings about Caelym's going on his spirit quest that year, but each time he tried to suggest putting it off, Caelym turned to Olyrrwd and Olyrrwd said, "No weather is bad weather so long as you are prepared for it."

Possibly to reassure himself, Olyrrwd said those exact words again while he and Herrwn were waiting for Caelym to finish his final cleansing bath, don his ceremonial robes, and emerge from the priests' bath chamber ready to leave for the Sacred Grove.

The shutters were closed and the priests' quarters were lit with a single candle, symbolizing the concept that in venturing out first to the shrine's Sacred Grove, where the chief oracle would carry out the augury divining the initiate's quest, and then up into the equally sacred northern mountains to accomplish that task and acquire his spirit guide, Caelym was leaving the limited vision of an ordinary priest for the limitless horizon of a disciple on the path to ultimate wisdom.

Standing with Olyrrwd in the darkened classroom, Herrwn was reminded of Caelym's arrival there—shrieking and kicking—ten years earlier. This time, however, the shrill screams were the winds outside the window and the banging was the shutters being pounded by hail stones.

"I am ready!" Despite the storm outside, Caelym's voice resounded with excitement when he swung open the great double doors—scrubbed, perfumed, and radiant in the robes that Herrwn had worn on his own Divining Day.

Olyrrwd nodded proudly. He shouldered the healer's bag, which was as much the symbol of his rank as the shrine's chief physician as Herrwn's staff was the symbol of his as their chief bard, and gripped his walking sticks—looking as eager as if he were starting the journey along with Caelym.

With a final glance at the bulging pack that Olyrrwd had assured him held everything Caelym would need for his adventure, Herrwn took up his staff and led the way out of the shrine and through what was now a veritable gale of freezing rain to the altar, where Ossiam and the rest of the priests and priestesses were already gathered.

Even in the relative shelter of the grove, hail pelted down through the branches of the towering oaks, and a cutting wind tore at Herrwn's cloak and robes as he raised his staff, signaling for the ceremony to begin.

Whether the goat being dragged to the altar was shaking from fear or cold, it seemed too numb to struggle when it was lifted onto the stone slab. After its last tremors were over and its entrails had begun to darken, Ossiam continued to stare down at them. His audience pulled their cloaks tighter as they waited for the more or less expected proclamation that Caelym was to climb to the top of a mountain, recite incantations calling on his spirit guide to reveal itself to him in a dream, and go to sleep in order to have the dream.

Looking up, Ossiam opened his mouth, closed it, then opened and closed it again. Clenching his jaw, he gripped the edge of the altar. His whole body shuddered. For a third time, his mouth opened, and out of it the voice of the female spirit from the other world who'd been quiescent for almost five years shrieked, *"He must go now, at once, into the mountains to seek his animal spirit guide! He must go on this journey as animals go, without human clothes or weapons! He may not return until he has learned to speak the language of his animal spirit's tribe and to sing their songs and tell their stories!"*

With that, Ossiam's mouth snapped shut, his head sagged, and he collapsed to his knees. As his two assistant priests rushed to his aid, the priests and priestesses circled around the altar gave a collective gasp. Even if humans and animals could still talk to each other, which they could not, going into the mountains in this storm without clothes or tools or a flint was not a quest—it was a death sentence.

Herrwn thought fast. As the shrine's chief priest, he could override Ossiam in ordinary circumstances—a dispute at the dinner table or a debate in the council—but that authority had never, to his knowledge, been raised or tested when an oracle was making a divined pronouncement. It was a question even more complicated in this case, since it was not Ossiam himself who was speaking but the female spirit from the other world. The answer presumably hinged on the rank that spirit held, but while Ossiam had frequently alluded to the importance of the affairs his female familiar had in the realm beyond death when he explained her erratic entrances and exits, her precise position in the pantheon of divine beings was shrouded in mystery and remained unknown to anyone except, possibly, Ossiam himself.

With no way to resolve those questions short of a meeting of the High Council, Herrwn made up his mind. He would refuse his consent to allow his disciple to accept this quest. Whatever the consequences in this world or the next, they would be his and not Caelym's. He was lifting his staff for the crowd's attention, but before he could speak, Olyrrwd stepped forward to address the still-kneeling Caelym in the matter-of-fact voice he used in describing the treatment of a troublesome fever.

"But, of course, as animals have hide and fur, you will go dressed in leather and a fur cloak. And as animals have fangs and claws, you will go armed with a knife and spear. And as you are my disciple, not even the spirit of she who speaks through the lips of our great oracle will object to your going forth bearing a token of our sacred order."

Caelym, who'd remained uncharacteristically silent until then, spoke up, sounding very much his buoyant and enthusiastic self. "I will embark on the quest that has been divined for me to seek my animal spirit guide, and I vow that I will return having learned to speak the language of its tribe and to sing their songs and tell their stories!"

Rising up smoothly, as if in a long-practiced rite, he cast off his priestly robes to reveal that he was already dressed in snug-fitting deerskin garb, and instead of sandals he was wearing thick leather boots. Stepping away from the altar, he donned a fur-lined tunic and cloak that, as it turned out, Olyrrwd had been holding in a bundle under his own cloak, and then knelt down again and reverently held out his hands, palms up, to take the healer's bag that Olyrrwd presented with the grave pronouncement, "With this, the token of our sacred orders, I give you my blessing on the sacred task you have been given."

Of all the gathered priests and priestesses, only Herrwn was close enough to hear what Olyrrwd whispered to Caelym while handing him the bulging satchel—"Animals also have dens, and they have the wisdom to go to them, curl up, and stay dry when it rains." This sounded more like a specific instruction than a formal blessing, but Caelym seemed as heartened by Olyrrwd's parting words as Herrwn had been by his father's benediction—"Seek high, sleep deep, and dream well, my son, and may the Great Goddess watch over you as your mother would"—on the day he set off on his own spirit quest.

Still on his knees, Caelym was close to eye level with Olyrrwd, and the two exchanged a long look before Caelym rose to his feet again, bowed reverently to Feywn, waved cheerfully to the five young priestesses, and went skipping merrily off through the rain.

By then even Feywn, though standing under a canopy held up by her servants, was soaked, her thick woolen cape dripping water from its hem. She'd been silent throughout the ritual and remained silent now, as she raised her hand to signal that the ceremony was over and turned to lead the way back to the shrine. Ossiam, supported on either side by Iddwran and Ogdwen, staggered after her. Olyrrwd elbowed ahead of Herrwn to get in line next, hardly leaning on his walking sticks at all and humming a tune under his breath that Herrwn recognized as the refrain of a song he had made up years before to annoy Ossiam in the midst of a dispute.

Herrwn cast a final glance over his shoulder in the direction of the path Caelym had taken, murmured his father's blessing, and fell into the line hurrying to the shelter of the shrine.

◆◆◆

Back in their bedchamber, as Herrwn and Olyrrwd were changing into their dry robes, Herrwn ventured to wonder aloud whether the cedar branch shelters Caelym had practiced making during the past weeks happened to be located along the route he'd be taking out of the valley and into the northern mountains.

"Well, where else?" Olyrrwd answered cheerfully, apparently unconcerned about the severity of the weather or the fact that Caelym hadn't taken the backpack with extra clothes and supplies or his bow and arrows or fishing spears.

"No point in being weighed down with an overloaded pack," he went on in as jovial a voice as Herrwn had heard him use in years, adding, "Besides, it's half the fu—spiritual growth—to live on your wits and skill."

"But the task . . ." Even as he spoke the word, Herrwn shivered at the memory of the harsh voice of Ossiam's female spirit shrieking that Caelym's task was to learn to speak the language of his animal spirit's tribe.

Olyrrwd shook his head in mock consternation. "Herrwn, revered elder cousin, you who are our shrine's chief priest and master bard, I cannot believe that you of all people should have to be reminded that it was the animal tribes who, for entirely understandable reasons, vowed never to speak in human language ever again—or that there is nothing in any version of the tales to say that humans cannot learn to speak the language of animals. I myself can say without boasting that I am quite fluent in cat, dog, and owl, as well as being reasonably conversant in raven and squirrel."

With a smug grin, Olyrrwd sauntered off, his walking sticks under his arm, whistling the tune he'd hummed on his way back from the Sacred Grove, as cocky as if he'd just won a hard-fought game of Stones.

Chapter 59:

Ossiam's Ordeal

After Olyrrwd left the classroom, Herrwn began rehearsing his evening's recitation only to be interrupted by a sudden rapping on the door. Before he could give his permission to enter, Benyon burst in, crying, "Master Herrwn, Master Ossiam lies prostrate in his chamber, refusing food and mumbling strange chants. Should I send for Master Olyrrwd?"

Frustrated that the intrusion came just as he felt himself on the verge of a new and insightful rendering of the hero's opening declamation, Herrwn was unintentionally abrupt in replying, "Master Ossiam is always left fatigued following a difficult divination. His chants are no doubt a part of his self-healing, and—" Here he caught himself before saying anything that might give away the hostility between his cousins. Clearing his throat, he finished, "—I do not think sending for Master Olyrrwd's attendance will be necessary." Later he would regret his terseness, but at the time he was simply glad to have Benyon bow his way out of the room.

Herrwn had not recited *Gwalmwn and the Wolf King* in several years. Besides needing to practice it, he also had to decide on which of two alternate endings to choose. With equally sound arguments for the happier, more romantic conclusion on one side and the sadder, more realistic one on the other, Herrwn didn't think any more of Ossiam's condition until he made his entrance into the great hall that evening and saw that the oracle's place at the high table remained empty.

Was his lack of concern over his cousin's welfare due in some measure to his own feelings of dismay—even anger—for the part Ossiam had played in Caelym's undertaking so perilous a quest at so young an age? Herrwn was ashamed to admit that this might be so and determined to go to the oracle's tower when he finished his oration.

◆◆◆

As soon as he had taken his final bow, Herrwn hurried off and climbed the stairs to the oracle's tower. Finding the door to the oracle's chamber ajar, he pushed it open. Ossiam was lying against his pillows while Iddwran fanned him with a cluster of eagle feathers and Ogdwen knelt by his bedside, holding a silver bowl of broth in one hand and putting a spoon to his lips with the other.

Weakly raising his head, Ossiam whispered, "Herrwn, you have come before it is too late! I feared that all but my faithful Iddwran and Ogdwen had forsaken me!"

"Ossiam, do not strain yourself! I will get Olyrrwd."

Herrwn would have turned and rushed down the stairs then, but Ossiam cried out in a stronger voice than seemed possible in his wasted, pitiful state, "No!" and then, in a weaker, barely audible tone, murmured, "There is nothing he can do! This is the price I pay for attempting to defy her."

"Her? The Goddess?"

"Her! Her! She who speaks through me!" Ossiam struggled up onto his elbows and looked around wildly, as if expecting his inner spirit to be lurking in the surrounding shadows.

"Iddwran, quick—another swallow of the draught that she will sleep, and I may speak while I yet have the strength."

Iddwran, who was still kneeling at Ossiam's side, poured a spoonful of dark violet liquid from a small silver vial and dribbled it between the oracle's trembling lips.

Ossiam closed his eyes and breathed a shuddering breath, then opened them again and said in a rasping whisper, "When I saw that dreadful message in those cursed entrails, I knew this task was too perilous for a sixteen-year-old boy, even one born to our once chief priestess and embodiment of the Great Mother God-dess, and I determined that I would not speak it—instead I would declare that I saw nothing and that Caelym's quest must wait until his eighteenth birthday. But she commanded me that I must. *I won't!* I resisted her demand, clenching my teeth. *You will!* Her voice filled my very being, but still I fought against her until—after what I know now was moments but then seemed like hours—all went black, and I knew nothing more until I woke up here and my faithful Iddwran and Ogdwen told me what happened—that she had overpowered my resistance and spoke through me, making that fatal decree."

Ossiam slumped back. Staring at the ceiling, he moaned, "I should have withstood her. Even at the cost of my life, I should have held out. Now it is too late, and I must bear the weight of my failure forever more!"

"You must not be so harsh with yourself!" Glad that he could lift the terrible burden of guilt from his despondent cousin, Herrwn rushed on to give Ossiam the reassurance he himself had received from Olyrrwd—that Caelym had everything he needed for his wilderness trek, that he knew how to find shelter along his way and survive in any weather.

"So you see, the task is not impossible at all, because, as Olyr-rwd has reminded me, though the animal tribes vowed never to speak in human language, that is not to say humans cannot learn to speak the language of animals, and with Caelym's memory and facility for recitation, I believe—as Olyrrwd does—that he will accomplish all his quest requires of him."

The color returned to Ossiam's cheeks, and his voice, while still tentative, was no longer weak and shaky as he asked, "So, then, Olyrrwd does not blame me or hold me accountable for what the spirit which speaks through me has said today?"

"I'm sure he does not! I will go get him now, shall I?"

"No! That won't be necessary." Ossiam's voice was quite recov-ered now, and he sounded like himself again as he went on, "The news you have brought me has been more salutary than any potion, even one brewed by our master physician. I think now I simply need to sleep."

After bidding Ossiam, along with Iddwran and Ogdwen, a good night and good dreams, Herrwn returned to his own quarters, changed into his night robes, got into bed, and blew out the candle. The shutters of the classroom windows were no longer rattling, and the sleeping chamber was quiet except for Olyrrwd's rumbling snores and his soft wheeze—which sounded to Herrwn's ear like the purring of a contented cat.

Chapter 60:

Herrwn's Dream

The weather improved rapidly in the days and weeks that followed Caelym's departure, something Herrwn took as confirmation of his belief that the Goddess was "watching over Her own." Olyrrwd was, if anything, more sanguine than Herrwn, although he was inclined to give himself credit for seeing their disciple was fully prepared for his adventure—as he cheerfully repeated, "Come rain or come shine."

With the warmth of an early spring melting the last of the ice on the lake, bringing buds out on the trees and calling new shoots up from garden beds, there was a renewed sense of industry throughout the shrine. Priestesses were hard at work pruning and planting. Olyrrwd set Moelwyn to scrubbing out empty cauldrons in the healing chamber, and Herrwn began the opening epic of the nine great sagas, an interconnected series of stories that spanned five generations of semi-divine heroes battling against demons, ogres, and one-eyed giants.

Having already finished recounting the birth and childhood adventures of Elderond, the hero destined to be the first of the Goddess's mortal lovers, on the night of the full moon following the spring equinox, Herrwn gave a rendition of Dwrrwort's Deception, a story in which Elderond was lured into an ambush set for him by his nemesis, the ogre king Dwrrwort.

The performance went well, and the part in which the Great Goddess's divine granddaughter, Ethelwen, saves the gravely wounded hero with a magic spell that brings him back from the very brink of death earned a loud burst of applause.

As he fell asleep that night, Herrwn drifted into a dream in which he was lying on his back in a pool of blood. Before he could feel dread or pain, he heard an ethereal chanting, and the blood began to swirl around him and then flowed backward into his wounds, which closed and healed as he looked down at them. Looking up, he saw a shimmering figure he somehow knew to be Ethelwen standing over him, beckoning him to get up and come with her. The path she took led through the woods to the meadow where he'd once seen Annwr dancing with the shrine's little priestesses.

Annwr wasn't there, but the girls were. They were older now and dressed in the long gowns he'd seen them wearing the week before when he'd passed them at their lessons in the shrine's garden, but they were singing the same songs and were dancing just as gaily around the glade as they had that day all those years ago.

Gwenydd led the line, twirling gracefully, her long, dark hair blowing in the breeze. The twins, their hair plaited in braids, bounded along after her like a pair of leaping hares. Arianna and Cyri followed behind the twins—Arianna swirling and swaying with the sensuousness she'd inherited from her mother, while Cyri skipped along with the wholehearted enthusiasm of a child riding a hobbyhorse.

As he watched from the edge of the meadow, Herrwn realized there was a sixth little girl dancing among the rest—a dainty elfin child so pale she seemed almost transparent.

It was his daughter.

Lillywen had not aged since her death. She was still wearing the soft silk gown she'd been buried in, but despite her waiflike appearance, she leaped and frolicked as joyfully as the others— her light blond hair shining in the sun and her dark brown eyes alight with merriment. As the other girls danced past Herrwn, Lillywen stopped and looked up at him, drawing in her lower lip the way she had when something worried her. Then, seeming to realize the others were leaving her behind, she turned on her toes and darted after them just as the forest and the meadow were fading and changing back into his sleeping chamber.

◆●◆

Herrwn woke up gratified that Lillywen had visited his dream yet puzzled about what message she was trying to convey. The question weighed on his mind throughout the morning, and he was still pondering it while sitting at the high table at the start of the midday meal when Olyrrwd elbowed him in the ribs, muttering, "Spoon first, think later."

In keeping with the tradition that the chief priest ladled out the first bowl of soup, which a servant would then carry to the chief priestess, the silver tureen was placed directly in front of him. Herrwn picked up the ornately inscribed serving spoon and would have done as his cousin prompted, but, as he looked into the bowl, he realized something in the soup was looking at him. He blinked and the two bulbous eyes protruding above the chowder blinked back.

"Allow me." Impatient, Olyrrwd took the spoon from Herrwn's hand, plunged it into the tureen, brought it up—and muttered a word not normally spoken at the high table at the sight of the large frog who sat, equally startled, in the cup of the ladle. The frog recovered first, leaping back into the soup in a splash as gasps and exclamations (though none so vehement as Olyrrwd's) arose on all sides.

Herrwn sighed and raised a hand, signaling for Ceirog, the kitchen servant who was laying out platters of bread at the far end of the table.

Ceirog rushed up, stammering his apologies and insisting that he'd put the soup out on the table himself and there had been no frog in it then.

Olyrrwd, recovered from his initial surprise, chortled and said, "Perhaps you might take it back and either cook it better or turn it loose"—words that set off a ripple of laughter up and down the table.

Herrwn sighed again. It was bad enough to have a meddlesome sprite wreaking havoc in their shrine, without encouraging it.

Chapter 61:

The Meddlesome Sprite

Herrwn had no doubt whatsoever that the impish being that had taken up residence in their shrine, and so far evaded all attempts to exorcise it, was a sprite. Certainly other spirits could and did make their presence known by playing jokes on humans—but the acts of demons were more malevolent, while those of elves were often quite whimsical. The pranks of the invisible jester who had been plaguing them for months were neither evil nor charming but simply childish.

The frog in the soup was characteristic of this particular sprite's sense of humor, as was the live eel swimming in a vat of pickled ones (which did upset the cook) and the bread basket that chirped suspiciously and was found when taken outside to be full of a teeming mass of crickets.

While the pranks of a sprite were much to be preferred over the cruel and dangerous tricks played by a demon, things had gotten to the point where you couldn't unseal a jar of sacred oil without a swarm of flies buzzing out, or descend a dark stairwell without stepping into a mound of horse manure.

It was with this in mind that Herrwn cast a stern look up and down the table before assuring the distraught servant that no blame was to be laid at his door and asking if he would be so good as to exchange this bowl of soup for another. He would have added, "one without a frog in it," only he wasn't sure he could say the word "frog" with a straight face—and, glancing toward the women's end of the table, he could see that neither Feywn nor Rhonnon was among those laughing.

Just how seriously the upper ranks of the priestesses took the problem of the meddlesome sprite was brought home to Herrwn that afternoon when Benyon threw open the doors to the classroom without knocking and cried, "You are called! She wants to speak to you!"

During the years that Caelendra had been the chief priestess it had been quite usual for Herrwn, as the shrine's chief priest, to be called to consult on matters of consequence. That, however, had not happened since Feywn ascended, and Herrwn hurried to take up his staff.

After striding as swiftly as dignity allowed down the hall and across the courtyard, Herrwn opened the front doors to the women's quarters. "I am here to see—" he began.

Belodden cut him off before he finished, saying, "You may proceed. She's waiting for you in the birthing chambers!"

Having expected to be directed to either the priestesses' communal meeting room or to Feywn's private chambers, Herrwn was surprised and must have looked it, because Belodden said with poorly hidden impatience, "High Priestess Rhonnon instructed me to tell you that she awaits your presence in the birthing chamber."

"Of course! And now, having your permission, I will proceed there at once." Hiding his disappointment that it was not the chief priestess herself who'd sent for him, Herrwn gave a brief bow and headed down the hallway.

The birthing chamber had changed from the last time Herrwn had seen it. Everything that had to do with birth had been put away, and the room was now clearly used for other tasks. There were several worktables, some with embroidery materials and others with sheaths of dry herbs. Rhonnon was standing at a table with herbs on it, sorting sprigs into separate piles.

Though he saw the shrine's chief midwife at the communal meals, the High Council meetings, and all their shared rites and rituals, Herrwn had not spoken at any length with her since the night they'd taken part in the Sacred Summer Solstice Ceremony together. Unsure whether he should make any reference to that uncharacteristically intimate event, he returned her formal greeting and took the chair she offered him at the one empty table in the room.

It was a long, wide table, and when Rhonnon took the chair opposite his, there was enough distance between them that he felt it was safe to assume she did not wish to be reminded of their ceremonial consortship. Still, there was an undertone of approval in her voice as she began, "I gather from the . . . incident at the midday meal that you are not one of those who takes the . . . antics of our meddlesome sprite as a source of amusement."

There was no question in Herrwn's mind that there was exactly one correct answer to Rhonnon's implied question, and he gave it.

"I do not, and I am deeply concerned that these antics have continued in spite of all Ossiam's attempts to identify exactly what sort of sprite this is and what steps we must take to propitiate it and put an end to these most troublesome incidents."

"So in the meanwhile, may I assume that you are willing to do all within your power to keep these . . . antics from causing harm?"

Again, there was only one answer to this.

"Of course!" he said, nodding firmly, but added what he hoped would be a reassuring caveat, "though fortunately this sprite seems to act without any real malice."

"Are you sure? Have you not noticed their increasing frequency and cunning?" Rhonnon's response was sharp, almost accusatory.

"Well, now that you mention it, I suppose—"

"Well, I suppose that those at most risk are the five girls on whom all of our hopes for the future rest!".

The thought that the young priestesses-in-training might be a target of the sprite's attacks was very disturbing indeed, and Herrwn responded with sincere concern, "Have any of these incidents occurred within the nursery?"

"They started there!"

Herrwn was shaken. "Then we must call Ossiam at once!" He was halfway off the chair and ready to dash for the oracle's tower, but Rhonnon motioned for him to stay where he was.

"As you have already said, Ossiam's efforts thus far have been in vain, so it is my thought that we must instead watch closely over the girls until this sprite tires of its games and leaves of its own accord. I have spoken with Feywn and have received her permission to take whatever measures are necessary to see that the girls are well guarded."

Flattered to be included in the determination of what steps should be put in place to assure the safety and welfare of the shrine's precious priestesses-in-training, Herrwn rose and bowed. "I am deeply honored that you should call on my counsel in this most urgent matter."

Accepting the gesture with a somewhat impatient nod, Rhonnon went on to describe the measures she had already taken, beginning, "As you know, there is only one entrance into our side of the shrine . . ."

Chapter 62:

Precautions

L ocated on the north side of the shrine, the women's quarters were divided between an upper level with a long hallway lined with individual rooms of similar sizes that were mostly sleeping chambers, and a lower level that included several clusters of rooms, each with a small central courtyard. One of the clusters, the largest, served as the exclusive living quarters of the chief priestess; another was the shrine's nursery; the rest were communal work or meeting places.

Unlike the other three sides of the shrine, the north side had no outer wall or walkway, as it had been built along the very edge of the cliff that jutted out into the deepest part of the lake and formed the base of the entire shrine. Short of flying, or scaling both the rugged cliff and the sheer wall above it, there was no way into the north wing except through its only entrance, the doors of which were closed and barred at night and guarded during the day.

Priests invited into the women's quarters were received in one of the rooms or courtyards on the lower level. Even Herrwn, the shrine's chief priest and once the consort of a high priestess, had never climbed the stairs to the north wing's upper hallway, and it went without saying that the priestesses' exact sleeping arrangements there were not something he'd had reason to know before this. By the time Rhonnon finished her account, however, he had no doubt that—in the extremely unlikely event that he should need to—he could find his way to the girls' chamber blindfolded. In particular, he knew that the five young priestesses shared a room, which, like the other rooms on that side of the corridor, had a single door that opened to the main hallway and three windows that looked out over the lake.

When the first of the sprite's antics occurred, the five girls were still quartered in the shrine's nursery. Rhonnon confided that she initially had thought the pranks were being played by one or more of the girls themselves (and while she didn't specifically mention the twins, those two would certainly have been Herrwn's first suspects).

"But," she went on, "their nursemaid was adamant that she never let them out of her sight, and so . . ."

And so the girls had been moved from the nursery to a secure room on the upper level. The move had not stopped the pranks but *had* put an end to suspicions that any of the girls were involved, since the antics had continued—and spread to other parts of the shrine. Here Rhonnon interposed that "while a frog in the soup might seem amusing, a hole bored in the side of the chief priestess's chalice so the sacred wine dribbled down onto her robes when she drank from it was not!" before going on to describe the measures they'd taken to see to it that the young priestesses-in-training were shielded from the sprite's malevolence.

The windows of their bedroom, which were usually left open in the summer months, were kept closed and barred. One servant had been assigned the duty of staying in the girls' bedchamber to watch over them while they slept, while another was on guard outside their door. So now, besides being invisible, the sprite would need to be able to fly or pass through solid walls to get through the defenses that Rhonnon had set in place—and if it did, it would find itself facing protective amulets hung from the ceiling and around each of the beds, the steaming vapors of repellent herbs now kept simmering in a cauldron over the chamber's hearth, and two fiercely loyal servants, one of them ready to recite the shielding charms to keep it at bay while the other rang a bell summoning the priestesses to drive it off.

"And during the day?" Herrwn didn't doubt that Rhonnon had equally stringent oversight planned for the girls' waking hours and felt ready to move on to learning what part he was to be assigned.

"As you know, Gwenydd, the eldest of the girls, is already taking part in all but those rituals reserved to those who have made their first journey to the Sacred Pools. Beginning at tomor-row's Sacred Sunrise Ritual, the younger ones will now join her. Likewise, I am having a table set for them in the main hall."

"They will be eating with the rest of us? Is that wise?" Herrwn hastily amended the implied criticism by saying, "Not that I have any doubt of your wisdom, which is demonstrated in all you have done to assure the safety of the young priestesses-in-training, but as so many of the . . . antics of this shameful sprite have occurred at our communal meals, do you think it safe for them to be there?"

"It is that or keep them locked in their bedroom while we dine, and I doubt whether any of them, least of all Arianna, would accept that gracefully. But I have of course instructed that their table be placed in a secure corner well away from the kitchen, which seems to be a particular haunt of our unwelcome guest. Assum-ing that meets with your approval"—Rhonnon clearly assumed it would—"then, taking into account their daily lessons, there is, you understand, only the late afternoon to consider."

Herrwn did understand. Based on what Rhonnon had said so far, there was no time that the girls were not behind locked doors or under at least two watchful pairs of eyes except for the late afternoon, when the senior priestesses conversed in their private meeting room or relaxed, according to their wishes.

"So, it would be of some help if I were to assume responsibility for watching them at that time, perhaps entertaining them with children's tales as I once had the privilege of doing in an earlier time of need?"

"It would."

From the genuinely relieved look on Rhonnon's face, Herrwn could see she'd been expecting him to object or make some excuse. To the contrary, he was not merely willing but delighted, recalling as he did the moment in his dream in which Lillywen had looked up at him, biting down on her lower lip as she had in life—and going from that to picturing the five girls gathered around him, his daughter's spirit hidden among them and listening in, as he told them the stories he had never had the chance to tell her.

With the matter settled between them, Rhonnon stood up and said that she would make the announcement at the next day's meeting of the High Council. Taking this as his dismissal,

Herrwn rose as well, gave another deep bow, and left to resume his practice for that night's oration.

All five girls were at the Sacred Sunrise Ritual the next day, as Rhonnon had said they would be, and Herrwn was charmed to hear their pure, sweet voices joining in the chant to welcome the rising sun.

On his way to breakfast, Herrwn quietly filled Olyrrwd and Ossiam in on the new arrangements for ensuring the welfare of the young priestesses-in-training. Instead of continuing into the main hall, Ossiam turned aside and declared that he would retreat to his tower, determined as he was to spend his every moment evoking the names of the deities, both minor and major, to protect and defend them all from the perversity of this demonic predation. He was gone before Olyrrwd could say with a snicker, "And who, then, will protect and defend us against the spirits you call forth?"

Chapter 63:

Olyrrwd's Ruffled Feathers

Despite Olyrrwd's skepticism, the rest of the spring and summer was free of pranks—something that Herrwn attributed to the combined efforts of Rhonnon and Ossiam. Without the sprite's troublesome pranks to distract him, Herrwn found himself increasingly anxious about Caelym, and while Olyrrwd remained adamant that there was nothing to worry about, Herrwn noticed that his cousin spent the time not otherwise occupied pacing back and forth along the shrine's upper walkway or leaning against its wall and staring up at the ridgetop where any figure returning from the peaks beyond would first appear.

Joining Olyrrwd at the wall on an afternoon when the sky overhead was filled with geese winging their way southward, Herrwn ventured to suggest sending out a search party, only to have Olyrrwd bark so angrily at him that he dropped the subject and decided he would ask Ossiam to use his second sight to see where Caelym was now and when he would return.

Knowing how sensitive Olyrrwd was about any mention of Ossiam and Caelym in the same breath, however, Herrwn didn't say aloud what he meant to do.

◆◆◆

He waited until the next morning to climb the stairs to the oracle's tower.

After listening in silence to Herrwn's request, Ossiam stared into the steam from his boiling cauldron, the dense vapors rising up and veiling his expression. Finally, he said, "It is well that you've come to me today, for tonight is the last new moon before the autumn equinox, the day after which is the most auspicious time on which to conduct the divination you request, the name of which is not to be spoken to the uninitiated. Haste is of the essence! Leave me now, I must begin my preparations!"

Turning to his assistants, who were hovering in the shadows, Ossiam ordered Iddwran to tell the keeper of the shrine's herds to bring the firstborn of that year's goats to the shed for animals in waiting to be sacrificed, and Ogdwen to gather the ingredients for the sacred elixir and sharpen the ceremonial dagger.

The next morning's Sacred Sunrise Ritual was sparsely attended. Of the high priests, only Herrwn was in his place. Olyrrwd had grunted his usual excuse and rolled over to go back to sleep as Herrwn was getting up and preparing to go, while Ossiam's absence presumably meant he was absorbed in whatever arcane preparations were required for his coming divination. Gwenydd, Arianna, Cyri, and the twins were in the line between Feywn and Lunedd, but neither Rhonnon nor Aolfe was there. Herrwn wondered if he could inquire about their absence without seeming intrusive, but in the end the answer came without his asking.

Once Lunedd had the girls settled at their corner table, she came around on the men's end of the table, dropped into Ossiam's empty chair, and explained that both Rhonnon and Aolfe had been called to the village to attend to the weaver's daughter, who was in the throes of a difficult labor.

As the keeper of the sacred calendar, Lunedd spent her nights tracking the movements of the moon and stars, and unless there was a meeting of the High Council to keep her up, she went to bed after breakfast and slept until the midday meal. Stifling a yawn, she said that with Rhonnon and Aolfe gone, she would be overseeing the girls that morning, "Unless . . ."

Herrwn, taking his cue, offered to watch the girls so she could get some sleep.

Lunedd smiled. "I hoped you could and have already told the girls and their nurse that you will meet them in the herb garden after breakfast." Giving a grateful nod, she got up and went to her place while Olyrrwd, who'd managed to rouse himself in time for the morning meal and was in his usual place on Herrwn's left, muttered, "Take you a bit for granted, don't they!"

Neither of Ossiam's assistant priests had been at the Sacred Sunrise Ritual, but Iddwran, the elder of the two, came into the main hall midway through the meal to announce that Ossiam was fasting in preparation for carrying out a difficult and highly complex augury and that at noon the following day he would sacrifice the firstborn of that year's goats on the great altar in the Sacred Grove to divine where Caelym was and when he would return.

While Iddwran was speaking, Olyrrwd's face turned progressively darker shades of red. He finished his bowl of oatmeal—chewing harder than the mush required—and then got up and left the table muttering.

Supposing he would have to soothe Olyrrwd's ruffled feathers—and apologize for not telling him about the augury before its public proclamation—Herrwn put down his spoon and took his own leave, pausing on his way out to reassure Lunedd that he'd be at the herb garden as soon as he'd changed out of his ceremonial robes and that she could go to her well-deserved rest knowing that the girls would be alone in their servants' care for at most only a few moments.

Olyrrwd's feathers were more than ruffled.

Herrwn reached the classroom to find the physician stamping in circles around the hearth, ranting and raging, in a tirade that mixed curses with accusations that Ossiam was plotting against Caelym again.

When calling his cousin's name had no effect, Herrwn raised his staff and brought it down, striking the floor with a firm thump. "Olyrrwd, stop! Ossiam is only conducting this augury because I asked him to!"

"You what?"

"I asked him to!"

Olyrrwd's outrage changed to incredulity. "You asked him to kill and gut the best of this year's male kids, the goatherd's pick for the herd's next stud and the only one out of the lot he kept uncastrated?"

"Yes . . . No . . . I can explain—"

"It isn't me you need to be explaining to!" Olyrrwd snapped, and stamped out of the room.

As his cousin's walking sticks clicked furiously down the hall, Herrwn sighed and put "Express my sincere regrets to goatherd" on his mental list of things to do, adding, "Ask Olyrrwd what the goatherd's name is and where I am to find him."

First, however, he had to keep his promise to take Lunedd's shift with the young priestesses-in-training—which was just as well, since by noon Olyrrwd would most likely have calmed down and be ready to listen to reason. Glad of the reprieve, and a few hours of peace and tranquility, Herrwn changed from his ceremonial to his everyday robes and left for the garden.

Chapter 64:

Elderond

Neither peace nor tranquility lay ahead for Herrwn that day. Even before he reached the gate, he could hear heartrending sobs and wails. The girls' servant met him at the entryway, wringing her hands and pleading with him to do something. Looking over her head, he could see Gwenydd sitting on the ground with her arms wrapped around Cyri, who was weeping inconsolably. Arianna lay next to them facedown, kicking her feet and pounding the ground with her fists, while the twins huddled nearby, hugging each other and keening in unison.

Herrwn rushed over to them and, looking anxiously for some sign of illness, asked, "What is wrong?"

It was Cyri who answered, raising her tear-stained face from Gwenydd's shoulder.

"They're going to kill Elderond!"

Whatever answer Herrwn had expected, it was not that. All he could imagine was that when he was later than he'd promised, their nurse had started to tell some story from the tales of Elderond's battle against the giants, and she had not yet reached the point at which the frequently imperiled hero was rescued by an enamored nymph or wood sprite.

Thinking this, at least, was a matter he could easily resolve, he hastened to assure them that "as the greatest of heroes and the one destined to be the first and favorite of the Great Goddess's mortal consorts," Elderond would escape whatever perils so distressed them—but Cyri started to cry louder and Gwenydd spoke up in a quivering voice, "No, not that Elderond, *her* Elderond!"

"And mine!" Arianna broke in, while the twins nodded together, sniffing, "Me'glo Me'glo!" in the shared language they fell back on in times of stress.

Gwenydd continued to rock Cyri and pat her on the back as she told Herrwn that when the sheep and goats were giving birth in the spring, Rhonnon had taken them to watch, and that when the first baby goat was born she let them each hold it after its mother had licked it dry and let it nurse. The twins nodded and pantomimed how they'd cradled it in their arms. Going on, Gwenydd sniffed, "It was the dearest and sweetest little baby with the prettiest brown spots and the cutest wagging tail, and we all love him, especially Cyri, and she named him Elderond and goes to play with him every day, and now Ossiam—"

"Stupid, nasty Ossiam!" Arianna pounded the ground harder with her fists. "I hate him!" "Stubo nindo Ossiam! Stubo nindo Ossiam!" the twins chimed in, and stuck out their tongues in the direction of the oracle's tower.

"—is going to kill him." Clutching Cyri tighter in her arms, Gwenydd rocked back and forth as the younger girl sobbed, "He didn't do anything! It's not fair."

Gwenydd looked up at Herrwn. "You are the chief priest. Can you tell him to sacrifice something else?" Cyri looked up too, tears streaming down her cheeks, and whispered, "Can you?"

Herrwn was tempted to equivocate—to say he would try—but he knew that would do no more than give them false hope, since once a sacrificial victim was announced, making any substitution would be risking injured feelings in the next world. So, instead, he said the only thing he could—"I am sorry."

And he was deeply sorry, indeed was heartsick, to see the pain he had inadvertently caused.

Arianna pushed up on her elbows and glared. "Well, if you won't—"

Before she could finish whatever childish outcry she was about to make, one of the twins grabbed her arm and pulled her off behind a hedge of elderberry bushes while the other asked in quite clear words, "Will you tell us a story?"

"Of course I will."

Herrwn sat down next to Gwenydd, eased Cyri onto his lap, and began to recite one of the lighthearted tales he'd told Lillywen when her feelings were upset.

By the time the horn calling them to the midday meal sounded, the girls' sobs had been reduced to occasional sniffles and Cyri was even managing a wavering smile at the funnier parts.

Having successfully soothed the five young priestesses-in-training, Herrwn only hoped he could do as well with his middle-aged cousin.

By that afternoon, Olyrrwd had calmed down enough to accept Herrwn's invitation to go for a walk along the lakeshore. Grunting now and then, he listened to Herrwn's explanation that, in his almost unbearable worry over the time it was taking Caelym to complete his spirit quest, he had indeed asked Ossiam to perform this augury to see where Caelym was and when he would return.

"You understand I had no way of knowing what sort of animal would be required, nor could I have guessed that the one he chose was so beloved by the priestesses-in-training, but please—and I ask this of you as my dearest kinsman and my best friend—please lay the entire blame for this on me and please, please accept my most deep and sincere apology and convey my deepest regrets to the good goatherd as well."

It was, Herrwn thought, a quite well-worded and thorough apology and, as such, deserved more than Olyrrwd's grudging retort, "Next time tell me when you are planning to do something stupid so I can talk you out of it."

When Rhonnon returned with Aolfe late that afternoon, it was immediately clear that the chief midwife was no happier with Herrwn than Olyrrwd had been. While she let him repeat his explanation without interrupting and didn't exactly say it was up to Herrwn to face the girls again the next morning while their pet was being prepared for its sacrifice, he found himself offering to do exactly that.

"That would be good of you!" she said stiffly. "I suggest you avoid stories about goats or oracles!"

Olyrrwd, at least, came around to agreeing that Herrwn was paying for his error in judgment by returning to the garden and facing a new round of tears, and he was openly sympathetic the next morning as Herrwn prepared to leave.

Strengthened by the knowledge that his cousin was on his side again, Herrwn took up his staff and went out to *meet his fate*, as Olyrrwd jokingly called after him.

That was, in fact, how Herrwn felt as he approached the garden gate, so he was more than a little surprised—and very much relieved—to find the girls bravely reconciled to their pet's fate. Each one greeted him affectionately, even enthusiastically, and asked for a favorite story.

"Gwendolwn and the Honey Tree, please." Gwenydd took hold of his hand and looked up sweetly.

"What about the brave stallion who fooled the mean sprite?" Cyri had taken hold of Herrwn's other hand and had her head cocked to the side in a way that reminded Herrwn unexpectedly of Labhruinn—or would have, if he weren't immediately distracted by the twins jumping up and down and crying in unison, "The one about the giant one-eyed ogres!"

"No! No! Caerwyn and the Fairy Queen! That's the one I want!" Arianna announced with a toss of her head and stamp of her foot.

A veteran of responding to equally valid yet competing demands brought before the High Council, Herrwn responded with an alternative of his own.

"What would you all say to my telling you a story you have never heard before—the story of Rhiawana and the Lost Prince?"

The chorus of "oh yeses" and "pleases" that followed this suggestion quite warmed Herrwn's heart. He took the cushion that the girls' nurse held out to him, sat down, and, with the five of them gathered in a circle around him, began the tale of how Rhiawana, a beautiful and kindly forest nymph, used her wiles and cunning to save a king's son who had gotten lost in a deep and dark forest and was being pursued by a pack of voracious ogres.

The prince, whose name was Pendorffen, was the firstborn son of the great King Pendorwn. A skilled archer, Pendorffen had pursued a white stag into the forest unaware that it was not an ordinary stag but the spirit-king of the deer clan. As the chase went on, the stag dashed deeper and deeper into the forest. Then, just as Pendorffen spent his last arrow, it turned on him, lowered its horns, and charged.

Pendorffen's terrified horse reared, threw him to the ground, and dashed off.

"What happened then?" the five girls asked in a single voice.

Lowering his voice to effect the dread the hero would have felt, Herrwn answered, "The king of the deer could have trampled Pendorffen or gored him, but instead it strode contemptuously off into the mist and vanished—leaving him lost and alone."

"Ohhh," they all gasped.

Pleased to have captivated his young audience, Herrwn went on to tell how the prince's plight went from bad to worse—accidentally knocking over a hornet's nest, nearly drowning in a river he'd jumped into to save himself from the angry wasps, and then, finally, crossing paths with a pack of hungry ogres who pursued him as he had once pursued the stag.

They were gaining on him. He could hear their curses and war cries coming closer. As the last strength in his legs was failing, he saw an opening through the trees and in a final, desperate dash broke through the undergrowth to collapse in a flower-filled meadow, where Rhiawana, a wood nymph, was dancing in the twilight.

Although she was descended from the Rain-God on her father's side and from the Wind-Goddess on her mother's, Rhiawana was herself only a local deity and had nowhere near the power it would have taken to fend off the ogres who surrounded her, demanding that she give them the mortal who lay gasping at her feet. But looking down at him, she saw he was more handsome than any mortal she had ever seen, and so she resolved to save him if she could.

Fluttering her eyelashes at the chief of the ogres, she asked, "Have you thought of whether you would like to have him roasted or stewed?"

Herrwn's use of a coquettish falsetto here made the girls giggle. He was about to shift to a low, gravelly bass to give the chief ogre's answer when Benyon burst into the garden, gasping, "He's back!"

Chapter 65:

The Girls' Game

"Caelym is back?" Herrwn reached for his staff. "That is won—" "No, no, Master, not he, Master Caelym—he, the sprite! The wicked, wicked sprite! He's taken it!"

Dropping to his knees, the distraught servant grabbed hold of the hem of Herrwn's robe and twisted it between his fingers. "It was there! I know it was! And now it's gone!"

Startled by this alarming display of emotion, Herrwn could think of nothing to say but, "What is gone?"

"The goat!"

"Which goat?" Herrwn asked, although he'd already guessed the answer.

"The goat that is to be the sacrificial offering for Master Ossiam's augury! The wicked sprite has stolen it from its pen in the shed!"

Herrwn caught his breath. Until now, the sprite's misdeeds had done no real harm, but to steal an offering intended for the spirit guide who was Ossiam's link to the next world was an act that could have grave consequences—not just disrupting the day's difficult and delicate augury but making their chief oracle appear foolish in the eyes of the denizen on whom he relied for his prognostications. Hoping that there might be a natural rather than a supernatural explanation for the goat's disappearance, he asked the sort of questions he imagined Olyrrwd would ask, starting with, "Are you sure? Could it have found some way out of its pen?"

"I am sure, Master! I am absolutely sure!" Benyon continued wringing the hem of Herrwn's robe but spoke in a steadier voice. "Iddwran told me that Master Ossiam wanted the firstborn of this year's goats for the sacrifice, and I told Aonghus, the chief herder, and he went and got it and gave it to me, and I put it in the pen in the shed—but now it's gone!"

"When did you last see it was in its pen?"

"Last night. I gave it its last meal exactly at sunset."

"And could you possibly have left the—"

"No! No! I swear on my mother's grave I tied the gate to the pen closed, and I closed and barred the door to the shed! And the door was still closed and the gate was still tied shut when I went there this morning! But the goat was gone!" Letting go of Herrwn's robe, Benyon buried his face in his hands and rocked back and forth. "What am I to tell Master Ossiam?"

Herrwn pursed his lips and thought before he answered, "Nothing yet, as he is no doubt absorbed in his preparations for this ritual and must not be disturbed! For now, you must go quickly and find the goatherd. Tell him to get another young goat—one that is as much like the missing one as possible, so the spirits will have no cause to be disappointed—and see that it is prepared and ready when it is called for."

As Benyon dashed off, Herrwn turned back to his five young charges. They were sitting quietly in a circle, playing with a loop of string—making complex designs that changed as they passed it between them. It was a girl's game that Lothwen had once tried to teach him, laughing at the tangles he made in his clumsy attempts to take hold of the right thread at the right spot and lift or twist with just the right pressure. "You are too tense," she'd told him. "You have to relax and not worry so much!"

Watching the girls, all five of whom had been so distraught over the fate of their pet goat the day before, easily and deftly picking up the loops of string and turning one pattern into another as they passed it around their ring, his teacher's instinct tingled.

From Benyon's account, it was clear that the goat could not have escaped on its own, but the shed was not guarded and anyone—even a child—could have gone in, let the goat out, and closed the gate and the door behind them.

Herrwn cleared his throat and said sternly, "Now, girls, I know how fond you all were of the little goat, but this is an extremely serious matter, and if any of you have any idea of where it might be, you must tell me now!"

Five pairs of eyes met his without blinking or shifting away.

"We were all in bed!" said Arianna, her tone equally hurt and offended. "Ask Nonna!"

The nurse, who had already come over to listen to Benyon's account, reached out her arms, gathered the five girls close to her breast, and bristled like a mother bear. "They were—all of them—fast asleep in their beds all night long. I was there watching over them myself!"

"I am relieved to hear it, for I would have been very disappointed to think otherwise." Herrwn did not take his eyes off the innocent ("too innocent," a little voice in the back of his mind whispered) faces looking up at him.

Oddly, of the five girls, the only one to shift her gaze was Gwenydd. If it had been any of the others, Herrwn would have pressed further, but he could not imagine the best behaved of all the priestesses-in-training sneaking past her drowsy nurse, down the torchlit halls and stairways of the women's quarters, past the guardian at the entryway, and out through the shrine's back passages to take the goat out and hide it, all without being noticed.

Still, he hesitated, wondering what Rhonnon would say if he approached her privately and asked that she have the women's quarters searched for the missing animal. As he was picturing the affronted look on her face, Benyon came rushing back in, panting. "They're gone!" he cried. "They're all gone. The herder went to get another baby goat, but the whole herd is gone!"

"The whole herd has disappeared? How could—"

"He thinks they have run away to meadows on the upper slopes and has taken his dog and gone to get them back but . . . but . . ."

Here Benyon stuttered to a halt—but Herrwn knew what he was trying to say. It was almost noon! At any moment, Ossiam would be descending the stairs of the oracle's tower, starting the incantations that would draw an invisible audience from the spirit world.

They needed a goat, and they needed it now!

"I heard you might need a goat." Olyrrwd appeared at the garden's open gate, looking quite good-humored. Both his walking poles were in his right hand, and in his left he held a thick rope that was tied to the collar of a decrepit-looking ram.

"Where did you—" Herrwn wasn't sure whether to ask "hear that?" or "get that?"

Answering both questions at once, Olyrrwd explained that he'd just been to the shrine's kitchen to tend to the cook's toe, and he learned the strange story of the missing goat from her. "As we wouldn't want our chief oracle to get all dressed up for his augury and not have anything to gut," he went on quite cheerfully, "I asked whether there might be a goat in the kitchen's pen where they keep the animals to be stewed. Mind you, to get this fellow I had to promise Iddwrna on my word of honor that we'd have him back to her, cleaned and flayed, as soon as Ossie is done."

With that lighthearted admonition, Olyrrwd handed the lead rope to Benyon. He gave the animal a departing pat on its flank as it hobbled off.

"Are you going to the augury, the name of which is not to be spoken to the uninitiated? It's close to time." Olyrrwd's tone remained droll and it was clear to Herrwn, seeing his cousin's ordinary (not to mention stained) robes, that Olyrrwd had no intention of being there himself.

"I am," Herrwn said, picking up his staff, "but first I must go to the oracle's tower to advise Ossiam what has come to pass, assuring him that a substitute offering has been found."

Still chipper, Olyrrwd responded, "It will be my honor to take over their lesson. I have some quite useful things to teach them about the healing properties of willowwort and barthberry."

Intending to remind Olyrrwd that it behooved them to maintain an elevated and serious demeanor in the presence of the young priestesses-in-training, Herrwn gave a formal bow and, assuming the tone he used when addressing the High Council, said, "The girls will, I know, be honored as well."

As he was taking his leave, Herrwn looked over his shoulder and paused long enough to watch Olyrrwd lay his walking sticks aside and reach down to the string lattice Cyri was holding out toward Gwenydd. Picking up its outer threads deftly with his thumbs and forefingers, he hooked the innermost lines with his little fingers, turned it with a flip into a spectacular design, and with another flip changed it back into a plain but untangled loop of twine.

Chapter 66:

Only Fog and Mist

With no time to wonder how his cousin had learned to play the string game, Herrwn rushed off. After passing through the entrance to the oracle's tower, he took the stairs two at a time and got to the top just as the door was opening—and all but collided with Ossiam as the oracle swept out.

"Is there a problem?" In the shadow of the stairwell, with the light from the room behind him and steamy fumes shrouding him, Herrwn—who had to catch his breath—felt, just for a moment, that it was not Ossiam but the oracle's long-dead father who spoke.

Feeling like a pupil caught unprepared for his lessons, Herrwn stammered, "Yes . . . ah . . . No . . . That is to say, there was, but it is resolved for the best . . . You see . . . ."

After recovering himself enough to speak with reasonable clarity and succinctness, he explained Benyon's discovery of the missing goat and how they'd found a substitute, concluding, "So all should go well."

Ossiam's answer was to raise his staff and sweep down the stairs, leaving Herrwn to fall into line behind him.

Later, Ossiam would contend that the higher spirits to whom he called had indeed been offended by the meagerness of their sacrifice. There was certainly nothing Herrwn could see in the rigor with which the oracle carried out his incantations or the intensity with which he stared into the tangle of bowels—for what seemed like an eternity of time—that would account for his raising up his head at last and sighing, "There is only fog and mist! I cannot see through it!"

Herrwn's heart sank.

The day was bright and warm. Except for a few wispy clouds near the horizon, there was no hint of fog, at least not in the mortal world. What was there to think but that Ossiam did not see an ordinary mist but the veil separating the living world from the next? Did this mean that Caelym had crossed to the other side?

From the unhappy murmuring around him, Herrwn guessed his fears were shared by the other priests and priestesses, all of whom, like Herrwn, waited just long enough for Ossiam to finish his closing chants before leaving the grove, their heads bowed in despair.

Chapter 67:

Wolf Songs

errwn retreated to his quarters after a midday meal he barely tasted. He spent the next hours in solitude, reciting the lines of the final episode in the epic of the wandering minstrel. It was not a saga he had chosen for any particular reason, other than that it was traditionally told at the end of summer so its conclusion would coincide with the celebration of the start of the fall harvest—an occasion on which the Songs of Melamardd, the fabled bard for whom the tale was named, were sung.

Now he found himself deriving hope from the reminder that earlier generations of Druids had sent their sons on quests for mystical insight and had lost hope of their ever returning, but Melamardd had—and so might Caelym.

All the priests and priestesses were in their places when Herrwn made his entrance into the main hall that night. Only his own chair and Caelym's were vacant.

Receiving Feywn's nod, he began.

In the high, shining hall of the realm of King Maeclwdden of the Kingdom of Llancerddysul, there was a great gathering of those who had come together in final lamentations for the king's youngest son, Melamardd, from whom there had been no word for seven years and now was to be mourned as dead.

A bard of the highest order, Herrwn spoke the narrator's lines as if he were seeing the events unfold before his eyes. As each mourner rose to speak, he became that person—the queen recalling how she'd cradled her last-born and most beloved infant in her arms, the king as he recounted the childhood feats that had set his favorite son apart from his six brothers, each of those brothers admitting their envy and wishing for the chance to make amends, each of Melamardd's seven lovers recalling his ardor and forswearing their former jealousy to be sisters-in-mourning.

He had reached the climax of the final scene—the moment at which the darkly shrouded woman (previously only noted in passing as a dark figure sitting in the shadows) rises up from her stool and throws back her shawl to reveal Herself to be the Great Goddess.

Speaking in the narrator's awed voice, he said, *"As She reached out her snow-white arms, the hall's golden doors swung open and—"*

And at that moment the curtains of the entry to the hall parted and a tall figure, clad in furs and carrying a stained, battered satchel over his shoulder, stepped through.

He was almost unrecognizable. His hair was tangled and matted. His dark eyes glowed in the light of the hearth the way Herrwn imagined the eyes of a wild animal glowed in the forest at night. And when Caelym spoke, his words came out in an oddly warbling tone much like the voice Herrwn used when he recited the part of Namurran, the king of the wolves, in the second saga in the epic of Fondelwn and the Fairy Queen.

"If she who speaks through our great oracle is listening," Caelym began, "let her hear how I have done as she decreed, how I have found my animal spirit guide and how I have learned to speak the language of its tribe! And then"—he took the sagging, lumpy pouch off his shoulder and let it drop by his feet—"I will sing you their songs and tell you their stories!"

Stepping around the pack as though it were a rock in a stony mountain path and shivering in an imaginary wind, he pulled his fur cloak close around him. His teeth chattering, he described how he had climbed to the top of a peak in the northern mountains and heard the howls of wolves coming from a distant ridge.

"It was then I knew what animal was to be my spirit guide, and so"—he cast a resolute look around the room—"I set out to find their pack and fulfill my quest."

With that he pulled up his hood and began to pace, crisscrossing the chamber, leaning forward and backward as he mimed his climb up one ridge and down another. Coming to a sudden halt, he ducked behind a vacant chair, peeked over the top of it, and whispered, "After days of searching, I came to a rise, and there, in the valley below, I saw seven silver-gray wolves racing after a herd of deer, cutting out the hindmost and bringing it down," in a voice that carried both admiration for the wolves and grief for the deer.

Slowly, warily, he crept out from behind the chair and around the edge of the room, all the while describing how he followed the pack for weeks, spying on them to learn how they spoke to one another. Reaching another empty chair, he stopped again, crouched, and then rose just enough to peer at a spot in the center of the chamber floor as he told them how, on the day of the summer solstice, a light brown wolf he'd never seen before came out of the bushes and trotted toward the place where the pack was resting in the shade after their most recent kill.

"Smaller by half than any of the gray wolves, most likely the lost or orphaned cub of some other pack, it was too young and weak to fend for itself and too inexperienced to know the danger when the entire enemy pack rose as one and stalked toward it. As the pack surrounded it, the largest male in the lead, the little brown wolf dropped, rolled over on its back, and exposed its neck and belly as if surrendering to death. The great gray wolf drew back his lips in a fearsome snarl and closed his teeth on the pup's throat. The pup made no move save for a small wag at the tip of its tail. I watched with tears welling up in my eyes for the poor, doomed pup—but instead of biting down, the great gray wolf released his grip and walked away. The rest of the pack followed him, and the little brown wolf got back to its feet and crept along after them with its tail now wagging happily, even tucked as tightly as it was between its legs. And so the next day . . ."

Caelym crept out from behind the chair—stooped over, so it looked as if he were moving on four feet—and eased his way into the center of the room as he told how he, too, had bowed down to the leader of the wolves and had, likewise, been taken into the pack.

Shifting from cowering to exuberant, and interspersing his words with barks and whines, yips and yowls, he acted out how he had spent the rest of the summer living with the wolves—sleeping in their dens, wrestling with their cubs, joining in their hunts, sharing in their kills, and howling along as they sang their songs to the moon. For most of the time he was speaking, he moved crouched over, darting and bounding from one place to another, but then, upon reaching a group of chairs that his audience had come to understand as the ridgetop where the wolves sang at night, he froze in place, hesitantly lifted up his head and turned it, sniffing, listening . . .

"As the days grew shorter, there was something—an elusive scent carried on a chill breeze or the cry of birds flying south—that told them it was time to leave their summer abode in the high mountain valleys and journey down to their winter home. I might have gone along with them except that I, too, heard a call, equally compelling, to return to you, my human kin, and live again as a man."

As he spoke these last lines, Caelym slowly straightened up to stand erect, his gaze fixed in the direction the pack had gone.

Like the rest of the gathered priests and priestesses, Herrwn was held spellbound by Caelym's tale, so it took him a moment to realize the boy was finished.

As the shrine's chief priest and master bard, it was Herrwn's duty to welcome his disciple back and make the formal announcement that, having completed his spirit quest, Caelym was now a full-fledged high priest, with all the privileges and obligations that entailed. He would have been both proud and honored to do so—but Feywn spoke first, making that precise pronouncement with an undertone of warmth he'd not heard in her voice since Rhedwyn's death.

Feywn's declaration was followed by a spate of toasts and speeches, so it was well past midnight before Herrwn and Olyrrwd, with Caelym between them, made their way back to their sleeping quarters.

◆◆◆

Though obviously exhausted, Caelym balked at getting into bed. Instead, he drew his tattered fur cloak around him and went out into the courtyard, where he circled the garden bench three times before crawling under it, curling up into a ball, and going to sleep.

As Herrwn was about to kneel down and coax Caelym inside, Olyrrwd, who until then had said nothing except, "Hello, Caelie, nice to have you home," whispered, "Leave him be for now."

Taking that as a healer's instruction, Herrwn followed Olyrrwd back into their sleeping chamber, where he spent what was left of the night drifting in and out of very odd dreams about being a wolf running at the head of a howling pack.

Chapter 68:

Whatever Happened

"*I* wonder whatever happened to the little goat."
It had been a year and four months since Caelym's return from his spirit quest, and, with all that had gone on since then, Herrwn had forgotten about the missing animal, but he was reminded of its mysterious disappearance as he and Olyrrwd sat at the classroom table, watching their distraught disciple pacing around the chamber reciting snatches out of unrelated sagas—one of which Herrwn recognized as a stanza from Rhiawana and the Lost Prince, the story he'd been reciting to the girls on the day the goat vanished.

"I thought—" Olyrrwd's answer was interrupted by a paroxysm of coughing that went on for an inordinate length of time, during which his face turned from beefy red to dusky blue. Knowing how much it irritated Olyrrwd when people "made a fuss over him" whether by asking anxiously, "Are you all right, Master?" as Benyon invariably did or by pounding him on the back, as Caelym tended to, Herrwn held his breath and waited until his cousin leaned over, spat a greenish-yellow glob into a crock by his feet, wiped his mouth on his sleeve, and went on matter-of-factly, "you knew."

"Was it found? Where? When?"

"At the pools. A week or so later."

"The pools? You don't mean—"

"I do. The Sacred Pools. Fortunately, not by Feywn but by a servant who'd gone ahead to make sure all was in readiness for her next visit."

"What did she—I mean, the servant—do?"

"Hustled it off to the goatherd, who put it back into the flock, where it has taken on its responsibilities as the herd's new stud with admirable vigor"—Olyrrwd waited for Caelym to pace past them and on to the far side of the room, then lowered his voice—"something I would say our Caelie has done as well," with a chuckle that turned into another spasm of coughing.

While Herrwn would have phrased it differently, there was no denying the truth in what Olyrrwd was saying.

Chapter 69:

The Sprite's Last Prank

It had, at first, been surprisingly difficult for Caelym to read-just to living in the shrine. He didn't let Benyon cut the mats out of his hair until Herrwn admonished him sternly that he was "no longer living among wolves and was not ever again to growl at their servant!" and while he'd been persuaded to come indoors at night instead of sleeping underneath the bench in the classroom courtyard by the end of the first week, he'd still insisted on walking around his bed three times before he would lie down.

But after soaking off the leather shirt and pants that had stuck to him like a second skin, he emerged from the dressing chamber dressed in a full-fledged priest's formal robes, ready and eager to resume his work with Olyrrwd and his orations with Herrwn, and to take his place in the highest of their ritual practices.

Already tall when he left, Caelym had been even taller when he returned—eye level with Herrwn, which meant he towered over Olyrrwd—and even draped in the loose robes of their order, it was obvious that the lanky thinness of his limbs was now hardened and sinewy. When Herrwn commented on this to Olyrrwd, the physician's response was, "He left a boy and returned a man, and so . . ."

When Olyrrwd didn't finish, Herrwn prompted, "And so?"

"And so how old was Rhedwyn when Caelendra chose him to be her Sun-God?"

They both knew the answer was seventeen.

Speaking as if Herrwn had actually said the number out loud, Olyrrwd followed up with an equally self-evident question. "And how old will Caelym be on his next birthday?"

This time Herrwn—seeing where Olyrrwd was taking this line of reasoning—said,

"Seventeen, but that was different!"

"How?"

"Because . . ."

In spite of himself, the first objection that jumped to Herrwn's mind was that, as Rhedwyn had been Feywn's consort, Caelym was essentially her stepson, or would be if it had been Rhedwyn himself rather than the embodiment of the Sun-God who'd done Caelym's actual fathering. There was something that made the idea of Caelym assuming that same role with Feywn disconcerting. As Herrwn tried to picture the two seated next to each other at the high table, what he saw instead was the image of the chief priestess swearing by Rhedwyn's death wounds that she would be faithful to him until the end of time.

"Because?" Olyrrwd's question broke into Herrwn's ruminations.

"Because she swore an oath at the sacred altar that she would never love—"

"Another man," Olyrrwd finished for him.

And of course he was right. Caelym acting as the Sun-God would not count as his being "another man."

With that exchange as a forewarning, Herrwn was fully prepared when Feywn made the pronouncement Olyrrwd had predicted at the next High Council meeting. The surprise came when she added, "And he will be my consort."

When he and Olyrrwd spoke about it later (well out of Caelym's hearing), Olyrrwd admitted to being caught off guard by Feywn's pronouncement. Then he shrugged and muttered, "Well, I guess she doesn't plan to love him."

◆●◆

The ceremonial consecration of Caelym's union with Feywn took place on his seventeenth birthday and the first anniversary of the day he'd embarked on his seemingly impossible spirit quest.

Instead of going to breakfast after the Sacred Sunrise Ritual, the priests and priestesses, all carrying sprays of spring flowers, walked in a solemn line across the shrine's central courtyard and up the steep curving stairs of the shrine's highest tower to witness this most sacred of sacred rites.

Feywn, wearing the same silken gown she'd worn on the day of her union with Rhedwyn, led the procession, followed by Caelym, dressed in robes sewn especially for the occasion and positively reeking with fragrant anointments. Next in line were the shrine's three high priestesses, Rhonnon, Lunedd, and Aolfe. As the shrine's chief priest, Herrwn came next, followed by Ossiam and Olyrrwd.

Neither Herrwn nor Olyrrwd had gotten much rest the night before because Caelym—who'd effortlessly memorized epics a thousand lines in length—had lain awake, repeating over and over the brief and straightforward vow he was expected to say the next day, panic-stricken that he might misspeak a single word. Olyrrwd had eventually grown exasperated and left, grumbling that he was going to the healing chambers to get some sleep. Herrwn, however, understood completely, having experienced the same anxiety the night before the celebration of his union with Lothwen.

Caught up in his memories of following Lothwen up these same stairs, Herrwn walked into Aolfe, stepping on the back of her sandals, when she stopped at the chamber's entryway. Behind him, the priests and priestesses piled up, peering over each other's shoulders at the center of the room, where a goat wearing a wreath around his horns and draped with an embroidered cape—both fashioned in unmistakable mockery of Caelym's attire—was eating mash out of a bucket crudely painted to resemble a sacred chalice.

After a communal gasp, no one voluntarily took another breath or made a sound.

Ossiam broke the silence, hissing, "Get it out of here!" to his assistants. The other priests and priestesses made way, pressing back against the walls, and Iddwran led the ram out while Ogdwen hastily cleaned up the droppings it had left behind.

Once the goat was gone and the floor was scrubbed, Feywn took her place in front of the altar. As close as he was to his disciple, Herrwn heard Caelym drawing a deep, calming breath before going to kneel at her feet and swearing to be worthy of the honor being bestowed upon him, without missing a single word and with only the faintest quiver that could easily be taken for heartfelt passion rather than a threatened outburst of nervous laughter.

The ceremony flowed smoothly from there. Feywn declared Caelym her consort as she placed a pendant around his neck, the two shared the ritual drink from the sacred chalice, they clasped hands, and Caelym rose to stand. With their hands still locked together, they led the way back down to the shrine's great hall for the celebratory meal that waited there.

At the time, Herrwn assumed that the brazen prank was the work of the impudent sprite.

Recalling the incident nine months later, however, Herrwn wondered. There had been no pranks at all from Caelym's homecoming until the day of his union with Feywn, and none since then. And would a mere sprite have dared to pull such a crude joke at the expense of the chief priestess and embodiment of the Great Mother Goddess? Or could it have been, as Ossiam had darkly suggested, a villainous attempt by some evil demon to defeat their Goddess's plan to renew the life force of their shrine?

Herrwn hadn't been aware that he'd spoken his thought aloud until Olyrrwd, just recovered from his paroxysm of coughing, answered, "Guess it didn't work!" with a chortle that set off another coughing spasm.

Chapter 70:

Arddwn

I t had taken five years for Feywn to bear the fruit of her union with Rhedwyn, but within three months from the night Caelym first entered her private chambers, the chief priestess's belly was swelling.

Nine months to the day after Caelym swore his vows as her consort, she was in active labor.

Lunedd's announcement at breakfast that Feywn had entered the shrine's newly renovated birthing room had confirmed what they'd all suspected when neither Feywn nor Rhonnon nor Aolfe nor any priestess who might assist with birthings had been at the Sacred Sunrise Ritual. Already jittery, Caelym had dashed out of the main hall, only to come stamping back, tearing at his hair and decrying the injustice that Rhonnon had declared him too emotional to be allowed into the birthing chamber "or even in its courtyard!"

Now, with no patients in the healing chamber to keep him occupied and no hope of his mustering the concentration to rehearse even the simplest ode for that night's oration, he was all but wearing ruts into the classroom's stone floor as he paced from one end of the chamber to the other, alternating between reciting random lines of poetry and muttering supplications to the entire pantheon of known gods and goddesses (excepting, of course, the disreputable Christian one).

Herrwn had knots in his own stomach and was carrying on his superficial conversation with Olyrrwd to keep his memories of Lothwen and Caelendra at bay.

Olyrrwd seemed to understand. He answered Herrwn's irrelevant questions as though they were about vital matters, slipping in bits of lighthearted japery to pass the time even though laughing invariably set off his racking cough. He was still gagging and hacking from his most recent witticism when there was a rap on the classroom doors.

Caelym rushed to jerk them open just as Blodwen, Feywn's chambermaid, was raising her hand to knock a second time. Apparently accustomed to Caelym's vivacity, she brought her palms together in the courteous gesture of a servant about to speak to a high priest and began, "Priestess Rhonnon calls you to—"

Since Caelym was halfway down the hall before she could complete her message, Blodwen turned to Herrwn and Olyrrwd and finished, "come to the courtyard beside the birthing chamber, as she has an announcement to make."

It took Olyrrwd several moments to finish clearing his airway, and Herrwn wasn't about to leave without him, so the courtyard was packed by the time they got there.

There was no sign of Caelym, but as they made their way through the crowd Herrwn caught sight of Rhonnon, her apron damp and tinged with blood, standing in front of the closed birthing chamber door and looking impatiently in their direction, tapping her right foot.

"That's a good sign," Olyrrwd muttered reassuringly as they took their places in the front row of priests. "If it were bad news, she wouldn't be in a hurry to give it."

"Shhh!" Ossiam hissed. "Our chief midwife is about to speak!"

Giving Ossiam a cool nod, Rhonnon began to recite the formulaic announcement that they hadn't heard in the twelve years since Arianna's birth. She had just reached the all-important ninth stanza—the part where the gender and name of the newborn were announced—when the door behind her opened and Caelym stepped through, holding a baby-shaped bundle.

"It's a boy! His name is Arddwn!" His voice was soft and awed as he repeated, "Arddwn!"

Chapter 71

Ealendwr

Arddwn was an unusual name for a Druid. It generally denoted membership in the warrior caste and was best known as the name of the heroic though ultimately tragic king who rallied his besieged forces to victory in the third saga of the epic war between the Goddess and the Northern Giants.

Something about Feywn's decision to give her firstborn son a warlord's name troubled Herrwn. Why exactly wasn't clear to him, except that it somehow stirred up the memory of her standing before them at Rhedwyn's funeral—still wearing the gown stained with his blood—raising her staff and swearing eternal vengeance in a chilling voice.

While Herrwn wasn't able to keep his vague uneasiness from settling into some remote part of his mind, he successfully kept it buried for the next four months, only to have it spring up again with the chief priestess's unexpected announcement at the close of the first High Council following the spring equinox.

After leaving the meeting, Herrwn and Olyrrwd returned to the classroom and spoke quietly together.

"You don't think . . ." Herrwn stopped, not sure how to put his worry into words.

"That she has decided to personally give birth to the army she means to send against the forever-loathed king of Derthwald?" Olyrrwd finished for him. While he did digress to make the more or less predictable witticism that "since Ossiam seems to be predicting that Feywn's next baby will be a boy, she'd best have a girl's name picked out," he didn't dismiss Herrwn's worry out of hand.

From the stunned expressions Herrwn had seen up and down the council table, it had been clear that none of the other priests and priestesses had taken the oracle's invocation at the opening of the council, with its lush prose laden with metaphors alluding to fertility and birth—and even with its inclusion of references to stags and stallions—as anything other than routine and that they, like Herrwn, had been caught off guard when Ossiam sat down and Feywn stood up, lifted her staff, and proclaimed the coming of her third child.

Sitting on Feywn's left, Caelym had beamed and blinked his eyes—no doubt struggling against the temptation to leap up from his place and turn cartwheels around the room.

On Feywn's right, Rhonnon seemed as surprised as the rest of them. This in itself was odd, and while it passed quickly, her fleeting frown made it clear that she had either not been consulted or her advice had not been taken.

Feeling Olyrrwd's elbow jabbing into his ribs—and taking the hint—Herrwn had risen to his feet, lifted the chalice of sacred wine, and begun a carefully phrased homage in praise of the many gifts of the Great Mother Goddess and her unquestioned wisdom in deeming when they should be bestowed.

Despite Rhonnon's misgivings, Feywn showed no ill effects despite having embarked upon her third pregnancy so soon after the second. Radiantly beautiful to begin with, she glowed with vitality as the months passed and her belly grew rounder. All indicators—Rhonnon's prediction, Ossiam's prognostications, and what Olyrrwd reported of the wagers being laid in the village—pointed to Feywn being due to deliver in midwinter, within a week on either side of the solstice.

As the time drew closer, the atmosphere in the shrine grew increasingly tense. The solstice came and went. A week passed, then half of another.

Rising for the Sacred Sunrise Ritual, Herrwn made his way to the central courtyard. Caelym, a bare half step behind him, stopped in his tracks at the sight of Lunedd standing in Feywn's place. Without so much as a word to excuse himself, he whirled around and dashed off toward the women's quarters.

Lunedd seemed momentarily flustered but then waved her hand, signaling for everyone to fall into line behind her, climbed the stairs to the upper courtyard, conducted a thin-sounding chorus welcoming the return of the sun, and led them back down the stairs—pausing at the bottom to say that those who wished could accompany her to await the news from the birthing chamber.

They all did.

Olyrrwd joined the procession as they reached the entrance to the women's quarters.

Herrwn was expecting to find Caelym pacing in anxious circles around the chamber's courtyard. Seeing the space was empty, he glanced at Olyrrwd, who muttered, "It's either a good sign . . . or a bad one."

Just then, Aolfe cracked open the door and gestured for the two of them and Ossiam to come in.

"Not a good one, then," Olyrrwd whispered.

At first, it was hard to see what was wrong. Feywn was sitting up, holding her newborn infant in her arms. The baby seemed only asleep. Swaddled in silk, she was as beautiful as Arianna had been, though in a different way, with a paler complexion and wisps of dark hair instead of red. Caelym was sitting on the bed next to Feywn, crooning, "Ealendwr, Ealendwr," as he stroked the infant's cheek. It was the catch in his voice that explained the atmosphere in the birthing chamber—that and the tears slipping down his cheeks.

Rhonnon had been standing by the side of the bed with her hand on Caelym's shoulder. Now she whispered something to him, stepped away from the bed, and began to issue instructions—that Ossiam and his assistants start the preparations for the funeral rites in the Sacred Grove ("No animal sacrifices, just flowers and incense"), that Herrwn compose an elegy ("Her name is Ealendwr, and she lived long enough to hear it spoken and to look into her mother's face"), and that Olyrrwd see to Caelym ("He'll need someone to look after him, and I've got other things to do").

Rhonnon's voice was firm and steady as she assigned their tasks. It was still steady, but softer, when she stepped back to the bed and murmured, "I will go and tell Arianna and the other girls and see that they are prepared to come in and say their farewells as soon as you are both ready."

Herrwn wasn't at all sure what Caelym would have said given the chance to speak for himself, but Feywn answered, "We are ready now."

Nodding, Rhonnon backed away, turned, and went out to the courtyard.

Ossiam left by the door to the inner hallway, and Olyrrwd limped over to the bed and put a hand on Caelym's shoulder where Rhonnon's had been. That left Herrwn standing alone in the middle of the floor. As the shrine's chief priest, he should have said something more eloquent than "I am . . . so very sorry," but he couldn't think of any words sufficient to express how sorry he was, and, recalling the time he'd cradled Lillywen's cooling body in his arms, he knew how meaningless words were at that moment. He stood where he was, feeling their grief as if it were his own, until, remembering Rhonnon's directive, he cleared his throat and said, "I will go now and compose a song to sing for her."

"A beautiful song?" Caelym looked up, his eyes wide and childlike.

"A beautiful song."

Caelym looked back down at his dead daughter's face and whispered, "Herrwn, the greatest of our bards, will sing you a beautiful song."

Chapter 72:

Elegy for Olyrrwd

alendwr's funeral was the first to be held that year. The
second was for Ollowen, an elderly priestess mainly known
for having been Caelendra's paternal aunt. Olyrrwd's was
the third.

While Olyrrwd had attended the rites held for Ollowen at the altar
in the shrine's main grove, he hadn't gone on the steep climb
to their sacred burial chambers. "I can't make it on foot anymore," he'd muttered as he hobbled away from the gathering line
of mourners, "and I'm not ready to be carried up there just yet."

After the interment, Herrwn went to look for Olyrrwd. He
checked in the healing chamber and in the priests' quarters before
taking the lakeshore path to the secluded spot where they often
went to talk or think. That was where he found him, sitting on a
low bench the village woodworker had made for him out of gratitude for some past healing—leaning back with his legs stretched
out and his hands clasped behind his head.

After sitting down next to his cousin and drawing his own
knees up, Herrwn looked out across the shimmering waters now
and then ruffled by a stray breeze. It was just about here that
Olyrrwd had once picked up a stone, sent it skimming across the
surface of the lake, and counted the remaining years of his life
on the number of times it bounced.

"Skipping stones is not augury!" Herrwn had said it then, and he said it again now.

Olyrrwd's answer was a grunt that could have been either accord or disagreement.

Not about to let the matter rest, Herrwn persisted, "There are other things to be considered, equally or more significant."

"Such as?" From the sideways look Olyrrwd gave Herrwn—his head cocked slightly, one eyebrow raised higher than the other—and the skeptical tone of his voice, he might have been addressing a beginning apprentice with the temerity to question his master's assessment of a patient's ailment.

Herrwn, however, was not some novice in the healing chamber, and he had given this particular question a great deal of thought, especially as the end of the twelve years Olyrrwd predicted for himself drew closer.

"Such as the fact that we—Ossiam, you, and me—were born in the same year, myself first, Ossiam second, and you last, and each transition of our lives—entering training, moving up to discipleship, becoming chief priests—has occurred in that order, so it is only reasonable to assume that we shall continue in that pattern, myself crossing through the curtain into the next world first, then Ossiam, then you. So," he summed up what he felt to be a persuasive, even compelling, argument, "your dying young is simply out of the question."

"You can hardly say I'm dying young," Olyrrwd countered. "Fifty-six is older than most, what with . . ."

He went on to list the myriad and sundry causes of death of those who survived past childhood, beginning with bloody flux, proceeding through the seven deadly fevers and three ways wounds went putrid, then pausing to cough and spit before finishing, "and foul, festering lung rot."

There was an answer to that and Herrwn gave it.

"Most ordinary people, perhaps—but we are not ordinary." He augmented his argument by naming a dozen elder priests who'd earned the title by living to ninety or more.

"Although, as you may recall, our own fathers barely made it into their seventies."

"But that was the plague and even then they died together, or at least within a few days of each other, and in the order of their birth!" This was, Herrwn felt, an excellent and all but irrefutable point, and he allowed it a moment to sink in before answering Olyrrwd's litany of mortal afflictions with an equally long list of patients—priests and priestesses, servants and villagers—whose health the physician had restored with his extensive curative skills and medicinal knowledge of remedies. Carried on by the force of his argument, he asked, almost demanded, "So why can you not apply those remedies to yourself?"

"Do you think I haven't tried?" Olyrrwd snapped. "Regrettably," he continued in a tone softened to a grumble, "all of that excellent skill and knowledge is contained within a body that has always had quite annoying limitations and now is practically useless." Before Herrwn could protest, he went on, "Like it or not—and I, for one, do not like it—I am going to die."

There was something very final in the way Olyrrwd said this, so final that Herrwn didn't attempt to put forward any further rebuttal. He did manage, however, by strength of will, to ask, "When?" in a fairly steady voice.

"If I am right in my estimate—which I have no doubt that I am—I shall be joining our venerated ancestors in the sacred catacombs on or about the next autumn equinox." Olyrrwd coughed, spat, and sighed. "I will do my best to depart on the day before and save everyone the bother of making an extra trip up there."

Although increasingly weak and seeming to cough more than he breathed, Olyrrwd drove himself relentlessly for the rest of the summer and into the fall, stocking the healing chamber's shelves, sharpening and shining his collection of surgical knives and saws, and making sure that Caelym could recite from memory every treatment for every ailment he would be likely to encounter, along with the responses to all of the excuses he was going to hear from his patients for why they did not do as they were told.

Then, on the morning of the day before the autumn equinox, Olyrrwd didn't get out of bed.

Kneeling down next to him, Caelym asked, "Shall I have a stretcher brought to carry you to the healing chamber?"

"No, the healing chamber is too crowded. I'll just stay here and have one day in peace."

Since there were no patients in the healing chamber just then, Herrwn assumed that Olyrrwd meant it was too crowded with ghosts. That seemed to be what Caelym thought as well, since he nodded in agreement, pulled a chair over for Herrwn, and went to get another for himself.

Herrwn spent the day holding Olyrrwd's hand and listening to him discuss the ebbing of his life with Caelym as though it were just one more classroom lesson. Vaguely aware of Benyon stoking the fire in the hearth or Moelwyn refilling the pitcher of poppy juice, he had no sense of time moving forward until Olyrrwd reached over to pull his stained and battered healer's bag off of the bedside table, handed it to Caelym, and wheezed, "It's yours now."

Turning to Herrwn, Olyrrwd gasped, something that sounded like "Ossie" and then, "I've taken care . . . of everything . . . except Ossie . . . I meant to . . . I should have . . . but . . ." His eyelids fell closed, then opened again. "But I just . . . just couldn't . . . I'm sorry . . . now it's up to you . . . to watch out . . . to watch . . ." Looking Herrwn directly in the face, he repeated, "watch," one more time, dropped back on his pillow, closed his eyes, and gave one last, long, sighing breath.

Herrwn was not sure at first what Olyrrwd's last words meant, but as he thought it over he reached the conclusion that Olyrrwd regretted not making up his quarrel with Ossiam. Perhaps his urging Herrwn to "watch out" was not necessarily a start of his old admonitions that "Ossie is up to something" but the beginning of some thought concerning Ossiam's welfare.

Herrwn's belief in his cousins' reconciliation was strengthened by the eloquence of Ossiam's elegy for Olyrrwd and the passion with which it was given.

As chief priest, Herrwn was to have given the main eulogy for Olyrrwd, but when the time came for him to step forward and stand before the gilded litter with its sheaths of fresh and dried herbs covering over the shrouded mound—a shape so much smaller than Olyrrwd had seemed in life—his legs would not move. Instead of obeying his clear command, they shook beneath him, and they would have given way entirely if Caelym hadn't put a hand under his elbow to steady him and guide him into place.

Then his voice, like his legs, failed him. He could make his lips move, but nothing would come out. Again, Caelym came to his rescue. Speaking with bell-like clarity—but without any of his usual dramatic inflection—he summarized everything Herrwn wanted to say in a single sentence beginning, "If ever you need to remember that stature is more than height, that beauty is not in how you look but in what you see, and that wisdom is not in what you know but in what you ask," and ending, "then you will only need to say one word, and that word is 'Olyrrwd.'"

Ossiam spoke next. Stepping up to the altar, he raised his staff and proclaimed, "I stand before you not as your chief oracle but as the closest kinsman to he who lies before you." At this he flung his staff aside, covered his face with both hands, and, sobbing, said through them, "He who is lost to my embrace." Looking up, he thrust his arms skyward and shifted from tearful to triumphant as he sang out, "He who is now being welcomed into the next world, there to feast forever in the company of the eternal gods and goddesses!" He then dropped his voice, along with his arms, and, shaking his head, said, "Who am I . . . who are any of us . . . to wish him back from that so well-earned a reward?" before answering his rhetorical question, "I will not! And neither should you!" His voice strong and resonant again, the oracle spread both his hands in a gesture that encompassed the whole of his audience as he declared, "And yet he will live forever in my memory and in yours."

What followed was a passionate litany of accolades and honorifics that might have been out of an ancient epic and recited over the grave of a fallen hero.

"Quite a fine fellow he must have been—wish I'd known him." The words, spoken in Caelym's voice but with the sardonic inflection that marked Olyrrwd's gibes at what he'd called "Ossiam's puffery" startled Herrwn. When he turned to look, Caelym seemed unaware that he had said anything, in fact had tears trickling down his own cheeks as Ossiam ended, in a broken voice, "I do not weep for him but for those of us left behind, bereft and brokenhearted."

There was no other sign of it that day or in the months and years to follow, but just then, for a very brief moment, Herrwn thought it possible that—unwilling to leave his patients' care to anyone else—Olyrrwd had somehow done what no one other than a chief priestess had done before: sent his spirit across the chasm between life and death to take up residence within his chosen heir.

PART VIII

𝔓𝔯𝔦𝔢𝔰𝔱𝔢𝔰𝔰𝔥𝔬𝔬𝔡

Had some traveling philosopher seeking to discover and describe the ways of foreign and unfamiliar peoples found his way to Llwd-dawanden, and had he persuaded Herrwn to explain the education and training for boys selected to enter the priesthood, he would most likely have found himself quite exhausted after hearing about the rigors of those studies. Assuming he was astute enough to notice that the shrine had priestesses as well as priests—and was not too overwhelmed to ask for more information—and had then inquired about the education and training by which girls were prepared to become priestesses, he might have suppressed a groan to learn that the studies for becoming a priestess of the shrine of the Great Mother Goddess were, if anything, more exacting than those for becoming a priest.

Like boys, girls began learning simple recitations while still in the nursery. Unlike boys, who were abruptly taken from the nursery on the women's side of the shrine on the morning of their sixth birthday to enter the classroom on the men's side, girls remained in the women's quarters, where they advanced as quickly as possible through the basics of ordinary invocations and minor rites to increasingly intensive lessons in the songs and dances reserved for women, along with introductory instruction in midwifery, herbal lore, and keeping the sacred calendar.

The most important difference between a priestess-to-be and her male counterpart—the power to give life—was inherent and innate and its onset was marked by her first trip to the Sacred Pools. By longstanding tradition it was at this, the most important of a woman's rites of passage, that a priestess-in-training learned the last of the most secret and sacred of the women's songs and dances, and that she made her declaration of the great fields of women's endeavors she would enter.

"Then," Herrwn, who would have the advantage over his belea-guered listener of having spent most his life reciting lengthy and complex sagas and so would hardly need to pause for breath before going on, "having determined her life's path as a midwife, an herb-alist, or a keeper of the sacred calendar, she returns to the shrine to take her place at the high table and begin intensive studies with the chief priestess in her chosen field."

"But," the visiting philosopher, who would almost certainly have had his own training in oratory and argumentation, and possessed an ear for discrepancies in informant accounts, might well object, "you have said that a boy's discipleship—whether as an oracle, a bard, or a healer—is decided for him in a council of the three elder priests, and then not until he is sixteen at the earliest, and yet you say that a girl makes the same decision for herself at an age possibly as young as twelve or thirteen?"

"Well, of course! Is that not how it is among your people?" Herrwn would no doubt answer and, frankly, would be wondering why he'd agreed to waste his time answering foolish questions from someone either simple-minded or inexcusably ignorant.

It would have been unfair of Herrwn to dismiss the visiting philoso-pher's question out of hand and without considering the possibility that there could be a society in which it was not assumed that girls born to their highest class were gifted with an inner wisdom that emerged along with the capacity to become pregnant—unlike boys, who needed to be trained and molded to assume the responsibilities of priesthood and who could hardly be expected to know what was best for themselves and the shrine until well into their adult years.

As with most societal norms, the question of whether this supposition was true was distinct from the question of whether it worked—and for most of a millennium, the assumption that "what girls know, boys must be taught" had worked well, so well that the possibility that the generally appropriate choices made by young girls might be explained by the benefits of having deep, ongoing relationships with their mothers (or, for those orphaned at birth, by a close female relative) was never considered. With the inherent wisdom of girls taken for granted, no one realized that a test of that notion was underway in the aftermath of Rhedwyn's fatal charge.

That so much of life in the shrine had gone on apparently unchanged in spite of losing so many of the valley's young men was in large part because the elder priestesses—Rhonnon, Aolfe, and Lunedd—had quietly taken up the tasks left behind by the servants who'd gone to work in the fields and pastures. It was out of simple necessity that caring for the five girls on whom the future of the shrine depended was turned over to a nurse who, though doting and devoted, was not equipped to replace the individual nurturance and learning the little priestesses-to-be would have received from their mothers. The girls were by no means neglected and each one, in fact, thrived in her own way, but their lack of maternal guidance and the stronger than usual alliance they formed with each other would eventually have unintended consequences for everyone in Llwddawanden.

Chapter 73:

A Place at the Table

T
he morning after Olyrrwd's funeral, Herrwn got up and went to the Sacred Sunrise Ritual cushioned by the sense that his cousin was just off tending some patient and would be coming back around the corner at any moment. It was a self-deception he knew wouldn't last, and it didn't—it ended the moment that he arrived at breakfast and saw Olyrrwd's chair had been taken away from the table and no bowl or cup had been set out for him.

If, as Herrwn had somehow expected, he and Ossiam had been drawn closer in their shared sorrow, that would have been at least some compensation for Olyrrwd's death. But that didn't happen. Instead, their exchanges at mealtimes or when they passed each other in the hall could have been conversations between any two polite strangers—largely amounting to Ossiam saying, "Yes, we must do that sometime," whenever Herrwn suggested they play a game of Stones or take a walk together.

Through the fall and winter and into the spring, Herrwn spent his mornings rehearsing orations, conducting rituals, or presiding over council meetings and his afternoons shuffling the ritual implements on the classroom shelves or staring into the flames of the hearth—always answering, "No, thank you, but no," when Benyon asked if he needed anything.

That was not true, but what he needed—a companion of his age and rank—was not something a servant could fetch for him.

◆●◆

On an overcast afternoon some three weeks after the spring equinox, Herrwn was rearranging the shelf where Olyrrwd had kept his medicinals. Having done this numerous times before, he knew that when Caelym came back to their quarters he would put the vessels and vials back the way Olyrrwd had always kept them—sorted by their contents rather than their size and shape—but he found it soothing to finger the things his cousin had handled so often, and Caelym never complained about finding them out of order or showed any impatience when he moved them into their proper positions.

If Olyrrwd were there, he would have barked at Herrwn to "stop meddling with my potions! Just pour yourself something, sit down, and drink it!"

Hearing his cousin's gruff voice in his mind, Herrwn took down the flask of elderberry wine and two cups—his own and Olyrrwd's—filled each halfway, and carried them over to the table by the hearth, as he'd gotten into the habit of doing at this time of day, when everyone was busy somewhere else and no one would see him sitting alone at the table with two cups set out, drinking first from one and then the other—talking aloud to his cousin's empty place and listening to what he assumed Olyrrwd would say back to him.

Sitting down and taking a sip from his cup, he sighed. "Things did not go well at the High Council this morning."

"Another prank by our meddlesome sprite?" Herrwn imagined Olyrrwd would ask, in the tolerant and amused tone he reserved for childish escapades and his patients' unbelievable explanations of how they'd caused themselves embarrassing injuries.

Herrwn took a sip from Olyrrwd's cup and sighed again. "No, worse than that—it was quite dreadful, really, and I do not know what, if anything, I can say to remedy the situation . . . not, of course, that I would be called upon for my advice."

Realizing that he'd just allowed his buried resentment that Feywn had never—not once in the twenty years of her reign as their chief priestess—called on him for his counsel on anything to slip out, Herrwn drew a calming breath and a sip from his own cup before continuing, "Today's High Council was, as you may know, the first since Arianna made her first trip to the Sacred

Pools, so there was every reason to expect Feywn would make the pronouncement that her daughter was her chosen successor." He took a sip from Olyrrwd's cup. "Though perhaps she feels Arianna is not yet ready, as she comes to rituals late and unprepared, and shows no contrition at her mother's stern looks of reproach—indeed, appears on the verge of . . ."

Herrwn fumbled for the right word before finally choosing "disrespect," although "defiance" was actually closer to what he'd witnessed that morning.

Herrwn had, as usual, gone to the council chamber early to stand at his place, ready to greet the others as they entered.

As he watched Caelym, in his formal robes, conducting himself with the solemn dignity expected of the consort to the shrine's chief priestess, Herrwn was struck by how much they were expecting of a boy barely past his twentieth birthday.

That was a thought he would ponder later, when he was sitting by himself in the shrine's classroom—but then his mind moved on to noticing that Feywn, always exquisitely gowned, looked especially impressive that day, and he guessed it meant that this was the day she was going to name her daughter as her successor. The same idea must have occurred to Rhonnon, because she hesitated before taking her seat on Feywn's right—seeming somehow reluctant to take that place even after she got Feywn's nod to do so.

The next most likely announcement would be the naming of the priestess and priest who were to enact the parts of the Earth-Goddess and the Sun-God at the coming Summer Solstice Ceremony.

While Herrwn was nodding and greeting, half lost in his speculations, four of the five priestesses-in-training—Gwenydd, the twins, and Cyri—came in and took their seats at the far right end of the table, leaving only Arianna's chair empty.

Rhonnon glanced at them as though she were expecting one of them to speak up and explain Arianna's absence.

Ossiam shifted in his seat and drummed his fingers on the table.

Caelym slid his hand over to rest on top of Feywn's in much the same gesture that Olyrrwd had used to calm Caelym whenever he suffered from boyish fidgeting.

Just as Herrwn thought he should say something, perhaps suggest that one of the women servants be sent to see whether Arianna was suddenly taken ill, the curtain to the room parted and Arianna stepped through.

Instead of a simple, unadorned gown like the other priestesses-in-training were wearing, Arianna was dressed in the resplendent silk robes reserved for the highest of priestesses to wear on the most important occasions, so it was obvious to Herrwn—and everyone else in the chamber—that she, too, expected this to be the day that she took her place at her mother's right side.

But the chair next to her mother was taken, and the only place open was the chair at the far end of the table between the twins and Cyri.

It was a dreadful misunderstanding—one that would have been humiliating for anyone, and certainly must have been overwhelming to a sensitive girl at an age when even the slightest embarrassment was catastrophic.

For a moment Arianna stood still, looking at the chair where Rhonnon was seated, and then at her mother, her cheeks reddening as though she'd been slapped across the face.

Recalling the days he'd spent watching over the girls in the shrine's garden and how quickly the smallest upsets had sent Arianna into a sobbing tantrum, Herrwn more than half expected that she would betray both her disappointment and her age by turning and running off in tears.

But she didn't turn and run. She walked as proudly and deliberately toward the high table as if the chair next to her mother were pulled out and waiting for her.

If Caelendra had been in Feywn's place, Herrwn was certain she would have found something to say to ameliorate the situation and soothe her daughter's hurt feelings. Feywn, however, was not Caelendra, and her stinging question—"Why are you late?"—was clearly meant as a rebuke, since it was obvious to everyone that Arianna had been changing her clothes and fixing her hair.

Coming to a stop directly in front of her mother, Arianna met Feywn's censorious stare with one that was all but openly insolent.

There was a long moment of silence.

The tension in the room felt to Herrwn like the pressure in the air just before a lightning strike. He held his breath, waiting to see which of the two would be the first to look away.

Arianna was.

Her gaze shifted to Caelym, who looked back at her and made the slightest of gestures—a shrug, his right shoulder rising a little higher than the left—before cocking his head to the side and adding his stern look to Feywn's. At that, Arianna gave a slight, almost mischievous, toss of her head, turned as lightly as if she were beginning to dance, and walked around behind the table to take her place at the far end between the twins and Cyri.

Ossiam waited just long enough for Arianna to take her seat before standing up and giving a rigidly formulaic prophecy regarding the weather and the prospects for the fall harvest, and the meeting began.

◆◆◆

"And I know you will see that as yet another proof that Ossiam has come to a better understanding of what harm a carelessly worded prophesy can do." Herrwn, taking a sip from his cup of wine, managed to convince himself that Olyrrwd would have agreed to this as the one positive outcome of an otherwise painful meeting, rather than retort, *"Ossie never made a carelessly worded prophesy in his life."*

"In any case," he continued, "the rest of the council went without further upset, although the mood remained"—again Herrwn needed to search for the right word—"strained." So strained, in fact, that when Feywn made the announcement that Gwenydd and Moelwyn are to enact the parts of the Earth-Goddess and the Sun-God at this year's Summer Solstice Ceremony, no one—not even Gwenydd and Moelwyn—gave more than the stiffest nods of acknowledgment."

"Perhaps"—Herrwn took a final sip from Olyrrwd's cup—"you are thinking that I am making too much of an event that came and went in less time than it takes to tell about it, but it worries me." Knowing what high regard Olyrrwd had for their chief midwife, he added, "And I think it worried Rhonnon too."

It was at this precise moment that—with no more warning than a single knock—the classroom doors swung open and Benyon rushed in, crying out, "Master Herrwn, Master Herrwn!" Here he stopped abruptly, looked both ways as though to be sure there were no spies or eavesdroppers lurking nearby, and lowered his voice to a hushed whisper before announcing, "Priestess Rhonnon requires your attendance on a matter of utmost importance and says that you are to come at once!"

Alarmed, Herrwn sprang to his feet, took up his staff, and rushed in the direction of the women's quarters.

Belodden was already holding the main door open when Herrwn arrived. Whispering for him to follow, she led the way through an arched passage to a set of double doors that, like the entrance to the priests' classroom, was engraved with a pair of oak trees with intertwined branches. There was a disk representing the moon on the door to Herrwn's left, and that was the door that Belodden cracked open, just wide enough to let him enter.

Chapter 74:

The Women's Council

nder ordinary circumstances, Herrwn would no more
expect to be ushered into the priestesses' private meeting
room than to be given free access to their bedchambers.
Clearly, this was no ordinary circumstance.

Pausing to compose himself and straighten his robes, he drew
a breath and stepped past Belodden into a round room roughly
the same size as the shrine's High Council chamber. Its stone
floor was inlaid with strips of burnished copper, making three
concentric rings and divided into four equal wedges by two lines
that crossed in the center. There was a large table in the middle of
the room and a small one set close to the arc of each wedge. Each
tabletop was a thick disk of polished oak with a line of circular
symbols inscribed around its rim, glyphs that were similar in
size and identical in design to the pendants the priestesses wore
to denote their field of endeavor—three interlaced waves for the
midwives, three upright plants for the herbalists, and a crescent
moon enclosing three stars for the keepers of the sacred calendar.

The table on the east side of the chamber had only wave symbols, the one on the south side only plants, and the one on the
west side only crescents, while the large table in the center of the
room and the small table on the north side by the chamber's one
window had all three repeated in an alternating pattern.

Herrwn knew, because Lothwen had told him, that the glyphs
marked tables reserved for members of the separate vocations.
The large table was for formal meetings, and the table by the

window was where the priestesses sat if they wished to confer with those of different fields—the obvious exception being the chief priestess, who, it went without saying, could sit at any table she wished.

Rhonnon was sitting at the north table, staring out the window. The chair across from her was pulled back.

"May I?" Herrwn asked.

"Do!" she answered as she turned to face him. "Please," she added as an afterthought.

No sooner had he settled himself than she said, "We have a problem—one that is extremely delicate."

Now certain this clandestine meeting had to do with some further strife between Feywn and Arianna, Herrwn hastened to reassure her of his absolute discretion. "Whatever this problem is, know that you may speak to me about it freely and in the fullest confidence."

"I knew I could count on you." Rhonnon's typically brisk response was marred by an uncharacteristic stutter as she said, "It . . . it is about Gwenydd."

"Gwenydd?" he repeated, caught off guard. "Not Arianna?"

"You would have thought so, and so would I. Arianna almost certainly, sooner or later and probably sooner. The twins possibly, if only for the fun of creating confusion for all concerned. Possibly even Cyri, though not for another few years, I hope. Still, I would have understood if it had been any of them but Gwenydd."

Now completely bewildered, Herrwn could make no sense of what Rhonnon was saying. Was Gwenydd, the most reliable of the young priestesses, also rebelling against Feywn's divinely ordained authority?

As he was struggling to formulate that question, Rhonnon went on, "As you know, Gwenydd is seventeen. She made her first trip to the Sacred Pools three years ago and returned, as we all expected, ready to enter her advanced training in herbal lore with Aolfe, and since then, again as expected, has excelled in her studies."

While Herrwn was no longer involved in the young priestesses' daily life, he was well aware of Gwenydd's progress and that she was, as always, the best behaved and most responsible of the five girls. The thought that it was Gwenydd, rather than Arianna, who was the subject of this extraordinary meeting left him unable to do more than nod.

Apparently that was all Rhonnon expected. She nodded back and went on, "So there seemed no question that she had earned the honor of being named to enact the Earth-Goddess at the coming Summer Solstice Ceremony, and no reason to even imagine . . ."

Rhonnon drew in a breath and blew it out again. Herrwn waited for her to continue. When she didn't, he repeated her last words as a question.

"No reason to even imagine?"

"That she would come to Aolfe and me and say that she will not take part in the Summer Solstice Ceremony!"

"She will not? But why—or, that is, why not?"

"Because it seems she has already chosen a consort, and she views it as being . . . I don't know what . . . disloyal, or unfaithful, or some such nonsense, but she is adamant that she 'will not mate with another man or even the Sun-God himself.'"

Herrwn let out a sigh of relief. While it was unheard of—unthinkable, really—that a priestess named to be the Earth-Goddess would refuse that honor, the priest chosen to play the Sun-God could and often did change between the public announcement and the actual event as eager contenders vied for the part.

"Well, in that case, I will speak with Moelwyn. I am sure he will step aside so she may instead name . . ."

Herrwn left the line dangling as he waited for Rhonnon to name the priest who was Gwenydd's own choice.

Instead of responding to his implied question, she abruptly changed the subject, asking, "Do you know who Darbin is?"

"Darbin"—it was not the name of anyone he knew personally, but still it was a name he knew . . . a name Olyrrwd had used not once but several times when he was collecting the provisions for Caelym's spirit quest. "He is the village smith," Herrwn answered. "Olyrrwd thought highly of him."

"Indeed." Rhonnon's tone lacked any trace of warmth. "So, it seems, does Gwenydd."

Shocked, Herrwn could only stammer, "But . . . but she is . . . but he is . . ."

Rhonnon filled in the missing words. "She is a priestess born to the highest ranks of our order, all but openly acknowledged to be our next chief herbalist, and he is, as you say, the village smith."

"How could—"

"I don't know, and frankly it doesn't matter. What matters is what we are going to do about it!"

"You have spoken with her, explaining that such a thing is forbidden—"

"I have."

"And?"

"She says she does not care, and that if we refuse our consent to this . . . union . . . she will leave the valley with him."

"But that cannot be!"

"Indeed it cannot, both because Aolfe will not risk the loss of her best pupil and because we cannot afford the loss of the valley's only smith. That is why I have called you."

As shocked as he was, Herrwn couldn't help but feel flattered that Rhonnon was calling for his counsel regarding an issue that might be considered exclusively a woman's matter. Straightening his back, he declared, "I will give this quandary my deepest consideration."

"I already have."

Having been an advisor to two high priestesses and a consort to another, Herrwn recognized Rhonnon's response to mean that he was not being asked for his counsel but for his compliance. He folded his fingers firmly around his staff and listened as she went on to remind him how many of their greatest priests and priestesses had been born to young priestesses in the prime of their childbearing years whose consorts were elder priests and sometimes exceptionally elder priests, men in their eighties and nineties.

That was of course true, and it was one of the things Herrwn had always understood to distinguish those in their order from ordinary men. While Rhonnon's clarification was worded diplomatically, it left no doubt that what distinguished those extremely elder priests from ordinary men was their willingness to lend the distinction of their fatherhood to the children of their consorts, regardless of how those children might actually have been conceived.

As was expected of a man with his years of training in maintaining a neutral countenance in the face of unexpected disclosures, Herrwn did so, nodding gravely and only raising his eyebrows when Rhonnon concluded, "And you, I'm sure, will do the same!"

"I?"

"You!"

"You mean . . ."

"I do! Aolfe and I have talked it over at great length and decided it is the only way. Gwenydd will name you as the priest to play the part of the Sun-God and be her consort thereafter. You and she will be given a bedchamber at the far end of the hall reserved for priestesses with consorts and children. All that will be required is that you and she enter the room together. There is a back door that opens onto the courtyard, so she may continue whatever private arrangements she has already made and you may choose whether to sleep there or spend the night in your own quarters."

"I see. And have you spoken with Gwenydd about this?" Herrwn answered cautiously, reluctant to agree to being a party to a charade, however well intended.

"I have."

"And she is in agreement?"

"She is seventeen! She insists that she will take this smith as her consort openly and proudly, and that he and none other will be named the father of her children, but"—Rhonnon crossed her arms and looked Herrwn straight in the eye—"she likes you very much and will listen to you if she listens to anyone."

"So what you wish me to do is—"

"Go to her, use your powers of persuasion, and convince her that this is best for all concerned."

After a long moment of silence, Herrwn cleared his throat, tightened his grip on his staff, and said, "I will speak to her. It should, of course, be a confidential conversation, conducted somewhere private."

"Aolfe told Gwenydd to remain in her room while we conferred over this. Belodden will take you there." With that, Rhonnon returned to staring out the window, her back straight and her shoulders stiff.

Belodden was waiting for Herrwn when he opened the door. She turned to lead the way before he could tell her where they were to go.

Chapter 75:

Where's Gwenydd?

here had been a time in Herrwn's youth when the very thought of venturing up the stairs to the women's sleeping chambers would have set his heart racing. Now, as he followed Belodden up those stairs facing the prospect of doing something that seemed to him both profoundly wrong and absolutely necessary, each of his footsteps seemed to weigh more than the one before.

There was a heaviness in the tread of Belodden's feet as well, making it sound as if she were wearing boots instead of sandals as she took him down the hallway to the second to the last of a dozen identical doors.

She opened the door and stood back. He started in but stopped before he finished crossing the threshold.

The twins were sitting on one of two beds with their heads bent over a parchment star chart, and Cyri was at a table by the window, sorting through a tray of dried herbs. All three looked up, appearing mildly surprised.

Thinking they must be in the wrong room, Herrwn would have apologized except that Belodden brushed past him and demanded, "What are you doing here? Where is Gwenydd?"

As the guardian of the entrance to the women's quarters, Belodden wielded considerable authority over who was where on the priestesses' side of the shrine, and Herrwn would have been hard-pressed not to cower if she had challenged him in that tone. The girls, however, seemed unconcerned and answered, "Studying our lessons," in a single voice while they looked around the room and shrugged as if it were only at this moment that they'd noticed Gwenydd wasn't there.

Incensed, Belodden sputtered, "Priestess Aolfe said . . . Priestess Rhonnon will be . . . You will tell me where . . ."

While Belodden was fuming, Herrwn saw the girls' lips pinch into tight, resolute lines. Knowing that commanding them to answer would only guarantee their silence, he turned to the incensed sub-priestess, bowed, and thanked her for her assistance before going on to say, "You may return to your post reassured that I will carry out the charge Priestess Rhonnon has given me. I'm sure I can find my own way out after these priestesses-in-training and I have finished speaking together."

He wasn't at all sure that his authority as the shrine's chief priest held sway in the inner sanctum of the women's quarters, and he saw the same doubt in Belodden's face. Still, he didn't allow his look to waver, and after a long moment, the guardian gave a disgruntled humph and stalked out of the room.

From the corner of his eye, he saw the three girls exchange exultant smiles, which, needless to say, vanished and were replaced by sincere expressions of solemn innocence as he turned to look at them directly.

From his long experience as a teacher (much of it spent teaching Caelym), Herrwn knew that silent but intense regard was a better key to a delinquent's mind than a raised voice and frustrated recriminations. Accordingly, he straightened up to his full height and stood looking from one upturned face to the next. The twins managed to remain steadfast, but Cyri shifted her gaze down, then looked back.

Herrwn cleared his throat, chose his next words with care, and addressed them all so as not to give their weak link away.

"Like Belodden, who is the honored guardian of the entrance to the women's quarters, I am deeply concerned that Gwenydd, daughter of Gwennefor, is not where she is expected to be. There is undoubtedly a good reason for this, and undoubtedly you who are her closest cousins and confidants know what that reason is."

"She broke her"—the twins started together—"necklace," said one as the other said, "bracelet," before finishing in unison, "and she needed to get it fixed."

"I see. So then she has gone . . ."

"To the smith in the village," Cyri whispered.

Careful to maintain his outward composure, Herrwn thanked the girls for their help and left the room. He closed the door behind him, hurried down the hall to the top of the stairs, and then stopped, wavering.

Should he go to Rhonnon and warn her that Gwenydd had run off and perhaps even now was fleeing with her lover? To do that would raise a hue and cry—and to what avail? Gwenydd was of age and a full-fledged priestess. None but Feywn had the authority to command her to do something against her will. And if it came to that and she openly refused Feywn's command, then the chief priestess's imposing the penalty of banishment would only accomplish what they most wanted to avoid.

No! He had promised Rhonnon that he would speak to Gwenydd, so that was what he would do—if it was not already too late.

His mind made up, he descended the stairs, nodded confidently to Belodden as he passed her on his way out the main entrance, and only broke into a run after he was well out of her sight.

Chapter 76:

Darbin

Though not as familiar with the village as Olyrrwd had been, Herrwn knew the way to the smith's compound. He'd spent a sweltering day there watching Darbin's father hammering out a plow shaft from a glowing iron ingot when he was seventeen. His own father had taken him there with the instructions to observe a real smith at his work, in order to instill more life into his recitation of a saga in which the god of metalworking forged a magical sword that played a critical part in both setting off and resolving a war between the king of Llanmeddelyderth and a race of mountain trolls.

The cluster of buildings encircled by a low stone wall was much as he remembered it. The smith's cottage and an assortment of outbuildings were on one side of the yard that served as both a vegetable garden and a chicken run. The workshop, with its glowing forge, was on the other. Its door was open and Herrwn could see tools scattered on the workbench and a broken cartwheel lying on the ground as if dropped in the workman's rush to leave. Beside the chickens, the one sign of life was a slender, dark-haired child who looked to be about seven or eight, sitting on the cottage stoop and hugging a doll Herrwn recognized as being from Gwenydd's childhood collection. Perhaps it was just the doll, but there was something oddly familiar about the little girl, even though Herrwn was certain he had never seen her before.

As he opened the gate and crossed the yard, the chickens ran up to him, clucking for a handout, while the little girl edged back.

Hopeful that the child's presence meant he'd gotten there in time, Herrwn knelt down to be at her eye level before he spoke.

"I am looking for Priestess Gwenydd. Is she here?"

"I can't tell," she whispered. "It's a secret."

"It's all right, I know the secret," he whispered back. "And I have another secret to share with her, so I'll just go in very quietly and tell her what it is."

Taking the child's timid nod as permission to proceed, he stood up, pressed down on the door latch, and eased it open just as Gwenydd was saying, "They can cast me out! I don't care! We'll take Mai and go somewhere . . ."

Still dressed in the finely woven and skillfully embroidered robes she'd worn to the morning's High Council, Gwenydd looked out of place in the rustic room with its rough-cut furniture, shelves of plain clay bowls, and half-grown pig watching the goings-on from a far corner.

The man clearly belonged there. Of average height for a villager, he was shorter than Herrwn by two handbreadths. His clothes—a leather apron worn over a leather tunic and pants—were dotted with scorch marks. As was to be expected of a laborer who made his living working with heavy tools, his arms and shoulders were solidly muscled. His hair was sandy blond and his eyes blue, suggesting that beneath the soot from his forge he was fair-skinned. Guessing at his age, Herrwn would have put him in his early twenties, although if the child on the stoop outside was his, he'd have to be older than that.

Like the little girl, there was something familiar about him. It took Herrwn a moment, but then he realized it was that Darbin closely resembled his father.

He cleared his throat to let them know he was there and stepped forward. "Forgive my intrusion, but I have been asked by Priestess Rhonnon to speak with Gwenydd about a matter I believe concerns all three of us."

They turned, startled.

Darbin, who'd been clasping Gwenydd's hands, let go and stepped back, looking as guilty as a child caught taking a forbidden sweet. Gwenydd held her ground. She crossed her arms and started, "I already told her—"

Putting up his hand to stop what was certain to be an emotional tirade, Herrwn shifted his stance to face her lover. "Under the circumstances, I believe it would be proper that we be introduced. Might you be Darbin, the artisan of whom my beloved cousin Olyrrwd spoke so highly?"

The smith opened his mouth, closed it, and nodded.

Herrwn nodded in return. "I am Herrwn, chief priest of our shrine, to whom it has been given to find some way to resolve this difficulty that is best for all concerned—"

"I don't care what Aolfe or Rhonnon or even Feywn says," Gwenydd broke in, "I love Darbin and he loves me—"

"I know I'm just a smith—"

"Not 'just'!" Gwenydd reached out, took hold of his rough, callused hand, and pressed it against her cheek as she declared, "He is the most wonderful smith in the world! He can make anything and fix anything."

Having taken on the role of being a mother to her younger cousins when she was barely eight years old, Gwenydd had always been serious, even solemn, but now her face positively glowed with enthusiasm as Darbin gazed at her with a look that only a completely besotted man could achieve.

Herrwn set his staff aside and put up both his hands to interrupt their reverie. "Now then, as I was saying, I have told Rhonnon I would speak to you—"

"I already told her—"

Gwenydd, who had never, to Herrwn's knowledge, been defiant in her life, seemed ready to start now. This, however, was not the time for it, and Herrwn gave her the stern look he'd so often needed to use with the twins and Arianna.

"I am aware of what you told her regarding her proposal. Now I expect that you will do me the courtesy of hearing mine—"

"I—" she started, but changed to saying, "We will," with a stress on the word "we."

Granting her assertion with a brief nod, Herrwn continued, "which is that you both conduct yourselves with dignity and decorum while I find a way to resolve this issue without dishonoring your love for each other or requiring you to leave our valley. Can you do that?"

It was Darbin who answered, "We can."

Gwenydd nodded, still gripping her lover's hand.

"Now then, I will ask that you, Gwenydd, accompany me back to the shrine and tell Aolfe and Rhonnon that you are giving my words your thoughtful consideration and that you, Darbin, remain here and comfort your daughter—"

"Sister," they said together, sounding like the twins would have if one were a baritone.

"Sister," Herrwn amended, "who sits outside, distressed by matters she is too young to understand."

Leaving Darbin to tend to his sister, Herrwn set off up the path to the shrine with Gwenydd at his side. Once he'd seen the young priestess past the grim and glowering Belodden, he walked back to his own quarters and stood staring into the flickering embers in the hearth.

Chapter 77:

At Times Like These

It was at times like these that Herrwn most missed Olyrrwd. Whenever Olyrrwd sensed that Herrwn needed to talk, he would make the excuse that it was a quiet day in the healing chamber, so why didn't they go for a walk along the lakeshore. As they strolled along the path to their favorite spot, Herrwn would explain his quandary. Then, after they'd sat on their bench, looking out across the lake, for a while, Olyrrwd would come up with some practical solution that Herrwn would never have thought of on his own.

Lost in his longing for Olyrrwd, Herrwn was startled when the classroom doors swung open and Caelym came in, carrying Arddwn on his shoulders. "It's a quiet day in the healing chamber," he announced cheerfully, "so we're going to sail our boat in the lake. Have you time to join us?"

With the pressing urgency of solving Gwenydd's dilemma, Herrwn started to say, "I can't," but Arddwn—a miniature version of Caelym, except for having Feywn's sapphire-blue eyes—had inherited his mother's capacity for command. Gripping a lock of his father's hair with one hand and waving a toy boat with the other, he declared, "Herwun come!" and Herrwn changed to saying, "I would be most pleased to do so."

It was a decision he would always be glad he made.

Once they reached the lakeshore path, Caelym put his squirming son down. Arddwn, who'd crawled at six months, walked at eight months, and now considered anything less than a dead run to be too slow, darted up the path ahead of them.

For a while, Herrwn and Caelym walked along without talking, Herrwn wondering if it was right to share the burden weighing so heavily on his mind. He'd just decided it was not, when Caelym said in a quiet and confidential way, "I've just been seeing to our cook's toe."

Freed of any constraint that he might be revealing anything Caelym did not already know, Herrwn recounted the events of his day, finishing just as they reached the quiet cove where he'd stood so often with Olyrrwd.

After settling Arddwn with his toy boat at the edge of a shallow pool, Caelym cleared his throat and said, "I have been thinking about the oration for tonight."

Herrwn's shoulders sagged at the realization that he'd been so distraught over Gwenydd's plight he'd given no thought at all to the evening oration—something he'd often lectured Caelym was a master bard's first and foremost responsibility. Resisting the temptation to make excuses, he sighed. "It is fortunate that one of us was attentive to his duty. We must decide quickly and pick something from one of the less demanding tales—perhaps 'The Wizard's Ill-Fated Apprentice' from the sagas of the Great Flood?"

"I was thinking of that very saga, only"—Caelym stroked his chin in a gesture much like one Olyrrwd often made—"I had been thinking that we might do the fifth story." After a small but telling pause, he added, "The fifth story, that is, from the eastern version."

Of course! The fifth and final story from the epic of the eastern version of the Great Flood! Where had his mind been?

Caelym had continued to grow taller over the past year, and Herrwn now had to look upwards to meet his eyes. When he did it in this moment, it was to share a look of complete understanding.

From there it was mainly a matter of changing a few lines and working out the practical details—which, as it turned out, Caelym had mostly done already. So, with a quick rehearsal and a few final revisions, they had the evening's event planned down to the last detail by the time Arddwn had brought his bedraggled little boat back to shore and was ready to go home.

Chapter 78:

The Smith's Tale

errwn was changing into his formal robes—wishing he'd had more time to rehearse and wondering what was keeping Caelym—when the evening horn sounded. He murmured the narrator's last and most crucial lines to himself, took up his staff, both his own and Caelym's harp, and was starting for the door, when, to his relief, Caelym came bounding through, his hair rumpled and his robes obviously pulled on in haste.

"Forgive my being late, but—" While Caelym's words were duly apologetic, his tone as well as the gleam in his eye suggested smugness rather than contrition as he continued, "I have done my best to ensure that Feywn is in an agreeable mood this evening."

Under other circumstances, Herrwn's response "That comes as a great relief to me!" might have been sardonic, but in this case he was entirely sincere, knowing how much hinged on their chief priestess's mood that night. Since the meal would not start before Feywn arrived, Herrwn set his staff and the harps aside and straightened Caelym's robes. "Your hair," he said, and waited while Caelym retreated to the dressing room to comb his locks into place. Using the time to adjust his own harp's tuning, he felt calmer and ready to start when Caelym emerged, groomed and grinning.

Herrwn led the way to the main hall, stopping outside of the high-arched entry. He could hear the hum of restive conversation coming through the heavy curtains.

"Now, Master?" Caelym's hand was already on the edge of the curtain, and, with Herrwn's nod, he pulled it aside and they stepped through together.

The shutters to the chamber windows were closed and the hearth was glowing. The priests and priestesses were in their seats and waiting—now silent as Herrwn walked solemnly across the room and took the narrator's place just to the right of the hearth. Caelym moved to the left to stand in the shadows, half-hidden, waiting until it was time for him to step out into the light and say his lines.

"With your leave," Herrwn began, and, receiving Feywn's nod, went on, "tonight I, along with my worthy disciple, will tell a tale from the saga of the Great Flood.

Leaning forward and casting a sweeping glance from one end of the high table to the other, he said in a low, confiding tone, "As commonly told, this tale—the story of how the great King Dwrddwain sent his wisest wizard, along with his mightiest warrior, to find a way to force back the sea after the ill-fated wizard's apprentice had brought forth a deluge that threatened to cover the earth—is well-known to all. But the story we will tell tonight is not the usual tale but one told only on rare occasions, and then only to those in the inner circle of Druid priests and priestesses."

Turning slightly to gaze into the flickering flames of the hearth, he assumed the voice of someone looking into the distant past.

The story, as you know, is from an ancient time, a time when all humankind still lived together in a single kingdom, and that kingdom was ruled over by the first dynasty of kings, of whom King Dwrddwain was the twenty-first. Only a few ever knew—and few of those remembered later—that the actual cause of this calamity lay six generations earlier, when King Dwrddwain's great-great-great-great-grandfather, King Dwrfwyn, reneged on his promise to give the Sea-Goddess a crown of gold as tribute for granting his ships safe passage through a channel roiling with monsters.

Disregarding the dire warnings of his Druid counselors, Dwrfwyn ordered his craftsmen to make the crown out of lead instead of gold, gilding the base metal so it glittered. It was a grievous deception and a foolish one, as it was quickly unmasked when the salt water washed away the paint. The outraged Sea-Goddess exacted a swift revenge, but revenge does not heal, and while above the shoreline the kingdom prospered under Dwrfwyn's wiser descendants, underneath the ocean's restless surface the goddess continued to brood, both over the affront and over the crown, which had appeared wonderful and turned out to be a sham. So while the ill-fated wizard's apprentice should never have cast his imprudent spell, the result would not have been so calamitous had it not served to break open that festering wound, releasing the Sea-Goddess's pent-up rage and setting forth the immense wave of water that swept up over the land, driving humans and animals alike to take refuge on the top of the highest mountain."

With the background set, Herrwn stepped back into place and assumed the traditional narrator's stance.

A mountain, did I just call it? A mountain was what it had been the day before, but now it was a shrinking island, its edges being eaten away by the terrifying waves that surged ever higher, its trees lashed by terrible winds!

Wolves and sheep, eagles and song sparrows, the king's royal family and ordinary villagers huddled together, the divisions between them forgotten in their shared dread of the sea.

Standing apart, on a boulder at the peak of that last remaining outcrop of earth, King Dwrddwain looked out over what was left of his once vast kingdom.

A very different ruler from his great-great-great-great-grandfather, King Dwrddwain's concern was not what was left to him but who. Surveying his surviving subjects, he was relieved to see that along with his greatest wizard, Alhwradd, and his great warrior, Haedrwn, his royal smith, Sidwal, had somehow managed to outrun the flood and climb up the side of the mountain in spite of being weighed down with his heavy pack of tools.

At the mention of the word "smith," Rhonnon lowered her eyebrows and fixed Herrwn with an intense stare. He was expecting no less and went on without the slightest hesitation.

Calling the smith's name and pointing to the swaying trees, the king commanded, "Sidwal, build me a boat strong enough to withstand the storming seas!"

When the boat was built and its sail hung in place, the king called out, "Who will go forth to subdue the sea and win back the land?"

Haedrwn, the king's chief warrior, raised his sword and declared, "I will go and, with my strength and my courage, win victory over the sea itself!"

Hearing that, Alhwradd, the king's chief wizard, raised his staff and declared, "No warrior, however brave and strong, can defeat the sea! I will go and, with my wisdom and my powers of persuasion, I will make peace with the sea and convince it to go back to its proper shores!"

While the two of them argued with each other, the smith went about his work loading the boat and raising the sail.

As the winds swirled, catching the sail and blowing it full, the king made his decision, declaring, "You will both go, for our only hope is in the combined power of our warrior's strength and our Druid's wisdom!"

Momentarily turning to look directly at his audience and shifting back to a confiding tone of voice, Herrwn shared the king's inner thoughts, saying, *"And even as he spoke those words, the king realized that while the wizard was thinking and the warrior was doing battle, someone would need to sail the boat, but none of his sailors were among the surviving subjects and so—reasoning that Sidwal, having built it, would be the best one to sail it—he commanded the smith to go along.*

He reverted to his formal narrator stance and voice and continued.

So, picking up his sack of tools, the smith followed the wizard and the warrior on board, and, as all the tribes of humans and animals watched, the boat set forth into the raging seas.

On the first day of the storm-tossed journey, the angry winds tore at the sail and snapped the mast in two, and they would have been lost had not Sidwal splinted the shaft together and put it back up so they could sail on.

On the second day of their fearful venture, a sea dragon rose out of the raging waters, and when Haedrwn raised up his sword to fight it, the dragon stuck out its head with the speed of a striking snake, took the sword in its mouth, bit it in half, and spat the pieces down at the warrior's feet. As the dreadful serpent drew back, preparing to strike again, Sidwal swiftly grabbed the broken weapon, forged it back together with three strokes of his hammer, and threw it back to Haedrwn, who slew the dragon and mounted its head as a trophy on the boat's prow.

On the third day of their perilous quest, they came to the edge of a giant whirlpool and would have been sucked in had not the smith pulled an anchor out of his pack, the wizard imbued it with a magical spell, and the warrior cast it off behind them so that it held them in place at the edge of the swirling maelstrom.

While Haedrwn was fighting the sea dragon and Sidwal was repairing the ship's mast and the warrior's sword, Alhwradd had been thinking and pondering and doing deep and exhaustive divinations, and he had come to the conclusion that peace with the sea could only be earned by righting the ancient wrong.

Calling the smith to him, he explained what he needed. Following his instructions, Sidwal—with the aid of the wizard's complex magic spells—made a shining crown of gold inlaid with sparkling diamonds and sapphires, along with matching earrings and bracelets and a gold necklace studded with emeralds and rubies, as well as a golden harp that Alhwradd enchanted so that it both played and sang songs of peace and forgiveness.

Having divined that the whirlpool was the entrance to the Sea-Goddess's underwater palace, the wizard took the crown, jewelry, and harp and, with a final, impassioned invocation, cast them into the whirlpool, where they circled three times before sinking out of sight.

The three men stood, gripping the railing of the heaving boat, and waited.

Suddenly, all went still. The whirlpool vanished. The waves subsided. The wind died.

Their mission was accomplished, but they were stranded—becalmed in the center of the now motionless, windless sea.

Haedrwn turned to Alhwradd, asking with his eyes what he would not deign to put into words.

Alhwradd understood and answered, "I have used up my magic powers and do not have enough left to swim or fly back to shore, and even if I did I would not leave you—and so, knowing we have done what the king has commanded, we will face our end together as the receding seas carry us ever farther away from land."

Haedrwn raised his sword in a salute to the wizard, and Alhwradd raised his staff in return.

They turned back to face the western horizon, where the sun was emerging from the last of the dissipating clouds. Standing together, resigned to their fate, neither of them noticed at first that the boat was beginning to sway and move. When they finally did, they turned as a single man to see that Sidwal had pulled his bellows out of his pack and was using them to fill the sails and start their voyage home.

It was a slow journey, and the seas had already returned to their proper shores when they reached home—welcomed by the king, his royal family, and all his jubilant subjects.

Docking the boat, Sidwal dropped the sails and put his bellows away while Alhwradd and Haedrwn disembarked shoulder to shoulder. He followed, sack of tools in hand, as they strode through the cheering throng to kneel before the king.

Alhwradd told the tale of their adventures—how Haedrwn had battled the sea dragons and how he had placated the rage of the Sea-Goddess, as well as how Sidwal had mended the mast, made the sword, crafted the tribute, and pumped the bellows to bring them safely home.

Dwrddwain's response, "You have saved the earth and you must be rewarded!" was greeted by a resounding cheer from the gathered crowd, but all three men demurred, insisting that they wished nothing but to serve their beloved king.

"But you must have something to show for the deeds you have done!" Dwrddwain insisted, and he turned to his daughters, all three of whom were wise as well as beautiful, and he asked them what gift he should give the three heroes.

The youngest spoke first, saying that for his courage in battling the sea dragon, Haedrwn should be given a golden helmet bearing the crest of a wild boar. The king agreed and told Sidwal to make the helmet, which he presented to the warrior.

The middle one spoke next, saying that for his wisdom in placating the rage of the Sea-Goddess, Alhwradd should be given an oaken staff engraved with symbols of his order. The king agreed and told Sidwal to carve the staff, which he presented to the wizard.

The eldest remained quiet while her younger sisters were speaking. When she did finally speak, it was to say that without the sword the smith had forged, the warrior would have been eaten by the sea dragon, and without the crown and jewelry and harp the smith had crafted, the wizard would have had no tribute to give the Sea-Goddess. Then she asked a question that she spoke so softly, she must have been asking it of herself—"But what can you give to a man who can make anything?"

While she was speaking, the princess was—idly, it seemed—weaving a bracelet out of a cluster of flowers she'd picked on her way down the mountain. Finishing it, she took it over to Sidwal, who was gazing at her with worship in his eyes, and she held it out to him, saying, "I will give him my flowers, and, if he wishes, I will take him as my consort."

The king was shocked, but he had said that his daughter could name the smith's reward, so he declared that Sidwal would have the flowers and would be the princess's consort in a tone of voice that let the smith know that he couldn't say no to this reward even if he wanted to—which, of course, he did not.

"And that," Herrwn concluded, "was how the anger of the Sea-Goddess was finally assuaged and earth and sea were restored to their proper boundaries. And forever after, our greatest warriors have worn a helmet bearing the crest of a wild boar and each of our chief priests has carried an oaken staff engraved with symbols of his order."

Abandoning his narrator's stance, Herrwn stepped forward to stand before Feywn where she sat at the center of the high table. Normally, Caelym, who'd done his part speaking for the varied minor characters, would also have come forward, but tonight, as agreed, he remained in the shadows.

The voice that Herrwn used as a narrator was different from the one he used as the head of the High Council, putting a question to the chief priestess. It was his High Council voice he used as he delivered his last and most important lines.

"Now we have told you the tale of how a wizard, a warrior, and a smith acted together to save the earth from being drowned by the sea, and how each was rewarded in turn by the king's wise daughters—and yet, as I said at the beginning, the part that Sidwal, who is ancestor to all smiths everywhere, played in these heroic deeds has been all but forgotten. So it is my thought—if, in your boundless wisdom, you agree—that we should ask the eldest of our young priestesses what reward we should give to our own smith, not just for the many things he has made for us but as the son of a father who died fighting at the side of our greatest hero."

On cue, Caelym drew back the kitchen curtain and Darbin stepped out. With Caelym at his side, he crossed the room to kneel facing the high table. Glowing like a goddess from an ancient tale, Feywn stood up and nodded toward Gwenydd, who rose in turn and, producing the circlet of summer flowers she'd tucked into the folds of her skirt, said clearly, "I will give him my flowers, and, if he wishes, I will take him as my consort."

Gazing up at her, Darbin whispered, "I wish."

When the smith made no sign of rising on his own, Caelym put a hand under his arm and pulled him to his feet. Herrwn took hold of Darbin's other arm, and together they guided him out through the curtain of the main entryway.

Chapter 79:

Cyri's Calling

"Dou realize that the permission Feywn gave granting Gwenydd leave to take the smith as her consort does not extend to his being permitted to take the part of the Sun-God in the Summer Solstice Ceremony or release her from acting as the Earth Goddess."

As they got up from the breakfast table, Rhonnon had tapped Herrwn on the shoulder and said she'd like a word with him, which was how Herrwn found himself again seated at the small table by the window in the priestesses' private meeting room.

He had known this talk was coming, had his answer prepared, and gave it with confidence. "Of course what you say is true, but as you recall, her threatened refusal was due to her determination that Darbin be acknowledged as the father of her children. And as we both know"—Herrwn met Rhonnon's direct gaze with one of his own—"not all summer solstice rites result in children being conceived, and so I have no doubt that Gwenydd will accept that honor, along with your wise counsel that I be granted the privilege of taking part in that high ritual."

"Even knowing that if she should give birth as soon as eight months—or as late as ten months—afterwards, it is the Sun-God who will be deemed that child's father?"

"Knowing that a child born eleven—or, to be absolutely clear—twelve months afterwards will be credited to none other than her consort."

"Which is assuming that she and this smith have not already—"

"Which I am confident they have not!"

"And that they will restrain themselves for two months thereafter!"

"Which I am confident that they will!"

It was a first for Herrwn to speak so boldly to Rhonnon on a matter that was above all else the chief midwife's purview. He was relieved as well as pleased that she nodded and said, half to herself, "Well, in any case, Aolfe assures me she has seen to it that all the young priestesses have had the necessary instruction in both preventative and remedial herbs should their restraint slip, as it does for most people at one time or another."

Three weeks later, when Herrwn made his way to the altar in the center of the shrine's Sacred Grove wearing the Sun-God's golden robes and crown of summer flowers, it seemed to him that he was, for that night, transformed from a storyteller into a divine being with the power to bring about a happy ending for two star-crossed lovers. As Gwenydd put her hands on his shoulders to dance the ritual dance out of the crowd and into the shadowy woods, he imagined he could see the gratitude—and the approval—of the Earth-Goddess Herself shining in her eyes.

The next day, a dazzling blue sky and a balmy breeze, fragrant with the smell of summer flowers, greeted Herrwn as he was crossing the central courtyard on his way back to the classroom after the midday meal. It was not usual for him to act on impulse, but with nothing to do back in his classroom except move things from one shelf to another, he decided to sit outside for a while and, without consciously thinking about it, chose the bench in the secluded niche where he'd sat with Lothwen so often that they'd privately considered it their bench.

He'd just settled himself, put down his staff, and assumed a meditative posture when Rhonnon approached with a determined look on her face.

"May I join you?"

"Of course." Herrwn sighed. He started to stand to bow and add a more gracious, "Please do," but she waved him back down and took a seat at the far end of the bench.

Without any preamble or pause for breath, she said, "There is something you should know before it is announced at tomorrow's High Council. Feywn has not gone to the Sacred Pools this month. I have spoken to her and am pleased to know that she is again pregnant."

"Pleased" was not the word Herrwn would have used to describe the chief midwife's tone or affect. "Troubled" or "uneasy" seemed closer to the mark, and he phrased his response cautiously.

"I would be the last to question the wisdom of the chief priestess and embodiment of the Great Mother Goddess in matters of her own fertility . . . yet I must admit to some concern at her risking the dangers of pregnancy again."

This time it was Rhonnon who sighed before saying, "There are risks in any pregnancy, and, as you say, there is no questioning the wisdom of the chief priestess." But having said this, Rhonnon continued sitting in the kind of silence that meant there was something more to come.

Watching the midwife fiddle with a fold of her cloak out of the corner of his eye, Herrwn waited with increasing apprehension.

Finally, Rhonnon straightened her back and said, without looking in his direction, "And on the subject of the Sacred Pools, Cyri has just returned from her first trip there."

Since Cyri had not been seen in public for the past five days, this announcement was only a surprise in that the event that marked a girl's transition to womanhood was not something a priest was normally expected to comment on. Since Rhonnon had brought it up, however, Herrwn ventured, "Will she be a midwife like her mother?"

"She has asked that I accept her as an apprentice in midwifery."

"And is there any reason you hesitate?" Herrwn's question seemed to him only natural and, he felt sure, gave no hint of the special favoritism he harbored for Annwr's daughter.

"Midwifery is a demanding field for even the most capable and devoted of pupils."

"Do you doubt that Cyri is sufficiently capable?" Even-tempered by nature, Herrwn had never previously experienced the sensation that Olyrrwd had always described as having his hackles rise.

"Capable? Of course she is capable, and could well become the midwife her mother was meant to be, if only—"

"If only?"

"If only she wasn't insisting that she wants to take on two other fields of study as well."

"She wishes to study with Aolfe and with Lunedd too? That will undoubtedly be a challenge, but surely not insurmountable with hard work and perseverance. Indeed . . ."

Herrwn went on to offer what he hoped would be reassurance that he and Olyrrwd had quite successfully shared in Caelym's advanced training.

Rhonnon's expression and tone remained stern. "Indeed? Well, we'll see whether that holds true for the goals Cyri has set for herself, one of which is to enter training with Caelym and become a physician as well as a midwife."

"A physician as well as a midwife? That certainly is unusual, but if it is her desire and if Caelym has agreed—"

"If by 'agreed' you mean turning cartwheels and shouting, 'Yes! Yes! Yes!' at the top of his lungs, you could say that Caelym has agreed."

"So it is settled, then?"

"So that much is settled. As to her third wish, Cyri will be coming to speak with you."

"With me?" While Herrwn's expression remained neutral, his heart skipped a beat.

"With you! When or where or from whom"—Rhonnon cast a grim glance in Herrwn's direction—"she got these foolish notions, I can only guess, but in addition to being a midwife and a physician, she also intends to learn to recite sagas and become a bard."

Not one to shout and turn cartwheels, Herrwn momentarily reveled in the thought that Cyri's choosing to "learn to recite sagas and become a bard" placed him in the role of a teacher, a mentor, and almost a father to Annwr's daughter.

"So," he said, speaking in a calm—even sage—tone of voice, "have you any objections to this?"

"Oh, I have several objections, but none she was willing to listen to, so I have agreed that she may come to you with her request."

"And I will receive it and give it my fullest and most careful consideration—"

"Before you say yes!" Rhonnon finished for him with a humph. "Well, remember that her first obligation is to me, and if I think even for a moment that she is neglecting my lessons, she will need to choose what matters the most to her."

Herrwn waited long enough for Rhonnon to humph again, push herself up from the bench, and stalk away; then he reached for his staff and hurried back to the classroom.

He was standing by the hearth an hour later when Cyri arrived dressed in her new priestess robes and with her usually flyaway hair meticulously combed and braided.

Herrwn had meant what he said when he told Rhonnon that he would give her request full and careful consideration, and he did—in fact, he weighed her solemn entreaty to sit at his feet and learn to be a bard fully and carefully for the time it took for him to ask, "Is this truly what you wish?" and for her to answer, "Yes, please!" before he smiled, nodded, and put out a hand to touch her forehead with the tips of his fingers.

Chapter 80:

Words with Olyrrwd

The curtains to the sleeping chamber rustled so softly that the sound seemed a part of Herrwn's dream that he was sitting up in bed and Olyrrwd was sitting next to him. They each had a cup of mulled wine, and they were talking about whether to allow Caelym to take Arianna, Cyri, and the twins to the meadow above the shrine to go dancing with the wolves from his pack. Herrwn had just said he thought it was too dangerous because the wolves might fight over who they got to dance with, but Olyrrwd crossed his arms and said, "I told you it's not wolves you have to watch out for! I told—"

"I told the laundress you would need your best robes washed and ready this morning!" Benyon's voice broke in. "I told her that over and over, Masters, but she didn't get them washed and hung out until the late afternoon, and I had to go over and get them this morning so you would not have to come back to change after the sunrise ritual but can go directly to the High Council after you have had your breakfast."

Caelym's sleepy voice mumbled, "Thank you," his blanket rustled, and his bare feet plopped onto the floor and padded off to the latrine, but Herrwn kept his eyes closed long enough to see Olyrrwd scowl and hear him grumble, "Well, that's Benyon for you, never around when you need him and underfoot when you don't!"

Olyrrwd had always lacked patience with Benyon. He'd mutter, "Why can't he just hand you a dish without telling you how glad he was to wash and polish it for you?" when their chief servant spoke during the performance of his duties, but complained, "You never know when he's lurking around," if he came and went quietly. The closest thing to a compliment Herrwn recalled his cousin paying the servant was, "It only took two men to hold him down, and he hardly screamed at all while I cleaned out what was left of his eyeball," when Benyon suffered an accidental—and quite awful—injury, and even then Olyrrwd had added, "Of course, looking over the cook's shoulder just when she's yanking the skewer from a roast goat was a stupid thing to do!"

Now Herrwn sat up, took the robes Benyon held out to him, and thanked him with more warmth than necessary to cover the resentment he felt at being woken up before he could talk with Olyrrwd about what had gone on since the last time his cousin had appeared in his dreams.

In the first months after Olyrrwd departed for the next world (which is how Herrwn preferred to phrase it, even knowing Olyrrwd himself would have just grunted and said, "You mean *died*!"), Herrwn had often dreamed that his cousin had come back to talk to him, but over time those visitations had grown less and less frequent.

Why this dream, and why now?

While having visions and interpreting them was more an oracle's province than a bard's, all priests of Herrwn's rank were expected to ask—and answer—those two essential questions about their own dreams.

On the surface of it, the idea that there was a pack of wolves in the meadow above the shrine or that Caelym would take the four girls to dance with them was absurd. There were no wolves in the valley, and while Caelym might be impetuous in some ways, he was as protective of the young priestesses as of his own children. Still, it seemed to Herrwn that Olyrrwd was worried about something.

"If only we'd had more time," he thought as he was putting on the clammy robes, "I could have reassured him that things are, for the most part, going quite well here."

Which they were.

Caelym and Feywn's second son was safely delivered after nine nerve-racking months, during which it took Herrwn's stern and repeated admonitions to "be strong and remain calm for Arddwn's sake" to keep Caelym's agitation—elation alternating with panic—to a manageable level.

Recalling that Olyrrwd had been troubled by the warlike name Feywn had given her firstborn son, Herrwn would have liked to tell him how, when Rhonnon came out of the birthing chamber, she'd announced, as smoothly and authoritatively as if this were a part of the expected norm, "She and her chosen consort will be consulting with our chief priest on the matter of the infant's name."

Stunned and honored, Herrwn had crossed the threshold into the softly lighted chamber, where he found Feywn resting back against her pillows and taking sips of some reviving potion that Aolfe was spooning to her from a silver bowl. Caelym was kneeling at the edge of the bed, gazing down in radiant joy at the bundle he held cradled in his arms.

Rhonnon cleared her throat a few times, made increasingly louder "ahems," and finally said, "Our chief priest is here, as you requested!"

Pulled out of his reverie, Caelym shifted his position so Herrwn could see the baby, whose hair was damp but unmistakably red. It had not seemed possible for Caelym's face to beam any brighter, but it did when he looked up at Herrwn and whispered, "Feywn has said that I may choose his name, and I would like to give him the name Lliem, if you think it a good choice."

Herrwn's own cheeks must have glowed just as brightly as he replied, "It is the name of one destined to be a great bard, and I think it a very good choice."

Lliem's birth came at the start of a bountiful spring in which the crops came up early and frolicking lambs dotted the hillsides. Three months later, Gwenydd went into a long but, by Rhonnon's report, not exceptionally difficult labor and delivered a vigorous baby girl, who was given the name "Gwylen" in what Herrwn guessed was a blending of "Gwenydd" and "Darbin," as the infant herself was a blend of her two parents—blond and fair-skinned like her father but with her mother's exquisitely refined features.

"Arddwn is five and will be coming to the classroom in the fall," Herrwn would like to tell Olyrrwd now, "and Lliem and Gwylen have turned two, both of them walking and talking early, and they have been moved from their crib into a bed to make room for the baby Gwenydd is due to deliver at the turn of the next moon. None of the other young priestesses have chosen consorts or taken part in the Summer Solstice Ceremony. The twins are still a handful, but Lunedd has them in training as her apprentice keepers of the sacred calendar and seems to be keeping them more or less under control, and Cyri is doing quite well in all her studies. You would be pleased with her progress in the healing chamber, just as Rhonnon is with her natural skills at midwifery and I am with how far she has come in her memorization of the nine great sagas—especially considering she started her lessons at fourteen rather than at six."

"And Arianna?"

Olyrrwd would not have overlooked Herrwn's omission, and Herrwn would have had to answer honestly, suppressing a sigh to say, "And Arianna . . . well . . . Arianna has yet to find her calling . . . even at seventeen and three years past her first trip to the Sacred Pools. She flits from one field of study to another like a butterfly, some days tending the herb garden with Gwenydd, other days off with Cyri tending to pregnancies in the village and then sleeping through important rites because of being up all night tracking the movement of the stars with the twins."

Since this was just between him and his cousin's memory, Herrwn allowed himself to reflect, "I don't think even Rhonnon knows where Arianna is half the time," before continuing, "I spoke with her—Rhonnon, that is—about it the other day, urging her to advise Feywn to begin her daughter's formal training as her chosen successor and give her the guidance she must have to be ready when the time comes for her to receive the spirit of the Goddess."

"And what did Rhonnon say to that?" Herrwn could almost hear Olyrrwd's chortle and had to smile ruefully as he recalled Rhonnon's snappish retort that she had other things to do at the moment but that he was welcome to go to Feywn to discuss her getting old and dying if he wished.

Chapter 81:

Two Little Birds

errwn's imagined exchange with Olyrrwd was still running through his mind as he finished dressing and walked with Caelym down the corridor and into the central courtyard, where the other priests and priestesses were assembling in preparation for the Sacred Sunrise Ritual.

Ossiam was standing off from the rest, a tall, thin silhouette barely distinguishable from the surrounding shadows.

Seeing the oracle as remote and inaccessible as if he were behind the curtain to the next world, Herrwn remembered how, just before Benyon interrupted his dream, Olyrrwd had started to say something, and he suddenly felt sure that it was going to be a repeat of his cousin's dying admonition to "watch out for Ossie."

Olyrrwd's use of their cousin's nearly forgotten pet name had touched Herrwn's heart then, and the memory of it now almost moved him to whisper aloud to Olyrrwd's ghost—which might be lingering nearby—that he had not just watched out but had reached out to Ossiam, only to be rebuffed time and time again.

In contrast with the cautious sense of optimism that had come over the shrine since Lliem's birth, an impenetrable cloud of gloom seemed to have taken hold of Ossiam. Rarely emerging from his tower room except for rituals and council meetings, his visions, omens, and prophecies had grown darker and more ominous as their cult's future brightened.

"But," Herrwn said to himself, "how can we feel hopeless when the Goddess is still with us and the sun rises to her singing each morning?"

It was a particularly spectacular sunrise that morning, and their voices filled the valley as they sang their ancient round. Even Iddwran and Ogdwen, Ossiam's assistant priests, who mostly mimed his grim attitude and melancholy mode of speaking, stepped lightheartedly down the stone stairs on their way to breakfast after the ritual ended.

In part, Herrwn supposed, they were all buoyed by the feeling of spring around them, and in part, he suspected, they'd all become so accustomed to their oracle's unremitting gloom that they took his bleak foresights as a matter of course and no longer paid much attention to them.

Feeling uplifted himself, Herrwn enjoyed his porridge and was looking forward to starting his rehearsal of the always engrossing epic of Caerwyn and the Fairy Queen as soon as that morning's High Council meeting was over—something he anticipated would not take very long at all, as there were no contentious matters to be debated.

Herrwn's responsibilities for presiding over the High Council meeting included getting to the chamber ahead of time in order to greet the rest as they came in. That day, Ossiam was the last to enter, which was unusual, but not as unusual as the fact that the oracle's expression, if not exactly joyful, was considerably less glum than in the past months.

After a nod from Feywn, Ossiam rose to deliver his portent. He stood, lifted the ritual chalice above his head, lowered it to take a sip, and began, "I dreamed a dream last night . . ."

There was something in the pensive, faraway tone of those six words that made Herrwn feel as though his blood had frozen in his veins. It was the same tone—and almost the same words—Ossiam had used the day he'd had the vision that the infant Arianna must be sent out of the valley to be fostered among English-speaking Celts in order to be ready to rule the outer world when the time came.

So long as Ossiam held the chalice, however, there was no interrupting him. Herrwn could only listen in dismay as he went on, "It was a dream I dreamed before. I saw our shrine transformed into a colossal boat in the center of a vast lake. The boat had decks that rose seven layers high, and in the top of the highest deck was a woman with the sun behind her, its light shining all around her and her flowing hair glittering like gold. White birds soared in the sky above her and schools of silver fish leaped out of the lake's sparkling waters, swimming in circles around six smaller boats, each one laden with gifts and tribute, that were rowing toward the Goddess's floating shrine."

A chill ran up and down Herrwn's spine. It was the same dream, almost word for word, but what could it mean? Surely not that Arianna must be sent out again! Surely Ossiam would not suggest that, and surely Feywn would never agree if he did!

Bracing himself to reach for the chalice as soon as Ossiam set it down, Herrwn planned to say exactly that, but Ossiam went on, "Then the dream changed: I saw the Goddess lift up Her snow-white hands and release two small birds—one with black feathers and one with red feathers—that went off soaring over the cliffs."

Ossiam blinked as though he were just awakening, then looked at Feywn and said, as if there were no one else in the room, "I believe this means that the day is coming closer when the Goddess will again assume Her full powers, when once again all will worship Her—and that in order to prepare for that day, Her two mortally born sons must be sent out to be fostered among English-speaking Celts so as to be ready to lead Her armies and"—Ossiam paused and waited for the gasps around him to subside before finishing in a voice that sounded like the hiss of a deadly snake—"wreak Her vengeance!"

It was time for the oracle to sit down, relinquish the chalice, and let someone else speak. When he remained standing—gripping the vessel so Herrwn thought it might be crushed between his fingers—Caelym rose and pulled it out of his hands. As the wine sloshed and spilled over the top, he declared, "We cannot send Arddwn and Lliem to live among our enemies. It is too dangerous! If they must learn English, then Arianna, who is their sister—or someone else who speaks it—will teach them!"

The council was divided as if by a cleaver, with only Ossiam on one side and Caelym, Rhonnon, Aolfe, and Lunedd on the other—each of them taking the chalice in turn and adding their opposition. There was no question where the majority lay, and had this been some ordinary dispute, Herrwn would have been more than ready to use the power of his position to declare the matter settled. Ossiam, however, had not proposed this as an issue to be debated but as a prophetic vision. And what's more, Feywn, who was of all of them the most qualified to determine the meaning of the oracle's vision, remained silent as the dispute deteriorated into an unrestrained row.

When Ossiam snatched the chalice away from Rhonnon and, sneering, declared that a midwife's work was to deliver babies and she should stick to what she knew, not attempt to ordain their future, Herrwn decided enough was enough—he was still the chief priest, and he was still responsible for the conduct of the High Council. Standing up, he rapped on the floor with his staff, and when that had no effect, he leaned over and grasped the chalice by the handle.

At first, it felt like Ossiam would not relinquish his hold. Herrwn kept his own grip steady, matching the oracle's, until Ossiam gritted his teeth and let go.

Setting the chalice down squarely in front of him, Herrwn began, in his sternest chief-priest-and-head-of-the-High-Council voice, "We have heard our oracle's vision, and as we all know this vision is an omen and so, as all omens, may have more than one interpretation. Even more than most, however, the consequences of this omen are grave and perilous! Indeed, it has already led to such heated and unthoughtful dispute among us that I am disbanding this council. It is my expectation that we each will give due and serious consideration to the many meanings of this vision and that, when we come together at the next High Council, we will listen to each other, reach the right interpretation, and work together to determine the right actions to take."

Finishing, "With your gracious consent," he made a deep bow to Feywn and, upon receiving her almost imperceptible nod, left the chamber—and was relieved, as he went, to hear the scraping of chairs and shuffle of footsteps behind him.

Chapter 82:

Swatting Flies

" They're Caelym's children, so they can't take them away from him, can they?" Cyri was having trouble concentrating on her day's recitation, and Herrwn, after correcting her a third time for the same mistake, had asked her what the matter was.

Wishing he could simply say, "No, they can't," Herrwn still spoke reassuringly. "I cannot say what our chief priestess will decide, but I believe the case for keeping the boys here is a strong one, and there is every reason to hope it will prevail."

"But what if Ossiam . . ." It was a mark of just how upset Cyri was that she'd left off the oracle's honorific title. At the sight of Herrwn's raised eyebrow, she corrected herself, "If Master Ossiam still—"

Benyon's sudden arrival, banging the door open and gasping that Cyri was needed in the healing chamber, saved Herrwn from hearing the end of the question, for which he had no answer.

While clearly dedicated—and hardworking—in all of her studies, there was an eagerness in the way Cyri rushed off that made Herrwn wonder whether, at the susceptible age of sixteen, she might be as enamored with the teacher instructing her in healing as she was with learning how to heal. Only half aware of Benyon's profuse apologies for interrupting their lesson, along with his repeated avowals that he would not have done so if Master Caelym hadn't said that he must, Herrwn found himself musing about how well Cyri's solemn, steady personality balanced Caelym's impulsive exuberance and that, had things been different, this would have been a very good match for them both.

Realizing that Benyon was still standing in the doorway waiting to be dismissed, Herrwn sighed, thanked him, and sent him on his way. Then, with the thought of the next day's High Council meeting weighing heavily on his mind, he went over to the classroom window.

The cliffs that circled the western side of the valley poked up through a misty bank of clouds. Those cliffs, his father had once told him, were the shield that protected them from the dangers of the outside world. Picturing two tiny birds flapping their little wings and fluttering out of sight over those dark, jagged ridges, Herrwn repeated, "The case for keeping the boys here is a strong one, and there is every reason to hope it will prevail."

Ossiam's opening invocation the next day was a repetition of his previous vision, except for adding that he had conducted three separate auguries and each time the answer had been the same—that, in order to prepare for the day when the Goddess would again assume her full powers, Arddwn and Lliem must be fostered among English-speaking Celts.

Ossiam held the chalice out to Herrwn, who accepted it with both hands and gave his own carefully prepared speech acknowledging the compelling power of their oracle's vision of the Goddess lifting up Her hands and releasing two small birds to go soaring over the cliffs, agreeing that the one having black feathers and the other red made it almost certain that they symbolized Arddwn and Lliem but going on to point out that "while this could be taken in the literal sense of the boys being sent outside of the valley's walls, it could equally well be understood in the figurative sense that She is setting their minds free to learn all the wisdom in all the world, including, as our oracle suggests, the language spoken by Saxons."

"And so"—he paused to take a sip of the sacred wine and to let his point receive the consideration it was due—"the next and paramount question is how to heed this portent while fulfilling our duty as the guardians in whom She has placed Her trust to keep Her children safe. Who here can speak to that question?"

"I can!" Rhonnon rose from her place and took the chalice. "I have spoken to each of the women servants and found five who have ties with kin in villages outside our valley. Of those, two say that neither they nor their kin nor any others in those villages speak English. The others say that their kin and all who live around them have converted, and that they wouldn't dare take the boys there for fear of them being captured and made into Christians."

Succinct as she always was, Rhonnon handed the chalice back to Herrwn and sat down.

Although he knew that Caelym was chafing to deliver his own speech, Herrwn held on to the chalice long enough to ensure that the significance of Rhonnon's words was clear.

"So to your absolute knowledge, there is no longer anyone among your trusted servants who has kin ties in a place where English is spoken and where it would be safe for her to take these boys, disguised as her own, and keep them in safety while they learn to speak this new language?"

"Yes! That is what I have just said!"

Handing the chalice to Caelym, Herrwn sat down, nodding his own approval as his disciple rose and gave a smooth rendition of the lines he'd learned from Gofannon, a survivor of Rhedwyn's War who'd lived outside the valley before joining them and who had learned to speak the Saxons' language from a boyhood friend. While a recitation of an exchange between two boys agreeing to go fishing was not in complete accordance with what the vision suggested Arddwn and Lliem would need in order to be prepared for the day when the Goddess again assumed Her full powers, Caelym delivered it with a flare suggesting more than the words actually conveyed, and the response of everyone—except Ossiam—was warm, even effusive.

As Caelym bowed and took his seat, Ossiam stood up.

There was a moment when it seemed Caelym might refuse to relinquish the chalice, but he was obliged to do so and, reluctantly, he did.

Speaking in a solemn voice that was quite different from his usual shrill oratory and, like Rhonnon, looking directly at Feywn, Ossiam began, "Our ever-esteemed chief midwife has, I am certain, done as she said and searched among the women servants for any with kin in an outside village where English is spoken and where

Arddwn and Lliem may safely be fostered, but her failure to find one does not mean no such servant and nor any such village exists."

There was a faint snort from the priestesses' end of the table that Ossiam ignored as he continued, "I, too, have made a search, and I have found a servant—an honest, dependable servant in whom we can trust absolutely and who, by good fortune, has kin in just such a village."

Rhonnon took advantage of Ossiam's pause, which he no doubt meant for emphasis, to demand, "And who is she?"

"He"—Ossiam turned his gaze to meet hers—"is Benyon, chief of the men's servants, who as part of his many duties is entrusted with taking our artisan's goods to trade for salt and spices." Turning back to Feywn, he dropped his voice again, speaking as if she were the only one in the room. "It was on his recent trip to the market that he met one of his kinsmen and learned that he, a cousin of a cousin on his mother's side, practices Druid ways and not only lives in a village where English is spoken but one in which Saxons and Britons live at peace with each other and where those who worship the Goddess do so openly and without fear. Then—by a coincidence which, I am certain, must have been ordained by powers beyond my understanding—this cousin revealed that he is in need of help with his flocks. Thinking quickly, and acting out of selfless devotion, Benyon told his kinsman that he was widowed with two young sons and that, so long as there was no risk of either himself or his sons being forced to convert, he would return to his home, pack his wagon, and come to join him. Returning from this trip to the market, Benyon came to tell me what I have just told you and gave me his oath that he will take the boys there, care for them and protect them as he would his own children, and bring them back to you when they have learned to speak English as fluently as they do Celt."

When Ossiam raised his voice to address the rest of them, demanding, "Is there anyone here who does not wish the vision I have seen and the prophesy of the Goddess again reigning supreme to be true?" only Caelym spoke up, and his protests— that the boys were too young, that he could already speak enough English to teach them himself, and, the last desperate objection, that they needed Benyon to clean the priests' quarters—were dismissed by the oracle as easily as he might swat flies on a table.

Chapter 83:

Cyri's Worries

"How long will they be gone?"

Herrwn had just finished explaining the outcome of the High Council to Cyri. Her eyes glittered with tears.

His answer—"It's hard to say exactly; infants learn to speak in two or three years, so I should think it should be no more than that"—was meant to be reassuring, but clearly it was not, as the tears spilled over and ran in streams down her cheeks.

Chiding himself for forgetting that time, which passes so quickly when you are sixty, stretches out forever when you are sixteen, Herrwn tried a different tack. "But Master Ossiam assures us that his visions show them happy with their foster kin, and, although you were too young when this happened to remember, Arianna was also fostered when she was little, and she returned to us quite safe and sound, and speaking English as easily as Celt."

Knowing how close Cyri and the other young priestesses were, Herrwn expected the reference to Arianna to be comforting. He was surprised that, instead of being cheered, Cyri bit down on her lip and looked away. When she looked back it was with an expression he rarely saw on her face—an expression that almost always meant a pupil was hiding some wrongdoing.

"Cyri, is there something else that troubles you?"

"I—I . . ." she stammered. "She . . . We . . . I— I didn't practice my recitation like I should have. I don't remember how it begins."

Herrwn had a feeling from the "she" and the "we" that what Cyri started out to say wasn't about her failure to memorize the day's lesson but rather some strife with her cousin. Recalling how his well-intentioned attempts to mediate Lothwen's quarrels with her older sister had entangled him in emotional turmoil beyond his understanding, he didn't press further, but instead said soothingly, "Well, I can understand that, with your worries about Arddwn and Lliem, it is hard to keep your mind on your lessons, so instead of your reciting for me, I will recite a story for you."

Later, Herrwn would remember the troubled look on Cyri's face as she forced a smile—pressing her lips together as if she were afraid of their betraying her—and he would wonder whether he might somehow have prevented the end of their world if only he had asked the right question and found out what was weighing on her mind. But at the time, he had just assumed that Cyri and Arianna had quarreled over some minor thing and, like all their squabbles, it would be made up and things would be as before. After all, the relationship between the two girls had begun with a misunderstanding, and that had been resolved without undue difficulty.

Born a half year before Cyri, Arianna had been sent out to be fostered when Cyri was barely three months old, so the two had essentially met for the first time at the celebration of Arianna's return.

The burst of cheers that had erupted as Rhedwyn threw back his cloak, revealing their "most beautiful jewel," had been the start of an exuberant procession through the shrine's gates and on to the main grove, where priests and priestesses crowded around to welcome the child they already thought of as their future chief priestess. The next day they gathered again, this time having had a chance to put on their best clothes and pick out presents for the occasion. In the center of the jubilant crowd, Feywn and Rhedwyn stood together with Arianna in front of them, the girl glowing with delight at the noise and excitement around her and receiving each new gift with a heart-melting smile.

Annwr and Cyri were on the sidelines. Cyri, a cautious child, was clinging to her mother's skirts and clutching her little plaid blanket. When it was time for her to be formally introduced, Annwr brought her forward and, kneeling down next to her, urged her to give her "dear cousin, Arianna, a hug and kiss."

By then Arianna had given and received hugs and kisses from a long line of previously unknown relatives and had received a present from each in turn. She threw her arms around Cyri in an adorable gesture, kissed her cousin, to the applause of the gathered grown-ups—and left the embrace with the plaid blanket in her hand.

Cyri had stood still, her mouth open in shock, for a long moment before turning to her mother and crying out, "Lovie! She took Lovie!"

Watching from his side of the circle, Herrwn could see Annwr didn't want to hurt Arianna's feelings by taking back what the little girl obviously thought was a gift, and he understood that was the reason she took off her ceremonial shawl—the iridescent silk cloth embroidered with shimmering blue and green interlacing waves that she'd received on being ordained a full-fledged midwife—and gave it to Cyri, saying she was a good girl for giving her blanket to her dear cousin and she could have this instead.

The act of giving that priceless keepsake to a child not yet three years old momentarily silenced the crowd of onlookers. In that sudden stillness, the two girls stood facing each other— Arianna staring at the beautiful shawl in Cyri's hand while Cyri's eyes were fixed on the blanket in Arianna's.

With a beguiling smile on her lips and her head cocked to the side, Arianna put out her free hand toward the shawl.

Lowering her eyebrows and sucking in her lower lip, Cyri held it out but kept a tight grip until Arianna in turn held out the blanket.

Cautiously, each took hold of the thing she wanted—then, at some signal invisible to the adults around them, Arianna let go of the blanket and Cyri let go of the shawl.

A titter of laughter ran through the crowd and the adult celebration went on, but Herrwn kept his eye on the little girls, and he noticed that, as they settled into playing with Gwenydd and the twins, Arianna wrapped the shawl around her shoulders like a royal cloak, its meticulously embroidered corners dragging on the ground, while Cyri kept her blanket tucked tightly under her arm.

◆◆◆

Recalling that early scene, Herrwn felt sure that having success-fully resolved their first conflict—and having done so when they were hardly out of infancy—the two would certainly make peace with each other now. And to be fair, just a few days later, on the day of the Welcoming of the First Lamb, he saw Cyri whispering the lines of the sacred songs to her cousin, and while that was not something he could condone, he did feel justified in taking that to mean the two were friends again.

Chapter 84:

Welcoming the First Lamb

The Welcoming of the First Lamb, considered by scholars, including Herrwn, to be the most ancient of their shrine's sacred practices, was exclusively a female rite. It was conducted at whatever time of day or night the lamb from which the rite took its name was born and in whatever field the birth occurred. It was one of just two high rituals in which the villagers were present from start to finish—and the only one where the villagers knew the ceremony was going to take place before those who would be performing it did.

"It's born!"

Nimrrwn arrived at the classroom entrance with the announcement as Cyri was reciting the closing passages from the Triumph of the Sea-Goddess's Daughter. Heeding the summons, she made a hasty apology and was out the door before Herrwn finished giving her permission to go.

Since he had no active part in the coming rites beyond leading the other priests to join the villagers on the sidelines, Herrwn had the luxury of slipping into a pleasant state of relaxed anticipation as he washed and changed into his best robes—he even had time to stop and look out the window. He took the songs of the birds in the trees below as a sign that he was sharing in a joy that filled the valley and the world beyond.

The feeling stayed with him as he met Caelym and Ossiam and the other priests in the main courtyard and followed the son of the chief herder to a field where the villagers were already gathered as close around the mother and lamb as their shepherd would allow.

The Welcoming was among Herrwn's favorite rituals. In his mind, there were few sights more beautiful than that of the shrine's priestesses, young and old, dancing toward him, their ceremonial gowns and shawls—the blues and greens of the midwives, the greens and golds of the herbalists, the purples and silvers of the keepers of the sacred calendar—all swirling in synchrony, and few sounds more lovely than the interwoven snatches of children's songs and lullabies sung in the archaic form of their language used by mothers at the beginning of time.

As the priestesses arrived in the field, their dance steps changed, becoming slower but more intricate as they formed a semicircle on the far side of the ewe and lamb from the priests and villagers. The song that so far had been sung in a vibrant chorus shifted into individual parts, each in turn singing of some divine offering—the crystal streams of the mountains, the flowers in the meadows, the shelter of the trees—that the Goddess gave along with the gift of life itself.

From where he stood Herrwn had a clear view of the younger priestesses, and he was, to put it mildly, shocked to see that Arianna kept her eyes on Cyri's feet, copying her steps, and that when it was her turn to sing there was a fraction of a moment between when she parted her lips and when she sang, during which she cocked her head toward Cyri, who responded by whispering something out of the side of her mouth. The interchange was subtle, so subtle that it was unlikely anyone without Herrwn's experience and acumen would notice—so subtle that it must have been done many times before this.

The priestesses finished, turned, and danced off. Instead of staying to watch the village children come forward and feed bouquets of clover to the mother sheep, Herrwn slipped away and returned to his quarters to mull over what he'd witnessed.

◆◆◆

The next morning when Cyri arrived to start her lesson, Herrwn greeted her with a solemnly spoken recital of what he'd seen. She had come into the classroom bright-eyed and eager but seemed to wilt at his stern reproof. Bowing her head, she whispered, "I am sorry, Master, and ask for your forgiveness."

As tempted as he was to pardon what he knew was a well-meaning indiscretion, he remained somber. "When the day comes that Arianna must be ready to receive the spirit of the Great Mother Goddess, you will not be able to accept it for her."

Keeping her eyes cast down, she whispered even more softly, "I know that, Master, and I am sorry and I ask for your forgiveness."

"And do you understand that by whispering her lines to her you do more harm than good, as she will have no reason to learn them herself?"

"I do understand, Master, and I am very, very sorry."

"And have I your promise that I will never see this again?"

"Yes, Master, I promise you will never see this again."

"Then let us go on with the day's lesson—which is?"

"The first story in the epic of Caerwyn and the Fairy Queen," Cyri answered promptly and with a just-audible sigh of relief.

Herrwn was well aware that his admonition and her promise required only that she be more discreet in the future. While he did not approve of or condone Cyri's coaching her cousin, he saw no use in forcing a commitment that would put her in the position of refusing to give aid to a fellow priestess when it was asked for—and, in particular, to a fellow priestess who was both her closest kin and certain to be their next chief priestess.

No, he mused as Cyri began reciting the opening to Caerwyn's next adventure, the responsibility for insisting that Arianna be fully prepared for her part in sacred rites was not a burden to be laid on her younger cousin.

Still, it was something that needed to be addressed. But, just how—and with whom—to bring up this problem was a delicate issue.

For a concern regarding a daughter with a living mother—and not just any living mother but one no less than the embodiment of the Great Mother Goddess—the answer should have been obvious. Herrwn, however, had no intention of saying anything to add to the simmering tensions between Feywn and Arianna, so, seeing no better alternative, he decided that he would have to say something at his next meeting with Rhonnon.

◆◆◆

What had begun as occasional encounters with the chief mid-wife had become regular meetings, or at least as regular as their respective duties and obligations allowed. Herrwn found that their conversations, which always opened with Rhonnon asking how Cyri was progressing in oratory and his answering, "Most satisfactorily," helped fill the void of Olyrrwd's absence, and he suspected that for Rhonnon they provided a sounding board for the decisions she was having to make in her unacknowledged role as the overseer of the shrine's practical affairs.

Almost a month went by after the Welcoming before the two had a chance to sit together after the midday meal. It was an unusually hot day for early summer, and while their bench was in a shaded nook in the north corner, the rest of the courtyard was in the direct sun and the others had left to find things to do in cooler places. Relieved to have the extra privacy, Herrwn answered Rhonnon's opening question as usual, saying, "Most satisfactorily"—but then plunged on, "in her own studies, of course, but also in those required of others."

"Arianna, you mean?"

"You knew?"

"I've wondered, though I've never caught them at it—but then I've never caught Arianna at any of her lessons."

It was an odd response, one that seemed to change the question from whether Arianna was studying enough to whether she was studying at all. Herrwn waited, expecting Rhonnon to say something further. It wasn't like her to leave an important, in this case crucial, question hanging.

"Have you . . ." He stopped.

"I have spoken with Feywn, urging her to begin her daughter's formal training as her chosen successor and give her the guidance she must have to be ready when the time comes for her to receive the spirit of the Goddess!"

"And she said?"

"Nothing! She looked through me as if I were a servant pestering her about what meat to cook for supper and walked away."

Herrwn did not know what to say to this—but having told Rhonnon what he'd seen, he could do no more, and so he changed the subject to Ossiam's most recent predictions.

Though still hazy, the oracle's visions and portents had remained more hopeful than not. And with everything else they had to worry about, at least—

"At least Ossiam sees that the boys are safe, that they are thriving and well-loved in the hearth of the loyal kin of Benyon." He thought saying this might lift Rhonnon's gloomy mood, but even though she seemed to be agreeing with him, there was no cheerfulness in her voice when she echoed, "At least Ossiam says the boys are safe."

If her tone had been sardonic instead of simply tired, it could have been something Olyrrwd would have said, and for the first time it occurred to Herrwn that Rhonnon might have doubts about the reliability of Ossiam's powers.

For a while they sat in silence on opposite ends of the bench. Then, sensing that their conversation was finished, Herrwn got up and bowed. He started across the courtyard to begin his rehearsals for that night's performance but paused and glanced back to see Rhonnon, her midwife's shawl fallen off her shoulders, looking like a weary old woman longing to lay down her burdens and rest.

Chapter 85:

The Last Stalk of Wheat

he rest of the summer sped by. As he put on his robes
to celebrate the cutting of the first stalks of the fall harvest, it seemed to Herrwn that he'd just watched Moelwyn
dance nervously off with one of the mischievous twins at the close
of the Summer Solstice Ceremony.

Llwdd, head of the village delegation to the Low Council, had
urged them to hold the ritual early, citing the throbbing of his
arthritic knee, the shift in the direction of the winds, and the fact
that droves of wild ducks and geese were already taking off from
the lake and winging over the crest of the southern ridges.

"When a farmer of Llwdd's knowledge and experience says it's
going to rain, we need to listen." Rhonnon spoke up on Herrwn's
right while Ossiam sniffed dismissively on his left.

Sensing a dispute about to break out, Herrwn, who had strong
feelings about members of their rank arguing in front of the village
delegation, intervened, saying, "Our chief midwife speaks for all of
us, as do I in giving my thanks to you, Llwdd, Honored Overseer
of the Goddess's crops, for bringing this matter to our attention.
Understanding the need for urgency, I will dismiss this council
now so that our oracle may conduct his augury and discern what
the omens presage."

With that he rose, bowed to the village delegation, and stood
at attention as they trooped out of the room, muttering amongst
themselves.

As soon as the last of the villagers was gone, Herrwn turned to Ossiam, ready to soothe any injured feelings he might have.

There were, apparently, none. Ossiam simply took up his staff and announced, "I will make the necessary sacrifices and discern what the omens presage."

"Do that." Rhonnon's voice was quite even for someone speaking through gritted teeth.

Ossiam responded with a deep bow and swept out of the room.

Ossiam skipped the midday meal and withdrew to his chamber. All that day and through the night, the sounds of his droning chants could be heard from the tower's highest window and the fumes of burning herbs flowed under the edge of the barred doorway and down the stone stairs, spreading through the halls of the priests' quarters. He didn't appear at the Sacred Sunrise Ritual or at breakfast, but his assistants brought the message at the end of the meal that he would be conducting a sacrifice at the main altar at noon.

Gathered in the Sacred Grove, they watched the sacrificial sheep being led to the altar.

While Herrwn knew that Olyrrwd had set great store by Llwdd's judgment, there seemed little to support the alarm the farmer had sounded the day before, just the faintest wisp of clouds over the northern ridge and a bit of a restless breeze stirring the leaves overhead—leaves that had only the beginning touches of yellow at their outermost edges.

The sheep itself seemed calm and unconcerned—more curious than distressed even when it was hoisted onto the altar and rolled over on its back, and only mildly surprised when the sacred dagger struck home.

But as Ossiam stood staring down into the scattered entrails, a tremor passed over him. His knees began to buckle but straightened almost at once. He raised his face, his eyes turned to slits of white under half-drooped lids, and Herrwn braced himself to hear the voice of the oracle's female spirit, whose eerie messages never brought good news.

"A storm gathers in the north!" The words rolled from Ossiam's barely parted lips. "The spirits of ancient armies awake to clash again! The birds of the air flee in terror, calling out their warning as they go! Let those who cannot fly as the birds do gather their winter stores while there is still time!"

With a final, despairing wail, Ossiam collapsed into his assistants' arms.

Herrwn let out a sigh of relief. Stripped of its mystical imagery, the spirit's warning was the same as Llwdd's, so there need be no further time spent in debate. He looked to where the high priestesses were standing, and he saw Rhonnon whisper something in Feywn's ear and slip a small golden sickle into her hand.

Feywn nodded, stepped forward, and led the procession out of the grove, through the shrine's gates, and down the path through the village to the edge of the field, where a throng of villagers with full-size iron sickles were waiting.

Feywn knelt down, cut a single stalk, stood up, and laid it in Herrwn's palm. He bowed his thanks and spoke his lines, declaring the harvest begun.

And none too soon.

Even as they made their way back to the shrine, Herrwn felt a brush of cold wind on the back of his neck and looked up to see clouds spreading out from the north.

The rains didn't start for another two days, so as Herrwn commented in an afternoon conversation with Olyrrwd's empty chair, the villagers managed to get the last of the grain gathered as the first drops of what was to be a torrential downpour began.

"And what do you make of her cutting just a single stalk of wheat?" he imagined Olyrrwd asking.

He hadn't had an answer, but he later wondered if she had known that this would be their last harvest.

Chapter 86:

After the Storm

The season's first storm was, as both Llwdd and Ossiam predicted, a drenching downpour. Driven by howling winds and lasting five days, it turned the valley's streams into torrents and its lower fields into marshlands. Then, as abruptly as the tempest had begun, the rain stopped, the winds fell, and the sun returned.

The weather for the remainder of the fall was, if anything, milder than usual. Even so, the year's winter illnesses arrived early. While none of those in their highest circle suffered more than annoying coughs and catarrh, it hit the lower ranks of their order, most of whom were elderly and frail, with devastating harshness.

By the autumn equinox, they'd already made three trips up the cliffside path to the sacred catacombs, taking Inendredd, Maeddan, and Roddrwn to lie alongside the shrouded remains of their ancestors, and over the next two months they carried up another four of their number—Frengwld, Haeddrenn, Haerviu, and Bevwyn—leaving only Feywn, Rhonnon, Aolfe, Lunedd, and the five young priestesses on the women's side of the shrine and only Herrwn, Ossiam, Caelym, Moelwyn, Iddwran, and Ogdwen on the men's.

The servants suffered as well. While none of them died, Iddwrna, the cook who had reigned in the kitchen since Herrwn was a boy, was left so weak and debilitated that she turned her duties over to her granddaughter and told Rhonnon that she wished to spend her remaining days with a sister who'd married out of the valley years earlier.

"But how will she be able to make such an arduous trip, being so feeble and with her painful toe?" Herrwn was genuinely concerned when Rhonnon told him Iddwrna was leaving—and was also heartsick at the thought of losing one more link with his past.

"I have spoken with Nimrrwn," Rhonnon sighed and added, "Iddwrna's grandson," as if she did not expect Herrwn to know the family relations of his own chief servant. "I have told him that at the next break in the weather he is to take a horse and cart and adequate provisions, and accompany his grandmother to her sister's village—with your permission, of course."

This last bit was clearly a polite formality, and Herrwn gave the obligatory response.

"Of course, and he must stay with her as long as she needs him. I have no doubt we will be able to manage quite well while he is gone."

Rhonnon sighed again. "I'm sure you will do your best. In any case, I've made arrangements for young Fonddell, who has been a sub-servant in the kitchen, to tend to your hearth, bring your wash water, and see to your laundry."

Nimrrwn left things well-ordered, and with the hearth tended, hot water for bathing, and clean robes, Herrwn took some pride in feeling that he and Caelym were proving themselves quite self-sufficient—and said so aloud when he was sitting at the classroom table on the afternoon of the winter solstice with both his and Olyrrwd's cups of wine.

"*Well, who taught Caelie to look after himself?*" he imagined his cousin saying with a snort.

"You did!" Herrwn replied out loud. "And we've still got a room full of camping provisions to prove it."

While Olyrrwd was alive he'd refused to have so much as a single fishhook taken out of the room where he'd made his preparations for Caelym's spirit quest, always insisting that he'd get to it later. Since his cousin's death, Herrwn had found himself saying the same thing, first to Benyon and then to Nimrrwn. But when he had finally gone into the room, meaning to clear it out, he'd found that each waterskin and spear point held a memory of Olyrrwd too precious to part with, and that for him "the workroom" had become a shrine where he could feel the presence of his cousin's spirit.

Now, however, it needed to be made ready for Arddwn's return, so Herrwn set down his cup and went into the room, determined to do just that.

He was still in the room when he heard Caelym call, "Master, it's getting late!" and realized that what he'd thought were only a few moments spent reminiscing among the piles of leftover provisions and paraphernalia had in fact been hours.

Caelym, already in his ceremonial robes, was holding Herrwn's staff. After swiftly changing into his own ritual garments, Herrwn took the staff, drew a breath to compose himself, and put everything except for the all-important winter solstice rites out of his mind.

PART IX

The Winter Solstice

While all the great seasonal rituals required precision in their performance, in none were the potential repercussions of a false step or a missed cue as serious as in the Winter Solstice Ceremony.

The spring equinox rites had begun as a commemoration of the birth of the first child of the Earth-Goddess and the Sun-God but had taken on a broader connotation, recognizing the drive of life to renew itself through sexual union. As the vain attempts of less perceptive religions have proven, this is a force that is impossible to thwart, and in any case, the crux of their ritual observance lay in delivering the most lavish tribute they could, as it was assumed the gesture could be counted on to compensate for any minor errors or lapses in their accompanying invocations.

The pivotal event of the Sacred Summer Solstice Ceremony, celebrating that divine conception, was conducted in strict privacy by the designated priest and priestess, and it was simply assumed that, whatever form it took, that rite would be satisfying to those involved.

The outcomes of the autumn equinox and winter solstice rituals, however, could not be and were not taken for granted. In each, the slightest laxity—an invocation mischanted or an essential dance step omitted—could undo the whole of their labors.

Should that occur in the execution of the autumn equinox rituals—as it had once when Herrwn's great-grandfather had been the chief priest—the question of whose fault it was that the curtain separating the living world from the realm of the spirits did not part, allowing the spirits from the other side to pass through, was a cause for both individual and communal soul-searching, but that failure could be—and was—remediated the following year.

There was no known instance in which the winter solstice rites had been carried out with anything less than absolute fidelity, word for word, to the invocations spoken every year on the night that the first of their ancestors interceded in the lovers' quarrel between the earth and sun, persuading the earth to forgive the sun's misdeeds and calling on the sun to return to the earth and her children.

Despite the accuracy with which their priestesses could track movements of the sun, precisely pinpointing when the days would stop diminishing and begin to lengthen again, still there lurked the fear, *What if . . . ?*

What if, through some failure on their part, the sun and earth were not reconciled and the sun continued moving farther and farther away?

While Olyrrwd, during his lifetime, had frequently grumbled that most likely what would happen should that dreaded misstep occur was that the earth and sun would go about their business as they had before there were any Druids to nag at them about it, even he had carried out his part in the winter solstice rites with the exactitude with which he had recited his healing invocations.

Chapter 87:

Betrayal

$\mathfrak{J}$t seemed to Herrwn that even the echoes of their footsteps as they climbed the dark stairway to the shrine's highest tower were exactly the same as they had been when he'd followed his father up to the first winter solstice he'd been allowed to attend.

Entering the darkened room, they began the ritual by milling around the unlit hearth in what to an outsider would have appeared to be aimless wandering and a cacophony of despairing wails but were actually rigidly choreographed dance steps and overlapping lamentations portraying the despair of humankind left abandoned to freeze in eternal night.

At the prescribed moment, Feywn took her place beneath the window in the eastern wall—through which, so long as all went well, the first beams of the rising sun would enter at dawn. Following suit, the others moved to their assigned spots.

The only light they had to see by was from the window, but with a full moon at its zenith, a shaft of soft, shimmering light flowed in around Feywn.

Herrwn took his place at the centermost position in the men's arc, with Iddwran and Ogdwen to his left and Ossiam and Caelym to his right.

Rhonnon, as chief midwife, was at the center of the women's arc directly facing Herrwn with Lunedd and the twins to her right and Aolfe, Gwenydd, and Cyri to her left—each in their ordained place except that the space between Cyri and Feywn where Arianna should have been was empty.

Then, to a communal sigh of relief, there was the sound of footsteps on the stairs, and Arianna appeared in the doorway. But instead of taking her place between the other priestesses, she swept into the center of their circle to stand facing Feywn, the hood of her cloak thrown back and her hair curling around her head and shoulders.

"I have come—"

"Late, as usual!" Feywn cut in. "Take your place! We will speak of this after the rites to the Earth-Goddess and the Sun-God are over!"

"There will be no heathen rites," Arianna proclaimed, "for I have come to stop you in the name of the Lord God, Jesus!"

With those words—and to gasps of shock and horror—Arianna pulled out a silver cross on which the body of a dead man wearing only a loincloth was impaled, thrust it toward Feywn, and shouted, "There is no Goddess! There is only the Lord God, Jesus Christ, in whom you will believe or be damned!"

While the rest of the priests and priestesses stood frozen in their places, Arianna began to rant that they must convert "as I have done"—and while this clearly was directed to all of them, she remained facing Feywn, holding up the cross as if it were a war club.

Feywn matched the gesture, raising her staff, and declared, "What you see before you is a demon sent by our enemies' god to stop our sacred ritual and cast us into eternal darkness!" Stepping forward, she hissed, "I curse you, Demon! You will leave this place, and you will never return!"

"It is you who will leave, for I am saved, and I am going to marry a Christian prince. He is greater than you. He is the son of the Saxon king who rules all the lands beyond this paltry valley, and he will send his army to destroy you!"

"No! Arianna, stop!" Cyri thrust herself between Arianna and Feywn just as Feywn began the dreaded chant of banishment. Heedless of her own peril, she faced Feywn, pleading, "No, don't! She doesn't mean it!" With her back turned, she didn't see Arianna drop the cross and draw her knife.

Herrwn watched, aghast, as Arianna grabbed hold of Cyri, put the knife to her throat, and, dragging her along, backed out of the chamber, calling defiantly, "My prince will destroy you all!"

"Caelym," Feywn cried. "Take your bow! Slay the demon!"

Caelym stood looking bewildered, as though she were speaking some language he didn't understand.

"Slay her!" Feywn screamed louder.

Her shriek broke through Caelym's daze, and he grabbed the bow and quiver that were lying by the doorway along with the other things—shields and swords, slings and lances—spread there to symbolize how helpless human weapons were against the dark, and ran out of the room.

Then, when it seemed their dismay could be no worse, Feywn clutched at her chest, staggered, and collapsed down to her knees. Rhonnon and Aolfe started toward her, but she waved them off, and though as pale as death itself, she pulled herself, hand over hand, back to standing, and in a breathy whisper completed the chant expunging Arianna's existence.

Herrwn could not say later how much time went by—more than moments certainly, but less than hours—before they heard footsteps stumbling up the stairs and Cyri and Caelym appeared together. Cyri was shaking and disheveled, her shawl gone. Caelym was dragging his bow and quiver, and his face was streaked with tears.

In a gesture that was remarkable for its normalcy, Feywn pointed to their places.

From there the rites ran on through the final declaration of their faith in the Goddess as if nothing out of the ordinary had happened.

But, of course, it had.

◆◆◆

As they descended the stairs, Herrwn saw Gwenydd stoop to pick up Cyri's ceremonial shawl, which was lying in a twisted heap on the last step down.

Instead of dispersing to their separate quarters, they all followed Feywn to the main hall to begin a hushed debate over how to defend the shrine and whether to alert the villagers that night or wait until morning.

The villagers had to be warned, of course, and Herrwn would have spoken up to say so except that Rhonnon said exactly that before he could, and Feywn nodded vaguely in what seemed to be accord.

Those with assignments left to carry them out.

Ossiam withdrew to his tower muttering about curses and counterspells.

"Is there anything you wish of me?"

Herrwn's question was directed to Feywn, but it was Rhonnon who answered, "Not now. Go to your chambers and get some sleep."

Chapter 88:

Cwmmarwn

It was dark and cold when Herrwn woke up the next morning. His first thought was to wonder why Nimrrwn hadn't stoked the classroom hearth. His second was to recall that Nimrrwn was gone and that it was Fonddell, the young kitchen servant, who should have started the fire, opened the curtain to let the heat and light from the hearth into the bedchamber, and laid out his and Caelym's best robes for the most important sunrise ritual of the year—the one held on the dawn of the day after the winter solstice.

The winter solstice! Their shrine betrayed! Enemies massing to attack! Sitting up, Herrwn groped for his staff just as the curtains parted and Caelym came through, dressed in a heavy cloak and carrying a candle.

Of the questions flooding his mind, Herrwn chose what he assumed was the least painful to answer.

"Where is Fonddell?"

"He's gone. They are all gone."

"They?"

"The servants and the villagers."

"All of them?"

"All except for Darbin and his sister."

"Then . . ." Herrwn stopped short of groaning, "What are we going to do?" Instead, he said firmly, "We need to call a council to decide what must be done."

"Rhonnon thought you would say so and sent me to get you."

Instead of his ceremonial robe, Herrwn donned the heavy woolen one that Caelym handed him. Then he pulled on his fur-lined winter boots, took his cloak from its hook, and hurried after his disciple—out through the unlit hallway, across the courtyard, and up the dark stairs to the High Council chamber.

By the flickering light from a trio of candles, he could see the others were seated in their regular order. Except for Feywn, who was pale but as imperious as ever, they all looked to be in varying stages of shock.

Following a grim opening omen (and a morose reminder that he'd warned them to beware of demons in their midst), Ossiam passed the speaker's chalice to Rhonnon.

"The servants left in the night," she began, and went on to deliver one piece of bad news after another in a dire litany that made the oracle's words seem cheerful. "They took most of the shrine's food and all the spare blankets. The village is deserted."

"And the guards did nothing?" Ossiam shrieked, his voice as shrill as that of his female inner spirit.

Madheran rose from a side bench to protest, "There were only two of them at the upper gate—" but stopped midsentence and dropped back to his seat, his head bowed in shame.

"The two guards assigned to the upper gate are gone as well, and since there is no sign of a struggle, we must assume they fled along with the servants and the villagers." Rhonnon sighed. "Except for the smith's compound, which was left untouched, everything that could be carried, hauled in carts, or herded is gone."

"And the smith just stood by and watched them leave without coming to warn us?" Ossiam's voice had, at least, lowered from a screech to a sneer.

"Darb—" Gwenydd was on her feet, glaring at Ossiam, but she got no further before Aolfe put a hand on her shoulder and pressed her back into sitting.

Rhonnon gave Ossiam a quelling glance. "Darbin, as I don't need to remind you, is the consort to the Priestess Gwenydd, and he—as is his duty—was in their bedchamber in the hall reserved for priestesses with consorts and children. He and his sister have gathered the goods from their cottage and sheds and brought them to add to what the servants left behind."

Ossiam crossed his arms and hissed something unintelligible.

Rhonnon continued in a steady voice, "From what I can tell, we have enough food to last us two weeks, possibly three." She sat down without saying what they all knew—that between the threat of attack looming on one side and the certainty of starvation on the other, they were doomed.

Glancing up and down the table, Herrwn saw some people exchanging looks with their neighbors, some gazing down at their hands, and some staring at the small fire flickering in the hearth. Only Caelym directed his gaze toward Feywn.

While Herrwn and the others were wearing their heaviest cloaks over their winter robes, the chief priestess was still dressed in the silk robes she'd worn to the solstice rites, yet she showed no sign of being cold except for a bluish tinge around her lips. She looked, Herrwn thought, as if she were already reigning in the next world—so aloof that no one, except for Caelym, expected her to speak, and certainly no one, not even Caelym, understood what she meant when she said, "It is time."

When she didn't go on, Rhonnon said, "Time?"

"The time our oracle has seen coming—"

Glancing at his cousin, Herrwn was almost certain Ossiam was as confused as the rest of them, though he lowered his eyebrows and nodded sagely when he caught Herrwn looking at him.

Herrwn's attention returned to their chief priestess as she said in a soft but compelling voice, "The time that we leave this place and return to the world. We will do so now, while our enemies are still sharpening their swords. And when they swarm through our gates they will find nothing but empty walls, the shed skin of a sacred serpent, while we and all of those who have remained faithful to us will have returned to our rightful place—to Cwmmarwn."

"Cwmmarwn!" As Feywn spoke the name of their original shrine in the sacred valley of Cwddwaellwn, the air in the chamber seemed to grow warmer and to become faintly scented with the smell of spring flowers. That could of course have been the enchantment of her voice stirring the long-buried call of their ancient home or merely their sheer desperation, but they all listened, nodding, as she decreed that they would pack what they could carry and begin their journey home.

When Feywn fell silent again, Ossiam rose to repeat a variant of his prophesy of the Goddess's return to greatness, and they began to make their plans.

Herrwn, who'd had little to contribute until this point, stood up to say that the legendary accounts were quite clear that the valley of Cwddwaellwn was located high in the northern mountains—in some versions above and in other versions below a series of sheer black cliffs—but less so about the exact route between Llwddawanden and Cwddwaellwn, other than that it ran for part of the way along the route traders from the western seaports took to bring their wares across those mountains and on to the central and eastern kingdoms.

"I know those cliffs!" Caelym sprang to his feet, excited. "I stood above them with my wolf pack looking down into the valley—a sad and dreary place, half swamp and the rest barren slopes, save for a scattering of shabby huts. That could not be Cwddwaellwn, but above the cliffs, following my wolf brothers and sisters along a path through the high meadows in our search for prey, I saw what must have been that ancient sanctuary, long abandoned but protected from Christian desecration by the spirits of the mountain and the will of the Goddess."

"And I know that valley, the one below the cliffs!" It was Madheran's turn to jump up. "It is called 'Codswallow.' I've been there more than once, riding at Rhedwyn's side and seeking men with the courage to join us. That is where Gofannon is from." Here he broke off to face Ossiam and stated stoutly, "Gofannon—who kept watch with me at the lower gate last night, and who is as loyal to the Goddess as the sea is deep and the sky is high."

Herrwn was impressed by this poetic outburst from his once disciple and would have said so, but Rhonnon spoke first.

"So we know where we are going and, I hope, how to get there, but we still have enemies to contend with and dangerous lands to cross, so who has thoughts of what we must do next?"

From there the ideas formed and fell into place.

Caelym would go separately to get Arddwn and Lliem. The rest of them would travel in small groups, each taking a different route and each including at least one priest and one priestess capable of restarting their ritual practices.

Rhonnon was reluctant to agree to their splitting up, arguing that while there was certainly a risk in traveling as a large and noticeable group, only Madheran, Gofannon, and Caelym actually knew the way to the village below the cliffs and only Caelym knew the way from there.

Once again, Madheran made Herrwn proud by offering the needed solution to what seemed an insolvable problem. Standing before them with the confidence of a fully trained priest, he said that Gofannon had been back to visit his family more than once, "and on returning the last time, he told me there is an inn, marked by the sign of a sleeping dragon, whose keeper is thought by Gofannon's kinsmen to be a secret worshipper of the Goddess." After concluding, "We can meet there and Caelym can show us the way to Cwddwaellwn," he turned to Herrwn and asked, "And you, Master, can you not draw maps from the old tales and what Gofannon can add?"

"I can!" Herrwn answered with more certainty than he actually felt.

Perhaps sensing that this was not a time for uncertainty, Rhonnon nodded. "That is settled then. Madheran will send Gofannon to Herrwn, and Herrwn will make maps—one for Caelym to find the village where Arddwn and Lliem were being fostered and one for each of the other groups."

"We will need sacks or bags for packs," she went on, turning to Gwenydd. "There are twenty-four of us, counting Darbin, his sister, and your two little ones. Is there any chance that there are more to be had from Darbin's sheds, since the servants took what we had here?"

Gwenydd shook her head. "Some, I'm sure, but not enough for all of us."

Hearing this, Herrwn surprised himself, and no doubt the rest of the priests and priestesses, by having a practical contribution to make. Taking hold of the speaker's chalice, which had been left forgotten in the rapid exchange of words, he explained about the provisions Olyrrwd had gathered for Caelym's quest that remained stored in what had been the sleeping chamber of their young priests-in-training, concluding, "As Fonddell, the servant doing Nimrrwn's chores, would not have known they were there, I am quite sure we have ample packs and other useful items for the journey ahead."

"Very good, then we will need to . . ."

Rhonnon's tone was more grateful than her brisk words implied, but with so much to be done, and given the threat of the approaching enemy, she resumed giving directions, some of which were straightforward, others unexpected, but none unreasonable in view of the desperate circumstances. Ending with the words, "We have no time for regular meals—you will each need to come to the kitchen as soon as you are able," she looked at Herrwn, who took his cue to lift his staff, declare the council ended, and urge them all to make haste.

Chapter 89:

The Sorting

"We will leave nothing to be defiled by our enemies!" Ossiam broke off his emotionally charged outcry, collected himself, and finished, "We will burn what we can and cast the rest into the lake!"

The idea of destroying precious relics handed down to them through countless generations tore at Herrwn's heart, and he was relieved when Rhonnon put up her hand.

"That will not be necessary. I have spoken with Feywn, and it has been decided that Lunedd and Aolfe will hide what we must leave behind, keeping that location secret from all but the inner-most circle of our sisterhood."

"I have spoken with Feywn, and it has been decided . . ." was the opening line to all the pronouncements Rhonnon made at that late-night council, held at the only table in their main hall that was not covered with goods being sorted for their departure.

Feywn, sitting across from Herrwn with Rhonnon on her left and Cyri on her right, was silent but composed—almost serene. The rest of the faces he could make out by the flickering light of a single candle were drawn and haggard, as no doubt was his own.

That they would be traveling in small groups and going in disguise was already known. Who was to be assigned to which group and how they would disguise themselves was what Herrwn had assumed they were gathered to discuss and determine.

He was disabused of that notion when Rhonnon said, "I have spoken with Feywn, and it has been decided that we will follow the advice Gofannon has given us."

Gofannon? Herrwn was at a loss for words. Had Rhonnon actually conferred with one of the shrine's guards rather than with himself or—

A glance at Ossiam's livid countenance told Herrwn their chief oracle had not been consulted either.

Rhonnon cleared her throat and arched an eyebrow at him.

Feeling like a pupil brought back to task, Herrwn folded his hands on the table and nodded to assure her that she had his full attention.

"According to Gofannon, both Saxon and Celt Christians have lesser priestesses whom they called 'nuns' and lesser priests whom they call 'monks,' and it is a common practice for groups of these priests and priestesses to go on what they call 'pilgrimages' to perform rites for their minor deities, whom they call 'saints.'"

"And what have these quaint practices to do with us?" While Ossiam was the most obviously restive, it was clear he spoke what others were wondering.

"Everything," Rhonnon said in what was, even for her, a short and abrupt manner. "The garb they wear is not unlike our own ordinary robes and cloaks. They are mainly distinguished by"— for a moment Rhonnon seemed unsure of her next words, but she went on—"by wearing the emblem of their chief god, which Gofannon says need only be two crossed pieces of wood hung like a pendant, and these 'monks' carry wooden bowls for collecting tribute of food and coins from villagers along their way."

"So?" Ossiam snapped.

"So I have spoken with Feywn, and it has been decided that we will go in disguise as—"

"As lesser Christian priests?" Ossiam interrupted, despite Herrwn's nudging him in the ribs. "We will *not* venture into Christian abodes, nor will we go as beggars!"

"That is precisely what we will do!" Rhonnon snapped.

"But . . ." Herrwn interjected, shocked that neither Rhonnon nor Feywn had realized the obvious flaw in the plan. "We do not know the incantations of these Christian priests and priestesses— much less their rites and rituals—so surely this risks not only our discovery but our offending those deities, which we must assume to be no less prideful than our own!"

"We have thought of that. Gofannon, who was raised by converted parents and whose elder brother is one such 'monk,' stands ready to instruct us on just those incantations and rites. So if there are no other objections . . ." With a quelling look around her, Rhonnon said, "The next thing to discuss is the composition of our groups."

Since her next words were *"I have spoken with Feywn, and it has been decided,"* Rhonnon's use of the word "discuss" was simply a matter of courtesy.

Herrwn had thought about the matter at some length, and while it was now clear that his judgment was not to be called on, he felt quite certain he knew the gist of what she was about to say.

Each group had to include at least one priest and one priestess capable of restarting their ritual practices, so there could be no more than five groups—more likely four, since he anticipated that Feywn, Rhonnon, Aolfe, and Lunedd would each lead one.

Assuming that to be the case, it would follow that each of the latter three would take along her designated priestess-in-training, meaning Cyri would go with Rhonnon, Gwenydd with Aolfe, and the twins with Lunedd. Gwenydd's children would certainly be included in her group. And Belodden? In Feywn's group.

With Caelym leaving on his separate mission to get Benyon and the boys, that left Herrwn and Ossiam, along with the ordinary priests, Moelwyn, Iddwran, and Ogdwen.

At least two of the ordinary priests would be doubled up, presumably Iddwran and Ogdwen. Darbin and his sister and Madheran and his guards would be spread among the groupings in some way to compose a numerically auspicious balance.

So really, the only uncertainty in Herrwn's mind was whether he or Ossiam would be in Feywn's group. As chief priest, it was certainly the proper place for him, but given Feywn's preference for consulting with Ossiam, as well as the underlying tension between their chief midwife and oracle, he was prepared to graciously accept a place in Rhonnon's group for the sake of avoiding dissension.

Having this sorted out, Herrwn allowed his attention to wander momentarily. Glancing to his right, he saw that Caelym wasn't looking at Rhonnon but at Feywn, no doubt committing her every skin pore and eyelash to memory. On his right, he sensed Ossiam stiffening and returned his full attention to Rhonnon's pronouncement.

"As each of the four groups must have a guard, we began there," she was saying.

That was a different starting point than Herrwn had ever considered, and he guessed that Ossiam was not just surprised but offended. The oracle restrained himself, however, remaining stonily silent as Rhonnon went on, "Madheran will be in Feywn's group, Gofannon in mine, Barddwel in Lunedd's, and Darbin in Gwenydd's."

Surprised that Gwenydd rather than Aolfe was to lead a group, Herrwn started working out the reasoning for it in the back of his mind while staying attentive to the rest of the sorting. Other than the assignment of Belodden, the indomitable guardian of the women's quarters, to Feywn's group, it was not at all what he'd expected.

Usually meticulously organized, Rhonnon seemed to be assigning them their places randomly and with no method that Herrwn could follow. The groups were numerically unbalanced, for one thing—and they were not composed in anything like the way he'd expected. Gwenydd's group was simply her family—her children, Darbin, and Darbin's sister. Lunedd's had two priests—Moelwyn and Ossiam's assistant, Ogdwen—while Aolfe was in Rhonnon's, giving that group two priestesses. The twins were separated, the older going with Feywn and the younger with Rhonnon.

That left himself, Ossiam, Ossiam's other assistant, Iddwran, and Cyri yet to be assigned.

Iddwran would no doubt go to Gwenydd's . . . but no . . . Iddwran went to Feywn's as well. Did they mean to leave Gwenydd without a priest? Before Herrwn's mind could fully form that question, Rhonnon was saying, "I have spoken with Feywn, and it has been decided that, as our chief priestess's closest female kin and her heir, Cyri will go in her group."

Looking down the table to acknowledge the significance of this pronouncement, Herrwn caught Cyri's eye, only to see her drop her gaze as if she'd been shamed instead of honored. Meanwhile, Rhonnon was saying, "Ossiam"—Herrwn felt Ossiam's tension, his every muscle as taut as a bow string pulled back to the breaking point, perceptively sag when she finished—"will join my group."

So then he was to take his place at Feywn's side after all.

"And Herrwn will join Gwenydd's group which, following Gofannon's advice, will be disguised as a metalsmith traveling with his family, with Gwenydd as Darbin's 'wife' and Herrwn as her father and the grandfather to their children."

While he was nodding to Rhonnon's concluding announcement that Gofannon would now come in and teach them the rites and incantations they must know to pass as Christians, Herrwn could almost hear Olyrrwd grumbling, "Oh drat, Ossie got the higher place after all."

Chapter 90:

The Shawls

As he was dutifully repeating *In nomine Patris, et Filii, et Spiritus Sancti, Amen*, along with the associated hand movements, Herrwn's spirits were momentarily lifted—not by the actual rites but at the memory this brought back to him from his middle childhood.

Almost a year had passed since his father had returned from what was to be his last trip outside the valley, and the elder Herrwn's outrage at his two brothers' defection to Christianity had for the most part died down into composed resignation. Something someone said had reminded him of it, but instead of speaking out in anger, Herrwn's father had shaken his head and said, "One can only suppose those Christian priests who spend so much of their time in prayers for forgiveness—not just for deeds but for thoughts—must be also spending a great deal of time thinking about those things that they are telling the rest of us not to do."

Their abbreviated lesson in the Christian catechism went on until it was time for Gofannon to take his shift on guard at the lower gate. As Herrwn stood up to leave the table, he looked around for Cyri. Even coming in the midst of an anguished time when public celebration was not possible, his disciple's elevation to the second-highest position in their order made him proud, and it was both his honor and his duty to tell her so.

Catching sight of her green-and-blue shawl fluttering out the chamber's door, he hurried after her, distressed that she should be leaving the chamber with no blessings and barely even an acknowledgment of what should be the most important moment of her life, save conception and giving birth. With the chamber dimly lit, others milling around, and the floor cluttered with piles of things being packed, it cost Herrwn several "pardon me's" and a scraped shin before he made it into the hallway to see her hurrying away.

"Wait," he called. "Wait!"

A moment more and he would have called her name, but the girl he thought was Cyri stopped and turned, and Gwenydd cried out, "Oh, Herrwn, I'm so glad you've come."

Given the opportunity, Herrwn would have explained his mistake and returned to the main chamber to find Cyri, but Gwenydd ran back, caught hold of his hands, and burst out, "I was just going to tell Darbin! He will be so honored that you are coming with us!"

Herrwn had put his assignment to Gwenydd's group—indeed, to her family—out of his mind, burying the thought along with the sense of disregard for his position that it implied.

Not about to admit either that or how he'd actually wanted to talk to Cyri, he faltered, "I . . . I just wanted to ask if my being a part of your group for this journey met with your approval."

"Does it meet with my approval? Why, of course it does!" Gwenydd clasped his hand and pulled him along, telling him in a confidential whisper how Darbin had never felt he'd been worthy of her and how Feywn's naming Herrwn to be in their party would prove to him once and for all that he was as good as any priest.

Darbin met them at the door of their rooms holding a sleepy, tousle-haired boy. While the young smith, who was every bit as flattered as Gwenydd said he would be, stammered about proving himself worthy of the honor of Herrwn's being the priest in their group, Gwenydd took their son, crooning that it was time for him to be in bed. As she was walking away, Herrwn saw why he'd taken her for Cyri. Although she was an herbalist, Gwenydd was wearing a midwife's blue-and-green shawl.

Of course! Now he remembered! After rallying to recite her part in the Winter Solstice Ceremony, Cyri had stood shaking from shock and cold, and Gwenydd had taken off her shawl and wrapped it around her cousin's trembling shoulders. Then, coming down from the tower, Gwenydd had stooped to pick up Cyri's shawl where it lay crumpled at the bottom of the stairway. No doubt she had put that shawl on in place of her own, and with so much else to think about and do, the two had not changed back.

It was a small matter, and not one worth mentioning as he assured Darbin that he counted it an honor to accompany them. Clearly assuming that his responsibility for Herrwn's welfare began at once, Darbin insisted on escorting him back to the main hall and—finding the hall already empty—through the dim passageways to his quarters.

Caelym was there, curled up in his bed the way he'd slept for months after his return from living in the wild. Tiptoeing through the dark, trying not to wake his exhausted disciple, Herrwn changed into his night robes, lay down, and pulled his blankets up against the cold.

After all the horror of the previous night, it was odd that Gwenydd's wearing Cyri's shawl was still weighing on his mind. Staring into the dark, he wondered about why until exhaustion—both physical and emotional—overcame his fretting and carried him off to sleep.

◆◆◆

Herrwn dreamed of Annwr that night. She was standing at the parapet of a white stone fortress, her long blond hair and her silken green-and-yellow shawl blowing in the wind. Although he seemed to be at a distant vantage point, he could hear her beseeching him for help and see that her arms were shackled.

He woke up with the words "green and yellow" repeating unrelentingly in his mind.

Green and yellow! The shawl Annwr was wearing in his dream was green and yellow! The shawl the searchers had found floating in the river—and that they'd taken as proof that Annwr had drowned along with Gwennefor and Caldora—was a green-and-blue midwife's shawl.

What if, in the chaotic aftermath of Rhedwyn's death, Annwr and Gwennefor had inadvertently changed shawls, as their daughters had now done? What if Gwennefor had been wearing the green-and-blue one they'd found? What if Annwr was alive—had been alive all these years, crying out for help that never came?

The bedroom was still dark, but the curtain was pulled back. A small fire was crackling in the classroom hearth—lit, Herrwn guessed, by Caelym before he went off to finish his preparations for his departure. Sitting up and looking at the empty bed next to him where Olyrrwd used to sleep, Herrwn missed his cousin desperately. If only he were here so Herrwn could tell him about his dream and ask him what to do.

The one thing Olyrrwd would never suggest would be for Herrwn to go to Ossiam. Olyrrwd, however, wasn't there, and Ossiam was an oracle, and oracles knew dreams and how to interpret them.

Herrwn swung his legs over the side of his bed. With some fumbling, he found his slippers, wrapped his cloak around his shoulders, took up his staff, and started off, pausing only long enough to light a taper on his way past the hearth.

With the candle in one hand and his staff in the other, he made his way through the dark hallways and up the steps to the oracle's chamber, where acrid fumes were seeping from under the closed door.

Ossiam answered his knock and stepped back to let him in.

Despite the heat in the room, Ossiam's hood was pulled up, shadowing his face and hiding his expression, as Herrwn recounted both his dream and his conviction that Annwr was alive.

"Does this dream mean I should go to Feywn and have her send our guards with Caelym to rescue Annwr on his way to get Arddwn and Lliem?" he paused for a moment. "Or should I go myself?"

As he spoke this second thought, Herrwn realized how foolish it sounded, and yet, suddenly, he burned to be the one to go and find Annwr and rescue her from her prison.

"In this dream, did you actually see the symbols on the shawl this woman whom you took to be Annwr wore?" Ossiam's tone was sharp and demanding.

Although sure of what he'd dreamed, Herrwn had to admit that while he had seen the colors clearly, he had been too far away to see the symbols.

"And this woman you took to be Annwr—did she say anything to you that proved who she was, or did she merely ask for help as any impostor seeking your sympathy might?"

"No, nothing to prove who she was—but she was Annwr, I felt it in my heart!"

Feelings, however heartfelt, were a weak basis from which to assert any conviction, so Herrwn added, "And then there was the white stone fortress! What else could it have been than the stronghold of the Saxons who attacked us?"

"What indeed?" Ossiam raised his hands, palms together, and pressed the tips of his forefingers against his lips.

Feeling he'd scored his point, Herrwn went on, "So you see, it was Annwr I saw!"

"No! What I see is the purpose behind this false vision you have been sent!" Stroking his chin, Ossiam continued in a pensive tone, "The white stone fortress is undeniably the stronghold of the Saxon king whose name we revile and whose descendants we have cursed, but as for the rest, it is a deceit sent by demon forces to draw you into a trap or else"—and here his voice dropped so low he might only have been speaking to himself—"to turn our beloved Caelym's journey to find his most precious little boys into a suicide mission."

"But what if it is true?"

"It is not! It is an evil deception!" Ossiam's voice returned to full strength as he reached out and gripped Herrwn's shoulders. "You must swear to me that you will speak of it to no one!"

Herrwn hesitated. Somewhere in a distant part of his mind he could hear Olyrrwd saying, "Ossie's just jealous because you had a better dream than he did!" But that was unkind and unjust, so when Ossiam softened his tone to ask, "You trust me, don't you? You know I would give my life for hers if this dream were true?" Herrwn found himself nodding and heard himself agree to say nothing of this to anyone.

If he had known this was to be the last private conversation they would have with one another, Herrwn might have said something more to Ossiam—how deeply he cared for him and how much he regretted the distance that had grown between them—or at least he would have embraced his cousin before leaving him.

Chapter 91:

Herrwn's Task

eeping his word to Ossiam, Herrwn said nothing of his dream during his hurried breakfast in the kitchen.

Moelwyn was stirring a kettle of boiling oats as methodically as if it were a vat of healing potion, while Aolfe cut parsnips and Rhonnon sorted hard-baked cakes into sacks. Rhonnon glanced in Herrwn's direction as he was getting his bowl and spoon, but Aolfe kept her eyes on her task.

Madheran sat at the table, a bowl of mush in front of him, his hand clasped around a half-drunk cup of ale. His drooping eyelids told the story of a long night spent guarding the lower gate, and Herrwn hastily dismissed the usual protocol, saying, "Please don't get up."

Roused enough to mumble, "No sign of them yet, but we are ready and will fight to the . . . the . . ." Madheran brushed his free hand across the table in a gesture that might have been meant to mime the sweep of a sword or simply to push his bowl away so he could cross his arms and lay his head down.

Looking over, Rhonnon sighed. "Let him sleep while he can. Barddwel and Gofannon are at their posts and will sound the ram's horn if . . ."

There was no need for Rhonnon to finish the "if." The first of her pronouncements at the previous night's council was what they would do if the attack came before they could make their escape.

"Should that happen," she'd said in her dry, succinct fashion, "Madheran will sound the ram's horn three times. He has assured me that he and his guards will be able to hold the gate long enough for the rest of us to take refuge in the highest tower. With its doors barred, we will have sufficient time to drink the potion that Aolfe has prepared, and so avoid the indignity of being taken alive."

Herrwn had nodded at the midwife's words then and did so now, agreeing, "Of course, Madheran needs whatever rest he can get," as Rhonnon turned back to her work.

Finishing his breakfast to the rumble of Madheran's snores and the staccato sounds of Aolfe's chopping, Herrwn had enough time to wonder if there was some friction between Rhonnon and Aolfe. He hoped not, since the close and harmonious bond between the two had always impressed him and now—with Rhonnon shouldering so much of the burden for all their welfare—seemed vital.

Iddwran and Ogdwen, wearing heavy fur-lined cloaks with the hoods pulled up, were carrying the last of the provisions out of Olyrrwd's workroom just as Herrwn returned to the dimly lit classroom. As they bowed to him and hurried off, he was reminded of busy, bustling moles in a story he'd once made up for Lillywen.

With no time for frivolous thoughts, he shook his head and sat down at the table where his parchment, inkpot, and quill were waiting for him.

Once he took up the task of bringing the fabled accounts of their ancestral home together with the prosaic descriptions Madheran and Gofannon had given him of their more recent excursions, Herrwn lost track of everything save the worry that he would run out of ink before he finished. There was, it turned out, just enough. Pleased with what he'd accomplished, he was laying the last of the maps out to dry when Caelym arrived in the late afternoon, dressed for travel and with what Herrwn still thought of as Olyrrwd's satchel under his arm.

Herrwn had drawn Caelym's map first, knowing that he would leave ahead of the rest. As with all the maps, he'd encoded their meeting place with an illustration of a sleeping dragon in the upper-right corner. He'd sketched the village where Arddwn and Lliem were being fostered in the lower left, and to fill in the main part of the page, he'd chosen a mix of scenes from the tales of the eastern sagas that seemed the most relevant to the quest at hand. Careful not to include anything that might betray their plans if the map fell into the wrong hands, he had put in nothing of what Benyon had said about the route from Llwddawanden or the peaceful village where his kin raised their sheep—that he'd committed to memory, and now repeated word for word to Caelym before rolling the map in a sheet of kidskin and presenting it to him.

"As for your journey to rejoin us at the inn in Gofannon's childhood village," he added, hoping what he said would prove to be true, "you will have our faithful Benyon at your side and his kin's knowledge of the local lands for guidance, and so it should be a swift journey from there."

Sitting on the edge of his chair, Caelym repeated Herrwn's words and accepted the map, solemnly swearing that he would be at the appointed meeting place, his sons at his side, no later than the spring equinox, and from there would lead them on to Cwddwaellwn.

While his words were worthy of any fabled hero, Caelym looked more to Herrwn like the fidgety boy he'd been when he was preparing for his spirit quest—a quest that had proven far more perilous than expected.

For a moment, the image of Annwr imprisoned in the stone tower rose up in Herrwn's mind, but this time he saw her clasping her hands over her heart in a gesture expressing her love for children. Suddenly certain that the real Annwr would never have wished the life of Caelendra's son to be put in danger on her behalf, Herrwn put away any lingering thought of revealing his vision—now or ever.

Sensing Caelym's restiveness, Herrwn delivered his blessing, along with a few more teacherly admonitions, before asking, "Are you leaving at once?"

"Shortly, after I have paid my last regards to Feywn." While Caelym didn't actually wink, he might as well have, given the poorly subdued lilt in his voice as he answered and the hint of dance in his step as he left the room.

◆◆◆

Herrwn had forgotten his worry about the tension between Rhonnon and Aolfe until he took the rest of his maps to the main hall, where their goods were being collected, sorted, and packed.

The usual harmony the two shared—mostly shown in Aolfe's approving nods at whatever Rhonnon said or did—was missing. Instead, anything Rhonnon said to Aolfe about their preparations was cordial but stiff, and Aolfe's usually placid demeanor had a chilly edge to it as she busied herself sorting provisions into packs at the side table where their group's things were piled.

While most of the shrine's shutters were closed and barred, as though that would somehow stave off the attack that threatened at any moment, one of the room's windows was open.

It struck Herrwn how much the atmosphere in the room seemed to mirror the weather outside—deadly calm in a way that warned a storm was brewing.

Chapter 92:

Ossiam's Tribute

hether by chance, as Olyrrwd would certainly have insisted, or by the Goddess exerting Her will to hold off the storm's onslaught long enough for Caelym to be well away, the dark, roiling clouds gathering behind the western ridge didn't spill over until the next night—but when they did, it was terrible.

Winds tore at the shrine's walls and shutters, and rain hammered its roof. Except for Feywn, who remained secluded in her private chambers, Madheran and his guards, who remained on watch at the lower gate, and Ossiam, who circled restlessly around the hearth in the center of the main hall muttering about evil signs and ominous portents, the rest of the refugees-to-be huddled together at their designated tables in their assigned corners.

At a momentary lull in the sounds outside, Ossiam abruptly stopped his pacing and cried out, "What is the meaning of this storm, and why does it come over us now?"

No one had an answer to that. Even Rhonnon remained silent, though she did move closer to Aolfe and put an arm around her waist as a sudden blast of wind seemed to shake the shrine on its foundation.

"The gods are angry!" Ossiam called out above the howling wind. He stopped next to the table where the last of their ritual implements were stacked, picked up the golden chalice that held wine at their highest rituals and blood at their most important sacrifices, and, raising it over his head, shouted, "They must be appeased! I must take them the tribute they demand!"

Horrified at the thought of Ossiam doing what this declaration implied☐taking a boat out on the lake, which must be churning and heaving in the winds of the storm—Herrwn grasped his cousin's arm and pleaded with him not to go, but Ossiam shook him off and swept out of the hall.

Herrwn started after him, calling, "Wait, I will go with you," but Darbin stepped into the doorway, blocking his way, and said with unexpected force, "No, Master, you are needed here!"

Gwenydd came up on one side of Herrwn and Cyri on the other, and each took hold of one of his elbows and held him back, repeating Darbin's words. Feeling his strength draining away, he let them guide him to a bench by the wall, where they sat with their arms around him while the winds and rain continued to batter the shrine.

◆◆◆

The storm subsided overnight.

They hadn't celebrated the Sacred Sunrise Ritual since the night of what they now referred to only as "The Betrayal," but they did that morning. Feywn's voice was strong and bell-like as ever. The rest of them did their best. Afterwards, those who could be spared from other duties set out with heavy hearts to look for Ossiam.

They found the priests' ceremonial boat drifting upside down at the far end of the lake.

Lunedd, Gwenydd, the twins, and Cyri went back inside to finish the final packing, leaving Herrwn, Darbin, Moelwyn, Iddwran, and Ogdwen to continue searching up and down the lakeshore. One by one, the others gave up, but Herrwn kept on, unable to bear the thought of his cousin, who'd been so concerned with ceremonial observance, lying unburied.

Hours later, having all but given up any hope of seeing Ossiam alive, his heart stopped at the sound of footsteps on the path behind him.

Turning, he saw it was Rhonnon.

Answering the question he assumed she'd come to ask, he shook his head. "There is no sign of him, but I will continue searching . . ."

She, too, shook her head. "I have come to tell you that Mad-heran has sent Barddwel and Gofannon to find out if it is safe to leave. We will need to be ready to go when they return."

"I see," he said. "Then I have a little more time?"

"No, really you must come back. With Ossiam gone, we will need to move someone into his place. I have spoken with Aolfe, and it is agreed that you may go with us and Ogdwen may take your place in Gwenydd's group."

"Oh, I see." And he did. While it had never occurred to him before that Aolfe had taken his meetings with Rhonnon as anything other than discussions of matters concerned with Cyri and the other young priestesses, he now understood she'd come to see him as a rival for her closest friend's affections.

What had passed between the two either to change Aolfe's mind or to overcome her objections, however, was something he had no need to ask. His presence in their group would be a source of ongoing friction—the last thing any of them needed. And even if that were not so, what would Gwenydd and Darbin think if he left them now?

Drawing himself up and making a formal bow, he spoke in a tone as firm as the one Rhonnon had used, saying, "That is most kind of you, but I must decline the honor, as I am well satisfied with the sorting as it is. I will remain where I was placed."

"If that is your choice." While her words and tone were formal, Herrwn flattered himself there was a flickering of regret mingled with the more obvious look of relief on her face. In all the years they'd known each other, Herrwn had only touched Rhonnon once—the time they'd danced the ritual dance in the Summer Solstice Ritual six and a half years earlier. He hesitated to do so now but tentatively put out a hand. Before he could touch her shoulder, however, she'd turned and was striding back toward the shrine.

Herrwn followed, his feet dragging and his face turned toward the lake, scanning the surface for the thing he most dreaded seeing—Ossiam's drowned body with its robes swirling around it. Reaching the place where the path turned toward the shrine, he stopped and stared at the now mirror-smooth lake, trying to imagine that he might see Ossiam emerge from the reeds, his expression smug as it had been any time he'd triumphed over Herrwn and Olyrrwd in their boyhood games.

The cries of the birds overhead seemed to echo out of the long-ago days when they played here on the banks of the lake, laughing and shouting with each other.

Now only he was left.

This time he didn't turn at the sound of approaching footsteps, knowing that it would not be Ossiam and that whoever it was would break the spell he was weaving, calling him back from a joy- and hope-filled past to a lonely, desolate present.

The footsteps stopped at his side. A callused hand touched his elbow.

"We have to go now."

Darbin had his large pack on his back and Herrwn's smaller one in one hand. He held two plain staffs in his other hand. Herrwn was momentarily puzzled when the smith set down the pack and held out one of the two ordinary poles for him to take.

"The Priestess Rhonnon said that all the ceremonial staffs have to be left in hiding with the other ritual things and you must have one that will not give you away." Darbin's words were apologetic, but he didn't lower his hand until Herrwn took the staff. Then, with the sigh of a man with one task done and more ahead of him, he helped Herrwn get his pack onto his back.

The pack was heavier than Herrwn expected, but there was nothing in it he was willing to leave behind. Gripping his new staff, he thanked Darbin for his assistance and started along the path out of Llwddawanden.

Chapter 93:

The Divide

The sound of skittering gravel woke Herrwn up.

With the vestiges of his dream lingering, he seemed to be in two places at once—on the brink of a windswept cliff and by the edge of a blazing bonfire. His left hand was still clutching the bush that he'd taken hold of hours earlier; his right was reaching out to the fading image of a beautiful boy, engulfed in flames, who was in turn stretching a hand out to him.

He hadn't meant to fall asleep. In fact, just before he did, he'd made up his mind that it was time to stop thinking about the past and go back to the hut where he'd left Gwenydd and Darbin arguing over which path to take in the morning—the more direct upper route or the longer but less rugged lower one.

There were strong arguments for—or, rather, against—either choice.

The upland route, with its steep climb up a slippery trail and long, treacherous traverse across the crest of the nearly sheer rock wall above them, was perilous. The rain that had soaked their outer clothes earlier in the day had turned that higher ridge white. Staring up at it by the failing daylight, Darbin had shaken his head while Gwenydd, hugging her daughter to her chest, declared that a single snowfall didn't mean the trail wasn't passable. Darbin's set expression had made it clear he was unconvinced.

Herrwn could see both sides of their dispute, and he under-stood Gwenydd's vehemence. The lower path would take them leagues out of their way and force them to circle around the valley below them—which, though it appeared innocent from their van-tage point, was the stronghold of their worst enemies and far too dangerous to consider crossing, even in disguise.

The question was not whether the lower route was the safer one. The question was how much longer it would take.

They'd never expected to be the fastest group, not with having to carry one or both of the children for much of the way, and not with Gwenydd being pregnant and tiring as quickly as she did. Those were the first two reasons that in over two months of travel, they had covered only a fraction of the distance to their destina-tion. The third was that the pretense that Darbin was a traveling tinker worked entirely too well.

•◆•

The first day of their trek, they'd covered no more ground than a man without packs or children could cross in a few hours. By evening, it had begun to drizzle, and the temperature was falling. Weary and footsore, with little Gwylen whining and littler Darfel on the verge of a tantrum, they had risked seeking shelter at the outermost of the half dozen huts that constituted the first habi-tation they'd encountered.

At their knock, the rough-hewn door had cracked open, a griz-zled face had peered out, and a guarded voice had muttered, "We gave all we had to spare to the last beggars who passed through."

While Gwenydd started to back away, Darbin held his ground, pleading that his children were cold and offering to share the food they had in exchange for a place on the floor for the night. There was a long pause before the gruff voice muttered, "Just one night!" and the door opened.

Once inside, Darbin had said, with reasonable honesty, that he was a smith traveling with his family from a distant village in the southeast, where he'd been displaced by a Saxon rival, to begin a new life with kin in Celtic kingdoms to the north.

"A smith, you say?" Their host's sullen expression brightened. "Maybe you could fix a thing or two while you're here."

The problem, it turned out, was not getting shelter for the

night but leaving in the morning—in fact, it was midday before Darbin finished enough tinkering to be able to make a polite exit.

That had set the pattern of their journey. Wending their way from one small settlement to another, Darbin had bartered his skills for food and shelter. Most of the places they'd stopped in were, like the first, without a skilled artisan of their own, and the backlog of metal utensils in need of repair could and sometimes did keep him working for days. In the last village, there'd been a smith, an older man with no sons, who'd all but adopted Darbin on first sight and would have been more than willing to have them stay on and make their home with him.

It had been, so far as Herrwn could see, only out of courtesy that Darbin had sounded so regretful at declining the offer— and he further supposed he'd felt a need for extra civility after Gwenydd had turned her back on their host mid-conversation, gathered the children, and hustled them out the door.

Herrwn assumed that Gwenydd's uncharacteristic abruptness was a reflection of her worry over whether they would get to their meeting place by the spring equinox. He himself was worried about that—and about what they would do if the others went on without them.

As tired as he was after a hard day's travel and a long night spent in contemplation, Herrwn realized that it was his responsibility as their chief priest to go back inside and see whether the two had managed to reach an agreement on their own and to adjudicate the unresolved issues if they had not. He certainly did not intend to fall asleep, but only to gather his strength when he closed his eyes. And it had seemed that he was awake rather than dreaming when he heard the sound of footsteps. In that dream, he opened his eyes to see Darbin rush by, his shoulders hunched with the weight of a leather pack that towered above his head. After him came Gwenydd, her pregnant belly bulging out in front of her as though she were carrying an ox calf instead of a human baby. Behind Gwenydd came Gwylen and Darfel, holding hands and skipping merrily along the path. Darbin's sister, Mai, who'd grown taller in the hours since Herrwn had seen her last, skipped along after Gwylen and Darfel, calling out, "Hurry, Grandfather, hurry!" as she passed.

Afraid of being left behind, he struggled to his feet, picked up his staff, and started after them. The trail they were taking went neither up nor down but straight into a forest so thick and tangled he had to fight his way through its grasping branches. He finally broke out of it and into an open meadow just as the others reached the entrance to a cave in the side of a cliff on the far side of the field.

Still at the end of the line, Mai turned to wave him on, again crying out, "Hurry, Grandfather, hurry!"

Dashing through waist-high grass and flowers, he entered the cave just moments behind her, only to find that the group had once again gone on ahead but had left him a lighted candle.

Taking the candle in one hand and gripping his staff in the other, he trudged along the long, dark corridor, which seemed to twist and coil as if he were in the bowels of a gigantic snake.

Suddenly the way straightened, and he saw a light, flickering and faint, in the distance. His first thought was that it was the others coming back for him, but as he moved toward it he realized he was coming to the end of the tunnel, and light, bright and welcoming, was pouring in from outside. He rushed the rest of the way, stopping only when he reached the end to look before he stepped out.

He expected to see the sun, but it was still night. The light pouring through the cavern's entrance came not from the sun but from a blazing bonfire. Drawn to its warmth, he left the cave and joined a surging, noisy throng of villagers. Guessing he'd stumbled into a rustic festival, he pushed his way through the crowd. It was only when he got close enough to feel the welcome heat of the fire that he saw, to his shock and dismay, there was someone tied to a stake at the fire's center, writhing in agony and struggling to break free.

As horrified by the cruel taunts of the other onlookers as by the suffering of their victim, Herrwn watched the ropes give way. Suddenly free, the captive stepped away from the stake and walked toward the fire's edge, his body encased in flames.

The crowd's jeers turned to shrieks of terror that filled the air as they turned and fled into the forest, leaving Herrwn alone. Dazzled by the dancing light, he rubbed his eyes, squinted, and leaned as close as he dared, trying to see the strange figure through the fiery wall that separated them.

As the blazing man came closer, Herrwn saw that he was young, hardly more than a boy, and had red hair that waved and curled. Smiling a sweet, elfin smile, he held out his glowing hands. Without hesitation, Herrwn stretched out his own hands—determined to pull his brother to safety or else to reach across the barriers of space and time and join him.

Just before their fingers touched, an urgent voice intruded, calling, "Wait, Master, stay still. Do not move."

•◆•

Later, after they'd come to talk freely with each other, Darbin would tell Herrwn how he'd only come out to look for him as an excuse to break away from arguing with Gwenydd, admitting, "I thought you'd be practicing your recitations and was hoping you'd let me listen while Gwenydd calmed down—but when I saw your staff laying there at the edge of the cliff, I ran to look over the side and saw you sitting on a ledge that was about to give way and hanging on to a bush that was going to go along with you when it did."

With no time to run for a rope, Darbin had taken off his belt, looped it around a stump he thought might hold, wrapped the other end twice around his hand, and leaned over the bank, the rocks and gravel slipping out from under him as he pleaded, "Please, Master, you must give me your hand, and when I have it and say, 'Now!' you must let go of the bush."

It was the compelling urgency in Darbin's voice that made Herrwn obey. He held up his free hand and felt the smith's hand clamp, viselike, around his wrist at the same time that earth and gravel crumbled away beneath him.

With one hand holding the loop of his belt, one knee set on solid ground, and his other foot hanging over the edge, Darbin hauled Herrwn onto the bank, getting him fully onto it before he let go of the belt, shoved off with his heels, and rolled them both safely back from the ledge as the lower part of it gave way and slid into the valley below.

Now fully awake, Herrwn sat up and gave what he hoped was the proper response to a rescue he wasn't sure he'd wanted. "That was most kind of you—only did you not put yourself in undue danger on my behalf?"

"Not as much danger as I would have been in if I'd had to tell Gwenydd I'd let you fall off the cliff!" Clearly appalled at what he'd just said, Darbin clapped his hand over his mouth. Herrwn, however, nodded solemnly as he replied, "I, too, have been the consort to a high priestess, and I believe you are right."

For some reason this struck them both as hilarious, and they sat there side by side, their legs stretched out in front of them, and laughed until they had to stop to catch their breath.

Recovering first, Darbin got up, retrieved Herrwn's staff, and helped him to his feet.

Herrwn gripped his staff with one hand and wiped the tears from his cheeks with the other. "So then, Darbin, on which road will you take us this morning?"

Darbin sighed. "You are asking me?"

While there had not yet been time for Herrwn to fully examine the layered meanings of his dream, the first part of it—Darbin leading the way and carrying the enormous pack on his shoulders—was clear.

"It is you who has spoken with those who have knowledge of the outside world, and you on whom we all depend for our survival."

"You agree with me, then? And will tell Gwenydd to be reasonable?"

"I agree the burden is yours and so the choice must be. As for telling your consort, a high priestess in the early throes of pregnancy, to be reasonable, I would not attempt it. But if you will remain out here, I will go in to speak with her—having, I believe, some power of persuasion and also having had the honor of being one of those to whom she swore quite vehemently that, loving you as she did, she would follow you anywhere." Herrwn cleared his throat. "When we come out, it is my advice that, should Gwenydd say she wishes to take the lower and safer route, you have the wisdom to nod and say no more."

Whether it was due to Herrwn's powers of persuasion or Gwenydd's recovery of her common sense, they took the longer path when they left the wayside hut in the morning.

Translation of Latin Text

CHAPTER 91

In nomine Patris, et Filii, et Spiritus Sancti, Amen.
In the name of the Father, the Son, and the Holy Spirit, Amen.

Acknowledgments

My heartfelt thanks . . .

To my writing partner, Linda, without whom Caelym, Annwr, and Aleswina would still be languishing in word-processing purgatory.

To my husband, Mark, for his unstinting support and his invaluable advice.

To my sister, Carol, for believing in this book before I did.

To my incredibly kind readers, Anne, Carrie, Connie, David, Jack, Jim, John, and both Joans for their insights and encouragement.

To Bev Connor of Dreaming Otter Arts for her fabulous owls.

To Mirko Donninelli, scholar of classical languages and ancient history, for his generous help with Latin translations.

To my editor, Krissa Lagos, my publicist, Caitlin Hamilton Summie, and to the SheWritesPress team, with special thanks to Julie Metz for a wonderful cover, Shannon Green for managing to make this all come together, and Brooke Warner for taking on the quest to give women a voice.

About the Author

Ann Margaret Linden was born in Seattle, Washington, but grew up on the East Coast before returning to the Pacific Northwest as a young adult. She has undergraduate degrees in anthropology and in nursing and a master's degree as a nurse practitioner. After working in a variety of acute care and community health settings, she took a position in a program for children with special health-care needs where her responsibilities included writing clinical reports, parent educational materials, provider newsletters, grant submissions, and other program-related materials. The Druid Chronicles began as a somewhat whimsical decision to write something for fun and ended up becoming a lengthy journey that involved Linden taking adult education creative writing courses, researching early British history, and traveling to England, Scotland, and Wales. Retired from nursing, she lives with her husband, dog, and cat.

SELECTED TITLES FROM SHE WRITES PRESS

She Writes Press is an independent publishing
ompany founded to serve women writers everywhere.
Visit us at www.shewritespress.com.

The Oath by A.M. Linden. $17.95, 978-1-64742-114-4. Caelym, a young Pagan priest, leaves his cult's hidden sanctuary on a critical mission and ventures into a world where Druids, once revered as healers, poets, and oracles, are now reviled as wizards and witches.

Conjuring Casanova by Melissa Rea. $16.95, 978-1-63152-056-3. Headstrong ER physician Elizabeth Hillman is a career woman who has sworn off men and believes the idea of love in the twenty-first century is a fairy-tale—but when Giacomo Casanova steps into her life on a rooftop in Italy, her reality and concept of love are forever changed.

Size Matters by Cathryn Novak. $16.95, 978-1-63152-103-4. If you take one very large, reclusive, and eccentric man who lives to eat, add one young woman fresh out of culinary school who lives to cook, and then stir in a love of musical comedy and fresh-brewed exotic tea, with just a hint of magic, will the result be a soufflé—or a charred, inedible mess?

Dark Lady by Charlene Ball. $16.95, 978-1-63152-228-4. Emilia Bassano Lanyer—poor, beautiful, and intelligent, born to a family of Court musicians and secret Jews, lover to Shakespeare and mistress to an older nobleman—survives to become a published poet in an era when most women's lives are rigidly circumscribed.

Elmina's Fire by Linda Carleton. $16.95, 978-1-63152-190-4. A story of conflict over such issues as reincarnation and the nature of good and evil that are as relevant today as they were eight centuries ago, Elmina's Fire offers a riveting window into a soul struggling for survival amid the conflict between the Cathars and the Catholic Church.